RECLAIMED

JENNIFER RODEWALD

WORDS THAT EDIFY
Rooted Publishing

Printed in the United States of America
First Printing, 2015

Cover Design by Jennifer Rodewald and
Roseanna White Designs, www.RoseannaWhiteDesigns.com
Cover photos from www.Shutterstock.com

Author Photo by Larisa O'Brien Photography

Published by Rooted Publishing
McCook, NE 69001

Opening quote taken from *Morning and Evening* by C. H. Spurgeon and revised by Alistair Begg, © 2003, from October 18. Used by permission of Crossway, a publishing ministry of Good News Publishers, Wheaton, IL 60187, www.crossway.org.

Scripture quotations taken from the New American Standard Bible®, Copyright © 1960, 1962, 1963, 1968, 1971, 1972, 1973, 1975, 1977, 1995 by The Lockman Foundation. Used by permission.

For my Superman,
because you show me
A more excellent way.

CONTENTS

RECLAIMED

Rodewald

CHAPTER ONE

"Starving souls live at a distance from the Mercy-seat and become

like the parched fields in times of drought."

-*CH Spurgeon*

Maybe today I will find peace.
Suzanna Wilton fingered the ring dangling from a chain around her neck. The metal pressed cold against her skin, and the bitter taste of resentment soured in her mouth.

Nope. Country life didn't fix the heartache. Even after living in Rock Creek, Nebraska for four weeks, Suzanna couldn't claim peace. But, then again, it'd been years since she'd lived with anything she could label as peace.

She stepped out of her front door onto the wood-planked porch, amazed to hear nothing but the gentle rustle of a hushed morning. Echoes of city life still reverberated in her mind— busy streets, sirens and the footfalls of hundreds of people as they passed below her third-floor balcony. Another life. One she did not intend to revisit.

A kitten bounded onto the porch and wove its velvety body around her ankles. Suzanna bent to lift the little tabby, tucking it under her chin to feel its silky coat against her skin. Beyond her front yard the pasture seemed to never end, and she drank in the view. Emerald waves rippled along the hills, which heaved and sighed to the horizon. Autumn-blazed treetops clustered on her left, protecting the spring-fed creek nestled in the small ravine.

All the harmony one could imagine, and yet she was, as ever, unsettled, dissatisfied. Restless.

The gravel road crackled as an engine rumbled from the south. No more than three vehicles passed the farmhouse on any given day, so it commanded Suzanna's attention. A blue truck slowed as its nose peeked through the tree line, stirring behind it a brown cloud which billowed toward the far pasture.

Dust. She'd traded smog for dust. Even after a rain, the clay roads would suck the moisture in deep, leaving the surface dry and cracked. Within a day her Jeep Wrangler would be kicking up the dust.

Suzanna scowled as the vehicle turned into her dirt-packed driveway. Setting the kitten on the porch railing, she stepped down the porch stairs. The driver put his early nineties Ford in *park* and slid his Stetson over his cropped hair. Another middle-aged cowboy. She could guess what the stranger wanted as his booted feet touched the ground, so she couldn't muster a friendly greeting.

"Miss Wilton?" He reached toward her as he strode away from his truck.

She dipped a curt nod while she gripped his hand, intending to send a message. Maybe she was a city girl on her own in the middle of nowhere, but she wasn't an idiot.

"Paul Rustin," he continued smoothly. "I'm your nearest neighbor to the south."

Hmm. It'd been a month since she'd moved in. He just now decided to be neighborly? And they say small towns are so friendly. She'd met her city neighbors within twenty-four hours of moving. Must be a different standard 'round these here parts.

"So, you're Mike's daughter."

Obviously. "The younger of two, yes."

"I'm sorry about your dad. He was a good man, a good neighbor. I feel bad that I missed his services. I've been away."

A stale excuse. Away where? She'd learned quite a bit in the short time she'd been on the land. First rule: animals need daily care. Mr. Whatever-his-name-is was blowing dust in her face. She really hated dust.

"You doing okay out here on your own?"

Suzanna crossed her arms. "Managing, so far."

"I imagine it's quite a shock, with your dad passing and you suddenly moving. I thought I'd let you know I'm available if you need help."

Uh-huh. Wait for it. "Sure." Suzanna barely held her sarcasm. "Thanks."

The cowboy kicked at the dirt beneath his boots, shoving his hands in his denim pockets. "Also wanted you to know if you need an out, I'm prepared to make you an offer on this place."

And there it was. *Get in line, buddy.* She'd had enough. Tossing her shoulder-length hair, Suzanna pinned him with a glare.

"Why is it you cowboys see some city girl and assume she's a sucker?"

The man drew back, his eyes growing round. "Excuse me?"

Shocking, isn't it, cowboy? Yes, a city girl can have a backbone—and a brain. "Land's not for sale, mister." Suzanna bit off each word as she stepped into his space. "I'm fine. Thank you for the concern."

He stared, his mouth sagging open. "Yes, ma'am." Still looking dumbfounded, he tipped his hat and backed away. "You have a good day, Miss Wilton."

"Oh yes," she muttered under her breath, "you too."

The truck growled to life, and her neighbor pulled out, returning the way he'd come. She had yet to meet a man on this pathetic dot of earth who didn't offer an introduction only to present her a deal——one certainly tailored to benefit himself. Friendliness evidently came as a pretense in this small town.

Well, she had no intention of selling.

Wow. She was pricklier than a yucca plant.

Paul passed the tree line and floored the gas pedal. Irritation exploded inside his head. Where did she get off jabbing him with her spiny rudeness? Especially after he'd made it a priority to visit her first thing. Such a waste of time. He had nothing in his fridge worth chewing on, and catching up on business in town would take at least a week, but he'd deferred it all to say how' do. What a rip.

And to think Andrea had told him he had a pretty, new neighbor. Apparently Dre hadn't met the woman. His sister knew he wasn't that desperate. Or stupid.

What was the bur with that girl, anyway? She hadn't even smiled. Eyes cold enough to warrant a parka in August. He was a perfect stranger. Didn't she know it was rude to treat another human being that way?

Okay, she'd lost her dad. Maybe that gave her a little latitude. A smidge. Anyway, he didn't need to let it ruin his day. He had too much to do.

RECLAIMED

Nearing his home, Paul kept the pressure on the gas and bypassed his driveway. Two miles down the road, Dre would have some breakfast about ready by now. A full stomach, some laughs with the kids, and a mug of coffee with Tom should set his day straight. Miss Wilton could pickle away in her sourness. It didn't make a whole lot of difference to him.

CHAPTER TWO

"So, you met her?" Andrea leaned against the table toward Paul, her tone too cheery for innocent curiosity.

"Yep." Paul wiped his face with a napkin to mask his scowl.

Dre's eyes gleamed as if fate had just taken a twist. "And?" What was with her? She knew better than to poke at his singleness. Why did she suddenly think he needed a woman in his life?

"She tried to take my head off."

Tom rested against the back of his chair as a small chuckle escaped. "Heard she was a bit of a pickle."

"You did?" Dre's head whipped toward her husband. "Who told you that?"

"Chuck. He and Jim both had, shall we say, interesting conversations with her."

Dre's face puckered. "What reason did they have to meet her?"

"Business."

Paul watched his sister as she challenged her husband with a look. She was as feisty as she was kind, and for some reason, she had his new neighbor's back. What was that all about?

"Have you met her, Dre?" Paul asked.

Her expression relaxed. "No, not yet, but I saw her at Holeman's. She stopped her shopping to help old Mrs. Blake with a ten-pound bag of flour, and when she was checking out, she bought a Coke and gave it to the clerk. Just because. Pickled people don't do things like that."

True. That was a bit mysterious. Paul tried to imagine the bitter Miss Wilton helping poor, arthritic Agnes Blake. He couldn't picture her doing it with a smile. Actually, he couldn't picture her stony face with a smile at all.

"Maybe she's got a sore spot for men." Tom got up, poured a fresh mug of coffee, and then slid onto the stool at the kitchen island. "Mike lived here for almost six years, but I'd never seen her around. You'd think his daughter would show up for a visit every now and again."

A sore spot for men? Could be.

"Old Jerry Tripp was working the checkout that day." Dre shook her head. "She was perfectly kind to him. Like I said, bought him a Coke and everything."

Or not. Intriguing. But not enough for a return trip.

Dre planted her chin on her fist. "I'm gonna go say hey."

Paul raised an eyebrow. "You are, huh?"

"Yep." Dre nodded as she stood to clear the breakfast dishes. "'Bout time too. I'll take some of my double chocolate chip cookies, and we'll just see about this pickle rumor."

Oh, Dre. Always on the lookout for wounded puppies and lost kittens. And vinegar-soaked spinsters.

Paul grunted. "Wear a helmet."

Andrea spun from the dishwasher, scowling at him. Her hands came to her hips. "Kindness goes a long way. I won't need it."

Across the counter, Tom rolled his eyes and grinned all at once. Thirteen years and he obviously still adored her. It pleased Paul that his baby sister was well loved, but it also pricked a little jealousy way down deep. It seemed God had passed him over when it came to the two-by-two pairings.

Ugh. It was all right. He had a good life. Tom and Dre took him in as a part of their home whenever he was around. They were all the family he needed. He wouldn't have this nip of melancholy if Andrea hadn't unintentionally stirred up regret.

He was happy. And he had stuff to do. It was time to get after it.

Suzanna set a fresh pot of coffee to brew and stretched her fingers. Who knew typing could give you cramps? She'd met her entry quota for the day, but a new reservation request had blipped on the resort database, and she'd snagged it. Heaven knew she could use the bonus.

Rocking her head back and forth to work her neck muscles, she left the kitchen, heading for the makeshift office she'd erected in the front room. A white truck covered in a thin film of dirt rolled by the picture window. It turned in her drive, and Suzanna groaned. Two vultures in one day. She must have inherited the most sought-after two hundred acres in all of Cottonwood County.

Sighing, she pushed her loose hair off her face. She stepped out the front door prepared for another battle. Crisp fall air cooled her skin, sending a ripple of goose bumps down her arms.

The truck door swung open and a woman jumped out. She wore cowboy boots with faded jeans, and her long blonde hair fell in an attractive cascade down her back. Reaching into the cab, she emerged with a Saran Wrap-covered plate and a smile stretching across her face.

Could it be? An honest hello, a sincere welcome, rather than a "nice to meet you, now get out"? What took so long?

"Hey there." The woman approached with easy confidence. "I'm long overdue. My name's Andrea Kent. I live three miles down the road."

Genuine friendliness gleamed from the woman's blue eyes, melting Suzanna's reservations.

A smile tickled the corners of her mouth, the first one in weeks. "Suzanna Wilton." She met Andrea's hand with a warm shake.

"Well, Suzanna, it's real nice to meet you. I thought you might enjoy these." Andrea handed Suzanna the plate. "I hide them from my kids so's I can have me a chocolate fix whenever the need arises. Living out this far, a girl's gotta stock up."

A friend. *Oh, please, let her be a real friend.* It'd been so long since she'd had an honest friend.

Suzanna traced a cookie under the plastic wrap. "Rock Creek is a good drive from out here, isn't it?"

Andrea plopped down on the front porch step as if she'd nothing better to do with her day. "You'll get used to it. I do my best dreamin' and schemin' during that twenty-minute drive. It's good for the soul. Just me, a good set of tires, and the radio. Oh, and my kids. But I'm pretty well practiced at tuning them out."

Andrea's easy chatter drifted over her chilled soul like a warm breeze. A sigh rolled off Suzanna's muscles.

"I just brewed a fresh pot of coffee." She made a move toward the front door. "Would you like to come in?"

A laugh lit her face as Andrea bobbed her head. "I never turn down a cup of coffee." She followed Suzanna through the door. "I haven't been in this house since I was a girl. We used to come here to dig dandelions. Mrs. Hawkins would give us a nickel for every root, and then she'd make us fresh lemonade."

Suzanna had a mug of coffee poured by the time Andrea finished. Settling at her small kitchen table, she marveled at their instant familiarity.

"Was that who my dad bought the property from?"

"Goodness no." Andrea sipped her coffee. "Poor Mrs. Hawkins would have spit nails if she'd seen what had been done with her place. This was a feedlot when your dad bought it. Took only three years to ruin the land, and your dad spent almost six years reclaiming it."

"I thought it looked different." Suzanna passed cream to Andrea, who skipped the indulgence. "I came out right after Dad moved, and all I remember was mud. And stench. Dad talked a lot about planting, but I guess I didn't understand."

"Grass." Andrea's head bobbed once. "He planted grass. And replanted. He tested the soil, amended the dirt, and planted—for years."

"Is it recovered?" Suzanna's gaze drifted out the window. "The land, I mean? Did he do it?"

"He did it." Approval rang through Andrea's voice. "Reclaimed an acreage that had been written off as miserable. People couldn't believe it when Mike bought this place. Said it was a fool's dream: See that creek you have on the south side?" She nodded toward the tree line.

Suzanna dipped her chin.

"Water was turning up tainted downstream. The EPA was hunting to shut the feedlot down, so the owners put the property on the market. 'Course, everyone local knew about it, and they weren't gonna touch it. Figured it was worthless dirt. Too valuable to abuse, too hard to reclaim. Useless."

Suzanna frowned. "Did my dad know any of this?"

Andrea shrugged. "Not sure it woulda mattered. Seemed set on it. Jack, down at the Department of Natural Resources, he warned Mike about what it would take to sprout seed here. Mike just listened, thanked him politely, and got to work."

Drawn to the view outside her window, Suzanna scanned her inheritance. Green pastures waved against the afternoon sun, tinted with the golden hues of fall. The ground looked virgin, full of potential.

Reborn and beautiful.

Her breath caught in her throat as the vista whispered a promise. Was that why Daddy had given her his property?

God takes the broken things, Suzie doll. He can do wonders with hearts that have nothing left. Tears stung her eyes as her dad's voice rolled through her memory. Nothing left. At twenty-seven, that was exactly how Suzanna felt. Drained, used up, and broken.

"Mike turned this piece of Nebraska from scorned to coveted." Andrea brought Suzanna back from the past. "One of the prettiest little spots in Cottonwood County."

Coveted, yes. No fewer than five pressure-laden offers in the past month.

"Seems a good section," Suzanna observed, burying her resentment.

"Not a whole section, Suz. Little less than a third. But, yes, it's a good one. Thanks to your dad, you've got good grazing ground. What was he hoping to put on it?"

Suzanna shrugged. Sorting through what her father had been doing tangled up her mind. She couldn't make sense of her own life, let alone his.

Andrea finished her coffee and stood. "Well, Suz, knowing how hard your dad worked on this place, I'd say he had a plan. I'd bet on it."

Curiosity nipped at Suzanna. What had he been up to? She'd been so wrapped up with Jason and wounded by the past that she hadn't paid much attention to her father's endeavors. Had he left her any clues?

Suzanna followed Andrea to the front door. Andrea spun on her toes. "I don't use one of these very often. I feel all formal."

"What? The door?"

"The front door. Farmhouses only have them for looks."

Laughter bubbled up, rusty and unfamiliar. "Well, in that case, you're welcome to use the side door anytime."

"Good." Andrea tipped her head. "I'll stop by again soon." She turned to exit, but her boots stopped just outside the door. "Do you go to church at all, Suzanna?"

Ah, church. A preacher's kid ought to go to church. It'd been awhile though. Suzanna shrugged without a word.

"Well, if you ever want to, we're over at Rock Creek Bible. I'd love for you to sit by me." Andrea touched her head as if she were wearing a hat before she dropped down the front steps. "I'll be seeing you, Suzanna Wilton."

The joy in her voice pulled at Suzanna's soul. Maybe it was time to go back.

"You met that neighbor yet?"

Paul pushed back a groan. "Yep. Stopped by on Monday." Chuck Stanton tapped the paperwork against the conference table. "Tell me she isn't a little bit of Colorado sunshine." His grunt accentuated his sarcasm.

Keeping his stare blank, Paul wondered what took Chuck fifteen miles on a gravel road to meet Miss Wilton. Business, Tom had said. Too bad he hadn't thought to ask exactly what the banker's *business* had been.

"She's a bit on the cool side," Paul said, "but some people are just wary."

Was he actually defending the Pickle Lady? Well, she was his neighbor, after all. When it came to business opportunities, Chuck was a predator.

"Ah, Paul. Always the nice guy …" Chuck smirked, his head shaking.

Never the right guy. Easy enough to finish. He'd heard it at every bachelor party he'd been a part of since they were twenty-one. How long ago was that? Sixteen years?

Ugh. Think of something else.

Chuck saved him from thinking at all.

"Hey, you gonna come shoot tomorrow morning?"

"Yeah, I might come fire a couple of rounds. I've got a bunch of stuff to catch up on, though, so I'll be gone before coffee."

"You've got a bunch of friends to catch up on, too, old man." Chuck slid his documents into a file folder and stood. "You're gone way too much."

"Work, buddy. Lots of work." Paul held his hand out, and Chuck took it. "I'll be seeing you."

"Hey, Paul." Chuck caught him as he neared the door. "Watch out for that city girl. She's got claws."

Good grief. A guy suffered one broken heart, and you'd think he couldn't handle an uppity woman.

Suzanna stared at her reflection. What did country girls wear to church, anyway? Tugging at the fitted jacket, she flicked the pleats at the bottom of her pencil skirt with her knees. The outfit was all wrong—way too business.

She glanced at the dress she'd laid on the bed. The delicate, green paisley print had been her favorite. Jersey knit, it would slide over her shoulders, drop into a V at the neck, and gather in an attractive knot at her waist. She never wore that dress anymore.

The only other option was her black wrap. The funeral dress. She'd rather burn the thing than wear it again.

Maybe jeans would work. Country churches were casual, right?

No. Not jeans. Not on her first Sunday. What if Andrea were dressed up? How would she feel if Suzanna plopped down next to her in work clothes? As if she didn't stick out as a misfit already.

Suzanna wiggled out of her suit and slipped the paisley over her head. It settled over her frame, fitting just like it had when she'd bought it a little more than two years ago. She fingered the knot at her waist, and the memory came tumbling back.

They had been celebrating. They hadn't had the money to splurge, but it'd seemed necessary. Jason's transplant was a success. He would recover. Live. That demanded a celebration.

She glanced at the woman in the mirror, and her focus fixed on the ring hanging at her neck. Cold and empty—just like her. Heat pulsed through her veins as tears blurred her vision. She was just a frame. Drained of energy, of joy, of life.

She tugged the jersey off and curled up on the bed. Clothes no longer a concern, Suzanna pulled a gray fleece throw over her shoulders.

Rodewald

Church would have to wait. Suzanna Wilton was not ready to fake it just yet.

CHAPTER THREE

"What's the matter, Bumpkin Girl?" Mother nudged Dre, who sat to her right. "You look mopey."

Tom sprawled an arm across the back of Andrea's chair and squeezed her shoulder. "You didn't really think she'd come, did you, hon?"

Paul studied Tom and then glanced back to Dre. "The Pickle Lady?"

"Stop calling her that, Paul." Dre's eyes narrowed.

He sat up a little straighter. Why was Andrea so wrapped up with this city girl? Mopping up the last of his gravy with his dinner roll, Paul worked to overcome his irritation. How had his rude neighbor managed to work her way into all of his conversations?

"What's going on with you two?" Mother's look bounced from Dre to Paul and back again.

Dre's eyebrows arched, and she kept her stare locked on Paul.

"Nothing between us." He rubbed at the tension knotting in his neck. Surely he could rise above it. Didn't need to let the Pickle Lady eclipse his Sunday afternoon. "Dre's just worried about my new neighbor."

Andrea slouched in her chair. "Suzanna Wilton. She moved into Mrs. Hawkins's old place. Did you ever meet Mike Wilton?"

"Yes." Mother's voice begged for more information.

"Suzanna is his daughter, and he left the place to her. Seems to me we haven't given her much of a welcome." Andrea's eyes sparked, and her accusation nagged Paul. "So I went over to say hi. She's the sweetest girl, but there's something about her. Something...tragic. Her eyes seemed sad."

Sad? What trick had the Pickle played on his sister? He saw an angry woman with sourness oozing from her pores. Had there been tragedy in her expression?

"She did lose her father suddenly." Tom leaned against the table with his free arm. "That would explain it."

Mother's forehead wrinkled. "How did Mike die?"

"Heart attack. Happened while he was driving to town. Sherriff found his pickup in the ditch."

"That *is* sad." Mother tsked. "Still a young man. Late fifties, I'd guess."

Tom nodded.

Shame heated Paul's skin. He'd been unfair in his judgment. Harsh in his thoughts toward the Pick—toward Miss Wilton.

"I don't know." Dre brought the conversation back around. "She didn't choke up when we talked about her father. I feel like it's something different. Anyway, Mama, I invited her to church. I'm super-bummed that she didn't show up."

Mother patted Dre's arm. "I know a determined young woman who could coax a badger out of a hole. You keep at it, Bumpkin."

A smile softened Dre's eyes until they settled on Paul again. Why did she keep looking at him as though he were to blame? He knew nothing about Suzanna Wilton—had nothing whatsoever to do with her problems.

Disappointment sagged in Andrea's expression. Paul's shoulders sank.

Sunday dinner with his family——the best part of the week. He missed it when he was working the river property, and now it was strained. Thanks to the Pickle.

Glancing at his mother, he examined her with careful thought. She looked more rested. He allowed satisfaction to calm his annoyance. His parents were doing okay——a massive relief after Dad's third stroke.

Looking around the table. His sister's kids were awesome—— funny, intelligent, and well mannered. He loved every minute he got to spend with his two nieces and one nephew. Man, they grew fast.

Kelsey was only a peanut in his arms twelve years ago. Now she was a willowy sixth grader. Prettier than any he knew elsewhere. Nine-year-old Kiera grew lovelier every day, complete with her retainer and glasses. And Keegan. What a rascal that boy was. Five years old and more get-up-and-go than anyone around him had to match. The little gus could charm Paul's meanest bull into a tutu.

The years had slipped by, and Paul assumed they were the closest to his own kids he'd ever know. Honestly, that was okay. Usually. Most days, he had enough work to do to fill the loneliness, but he sure was thankful for moments like this. What would he do without his family?

His survey came back to Dre. Her silence pleaded with him. *You're a better man than this.*

Letting his gaze fall back to the table, Paul resolved to try again.

Mother had always done laundry on Thursdays. Suzanna didn't know why she patterned any part of her life after the woman, but she'd assigned the task for the same day. As she pinned the last of her sheets to the line, a breeze ruffled the cotton against her face. She'd never used line-dried sheets before, and she wondered if they'd be as crisp and fresh as someone on Pinterest had claimed.

Dust billowed beyond the tree line, and the sound of tires on gravel grew more distinct with each breath. Mr. What's-His-Name neighbor-man's truck passed the creek, the dark blue paint gleaming in the sunshine. He slowed as he approached her drive, and Suzanna groaned when he turned in.

Persistent old bugger. She squared her shoulders, wishing Andrea had pulled up instead. Why did her only company the whole week have to be an opportunistic buzzard?

The engine cut, and by the time she rounded the front of the house, the man was striding toward her with the typical confidence of a self-important cowboy.

"Afternoon, Miss Wilton." He smiled as if they were friends.

Suzanna scowled. She met his handshake, gripping harder than necessary. "Hello."

Holding her hand, he looked into her eyes. There was something intentional about his gaze. Suzanna prepared herself for manipulation.

"I wanted to check on you," he said. "Wanted to make sure you're doing okay."

Really? Doubtful. Suzanna bobbed her head in slow measures and swallowed. "I'm fine, same as last week."

He smiled. The expression seemed genuine.

Oh, he was good at this.

"Good. Listen, I left in such a hurry last week. I didn't give you my number." He passed a slip of yellow legal paper across the space between them. "You know, in case you did need something. I'm only a mile down the road, and I wouldn't mind helping out."

Jaw set tight, she glanced down at his boots. Was he serious? "Thanks."

Her response sounded more like a question than gratitude, and her face warmed. How sincere was this guy? She forced herself to meet his eyes.

He nodded with a half smile and tugged at his cowboy hat. "Good day to you, Miss Wilton."

Suzanna stared at his back while he strode to his truck. What was he about? She skimmed the paper he'd handed her. *Paul Rustin.*

Well, Mr. Paul Rustin, let's see what you're up to.

"Mr. Rustin."

The truck's door chime dinged while he paused inside the opened door, one boot propped on the running board. "Yes ma'am?"

"There's a spigot over by the big water tub for the horse."

"The tank?"

Sure. What did she know? Her ears felt hot. "Yes."

Dropping his foot on the gravel he nodded. "Okay, the spigot?"

Oh yeah. That's where she was going with this. "Right. It doesn't work. I've been hauling water from the house."

His eyebrows pinched. "Hmm. Let's take a look." He shut the door, ending the incessant ding-ding-ding escaping from the cab. Did all country people leave their keys in the ignition?

Suzanna crossed her arms as he approached.

"By the barn?"

Stupid girl. He was waiting for her to lead the way. She cleared her throat and moved a half a step away. "Yes, inside the pen."

"Corral."

Now he was just showing off. She rolled her shoulders back as her lungs filled with indignation. Dipping a curt nod toward the back of the property, she set her stride toward the dadgum *corral.*

Mr. Rustin walked beside her, his relaxed stride irritating her with every step. She couldn't bring herself to check his expression, but she had no doubt there would be smug laughter in his eyes.

They reached the fence, and Suzanna fumbled with the gate. Mr. Rustin climbed on the bottom rung of a sturdy panel and sprung over. She dropped the carabiner that secured the slide-lock and watched the man saunter to the tank. He flipped the handle up and ... nothing happened.

Shocking.

"Sure enough." He leaned down close to the pipe, listening.

Did spigots whisper symptoms? Whatever was the man doing?

He shook his head. "It's not working at all."

Exactly. Suzanna was so glad she asked.

"Do you have a separate main for the barn?"

"A separate main?"

Leaving the spigot open, he covered the ground back to the fence and sailed over the top again. "A water main. There might be a separate valve that would need to be switched on."

Why would that be? Sheesh.

"Let's go check the house." He set off in that direction. "If there's a separate valve, chances are it'll be in the basement."

"Not in the barn?" Suzanna jogged to catch up.

"Maybe, but I wouldn't think so. More likely to freeze. We'll check the house first."

They reached the side door, and he pulled open the screen. He stepped back, and Suzanna stared at him.

He tugged it wider and swept his free hand to the side.

"Oh, sorry." She scurried into the house and led him past her kitchen. Pushing on the narrow basement door, she drew a long breath and tugged on the chain dangling to her left.

"Is it creepy?"

His voice drifted from just above her head, tickling her spine. She jerked against the sensation, snapping herself rigid. "I don't know." She cleared her throat, irritated that she sounded like some goofy teenager. "I haven't made it down there yet."

Because it was creepy. The narrow stairway was dark and steep. Cobwebs from spiders Suzanna didn't want to think about drifted between the dark, exposed studs. The concrete floor at the bottom looked cold and foreboding. She hadn't any intention of visiting the depths of gloom on her own.

She hadn't any intention of visiting it with her handsome neighbor, either. Wait. Handsome?

Mr. Rustin put a hand to her shoulder and pushed her against the doorjamb. He slid past her and dropped down the steps, his chest brushing against her arm. Suzanna scolded her heart for pounding ridiculously hard.

He ducked under the header as his boots smacked against the concrete floor. He was pulling on the light bulb chain in the basement before Suzanna realized she was still standing on the top step, staring at his broad shoulders. Shaking her head, which felt stupidly light, she forced her feet down the exposed wood risers.

"I got it, Suz." His grin flashed beneath the wide rim of his hat. "It's just around the corner here."

Suz? How did she feel about that one? Her heart continued its silly skipping, while her brain tried to conjure up indignation.

Forget it. What was wrong with her anyway? She paused halfway down the flight of stairs. He could take care of it, and she wouldn't have to descend any farther into the icky pit. But that would only add to his growing stockpile of ammunition. She wasn't selling. He'd have to get that set into his cowboy-tough head. She may be out of place and less than capable right now, but she wasn't letting go of the only thing her dad had left her.

She took the stairs with quick steps, ignoring the musty smell of dirt and old wood. Mr. Rustin stood around the corner to her right, studying a large tank and several pipes.

"This is your well pump." He pointed to the tank secured to the wall, and then his finger moved to three pipes. "And these are your mains. These two are open. That one's closed." He bent and gripped the lever, pushing it parallel to the pipe.

"What are the other ones for?"

"One is the house. The other—you'll have to go exploring for that. Maybe there's another tank in your west pasture."

"Why wouldn't they all be on?"

Shrugging, he shook his head. "Dunno. Let's go see if that fixed your problem, though."

He waited for her to lead and clunked up the stairs behind her.

Suzanna gulped in fresh air as her eyes adjusted to the sunlight. Her head cleared, and the silly woman who had behaved like a juvenile faded. She took to the barn with confidence, leaving Mr. Rustin to follow. The sound of splashing water filled her ears as they approached the corral. She climbed the fence panel, unable to leap it as Mr. Rustin had. But she landed without falling, a satisfying success. Leaning against the handle, she put her weight into it, shutting off the pump.

"Thank you, Mr. Rustin." She brushed her hands against her jeans as she walked back to the fence.

He grinned from his place on the other side. "You're welcome." His eyes held hers and his smile grew.

He was mocking her. Suzanna's back jerked straight as she folded her arms.

Mr. Rustin pulled on his hat. "Afternoon, Miss Wilton."

Suzanna stomped to a stall, refusing to watch him as he walked away. He was *not* handsome.

Paul shook his head as he pulled away. She was almost friendly. For about five seconds.

Was she actually afraid of the basement? He chuckled, and something warm bloomed in his chest. She'd looked so timid standing on that top step. Hesitation had softened her features—she was pretty.

It was short lived. What made Dre think the woman was sweet? And shy?

Paul glanced in his rearview mirror. Suzanna's house shrank as he traveled down the road. He wondered if he and Dre had met the same woman.

CHAPTER FOUR

"Hey there, Suzanna Wilton." A feminine hint of southern drawl drifted from behind.

She knew that voice. Suzanna turned in the aisle, clutching her box of Grape Nuts. "Hi." She smiled, unable to hide her relief. Aside from the smug Mr. Rustin, she hadn't spoken to anyone face to face all week. She'd prayed she would run into Andrea as her Jeep Wrangler kicked up dust on the drive to town.

Ironic. God would answer a small request. He'd ignored all of the big, important ones.

"I'm sorry I haven't stopped by this week." Andrea leaned against her cart. "I was hoping to, but my week went into overdrive. Fall Festival is this weekend, and we do a chuckwagon feed for the barn dance at Heritage Park."

Suzanna glanced at Andrea's cart. Number ten cans of beans and fruit cocktail nearly filled the space, and bags of buns were stacked on top, heaped to the brim. She wondered who "we" was. Did Andrea's family do all that on their own?

"I'd love to have you visit, if you get time." Suzanna wished she could swallow the words. So selfish. So needy.

"You bet." Andrea's smile seemed sincere, her nod determined. "How about coffee in the morning? I run the kids in for school at 7:30, and I could stop on my way home, if that's not too early."

Company. Good company. Suzanna would make daybreak work if it meant she'd get to smile, get to laugh again.

"Not too early at all. I'll have a pot ready for you."

Andrea's smile widened. "So, are you coming to the Fall Festival?"

"I don't know anything about it." She needed to get a newspaper or something.

"Well, let me tell you, girl. It's a blast." Andrea leaned toward Suzanna, grasping her arm. "Town strings up that old barn with lights. Saturday, the park is abuzz with vendors and games. Cotton candy and funnel cakes. Drum-line sound-off, battle of the bands, and solo sing-off. It's almost better than the county fair. Then at night, those lights blaze, and music sets the air in motion. Mmm, girl. It's so much fun. You don't want to miss it."

A hint of a smile tugged at Suzanna's lips. Small town charm. Something she'd hoped for.

But to go alone?

"Listen, Suz. You could ride in with us. Tom and I can stop and pick you up, and you could spend the day with us. You'll get to meet the whole town, and it'll be great."

So, she was transparent. "How about I follow you in? If you're doing the chuckwagon thing, I don't want to get in the way, but the festival sounds fun. Would that be okay?"

"Perfect." Andrea hugged her. "We'll talk more about it tomorrow. I'm so sorry, Suz, but I've gotta run. My daughter has piano in five minutes, and I still have to check out."

Suzanna nodded as gratitude lifted her cheeks. Thank God. She did. For the first time in countless months, she did exactly that. In the next heartbeat, though, she wondered why He had just now decided to listen to her pleas.

Her eyes and nose stung. It was too late. For Jason, for her, God was listening too late.

Paul shuffled the football to Jim Calloway and jogged off the field. Sweat dripped near his ear, and he rubbed it away with his sweatshirt. Dropping onto the picnic table near the water cooler, he watched while the guys tore around on the grass.

Man, they were getting old. High school had long since bid them good day. Gray speckled every one of their heads—well, except for Jim. His hair fell out the year his third daughter had been born. Paul ran a hand over his head. He was getting a little thin on top too. Where did time go?

Had it been nineteen years since they'd graduated? Nineteen years since they'd sauntered through this park, proudly flashing letterman jackets and guaranteeing each other that once school was done, they were leaving this small town for good?

Here they were. Six out of the twelve guys in their class. Still tossing a football around at Fall Festival. Still calling Rock Creek home.

For Paul, that was a good thing. He had needed some redirection in his life. For some of the other guys, though, being here meant they were stuck. Bad choices, hard luck, or a lack of courage. They just didn't get where they thought they'd go.

"Can you believe how sloppy these kids play?" Chuck filled his Gatorade cup and dropped next to Paul, his sides heaving like he'd been running a marathon. "We were so much more disciplined."

Probably not. Paul was sure he wasn't, anyway. Discipline hadn't been a part of his vocabulary at age eighteen. Paul dropped his head, hoping a shrug was both an answer and a deterrent. He didn't want to hear any of Chuck's "good ole days" speeches. They were long, centered on himself, and generally fictional.

"You didn't come shoot last week."

Bummer. That topic wasn't much better. "Nope. I went to Dre's for brunch, and Kiera asked to go riding."

"Man, that's nuts." Chuck shoved Paul's shoulder. "You managed to avoid the matrimony irons, and you still get roped into kid duty?"

"I had fun."

"Sure. I draw the line with my woman when it comes to Saturday shoots. I'm going. End of discussion."

Such a big talker. Paul leaned back against his hands, squaring a look on Chuck. "You've got a pretty good wife, Chuck. I'm sure Shelby gives you plenty of slack."

Chuck opened his mouth, but nothing came out. He smacked his jaw shut and let his attention roam over the park.

Paul surveyed the activity as well. The high school kids continued to pound the middle-aged has-beens. Holeman's had sponsored a bouncy castle, set up past the field under a trio of ash trees. Children screamed and giggled as they ran with abandon, zigging past booths and dodging adults as they chased through the crowd. Rock Creek High's drum line pounded away on the stage opposite the old barn. Nothing ever changed.

He loved that.

Tom and Andrea's chuck wagon was parked near the barn, and they were hard at work preparing food for the dance. Keegan climbed on the wheels and over the wagon tongue, and Kelsey followed him, no doubt having been assigned guard duty. Andrea hefted a roaster to a table by their rig and stopped to talk to Mrs. Blake. They chatted for a few moments, Dre touching the old woman's shoulder as she so often did with anyone, and then she waved to someone out of Paul's line of vision.

The Pickle Lady stepped around the wagon, responding to Dre's beckon. A groan vibrated his core.

Andrea introduced the pair, and the three women stood in a loose circle. Dre smiled and talked. Mrs. Blake nodded. The Pickle looked awkward. Timid. Exactly like she'd looked at the top of her stairway. He thought it cute then. Not so much now.

What was she doing out on that place all alone? She was clearly afraid—incapable. Fifteen miles from town, attempting work for which she'd never been seasoned. That kind of undertaking required confidence and strength—for a man or a woman. Timidity would only get her into trouble.

It didn't suit at all. Why was she so set on staying? It wasn't like she was stuck. He'd made an offer himself. So had Chuck. And Jim. Why was she being so stubborn?

"So, have you talked to her anymore?" Chuck nudged Paul's bicep with his elbow.

Caught staring. That can't be good.

"Stopped by earlier this week." Paul hopped to the ground, shrugging like the subject was inconsequential. Because it was. "She needed a hand with...something that wasn't working right."

Did he need to cover her ignorance? The sooner she figured out she was in over her head, the better—for her. He had no reason to feel bad about it.

"Did you get some sense talked into her?"

Paul scowled. "Don't know what you mean."

"She doesn't belong out there." Chuck seemed perfectly at ease slamming a stranger.

Paul's jaw clamped hard, and a muscle near his eye twitched. He couldn't understand his reaction. He'd just thought the same thing. "It's her property, legal and fair. Her dad worked awful hard to reclaim the land. Don't know that we have any right to begrudge her."

Chuck's eyebrows twitched. "Maybe so, nobleman, but you're not thinking of others."

He tossed his head, not trying to disguise irritation. "How's that?"

"Doesn't affect you the way it does those of us east of her property." Chuck took a swig from his paper cup before he crushed it. "That spring water doesn't flow to your land. Did you know she inherited senior water rights pertaining to Rock Creek?"

No. He didn't know that. Didn't know why that rumpled Chuck, either. "That a fact?"

"'Tis. Mike was a reasonable man, and the work he did on that place benefitted everyone. But now we've got this little upstart lady runnin' things and who knows——"

"How do you know she's not reasonable?"

Chuck unfolded his former linebacker body and planted his feet a little too close to Paul. "You think she's reasonable?"

Paul swallowed, hating that he allowed Chuck to intimidate him. The man was all wind. Well, no, that wasn't true. He was a cunning businessman, and he kept manipulation in his back pocket. He held notes on almost every business in town, including the Cottonwood County Sale Barn and Rock Creek Meats. Two operations necessary to Paul's.

"Don't know either way." Paul pulled his shoulders back and forced his eyes to meet Chuck's challenge.

"She's refused offers five times over. Offers that come close to doubling the actual value of the property. That's not reasonable at all, is it?"

Double the value? What was Chuck afraid of? Paul's fist closed behind his back as heat spread over his skin. He'd just landed himself in the middle of something, and he didn't want any part of it. Not for Chuck. Not for Suzanna Wilton.

He glanced back to the wagon——to the Pickle. She smiled at Andrea. A small, timid smile.

Chuck would run her over.

"Doesn't seem neighborly," Paul said, "to push a woman out of town before you know anything about her."

He met Chuck's dark stare and walked away.

Had he really just thrown himself in with the Pickle Lady?

"You don't have to help, Suz." Andrea filled buns with sloppy joe meat while Tom and Suzanna sliced watermelon.

"I don't mind." Suzanna took up another melon, tapping the rind out of habit. Heavy. Hollow. Perfect.

If she weren't helping, she'd be leaving. She dropped her eyes when tears began to burn. Andrea had introduced her to at least two dozen people. They smiled, shook her hand, and asked about her roots. Most were kind. A few, however, were definitively not.

Funny how those names stuck in her mind. She'd never remember the names of all the nice people she'd met. But Shelby, Kimberly, and Trish—those she couldn't forget.

All three belonged to the men who'd come out wanting her place. Friendly offers were one thing, although a sincere hello would have been nice. But these men had been aggressive. Their pressure tactics intimidated Suzanna.

Apparently they had schooled their wives in the art of persuasion. Each woman had raked her over with silent contempt, their scorn making her blood hot and her core tremble. Their scorching glances devoured every other kind word. Were it not for Andrea and the desire for a friend, she would have climbed in the Jeep and driven west to the state line.

"You've just earned yourself a devoted friend for life." Tom grinned first at Suzanna and then at his wife. "Dre is big on service. To her, it's a mark of a humble, generous soul."

Andrea smiled, nodding. "You bet, but you were already my friend, Suz."

Suz. She liked how Andrea kept calling her that. There was something familiar, cherished in a nickname. Only her father—and Jason—ever called her anything but Suzanna. Her mother, her sister, even the few friends she'd gathered as an adult all called her by her full given name.

Except for Mr. Rustin. Irritation tangled with some sort of secret pleasure as she recalled his slip into familiarity. She pushed it aside.

"Speaking of friends, and service—" Andrea nudged Suzanna with her elbow. "I'd love for my new friend to come with me to worship service tomorrow."

Suzanna dropped her eyes and sliced through the thick green rind. She wasn't going to get out of it. Truthfully, she wasn't sure she wanted to. Sundays always felt vacant. Maybe going back to church would plug the hole.

"What time?"

"Sunday school begins at nine and worship at ten thirty." Andrea stopped working and focused her attention on Suzanna. "We have sweet rolls in between if you wanted to do both, but if you're only comfortable with worship service, that's perfectly fine."

Worship service. Sounded like so much more than church. Church was a building, a habit. In some circles, a requirement. Worship sounded personal.

Suzanna examined her frayed emotions. She was tired of brokenness. Tired of pain pulsing through her soul. She'd tried emptying herself of it, but it stuck to her like the gummy sap of an elm tree.

Worship. Before a God who had disappointed her?

Suzanna took in Andrea's warm sincerity. She would go to the service, but not before she had her heart securely locked away. Worship was not something she could muster.

CHAPTER FIVE

Paul sat on the right side of the sanctuary near the back. The stained-glass window and the ten-foot cross behind the pulpit looked different from that side, that distance.

His Bible lay open to the third chapter of 1 Peter while his finger rested in Ephesians 4.

To sum up, all of you be harmonious, sympathetic, brotherly, kindhearted and humble in spirit; not returning insult for insult, but giving a blessing instead.

Brotherly. Kindhearted. Paul's attention floated to his regular seat. To where Tom, Dre and the kids sat with the Pickle Lady on the far end. His gut clenched, and he dropped his gaze back to the Bible. Pastor Ron had moved on to Ephesians, his cross-reference passage, as he continued with his sermon about unity in the body of Christ.

Paul stayed in 1 Peter. He read the first seven verses in chapter three, the verses preceding Pastor Ron's chosen text.

Was it ironic that particular passage addressed husbands and wives? Paul shifted and cleared his throat. What about it should make him uncomfortable? Unmarried all of his thirty-seven years, he had no reason to feel convicted. He'd only ever pored over Biblical marriage instructions once. Turned out, it wasn't necessary.

Maybe that was what made his insides twist. Maybe not. Hailey was long gone, and he was well past it.

Paul rubbed his neck and read verse seven again.

Show her honor as a fellow heir of the grace of life, so that your prayers will not be hindered.

His head jolted up, and his eyes fell on the Pickle. Suzanna Wilton?

How did that woman keep turning up in his thoughts? Her ignorance annoyed him. Her anger provoked him. Probably more than it should. His life would be smoother without her.

Why, then, did he keep thinking about her? Paul rubbed his upper lip and focused on the sermon.

"The way we treat each other is a testimony to what we believe about God. Is He quick to anger? Neither should we be. Does He hold on to resentment? We shouldn't either. Does He defend those who cannot stand on their own? We also should take up the righteous crusade. If we believe God is love, we should behave lovingly. If we believe He is kind, then kindness should pour from our lives. A disciple of Christ becomes more and more like Him."

Of all weeks, Pastor Ron chose kindness for his message. Avoidance was the easier path.

Paul squared his shoulders and swallowed. Yesterday's conversation with Chuck replayed in his mind, and Paul was still frustrated that he'd landed himself somewhere in the middle of a brewing mess.

Maybe he hadn't landed himself anywhere. God was pretty good at logistics.

Harmonious. Sympathetic. Brotherly. Kindhearted.

He slouched in the pew, leaning his elbows on his knees. Okay, fine. Be nice to the Pickle. Got it.

Suzanna slid out of the Jeep while her hand kept the skirt of her dress from flying. She glanced at the paisley print and jerked her eyes away in the next instant. The only way she'd made it out of the farmhouse that morning was by avoiding the mirror and ignoring her attire.

"Here we are." Andrea strode across the rocked drive, reaching for Suzanna's arm. "I'm so excited you're joining us. My parents will be here in a bit, and my brother said he was right behind us."

Suzanna's mouth curved halfheartedly. Sunday dinner. Childhood memories of pot roast and honeyed carrots flitted across her vision. Replaced in the next moment by visions of lonely Sunday afternoons with a bowl of cold cereal and a side of resentment. Her mother would be off riding, her sister, pursuing a coveted PhD, and her father—the preacher—tucked away in his study ... ignoring the obvious.

Andrea rescued Suzanna from her gloomy past.

"Fair warning, Suz. We're a noisy bunch. Daddy won't say much—the strokes have changed him. But the rest of us—we love to laugh."

Her subtle southern country accent provided Suzanna a distraction. "Did you grow up in Rock Creek?"

Andrea laughed. "Sure did. But I went to Baylor, and after four years in Waco, I brought a little bit of Texas home with me. Even shared some with my brother. He used to tease me about it—said I couldn't decide where I was in life. Then one day he spat out one of my Texan phrases, and that put an end to it."

"Ah. That explains it." Suzanna walked alongside Andrea to the house, her smile blooming.

Picturesque. Tom and Andrea's home had been plucked from a *Better Homes and Gardens* magazine. White clad siding shimmered as a beacon on a sea of billowing grass. A large bay window and a wide covered front porch dressed up the traditional two-story frame. The yard was tastefully landscaped with a narrow strip of manicured lawn stretching to a picket-fenced garden. Native flowers, tamed and orchestrated in an impressive symphony of deep purples, vibrant pinks and sunny yellows, bobbed against an island hedge of glossy-leaved lilacs.

Suzanna imagined the Kent home in springtime. The fragrant blooms of those lilacs would perfume the air while daffodils and tulips heralded the new life of spring. Maybe Andrea had fruit trees tucked around back, and the pinks and whites of apple and peach blossoms would sing of hope and bounty.

Suzanna's breath caught as her heart felt light and free. It'd been so long.

God takes broken things...

A familiar blue truck turned into the rock drive, and Suzanna's heart dropped. What was he doing here?

Andrea squeezed her arm. "Oh good. Paul's here."

Good?

She led Suzanna toward the door and they met Paul on the porch.

"You made it." Andrea grinned. "Suz, you've met my brother, Paul, right?"

Her brother? Suzanna's tongue seemed rusted in place. She nodded as her eyes set on his.

"We've met," Paul said. "I was surprised to see you in church, Miss Wilton."

Surprised? Of all the things the man could have thought to say—*it was nice to see you,* or *glad you could make it*—Paul Rustin chose *surprised.* Well, that about summed him up. Rude. Self-absorbed and smug. Suzanna's chin tilted up, and she forced something like a smile.

"I grew up in church, Mr. Rustin." She held eye contact, refusing to bow to his criticism. "It was nice to be in one again."

His gaze chilled although his smile stayed plastered in place. He tipped a curt nod as he pulled the screen door open.

Andrea looked at Paul with an odd expression before she led Suzanna inside. Paul followed them to the entry but then cut off for the front room where the stairs split the house. Following Andrea to the kitchen, Suzanna stifled a sigh. A Sunday afternoon with the arrogant Mr. Paul Rustin. She would have preferred cold cereal on her own.

"What did you do to that girl, Paul?" Andrea glared from beside the counter, her hands perched on her hips like she was lecturing her children.

Paul went rigid. The day had already been long. He didn't need his kid sister scolding him as though he were ten. "What do you mean, what did I do? I didn't do anything to the Pickle."

"I told you to stop calling her that." Her glare gained heat. "No wonder she's afraid of you."

Afraid of him? Ha! Andrea didn't know one thing about it. The woman was as spiny as a cactus and as bold-faced as anyone he'd ever met. Except when she was looking down spooky basement stairs. Or meeting strangers.

Was she afraid of him?

Brotherly, kindhearted. That lasted, didn't it? Paul swallowed a groan. What was it about her that made him so agitated?

"I haven't done anything, Dre." Pursuing an argument to alleviate guilt. Yeah. That made sense.

"You must have. She went completely stiff the moment she saw you."

"Maybe she's just a stiff."

"That's not the woman I met."

He knew they hadn't met the same person. "I don't know why you think this is my fault. I told you I haven't done anything."

"I hate to argue with you, Paul." Tom appeared in the doorway, leaning against the frame. "But it did get pretty icy as soon as you came on the scene."

Um, yeah. She could have frosted a July afternoon with her cold blue eyes. How was that his fault?

"You're in on it, aren't you?" Dre stepped toward him, dismay tinting her voice.

"In on what?" This just kept getting better.

His little sister's scowl deepened.

Tom stepped into the kitchen, moving between the siblings. "Dre, you know better than that."

Paul propped his hands on his hips. "What's going on?"

"Trish Calloway," Tom said as though that should explain everything.

Granted, the woman talked more than a rooster crowed at dawn, and trouble clung to her like Gorilla Glue, but just hearing her name cleared up absolutely nothing. Paul shifted, waiting for Tom to give him a little more to work with.

"She was talking with Shelby just behind us before Sunday school." Tom pulled a stool from the breakfast bar and slid onto it. "Something about a plan to see that the sale happens and making sure that water rights were redistributed. By any means. Those were her words."

Andrea's brow hiked. "It doesn't take a stellar IQ to figure whose land they're after. I saw you talking with Chuck yesterday, Paul. Are you in on whatever they're scheming?"

Paul's ears rang as if she'd smacked him. "How could you even ask, Dre? Is that what you really think of me?"

"No." Anger sizzled in her glare. "That's not at all who I know you to be, but I also haven't known you to be cold. Hard. Something's gotten into you where Suzanna is concerned. You intimidate her, and you seem to like it that way."

Intimidate her? Good grief. Dre couldn't have misread the situation more if it had been written in a foreign language.

"Look. I told you everything. I've met her twice. Once, the first day when I got back. I think she would have taken a bat to my head if she knew how to swing one, and—"

"Why?" Dre pounced.

"Why what?"

"Why was she mad at you that first day?"

Paul rolled his head back and growled. "That's what I'm telling you. I. Don't. Know. She's a pickle."

Andrea pursed her lips and speared him with disapproval. "That could be part of your problem, Paul. Stop saying that."

His problem? Scowling, he stared at her. She met his challenge, unrepentant. This was going nowhere, and he was done with it.

"Okay, Dre. You win. No more pickle talk." He grabbed his half-empty glass of tea and took it to the sink. Snatching his Stetson, he made his way to the door. "But it doesn't change anything. I said hello to her, introduced myself as a neighbor, and even made an offer on her property, if she needed an out."

"You made an offer?" Dre's voice caught him halfway out the door.

He glanced back. She stepped toward the door, incredulity lifting her eyebrows. Swinging his eyes to Tom, he caught the man mashing his lips between his teeth.

Bingo.

...and humble in spirit

He *had* started this. Time to go mend some fences.

Paul knocked for the second time, sure Suzanna was home. The Jeep sat outside the garage, and the side-entry door hung open. She was probably ignoring him. Figures.

He turned away, intending to try the side entrance when the doorknob rattled. Dressed in sweats and eyes red rimmed, Suzanna wedged herself between the door and the frame.

She'd been crying. Because of him? He had been aloof with her—okay, maybe cold, but he hadn't said anything mean. Why would she cry?

Something burned near his stomach. Not guilt though. Resentment. If she couldn't handle herself, she shouldn't be here. She needed to run on home to the coddled city life she was accustomed to.

"Did you need something, Mr. Rustin?"

Just like that, she was as stiff as a branding iron, and the heat from her glare could have scalded cowhide. And Dre thought the woman was intimidated by him.

"Yes, ma'am." Paul gulped back annoyance. He could be chivalrous, even if she didn't deserve it. "You and I seem to be at odds. I can't leave it that way, seeing how we're neighbors, and you're my sister's friend."

One well-shaped eyebrow curved upward. She stepped onto her porch, parallel to him. "I see." Challenging him with a suspicious gaze, she crossed her arms. "What is it you're really after?"

Whatever could the little spitfire mean? "Excuse me?"

"Since the day we met you've had an agenda, Mr. Rustin. Quit playing the gentlemen and just spit it out."

"I'm not after anything, Miss Wilton." Paul stepped forward, matching her glare. "You've had it out for me from the beginning. I only came by to introduce myself, and you opened fire on me. Perhaps *you* should explain."

"I shouldn't have to explain myself." She drew her shoulders up, refusing to back down.

The timid woman, afraid of spider webs and creepy basements, held his challenge. She wasn't weak at all. Paul studied her eyes. Blue—like a clear sky at noon on a summer day. Intelligent. Fierce.

"You've been after my property from the first day, Mr. Rustin." Anger animated her voice. "I'm not going to be manipulated because you pretend to be a gentleman. I know your kind. So, hear me plainly. I'm not selling."

I know your kind? Paul's pulse jumped while heat poured through him.

"Look, lady." He leaned into her space. "I own over three thousand acres of prime grazing land, including river frontage. I don't need your piddly two hundred acres. My offer that day was exactly what I told you—an out if you needed it. If you want to stay here, miserable and alone, go for it. It makes no difference to me."

Suzanna flinched, and her crimson face lowered. Were tears pooling in her eyes? That was great. What had that verse said? Kindhearted.

Backing away, she darted down the two steps and moved across her front lawn.

Well done, Paul.

His boots slapped against the cracked pavement of her front walk as he set out after her. She rounded the house and left the yard, heading in the direction of the barn. Paul's long strides closed the gap between them.

"Suzanna."

"Go away." She kept her pace, refusing to look at him. Nearing the corral, her feet suddenly swept out from underneath her, and in the next instant she was up to her waist in mud.

Mud? It hadn't rained in two weeks. Jogging the remaining distance, he stopped with a lurch. She hadn't slipped. The ground had caved under her feet. Paul reached to pull her out of the pit while he surveyed the hole. Three feet in diameter, the sopped earth had dropped at least two feet.

Suzanna took Paul's hand and turned to crawl out of the muck. The edge of the hole collapsed opposite her, mud plopping into the sludge, and then water shot skyward like Old Faithful.

"Whoa!" Paul yanked her to solid ground just as the fountain died back. Water continued to sputter, though it looked more like a gymnasium water fountain than a geyser.

Covered in mud and wet from the top down, Suzanna stared at the mess. Her face looked stoic, but her shoulders slumped.

"Guess we know why that water main was closed." Paul tried to make light of it.

Her eyes moved to him, and giant tears spilled onto her cheeks. "You're right." She sniffed, shaking her head. "All of you are right. I don't belong out here."

Leaking pipes forgotten, Paul's lungs emptied, and his shoulders dropped.

Suzanna lowered her eyes. "I don't know why my dad left me this place. He left all of his cash holdings to my sister, and this"—she spread her hands wide—"to me. I thought he must have meant for me to have it, but I don't know what I'm doing out here. I don't belong, and I can't do it."

Paul's heart slowed so that he was sure to feel guilt more acutely with each beat. "You're doing fine."

She laughed. A derisive, defeated exhale that said more than words. Taking her elbow, he eased to her side. Her shoulders shuddered, and she sniffed.

"Really, you are." He pulled her into a one-armed hug, rubbing her arm. "Any woman who can stand up to me and Jim Calloway and Chuck Stanton will do just fine out here."

She tipped her head into his shoulder—a sort of silent thank-you. He slid his hand to her shoulder and squeezed.

"Listen, Suz. This kind of thing just happens. To cowboys and city girls alike—it's just life. I've got a backhoe for my Deere. I'll come over tomorrow, and we'll fix this. Okay?"

She glanced up at him. "Your deer?"

He chuckled. "My tractor. John Deere."

"Oh." Her head fell, and pink crept over her neck.

Paul squeezed her against his shoulder. "You'll learn, kid. Don't give up."

She pulled away and swiped at the last of her tears, smearing mud over her cheek.

Paul bit the inside of his lip as a smile tugged at his mouth. "So, since I didn't take a mud bath, I'll go shut that main off."

Suzanna turned, her eyes growing as she took him in. "You're still in your church clothes."

He looked himself over. Mud had splattered over his dark Wranglers, and his western button-down was smeared where she'd brushed against him. He was speckled with water spots that would probably dry brown.

"No worries." He shrugged, smiling. "I don't own anything that can't go through the washing machine. It'll be fine."

She looked up at him, her expression pathetic—miserable. "I'm sorry, Mr. Rustin."

"I told you it's fine."

"No, I mean I'm sorry..." She dropped her gaze. "I'm sorry I've been so nasty."

Paul pulled his handkerchief from his back pocket. "We didn't get off to the best start." He brushed at the mud near her nose and then pressed the material into her hand. "It's not all your fault. I didn't know about Chuck and the others. Honest. But I have to admit, even without that, offering to buy your place probably wasn't the best way to introduce myself. Will you forgive me?"

Suzanna nodded, and a small smile touched her mouth.

Fierce and Timid. Suzanna Wilton was a bit of a pickle. Maybe not the sour kind though.

CHAPTER SIX

Suzanna tugged on her earbuds and pushed pause. Sitting still, she listened. Yep. There had been a knock. Leaving her computer, she moved toward her kitchen door.

"Mr. Rustin." She pulled the door open wider.

The man smiled, tipping his hat. "'Morning. Too early for you?"

Suzanna stepped back and swept her hand toward the kitchen. "Not at all. I work on Eastern Standard Time, so I'm up by five."

"Eastern? Why?"

"I work for a resort company in Florida." Suzanna followed him in and went straight for the coffee pot. She tipped it to him. "You a fellow caffeine addict?"

"I never turn down coffee."

She laughed. "That's what Andrea said."

His grin spread wide, tucking a dimple into his left cheek. "Yep. That's what our mother always says too."

Suzanna smiled and moved to the sink to fill the pot. He wasn't bad at all. How had she mistaken his friendly overtures for manipulation?

"So, Florida... how does that work?"

"I fill in reservation entries. Dates, locations. Really boring, mindless work." She opened her coffee tin and inhaled the nutty smoothness out of habit. "But it's a paycheck."

He dropped onto a chair at her kitchen table. "How long have you done that?"

"About four years." She leaned against the counter while the coffee gurgled and steamed.

He nodded, laying an arm on the table. A dozen questions bubbled to her mind. Had he always been a rancher? Three thousand acres—that seemed huge. How had he acquired so much so young? How old was he, anyway?

His face, though weathered from the life of an outdoorsman, looked to be not much older than thirty. His hair, cropped short and indented with the ring of his hat, had a few grays peppered near his ears. Her eyes dropped to the hand resting on her table. His ring finger lacked the pale markings of a wedding band. Had he ever been married?

Her thumb rubbed at her ring finger. It still felt empty. Turning to the fridge, she reached for the chain hidden under her collar and fingered the thin, simple band.

"Do you use cream, Mr. Rustin?" She hoped he hadn't noticed the wavering in her voice.

"Paul, Suzanna. If we're going to be friends, you should call me Paul."

Friends? She spat nails in his face the first day they'd met, and he was still willing to have a go at friendship? Suzanna grappled with the anomaly.

Forget it. Maybe country boys were just different stock altogether. "Cream?"

"Only if it's flavored."

Weird. Jason hated the stuff, of any variety. He called it slime. "Sorry. I only have the plain kind."

Paul held up his hand. "No problem. Just sugar, if you have some."

Sugar? What a terrible thing to put in a good brew. "Sweet tooth?"

"Huge. Candy, soda, cookies." He laughed. "I still put sugar on my cereal."

Yuck. Suzanna ate her Grape Nuts plain.

"I have an affection for Lucky Charms," he continued. "Just in case you ever wonder what to get me for Christmas. I can go through a whole box in a day."

She wrinkled her nose. "Don't tell me you drink the sugary milk when the cereal's gone."

"You bet." He gave her a playful *duh* look. "It's the best part."

Suzanna took down her sugar tub and snagged a soupspoon from the silverware drawer. "Heap it in when I'm not looking."

"Health nut?"

"No. Just not a sugar fiend."

She hadn't ever been, really, but she'd basically lived without it while she was with Jason. Suzanna grabbed two mugs and redirected her thoughts. Sliding onto the chair across from Paul, she wondered what to say next.

Two heaping spoonfuls drowned in his black coffee. Suzanna wrinkled her nose.

Paul grinned. "You said you wouldn't watch."

"That is disgusting."

"Have you tried it?"

"No."

"Then how do you know?"

Suzanna looked at his sugar-laced coffee and shook her head.

Paul laughed and took a sip. "So, did the mud hole dry up?"

Oh yes. The broken pipe. That was why he was here. "I haven't been out there yet."

He sat back against his chair, his posture easy. Likable. "I wanted to check the damage before I drove the tractor down here." He tipped his mug for another swig and grinned. "Actually, I thought you'd like a go at it."

"A go at what?"

"The tractor. Do you want to drive it?"

Drive a tractor? Was it a stick shift? Do tractors shift? Suzanna didn't know the first thing about farm equipment.

"I wouldn't—" She traced the handle of her mug. Paul was offering her help. Dignified help. A learning experience, which was more than a pat-on-the-head, I'll-indulge-you kind of gesture. "I don't know anything. Will I break it?"

"You can't do anything I haven't done myself." He drained his sugar-with-coffee. "I'll go look at the damage. Do you need to finish up?" He tipped his head toward her office.

She did. "I have about thirty minutes of work left, and then I can take a break. Will that be okay?"

Paul nodded. "Like I said, I wanted to inspect the problem first anyway. That way, I'll know what else we'll need to fix it. Are you okay with me poking at it without you?"

He was asking? During a single cup of coffee, he'd managed to blow away all her despised assumptions about him, and arrogant cowboys in general.

No, she didn't mind. Help would be a welcomed relief.

"Miss Wilton."

Suzanna froze, her hand still clutching the deposit slip. Though they'd only spoken twice, she knew that voice. It set the hair on her neck on end.

"Yes?"

"I'm glad to run into you today." Chuck Stanton stepped closer, his black boots slapping against the tiled floor. "Did you get what you needed?"

They were in a bank, not a warehouse. Did he think she needed help reaching the deposit envelopes on the top shelf? "I did, thank you."

"Good. We strive for excellent service, even out here in the sticks."

Sticks. That was ironic. Only the windbreaks and narrow creek banks had trees; the rest of the prairie was as wide open as an empty stadium. Suzanna nodded, biting her tongue as she stepped away.

"How are things out your way?"

Her feet halted, and she forced her gaze back to him. The man was a bit on the strange side. He gelled his hair and combed it smooth; a style he must have found on a poster of *Grease*. She imagined a wifebeater tee shirt clinging to his broad shoulders under his silver button-down. And those boots? Never saw a speck of dirt. He was one confused, creepy man.

Why did he want to buy her land? She glanced out the full-length window at the front of the bank. Certainly, he didn't drive that shiny Dodge down a dirt road much. The chrome on the wheels gleamed way too much to have kissed the gravel on a country road.

"Things are fine, thank you."

"Having any problems?"

Like he cared. Actually, he did. His eyes glinted with a sinister hope that put her spine straight. "Nothing that hasn't been handled."

"Really?"

Nuts. She'd said the wrong thing.

"What'd you run into?"

"Just a broken pipe, but Paul Rustin helped me fix it." She tilted her chin. "It's good now."

Stanton stared, rudely calculating with a cool expression. "That's fine, Miss Wilton." His voice set her jaw on edge. "Glad to hear my buddy Paul is making himself useful."

Suzanna backed away. Her heart pounded, and her neck stiffened. How could a man make words that should have been kind sound so menacing?

Paul strode to his pickup with one loaded paper bag tucked in his arm. He'd caught up with Rodney down at the sale barn that morning, and they'd put together a sale bill for the end of the month. After lunch with his parents, he'd stopped at the farm supply store for some sweet feed. Holeman's was his last stop for the day.

"Rustin."

Paul dropped his groceries on the front seat and turned. Chuck smacked his way across the parking lot, looking like a missile trained on his target. Hanging a thumb on his jean pocket, Paul waited for the man to speak.

Drawing near, Chuck suddenly smiled and squeezed Paul's shoulder. A little too tight. "How you doing, buddy?"

"Fine."

"So I hear."

He did, huh? Paul looked at him in silence.

"Hear you're quite the handy neighbor." Chuck crossed his arms and leaned against Paul's Ford.

"Do you?" Paul arched an eyebrow.

Chuck nodded his slicked head and pulled himself straight. He stood a good three inches taller than Paul; he was taller than most, for that matter. Chuck loved to take advantage of that genetic quirk whenever possible.

"I thought we understood each other at the Fall Festival, Rustin."

"How's that, Chuck?" Paul crossed his arms, rolling his shoulders so they pulled at his tee shirt.

So he hadn't been a linebacker like Chuck. Running backs weren't exactly sissies. Not that any of that mattered twenty years past the glory days. Chuck had spent the majority of those years in an air-conditioned office in the back of the bank. Paul had been tossing hay bales, pushing cattle, fixing fences, and maintaining tractors. He wasn't about to be intimidated by a man just because he had longer legs.

"Suzanna Wilton."

Paul's stomach clenched, and his brow dropped. "I don't recall what you mean."

"Listen, Paul." Chuck balled his fists as he planted his feet. "You know exactly what I'm talking about. She doesn't belong out there. She has no claim to it, and I'm not real keen on your interfering. You don't want to help our cause, fine. But stay out of the way. The sooner she realizes she's out of her element, the better."

"Better for who?" Paul's eyes pinched. "Fact is, Suzanna has plenty of claim on that property. It was her dad's. It's never belonged to you, and, as I recall, you never wanted it. Not when Mrs. Hawkins's estate went to auction. Not when the feedlot put it on the market. What makes you think you're entitled to it now?"

"I was outbid. Those corporations have unlimited funds. Something you can't relate to because you inherited everything you've got. The rest of us have to pinch for ours."

"Yeah, you have to pinch." Paul snorted. "Your daddy left you plenty. And you could have bought the property six years ago, just like any of us. You didn't want to touch it. Didn't want to deal with the EPA, with fines, or with the undertaking required to reclaim all of it. Suzanna has more claim to that dirt than anyone, based solely on what her daddy did. You're out of line, Chuck, and I won't be intimidated by your not-so-subtle threats. If my neighbor needs help, I'm gonna help her. End of story."

Chuck's face went red, and his eyes narrowed. He stared Paul down, and then suddenly his brow smoothed. A malicious smile spread from one ear to the other. "You go down to the sale barn today?"

Paul scowled.

Chuck threw his shoulders back. "I know what goes on in this little town, Rustin. I may not have anything to bend you, personally, but I hold plenty on your associates. People you work with. People you care about. Rodney has more out on that little operation than it's worth. Know who holds it?" Chuck spit, aiming near Paul's boot. "Don't cross me, boy."

His boots clicked against the asphalt as he sauntered away.

Paul hopped into the cab, slamming his door. Yeah, he got himself into something all right. And if Chuck was going to wave fire in his face, he wasn't about to back down.

He'd stop by Suzanna's. Often. Just so Chuck would know he couldn't palm his neck.

Suzanna dumped the soapy water, wondering why her socks weren't black from the dirt she'd just scrubbed off the wood floor. Almost two months since she'd moved, and she hadn't gotten around to the floors. Yuck. Hopefully, the tree wouldn't mind the brown, soapy water.

Paul's truck peeked around the curve coming from town. He slowed to a crawl, and she stepped to the road.

"Hey there, neighbor." He set his vehicle in park and hooked his arm out the open window. "How's the new pipe holding up?"

Suzanna grinned. "No mud craters as yet."

"You're not hauling water for something else, are you?" He dipped his head toward the bucket she still held.

"No. Just doing some long-overdue cleaning."

"When you're done, you can just head on down the road. I have all sorts of dirt in my house."

Laughter tickled her throat. "I'll pass, thanks. Unless you pay well."

"Lucky Charms, lady. That's all I can offer you."

Suzanna wrinkled her nose. "Definitely not then."

"You can't blame a guy for trying." Paul tapped the outside of his door with his palm. "So, I was thinking about you today. Wondered if you've set eyes on all your property."

Warmth spread in Suzanna's chest. It was nice to be thought of by someone. "I've poked around here and there."

"Not everywhere?"

She smiled. "No, not everywhere."

Paul nodded. "I thought maybe not. Do you know how to ride a horse?"

"My mother is into equine, so I've been on one before. But I don't know the equipment—I wouldn't try by myself."

His smile held a hint of laughter. Had she said something funny?

"Well, I think you should see your place. And I happen to believe anyone living with a horse ought to be able to ride it. How about I come out on Saturday, and we take a ride together?"

Seriously? He'd put up with her again for a whole Saturday?

"Are you sure? I know you have better things to do than to babysit your citified neighbor."

"Nothin' better than sitting in a saddle, Suz." He rubbed at his chin. "Saturday work for you?"

"It will."

Paul nodded and tugged at his hat. "Evening, Suzanna Wilton."

"Paul—" She caught him by the elbow before he put the truck in drive. "Thank you."

He dipped his head again. "See you Saturday."

Suzanna stepped back and watched while he eased down the road. Holding her bucket with both hands, she swung it in front of her knees. How long had it been since someone worried about her out of the clear blue? Something fresh poked her dreary soul, like new blades of grass breaking through barren soil. It felt like life. Like hope.

CHAPTER SEVEN

Paul stirred the soup he'd heated, inhaling tomato and basil. Man, the things Dre could do with a tomato. She ought to give lessons.

Maybe Suzanna would like to learn.

Bizarre. Why should he care if Suzanna would like to learn how to make Dre's tomato soup? His brain had gone goofy.

He smiled in spite of himself. The little gherkin. *My mother was into equine.* Who talked like that? Wait, she said *is.* Not *was.* Is. Where did her mother fit into her life? Mike hadn't talked about a wife, past or present. Hadn't worn a wedding ring, either.

These days kids grew up with parents who had separated all the time. It still bothered Paul. Mostly because his home had been whole, and it was good. Mom and Dad had their spats, sometimes maybe a little more than that, but they were committed. Paul had never known the instability of a broken home.

Sadness weighed on his heart. Would he be intruding to ask Suzanna about it?

RECLAIMED

Suzanna shivered in her dark kitchen. Wrapping her grandmother's sweater around her thin frame, she wished the heavy cable knit would ward off the chill inside her. She reached for the coffee pot and slipped into autopilot while her mind replayed the words that taunted her in her sleep.

"Have you found a new church yet, Suzie doll?" Daddy leaned forward, closing the space between them on the park bench.

Suzanna picked at her chipped nail polish. Why had she painted them? She never went out. Hospital. Pharmacy. Home. A once-a-week trip to Whole Foods. Nothing ever beyond those stops, including church.

"Suz." Daddy's hand felt warm on her elbow. "You need a family."

Yeah, she did. They'd shattered, like the wedding platter she'd dropped after Jason fell two months ago. Did Daddy really expect a church to act as a surrogate for their family?

"I know, Daddy. I have Jason."

"You take care of Jason." His hand moved to her shoulder and squeezed. "You do it all on your own. You need help. Support. There are people in the body of Christ who would gladly offer it to you if they knew."

What people? Their old church? Not a chance. Daddy left for good reason. She was a daughter of shame, of scandal. Nobody would ever see past it. Suzanna swallowed. Tears built behind her eyelids, and her nose stung.

"Does your mother help?"

So, he'd let the church thing go.

"No." She ground her teeth, swallowing back her tears. "I don't want her help."

Daddy didn't argue. Certainly he shared her contempt.

"Suz." He dropped his hand and leaned his elbows against his knees. "God takes broken things and makes them beautiful again. He reclaims our desolate places. But you have to let him, hon."

The tears came back and there was no stopping them. Daddy would know. He was deeply connected with pain—with betrayal. But... but something. Her heart felt like it'd been shoved through a meat grinder. If God couldn't prevent it all, if He couldn't spare her, then why should she believe that He could heal her? And even if He could, she had no reason to bet that He would.

She'd been forsaken. Nothing fixes that.
Water ran over her hand. Coffee. She was making coffee.
Suzanna trembled again.

Daddy was wrong. Her life hadn't been fixed; she'd been
beaten down further still. What kind of a god takes a girl's
husband and her father in less than two years' time?

Beauty? God didn't take broken things and make them
pretty. He left them to decay. How could she love that kind of
god?

Paul slid from his saddle at the edge of Suzanna's front
yard, letting the split reins slip off Bronco's neck. His gelding
nudged his shoulder as if to say, "Done already? We just got
started." Paul chuckled, rubbing the horse's face.

"There's more, old man." He stepped forward, leading the
animal toward the barn behind the house. "But fair warning,
we've got a green gal today. It'll be a slow wander for us."

Reaching the small hitching post, he flipped the reins
around the cedar crossbar, letting them dangle loosely. "Hang
out here, old man. Oh, and you might be carrying our pretty
neighbor, so be nice."

Bronco nickered, dropping his head against Paul. Patting
the horse's neck, Paul leaned against his trusted friend before
he retraced his path back to the house.

Suzanna answered the door with her hair pulled back in a
short ponytail. An oversized sweatshirt swallowed her torso,
and her fitted riding pants were tucked smartly into a pair of
English riding boots.

Equine. He should have guessed she'd be set to go looking
like she was ready for a foxhunt.

"Hey there, Pip." Paul grinned. She looked cute, out of
place, but adorably so.

"Pip?" Suzanna's eyebrows pinched.

Paul laughed. "The first English name that came to mind.
Dickens, right?"

She laughed, though her face still looked befuddled. "Jeans would have been better, right?" She tugged her sweatshirt over her hip. "I wasn't sure how they would work with my boots, and I don't have the Western kind."

He'd made her feel silly. Paul's chest squeezed. "You look just fine, Suz." His gaze passed over her again. She was really quite attractive, especially without a wall of contempt shrouding her blue eyes. If she smiled more, she'd be the kind of lady who'd turn heads in town.

"I suppose you'll laugh if I put this on?" A riding helmet dangled from her fingers.

"No laughing, Miss Wilton." He tried to squelch a jovial grin.

"Liar. You already are."

He glanced at the ground and shuffled his feet, feeling bad that he couldn't stop the chuckle. "It's not a bad idea—protecting your brains. Accidents do happen. We just don't see much of your style in the pastures 'round here."

Suzanna snapped the helmet into place. "Laugh away, Paul Rustin. I've already known you to be a heartless cad." Her eyes actually danced, wonderfully complementing her smile and mock accent.

"She can tease." Paul held the door while she passed from the house. "Who knew pickles had a sense of humor?"

"Pickle?" She turned, her hands coming to her hips. "Is that what you call me?"

Paul kept silent while a grin tickled the corners of his mouth. Shrugging, he moved toward the corral.

Suzanna joined him, her chin coming up in good humor. "I've been called worse. Probably deserved it too."

They reached his saddled mount, and Suzanna's look darted as if she felt lost. She was trying to be a good sport. Very much so. But her effort didn't cover her nervousness—the chewing on her bottom lip or her hand tugging at her ponytail.

Compassion lifted Paul's heart, making him feel protective and somehow privileged. Honored that he got to glimpse this version of a woman who kept herself tightly locked away.

"Do you know anything about horse tack?"

She scanned the leather equipment fitted to his horse. "Not that kind." She nodded toward his horse. "Why is the saddle so huge?"

"Well, first off, it's sized for me." Paul held his hand above her head, level with his hairline. A good four inches separated them.

Suzanna glanced up, and her smile peeked out again.

"Second, it's Western." He dropped his hand and jerked his head toward the barn. "I know your dad rode from time to time. Let's see what he's got in the tack room."

Her eyes fell as some sort of sadness shadowed her expression. The lightness of the moment had vanished as she followed him in silence.

Paul opened the tack room door and stepped back, waiting for her to pass. Stepping into the twelve-by-twelve-foot room, he scanned the space. Two saddle trees and one western style saddle waited against the opposite wall, clean and well conditioned. A leather headstall hung on the right, and two halters filled the hooks beside it.

The room smelled of earth and leather and horse. Paul inhaled deeply. Home. Suzanna sniffed and frowned. She seemed confused or lost or angry. Paul missed the woman she'd been in the sunlight.

"You okay, Suz?"

"Fine."

He examined her. Her voice sounded angry, but her eyes looked ... *something tragic in her eyes.* Was this what Dre had seen?

"Are you still up for this?" he asked.

She lifted her chin. A week ago he would have described the move as defiant. Today, he saw determination.

"I am."

"Let's get to it." Paul reached for a bucket on a middle shelf near the door. Rummaging through it, he was satisfied with the currycomb, brush, and hoof pick. "Grab the saddle and the blanket just above it."

Back in the sunshine, he squinted to watch her drag out the saddle. Literally.

"Why are these so heavy?" She hefted it against her hip and dropped it near the hitching post.

Paul chuckled. "They're built for ranch work."

She squinted skeptically.

"An English saddle is built for speed. It's lighter and less complicated. On a ranch, we work cattle, so the equipment is different." Paul reached for Bronco's muzzle. "Did you ride much with your mom?"

"We took lessons when we were younger." Suzanna stared at nothing and then dropped her gaze.

Lessons in horseback riding should have been every little girl's dream. Suzanna seemed uncomfortable with the memory.

"Did your dad ride much?"

"Not with us." She looked at the ground, tugging at her sweatshirt. "He said he used to though."

She was growing more uncomfortable with every question. Paul dropped the interview. "So, this mare of your dad's—she seems solid, but I never rode with Mike. Are you comfortable on her, or do you want to ride Bronco?"

Suzanna hesitated and then shrugged. "I don't know. I really don't know what I'm doing. I've only ever ridden in an arena, and the horse was my mother's. I've never ridden in an open pasture."

What kind of lessons had she been given? Paul pulled at his chin. "Okay. So, I think we'll saddle the mare—I'll teach you how—and then you can do it once. Then, to start out, maybe you'd better ride Bronco. Just in case. We'll switch if everything goes well."

She watched him with uncertainty. Maybe she wasn't up for this. Should he offer her an out?

"Do we need the halter?" She gestured back to the tack room.

Guess she didn't need an out. "Yep. And a lead. Do you know how to do that?"

Nodding, Suzanna stepped back toward the barn. "We even practiced yesterday." Her shoulders relaxed, and her voice smoothed.

Paul waited for her to snag the synthetic lead, and then they started toward the corral.

Suzanna stopped at the gate. "Is that stupid?"

"Practicing?"

Her cheeks filled with rosy heat.

Paul grinned. "Naw. It's a good thing."

He pictured her fumbling with the knot, calling the horse like it was a puppy and taking it for a walk. With her helmet on. He worked to smother a chuckle.

Suzanna approached the palomino mare with a timid stride. Paul leaned against the gatepost, fascinated as the woman pushed her shoulders back, her posture contradicting her gait. She wanted to be brave, even if she wasn't on the inside. Wasn't that called courage? Fresh admiration tickled in his chest.

The horse dropped her head, a willing partner. Suzanna would be fine on that mount, but he'd leave their arrangement for now. If he could help grow that seed of courage, he would. She'd need it out here. Need it against the Chuck Stantons of this world.

CHAPTER EIGHT

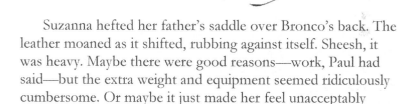

Suzanna hefted her father's saddle over Bronco's back. The leather moaned as it shifted, rubbing against itself. Sheesh, it was heavy. Maybe there were good reasons—work, Paul had said—but the extra weight and equipment seemed ridiculously cumbersome. Or maybe it just made her feel unacceptably feeble.

"Good." Paul nodded. "Now we'll see if you remember how to secure a cinch knot."

Her strength grew in the light of his approval. It would have been faster, easier, if he'd simply saddled her father's mare for her, and they'd set off. But he seemed to understand her desire to learn, to be able to manage on her own. He seemed to commend it.

Pulling the leather strap through the ring, Suzanna smiled. Paul should have been the last person to seek her as a friend. She'd been at her worst with him. Presumptuous, stubborn, and outright rude. Why had he pursued reconciliation? What was in it for him?

"Around the D ring." He guided her hand as she looped the strap against itself. "Right. Now pull it tight."

Done. She tugged on the cinch around the animal's girth. Two fingers slid snuggly between leather and hide, just as Paul instructed.

"Is it set?" she asked.

"Looks good." He squeezed her shoulder as if congratulations were in order. "Are you set?"

"Yes, sir."

She slipped her dusty boot into the stirrup Paul had shortened for her and tugged herself upward. Settling in the saddle felt strange. It rode different than the English gear, but it wasn't the equipment that spiraled discomfort through her gut.

Visions of her mother trotting in a manicured arena took her back ten years. Always the quintessence of perfection, Katrina Wilton graced her riding suit with enviable beauty.

A single scene, forever etched in Suzanna's memory, played. Mother cantered exquisitely, circling the course once and then entering the jump pattern. She performed with excellence and finished the exercise with a wide grin. Her eyes gleamed with something more than pride, and her stare settled on Mr. Pembroke. Their gazes held, too long for comfort, too intense for a married woman and her single trainer, too intimate for her teenage daughter to witness.

Something was not right. Suzanna should have known her world would crumble in the near future, but it didn't matter much. What was a seventeen-year-old supposed to do with that, anyway?

Paul relieved her of the memory, pulling his mount to a stop short of the gate. "South or west, Suz?"

She scanned the landscape, forcing resentment into a dark corner of her soul. Maybe she could let go of the hurt if the anger stayed chained and out of the way.

Yellows and oranges called an invitation. Suzanna loved trees, especially in the fall. "Can we go by the creek?"

"You bet." Paul dismounted and made for the gate.

Leaning into the cedar post with his shoulder, he pulled the loop over the corner post, and the barbed wire went slack. So, that's how that was done. Suzanna had buzzed around her property on the four-wheeler Daddy had kept in the barn, but she hadn't been able to open the gate so she could explore the pastures.

Paul pulled the gate back and handed Suzanna the mare's reins. She led his horse into the pasture and dismounted as well.

"Can I have a go?"

He had the post set in the ground loop but stepped back to let her take over. She leaned just as he had, but the loop fell short. She reset her boots and tried again. Still, a no-go. Her third effort proved successful, though it cost her a little sweat.

"Attagirl." He patted her helmet.

Suzanna breathed out a chuckle, and they both remounted.

"They make a cheater for the fence, if you want one." Paul nudged his horse, and they set in motion. "There's no shame in it. Several ranchers use them, especially with the gates they open often. I'll go with you to the feed store on Sunday after church, if you want. They usually have them in stock."

Church. Nothing magical happened last week. Of course, she and Paul weren't on friendly terms then, either. Not that he could make or break a worship service. But maybe she could give it another try. Her dad would want her to.

Paul stayed quiet as they descended a gentle slope. The trees met the terrain at the leveling point, and the creek gurgled quietly under a kaleidoscope of fall hues. They followed a game trail cut parallel to the water.

"Did you know this is spring fed?" Paul twisted in his saddle and spoke over his shoulder.

"I did."

"It originates on your property."

"The spring?" Suzanna pushed a low branch so it wouldn't catch her face.

"Yes."

Rock Creek bubbled up right here on her dad's land. Might explain some things. "Is that why all my neighbors want it?"

Paul grinned. "Not all. Let's just keep that clear because I'm not wearing a helmet."

What a rip she must have been. Poor man. "Not you, of course."

"Right." His hat bobbed with precision as if they'd settled something vital. "Yes, that's why they want it. You hold senior water rights. Seems that's become a concern."

"Has it always been a concern?"

Paul reined back, waiting until Suzanna's horse caught up with him. "Not always."

"I didn't think so. Dad never spoke of any issues." Suzanna scanned the property—or what she could see of it from the creek's depression. "He loved it here. Loved the land, the charm of small-town life and the opportunity. Intrusive neighbors don't figure into the picture. Made me jump to some conclusions about my own welcome."

His hand rubbed against his jeans. "I'm guessing they were something along the lines of chauvinistic cowboys and small-town snobbery."

Suzanna tipped her head. "Something like that, yes."

"Well, I can't say those conclusions were all wrong, but they weren't dead on, either. Rock Creek has its fair share of jerks, just like anywhere else."

Nodding, Suzanna pictured Chuck Stanton. Calculating, intimidating, and selfish. Yep, *jerk* about summed him up.

"Where exactly are you from, Suz?"

She glanced at him again, glad he continued to rescue her from the mental images that stirred her anger. "Fort Collins, mostly. I lived in Greeley for a while."

Paul looked surprised. "I assumed Denver. Mike talked about going to Denver the few times he went to Colorado."

"He did go there a couple of times. My sister lives in a suburb. Have you been?"

"A few times. National Western Stock Show over a few scattered years. When I was a teenager, I used to go as often as I could. Life changes though, and the city doesn't call to me anymore."

Suzanna pictured Paul taking the wide sidewalks of downtown under his long stride. He'd fit, actually. His strong profile and compelling good looks, complemented by the cowboy boots and hat, would make him blend. Until he opened his mouth and one discovered he wasn't numbered among the urban cowboys. No, Paul and the city would not be long-term companions.

"It used to?" she asked.

He smiled. "It took me a long time to grow up, Suz. I had some strong opinions about myself and this town that seemed incompatible." He cleared his throat. "The truth is, I was pretty much incompatible with just about everything and everyone in my life, and it was a long, tough road before I discovered the problem was mine, not everybody else's."

Suzanna leaned back in the saddle, comfortable in it. Comfortable with Paul. "That sounds like the overture to a story."

Paul laughed. "Such a gherkin."

"Gherkin? Why?"

"*Overture?* Fancy talk for a simple country boy."

He chuckled again, and she grinned.

"I've always had a fondness for words."

Paul ducked under a branch, holding his hat in place. The trees thinned on the trail ahead, and the ground heaved. The top of the hill sat barren of timber, and the grass swayed under the late morning sun. He guided them through the last of the trees to a body of water at the base of the hill. In a pool twenty feet wide, water rippled against the silt banks before it tumbled lazily down the creek path. A current bubbled near the center——the spring.

"Here it is," he said. "The source of the creek. Maybe of your troubles, too."

Maybe. Water rights were a big deal in Colorado. It wasn't hard to believe they'd be an issue here as well. But it seemed that they hadn't been. Not until she moved in.

Troubles, indeed. They could lie, for now.

Riding with Paul offered a reprieve. From everything. Her mother stayed locked away from her mind; the taste of bitterness didn't rise to her tongue. Grief didn't lodge in her throat. Anger didn't lurk near the surface of all that she did, all that she said. Suzanna held on to that relief; she'd keep it for as long as possible.

Standing in her stirrups, she let her gaze follow the movement of the creek. The sun glittered off the rippling water, and a soft gurgle harmonized with the rustling leaves. She soaked in the serenity—an unfamiliar feeling.

"Such a pretty secret," she whispered.

"I haven't been here in years." Crossing his arms against the saddle horn, Paul let his reins go slack, and the mare wandered to the edge of the pool. "Since I was a kid."

Bronco followed the other horse until the pair stood with their noses in the spring.

"Since you pulled dandelions for Mrs. Hawkins?" Suzanna unlatched her helmet.

"You know about that, do you?"

"Andrea."

His smile came easy. It seemed to be a natural part of his expression. "Actually, Dre did most of the pulling. I weaseled out of work every chance I got."

"Yes, you were hinting you were quite a devil. Did you plan on finishing that story, or were you going to leave it as an overture?"

"Not really a great story, Suz. You've already had a bad opinion of me. But..." He reached for a water bottle he'd packed in his saddlebag. After a long swig, he wiped his mouth and passed it to her.

She accepted the offer, squelching the paranoid germ-a-phobia she'd acquired from hospital sanitation standards. "But?"

"If you promise not to hold my rebellion against me...."

Swallowing the cool water, Suzanna nodded.

"I was a horrible brother. I don't know why Dre is so good to me now because I wasn't any good to her when we were growing up. But it wasn't just her. I failed school my senior year. Hard to pass classes when you don't show up. I came long enough to stay eligible for football, and after the season ended, I found trouble. Plenty of trouble. I'll spare you the details, but I ended up on a short stay with the state juvenile system. Have you ever heard of Boys Town?"

Suzanna shook her head.

"It's in Omaha. It's kind of like a crisis-intervention boarding school. I spent four months there."

"Why?"

"My parents didn't know what else to do with me. I'd been in legal trouble for underage drinking more than once, and then my dad caught me high in their basement. I had a record of being destructive, irresponsible, and disrespectful, and they'd had it. Dad said if I couldn't live with their rules, I couldn't live with them. He meant it."

Suzanna felt shock contort her face. Paul Rustin? The neighbor who had been kind to her even when she'd been horrible to him? She studied him, unable to picture him as anything other than the gentleman he'd shown himself to be.

Warmth shaded his complexion crimson. "See, not a very good story, right?"

"Why?"

"Why did I do those things?"

She pressed her lips together, wondering why she pushed him but nodded anyway.

"I don't really know, Suz. I was just angry, and I'm not even sure why. I didn't want to live here, I didn't want to be nothin', and I couldn't see anything beyond myself. I didn't have a real reason."

"What happened?"

Paul's eyes softened, and a smile crept over his features again. "I didn't graduate from Rock Creek—I went to Boys Town in March of my senior year. My grandpa came to Omaha to visit me in April with a proposal. If I studied and got my GED, I could come out and live with them. I would have to work like a ranch hand, but they'd keep me on until I figured out what I wanted to do with my life.

"It wasn't the out I was looking for. I didn't want to come back to Rock Creek. I thought, man, give me some money and let me go find a life. But Boys Town wasn't exactly Park Place, and it didn't look like I'd be passing GO anytime soon, so I agreed.

"I must have thought it would be like visiting my grandparents when I was a kid. You know, farm breakfast at nine every morning, Grandma always ready with a cookie, and I'd collect eggs or do some trivial chore as a token of work."

Paul chuckled and rubbed his neck. "Nope. My grandpa meant some w-o-r-k. I stayed in the bunkhouse, which was nothing more than a tin can trailer. If I wanted breakfast, I had to get up at six to eat with them because Grandma had things to do. They paid me what they would have paid a hand, and out of my earnings came the cost of rent, electricity, and food. When I slacked off that winter, my bunkhouse got awful cold because Grandpa didn't pay me enough to cover both heat and food."

Suzanna's eyebrows rose. "Seriously? Your grandpa put you out in the cold?"

He laughed. "Tough love, Suz. I found out later they'd set a threshold on the thermostat of around fifty degrees so the pipes wouldn't freeze, so it wasn't as bad as I thought. But it felt awful cold. I hated it. And then… I didn't."

He stopped, and Suzanna puckered her eyebrows. His attention wandered toward his place south of hers, and she wondered if the scenes unfolded in his mind as he recounted them.

"It came time for calving, and Grandpa said it was my responsibility." He rubbed a hand against his jeans, and the apples of his cheeks lifted. That look said it all—he loved his work. "I was so tired, but I knew he'd hold me responsible if something went sour. I wound up with a couple of bucket calves, and somewhere in between the late nights and early mornings while checking heifers and feeding orphans, I found myself. I found who God had made me to be, where I needed and wanted to be. It was right here the whole time."

Bronco shifted under her, and Suzanna slipped a hand around the saddle horn. Fierce rebellion melted away while Paul fed a few cows?

"As simple as that?"

Paul's gaze fell on her, his relaxed countenance contradicting his story. He looked toward the spring, then the trees, and finally to the hill rising before them.

"Not simple." He returned his attention to her. "That's the short version, but it wasn't simple. I wrestled everyone, including God, for things I thought I wanted. There was a whole lot of humbling that had to happen before I made peace with life. Pride made me useless; selfishness made me difficult."

His explanation created more questions than it offered answers. Suzanna longed for answers. His story, his life, looked nothing like hers, sounded nothing like hers, but he had peace.

Peace eluded her. She hadn't found it in church, not the lasting kind. She hadn't secured it in sacrifice. It wasn't in love. Love had made her ache all over again.

Where had Paul found this peace?

"Shall we take the hill, Pickle?" Paul gathered his reins and nodded toward the rise.

The mare perked her head, and Bronco followed. Opportunity slipped away, like the waters that rose from the depths of the earth and tumbled down the creek. Suzanna swallowed, pushing a smile across her lips. At her nod, Paul took the lead.

Peace remained hidden with the secret of Rock Creek.

CHAPTER NINE

Suzanna settled into the hot water, her hips and backside aching. Riding in a ring for twenty minutes was definitely not anything like riding over range for more than half a day.

Scooping up a mass of white foam, she inhaled the fragrance of the bubbles. Fresh-picked apples. She dropped back against the tub, sliding deeper into the water. Her eyes closed, and she let the fragrance stir her imagination.

She used to dream of picking them. Masses of apples, from her own orchard. Fruits of her labor. She would cultivate them in rows: Jonathans, Winesaps, Golden Delicious, and Lodis.

Their blossoms would hold promise in the spring. When the flowers dropped, tiny pommes would emerge and grow. She would check them weekly, tend them, thin them, and finally, when the temperatures cooled and fall ushered in the glorious culmination of spring's promise, she would harvest them.

Visions of her orchard faded, and the rows of trees dwindled to only two specimens in her mind. Daddy had worked faithfully with them, using the space he'd been allotted by the church. He loved anything green, but he'd been especially fond of the apple trees.

She'd worked beside him, and together they schemed of someday planning a mixed orchard. Cherries and peaches for late July and all through August. And apples. Fall harvest would bring the highlight of their hopes.

A fanciful dream. Someday never happened—would never happen. Daddy was gone. In truth, she'd smothered their vision long before he'd left the earth. Everything came unraveled after her mother had come clean, and dreams only fueled Suzanna's resentment.

There was a whole lot of humbling that had to happen before I made peace with life.

Peace. Oh, how she longed for it.

Hope deferred makes the heart sick.

The proverb rang true. Almost. Was anger a sickness?

Paul rubbed the oil from his hand with a smudged rag. His Deere had been due for service. So had the four-wheeler. And the mower. He usually did them all in one shot, but he'd only had about two hours of daylight left by the time he rode home from Suzanna's. Not that his shop wasn't lit, but the rest would keep.

It'd been a day. A good day, but a day. He hadn't planned on being so open with Suzanna, but her eyes begged for connection. Had she many friends back home? She seemed so isolated.

There's something tragic in her eyes.

Dre was dead on. A wound of great depth lurked beneath her pretty smile.

Replacing the oil plug, Paul rolled out from beneath his tractor and sat up. He wrung his hands in the old rag while his thoughts drifted to earlier in the afternoon.

"I'll see you tomorrow." He'd resaddled Bronco and was ready to mount up and head home.

Suzanna's brow furrowed.

"Church?" he prompted. "Are you going?"

Uncertainty crossed her expression before she brushed the hair from her eyes. "Yes."

Her answer had been less than enthusiastic. If he asked about it, would she open up?

"Good." He opted for the safe side. It'd been a good day. It should end on a good note. "I'll see you then."

Sitting between farm equipment with work surrounding him, he rummaged through their day together. Suzanna's hesitation still weighed on his mind. She'd started as a lighthearted, attractive woman. Funny, even. What had happened when she'd stepped into the tack room?

She was mystifying. Horse lessons, but she'd never ridden outside a ring. Her father rode, but never with them. And her mother... There. Right there. Suzanna had ducked after mentioning her mother, and she'd retreated from that moment on.

Suzanna was like a kaleidoscope—she seemed to change as the light and angles shifted. Rude, kind. Timid, fierce. Happy, heartbroken. Who was this neighbor of his? And why did he feel compelled to know her?

"Will you join us this afternoon?" Andrea's hand rested on Suzanna's elbow.

Suzanna glanced at Paul, who was engaged in another conversation across the church's entryway. Had he asked Andrea to invite her? She felt a little bit like a charity case, but he didn't treat her like one. Neither did Andrea. She seemed to accept her on a whim, embracing her almost as a sister.

Strange. Suzanna's own sister wasn't much more than a relative. Their relationship was bound by blood, but that was all. Could be because there was such an age difference between them. With seven years between them, they hardly shared a common interest growing up.

RECLAIMED

Sasha had an aversion to dirt and an affinity for glitz. Suzanna hated dressing up, never wore jewelry, and preferred digging in the earth to wandering through a mall. Their riding lessons with Mother were a forced and volatile topic. Suzanna would have rather been with her father. Mother fussed about her appearance nonstop.

Suzanna Korine, sit up straight in the saddle. When you slouch, your gut pokes out. An issue you must work on, young lady. Are you doing your sit-ups daily? Smooth your blouse. It shouldn't rumple at your neck. Why didn't you brush your hair before we left the house? Mr. Prembroke must think you are a gypsy.

Wednesdays, the dreaded days assigned for riding, were eternally miserable. She'd complained to her father once about it. He squeezed her shoulders with sympathy, but his advice left her alienated.

You're simply going to have to find a way to get along. She's your mother. She'll always be your mother. Make the best of it.

It didn't sound jaded to her fifteen-year-old ears. Maybe it had been though. She didn't know then all that she knew now.

Sasha fought Mother for different reasons. She hated horses. They were smelly, dusty creatures, and she had no interest in riding. Many a Wednesday she'd arrive with swollen eyes and splotchy cheeks. She never did accept that sobbing a tantrum would not give her an out. Of course, that ended when Suzanna was only twelve. Sasha graduated and never lived at home again.

"Please come." Andrea pulled her back into the present. "I planned for you, you know. Kelsey set an extra place at the table before we left this morning."

How could she turn that down? Suzanna forced a grin and nodded as Paul approached.

"Are you joining us for Sunday dinner, Pickle?"

Her face warmed, but her smile didn't feel forced anymore. "I am. Did you make your sister invite me?"

"'Course not." Paul slung an arm over Andrea's shoulders. "She does whatever she wants anyway. There's no point in attempting to persuade her."

Andrea eyed her brother with mock irritation, and then her expression turned to intrigue. She glanced from him to Suzanna and back again, a question certainly rolling through her head. She kept it to herself though.

Suzanna's ears warmed. Would Andrea approve of her emerging friendship with Paul? Or did it look suspect and flirtatious to her?

Flirtatious—definitely not. Suzanna had no interest in riding emotional roller coasters anymore. The sacrifice of marriage had been too demanding; she had nothing left to offer another man. Not even one as kind and gentlemanly as Paul Rustin.

CHAPTER TEN

Paul hooked an arm out to give Kiera a leg up. Bronco stood still, as he always did. Few things were as dependable in Paul's life as his equine friend.

Equine. He chuckled under his breath. Suzanna had done changed his vocabulary.

"Set?"

Kiera nodded, straightening the reins. Paul mounted Buck, the more flighty of the two horses. Taking a firm hold of the reins, he spurred the gelding forward, and he and Kiera set off westward.

Kiera loved to ride and asked to go more often than the other children. Paul rarely denied her requests, even after a hefty Sunday dinner. They'd cleared their dishes and hopped in his pickup while Dre and Suzanna cleaned up the kitchen.

What a difference a week made. Paul had enjoyed his family gathering again, and Suzanna relaxed. Somehow he needed to draw out her sense of humor. It was too endearing for her to hide it away. Why did she feel like she needed to?

Mike had been a friendly man. He'd been the one to initiate an introduction, stopping by Paul's house the very week he'd moved in. He could chat with the best of them and never seemed to feel awkward in a gathering.

Why was getting to know Suzanna more like playing a game of hide-and-seek?

"Miss Wilton's nice, isn't she?" Kiera looked up at Paul as the horses plodded toward his alfalfa field.

Paul nodded, forcing his questions back for another time. "She is."

Kiera's little forehead wrinkled. "She didn't seem quite so nice last week."

Perceptive. Paul didn't always take into consideration how much the kids could read into an adult situation. If he'd heeded the Word of God last week, he would have avoided the whole uncomfortable scene and spared Kiera some confusion.

"I had done some things to make her upset, Keys. It was my fault she was withdrawn last week."

Kiera bobbed a slow nod. Sandhill cranes called overhead, and she tugged on the reins. Bronco stopped, and Paul pulled his mount back as well. Buck danced sideways and then spun around before his hooves stilled.

"How do they know where to go every year?"

Cranes and snow geese cut a path above them twice every year. Seasons were marked by their migration. And every year Paul was fascinated with the birds' incredible journey.

"Instinct." He spoke to the sky and then glanced to Kiera. "God programmed them to know. Pretty amazing, huh?"

Kiera nodded, her eyes riveted on the flock above. In the air, the cranes weren't majestic birds—they didn't soar like an eagle—their bodies looked awkward in flight. But on the ground, their long necks bestowed a unique dignity, and their journey was indeed a marvel.

"When will you get married, Uncle Paul?"

From instinct to marriage. How was that for linear thinking? Paul cleared his throat and slowly brought his gaze to Kiera. She studied him with the kind of open curiosity most adults have been forced to tame. Her innocent intrigue made him grin.

"I don't know that God has marriage planned for me, kiddo."

She concentrated on that statement, her face betraying her focus. "Don't you want to get married?"

Ah. There's a tough one. Not his answer—yes, he'd wanted to get married. Kiera wouldn't remember that though. She'd been a baby when he'd been engaged. Explaining why he didn't have a wife—that would be the hard part.

It had taken years of wrestling to lay that one down. It was done, and he had real peace about it now, but letting go of it all—the desire for a wife, the hurt and anger when it didn't happen—had been far from easy.

"I thought at one time I'd be married, Keys." Paul pulled his hat off and rubbed his short hair. "Probably because that's what usually happens. Most people get married. I've learned God has something unique for all of us, though, and for me, it's to be single. I want to live the life God wants for me, so not having a wife is okay."

That should clear it up. Her sweet face pinched even more. Apparently he'd missed the mark.

"So, you don't ever want to get married?"

A grin slipped into a laugh as he wondered why Kiera was so intent on this. "Like I said, I want what God wants. He's always full of surprises, so I'll just live like I'm living until He shows me something else."

Kiera cast her eyes westward.

"Hey, Keys?" A sudden inspiration hit Paul. A teachable moment shouldn't be missed. "I'm not sure why you were thinking about that, but I want you to know something. Only God can complete a person. There isn't another human being on this planet who can make me whole, or you whole, whether we ever get married or not. I am complete in Jesus. He will make you whole too, if you let Him. Will you remember that?"

She looked at him with serious eyes. Approval filled her expression, and a small smile lifted her mouth. Kiera nodded, looking much older than ten.

She'd been worried about him—concerned that her old uncle wasn't happy. Warmth washed over Paul's heart, and he cherished the evidence of her kind spirit. So much like her Mama.

"Can I say something, Uncle Paul?"

"Always, kid. Hit me."

"I think Miss Wilton is special." Her face colored pink. "I'm not saying you should marry her, but I keep wondering why God would send a pretty lady from the city to be your neighbor. Seems kind of not normal, right?"

Did she think this up all on her own? Heat spread through his cheeks. "Maybe so. She is a bit of a puzzle."

"You mean a pickle."

He chuckled. "You pay way too much attention."

She shrugged, giggling. Paul nudged Bronco forward, they continued their ride. "Still, she *is* special. That's why Mama likes her. She says that God draws us to people for a reason. Mama says Miss Wilton is here by God's design."

This wasn't going away. He might as well ask. "Why do you think she's special?"

"I don't know." Kiera shrugged again. "She's not special in the wow-she's-super-fun kind of way. More like she's … she's hurt. Like a puppy who's been tossed into a ditch. Special because she seems sad, but she is the kind of person you want to be around anyway."

When did Keys grow up? Last he'd checked, her eleventh birthday was still a month away. A puppy tossed into a ditch? Yeah, she was onto something there.

"You're quite the observant girl, Keys." Paul glanced at her with affection. "I think maybe you're right. There's something sad in Suzanna's life. What do you think we should do about that?"

Kiera looked to him earnestly. "Mama says we're supposed to love on the widows and orphans. The people who don't have anyone else—because Jesus would."

Widows and orphans. Suzanna would fit one of those categories, sort of. Losing her dad left her alone, especially since her mom seemed to be out of the picture. Why exactly was that?

Orphaned. Maybe death wasn't the only way one qualified under that title.

"Do you miss Colorado?" Andrea wiped the long farm table while Suzanna covered the left-overs they'd divvied into Glad containers.

"Not overly. I miss the Aspens. They're really beautiful in the fall. And the coffee shop down the street from my apartment."

"How about friends? Have you been able to keep in touch with them?"

Suzanna's throat suddenly felt swollen. "I didn't have many close friends." How pathetic. Her skin warmed, and she scanned her brain recklessly for a recovery. "I talked to my sister last week."

Her gaze dropped to the floor. She'd called her sister all right, for the obligatory "happy birthday, how's whoever it is you're with these days" conversation. Was a false impression the same thing as a lie?

Having moved to the sink, Andrea ran steamy water over her dishrag. "I know city life is so different. Down in Waco, things moved faster, and people came and went as if we were never intended to have an impact on another human being. But here, I still see over half of my high school classmates running around town. Honestly, though, I don't keep up with them well either."

Suzanna's tongue felt too thick for use. She nodded, wishing she could bury the resentment from the past. What if she'd had a friend? What if someone knew all of the wounds in her heart, all of the bitterness stored up there and loved her anyway?

Jason had. For a while, he'd been enough, but he'd left her. No, God took him. That wasn't the same thing.

"I've upset you."

Glancing up, Suzanna found Andrea leaning against the counter. Compassion mingled with invitation on Andrea's face. Suzanna bit her lip, deliberating.

"My dad was a pastor. Did you know that?"

Andrea's eyes widened, and she shook her head.

"I thought maybe not. He quit preaching about a year before he moved." Suzanna swallowed and handed a short stack of containers with leftovers to Andrea. "Anyway, growing up in that kind of setting, as a preacher's kid, is different. There are expectations and assumptions. It makes it hard to bond."

Andrea shuffled things in her refrigerator, finding room for the loot. "What about school?"

"I went to private school. It was associated with the church."

Shutting the door, Andrea turned, empathy in her eyes. "Oh dear. I can see how that would make things difficult."

Suzanna braced herself for more questions. Why had her dad left the pulpit? What happened to her mother? Inquiries she wasn't ready to deal with.

"Well, Suz," Andrea said, "perhaps that will make it easier to make this home. Because you are staying—I'm going to have to insist on it."

Andrea moved to hug her, and Suzanna wondered how the woman knew exactly how far to prod and when to leave it alone.

"It's time for coffee, I think." Andrea pulled away and moved to the pot. "I have to warn you though, mine's not near as good as yours." She laughed while the water filled the carafe. "Whenever I drive by your house in the morning, I have to tell myself to just a keep on a goin'. You make some kind of magical brew, girl."

A grin eased the tension in Suzanna's face. "It's not me; it's all in the beans. My one indulgence. There's a little shop down the street from where I lived. I begged to buy to their coffee in bulk when I was getting ready to leave. They ordered wholesale quantities for me. I'm not sure they're supposed to, but I told them I'd be living in the middle of a pasture away from everything. Maybe they felt sorry for me."

"So I guess that means you won't be opening your own coffee shop anytime soon?"

"No. That would definitely not be my thing." Suzanna smiled. "But you stop over anytime."

The coffee maker gurgled and steamed, scenting the kitchen with the rich aroma of a fresh brew. Andrea slid onto a bar stool at the kitchen island, and Suzanna dropped onto one across from her.

"You and Paul seemed to be on better terms today."

Sheesh. Was there anything the woman missed?

"I'm sorry." Suzanna hung her head. "I must have ruined your family dinner last week."

"You don't need to be sorry. *You* didn't do anything."

Oh, if Andrea only knew. Suzanna fidgeted with her fingers. "We had a bad start, but it wasn't his fault. I can be... prickly. I wasn't very nice to him."

"I know you weren't made to feel welcome in Rock Creek. I'm sorry for that, especially since it took me a month to stop and say hi. Paul didn't know; he was working the river property when you moved, but it didn't excuse him for being cold."

He'd been gone. She'd thought of him as self-serving and snobbish because he hadn't stopped to welcome her until he wanted to buy the property. All the while, he'd been gone. She'd been entirely presumptuous—a total fool.

Suzanna looked at the floor and swallowed. Andrea was a different sort of woman than she'd ever known. Blunt, but compassionate. Honest, but tactful. She would call things what they were, pretty or not, but she could do it with the kind of grace that left you better, not shredded.

"Anyway." Andrea patted Suzanna's shoulder. "All that to say, I'm glad you're okay with him now. He is my brother. It'd be terrible awkward if you were to loathe him since you and I are going to be such good friends."

"Are you sure you want me for a friend?" The words slipped out before Suzanna processed them.

Andrea laughed. "Girl, you've no idea how long I've prayed for a girlfriend to show up down that dirt road. Here you are, neighbor. God's answer, in the flesh."

Another answered prayer? Maybe God had aroused from slumber.

Tom had a bonfire crackling in the backyard by the time Paul delivered Kiera home.

"'Night, Uncle Paul." Kiera moved toward the stairway. She had school in the morning and knew the drill.

"'Night, Keys."

She paused before she ascended from sight. "Hey, Uncle Paul?"

He halted his steps just before the kitchen. "Yep?"

"I won't tell anyone what we talked about today, okay? It can be just between you and me."

His warm grin matched the swelling of his heart. "Thanks, Keys. Just between us." He winked, and she climbed the remaining risers.

Paul moved past the kitchen, through the dining room, and out the French double doors to the patio. The fire burned orange against the twilight sky, and the air smelled of applewood smoke and hot cocoa.

"Hey, brother." Dre turned in her Adirondack chair. "Did you keep my girl from falling off?"

"Kiera wouldn't fall off." He dropped into the empty chair next to Tom. "And I didn't let her ride Buck. She's all in one piece and getting ready for bed."

Dre nodded. "There's enough in there for one more mug, I think." She bobbed her head toward the thermos sitting on the stone fire ring.

Paul poured himself a mug, anticipating Dre's homemade cocoa, like her tomato soup, a delicious masterpiece. Many years back, before he understood what a gem his sister really was, he'd questioned Tom about building a house with a very large kitchen, complete with an industrial cooktop, twin ovens, and two sinks. Over-the-top. That's what Paul had called it.

Tom had grinned. "Here's what I know: it makes my wife happy, and that somehow makes my stomach happy."

Made all of their stomachs happy. Paul ought to thank Tom when Dre was out of earshot.

"Did you know Mike had been a pastor?" Dre opened a conversation before Paul was done musing. It got his attention.

"No." A pastor?

"We didn't either." She sipped her cocoa.

"Did Suzanna tell you that?"

"Yep, just today."

Paul scratched his head. The Pickle got more peculiar every day. "How'd that come up?"

"We were talking about her home in Colorado. It just came out."

"Home?" The fire snapped and Tom shifted the wood with a long stick. "Didn't seem like it was much of a home from what you said, Dre."

"How's that?" Paul sat forward, leaning so he'd have a better view of his sister.

Dre shook her head with a sad face. "I asked if she was able to keep in touch with people back home. She didn't have anyone besides her sister."

She exchanged a look with Tom, and he took her hand.

"You'd figure if she grew up there, lived there her whole life there'd be at least one good friend she would still talk to."

Puppy in a ditch.

Paul's mind blipped back to the woman he first met. Angry. Maybe she had a reason. More than the legitimate irritation at the fact that she'd been made to feel unwelcome on her own property. Maybe anger covered a deep well of pain.

"Let's not let that be her life's legacy, Paul." Dre leaned toward him, still holding Tom's hand. "We're her closest neighbors, and thus far, her only friends in Rock Creek. Let's show her life doesn't have to be lonely."

Paul stared at the flames, tipping his head to acknowledge his sister. He wasn't focused on the future though. He was too puzzled by her past.

CHAPTER ELEVEN

Paul slowed his pickup and turned into the drive. Suzanna's house was becoming familiar.

He shifted his ride into park and sat deliberating. Eight in the morning was pretty early for calling on a neighbor, but she did say she got up at four. And she made some dang good coffee. Besides, it'd been almost a week since he'd checked on her last. He wouldn't guess she'd call for help if she needed it. He'd best check.

Cutting the engine, he opened the door. The October air nipped at his bare forearms. Time to pull out the flannel.

What would a city girl like Suzanna Wilton think of flannel? Surely it'd left the fashion world by now. So had cowboy-cut jeans, he guessed.

Did it matter what Suzanna thought? Who cared?

I think Miss Wilton is special. Kiera and her innocent comments. They'd set his brain off-kilter all week, and somehow Suzanna made it into his musings more often than she should.

He cared, apparently. Truth was he had to force himself away from her driveway for five days straight. It'd been a relief when he discovered his milk was running low. Now he had an excuse to drive her way. If he could only make up one for why he'd stopped.

He was being neighborly. That was why. No need to get all twittered over it. Good grief, what had gotten into him?

Paul flung the pickup door shut with a little too much gusto. His boots pecked at the cracked concrete as he walked to her side door. Surely she wouldn't expect him to use the front door, would she? Those things were for lost salesmen and determined missionaries.

Suzanna met him at the screen door. Good. They were on a side-door-use basis.

"Hey there, Pickle." Paul tugged at the brim of his hat. "Was heading into town and I thought I'd stop real quick."

She smiled, pushing the door wide. "Come in. I was due a break. Coffee?"

He chuckled. "You know the rule."

"Never turn down a cup."

Paul nodded as he clomped into her kitchen. Inhaling, his eyes slid shut. Ah, go-mud. Good go-mud. No, he shouldn't call it mud. Suzanna's coffee was way too good to be labeled mud.

"I was hoping you'd stop by at some point." She filled a blue mug and passed it into his hand.

"You could have called."

Her cheeks turned rosy. "No, it wasn't important, and I know you've got a place to run. A really big place."

Dropping onto a chair at her table, he pulled his hat off. "Nothing's so important I can't help a neighbor. What's up?"

Suzanna filled her own mug, a cream-colored ceramic vessel with painted leaves scattered all over and the words *grow hope* etched on the front.

She sat across from him. "Two things, actually."

Paul nodded.

"First, I tried putting that cheater on the gate, but I couldn't get it."

"Oh shoot, Suz. I forgot about that." Dimwit. He'd gone crazy the whole week telling himself he didn't have a good reason to go over. Here she'd been waiting for his promised help. "I can do it as soon as I finish."

"No hurry." She tipped her cup and took a drink. "I'd like to go too."

Too timid to plunk down to her basement by herself, but stout enough to want to know how to work things. Paul smiled. "And the second?"

Suzanna scooted her chair away from the table. "I finally started going through some of my dad's stuff. He had a notebook labeled 'Rock Creek Property.'" She grabbed a binder from her desk in the front room. "He was looking at cattle. I wondered if you could tell me about them."

Paul leaned his forearms against the table. "Sure. I'd be glad to."

He took the notebook and opened the front. Information sprawled over pages printed from Internet sites. Angus, Maine-Anjou, Highland, Hereford, and at least six other breeds were represented in a one-inch-thick stack of papers. Mike had highlighted certain aspects of each breed: benefits in calving, susceptibilities to various illnesses, finishing rates.

"Your dad's research looks thorough." Paul continued to shuffle through the pages.

"He liked research."

"What was he looking for?"

Her brows rose. "I was hoping you could tell me. Dad didn't do much with animals. He had some when he was younger, but it wasn't his passion. He liked growing things."

"Growing things?"

"Yes, growing things." Suzanna smiled, and it reminded Paul of the first rays of morning sun. "We even had our own miniature greenhouse. He loved the dirt, and anything green that came from it."

Intriguing. Mike knew exactly what he was doing as he reclaimed this run-down property. All the while his neighbors thought he was on an ignorant fool's mission. They'd all thought it was a city slicker's attempt to get "green" in his blood. He'd already had it.

"Did he have any training?"

"His family owned an orchard on the Colorado Western Slopes, and he researched. Like I said, he loved research." Suzanna sipped her coffee.

An orchard? Mike had lived here for six years. Paul hadn't known his neighbor at all. "Why did he leave the family business?"

Suzanna traced the wood grain on the table. Her expression seemed distant—sad. "He didn't plan to at first. He was managing it when he and my mother got married, but I guess somewhere in between my sister and me, he felt called."

"Called?" Paul yearned to see her eyes. Would they tell him more than her flat voice?

"To the church." She looked up. A storm brewed behind those blue windows.

Had she hated being a preacher's kid?

"What happened to the orchard?" he asked instead.

"It was auctioned off. I guess my uncle took over after Dad left. Mortgaged it beyond what he should have to expand and then couldn't pay when a late-spring frost wiped out an entire crop. Insurance didn't cover the whole amount of the loss or the loan payments."

One year? They lost everything in one year? How much had the uncle gambled?

Paul watched her gnaw on her lip. She kept her eyes averted and traced the leaves on her coffee cup.

"How old were you?"

"When they lost the orchard?"

He nodded.

"Two or three. I don't remember."

"But you remember what happened?"

"No." The storm surged in her eyes, and her tone suddenly cut hard. "No, I don't have any memory of the orchard. My mother told me about it."

She was angry. Paul tried to put the puzzle together, but there weren't enough pieces. She didn't remember the orchard and had no emotional connection to it. Why would something so distant provoke her?

Suzanna pushed a hand through her hair and came to her feet. "Do you need more coffee?"

Subject closed.

"No, I'm good. Thanks, Suz." He drained the last bit and pushed away from the table. "I can come by this afternoon, if that works better for you."

Confusion wrinkled her face.

"To put that cheater on the gate?"

"Oh." Relief smoothed her expression. "Yes, that would work. I should be done for the day by two."

Nodding, Paul ducked into his hat. "Can I keep this?" He held up the binder. "I can look it over a little more this week. Maybe I can figure out what your dad was after."

Her smile removed the last trace of anger from her eyes. "I'd appreciate it, Paul."

Paul stepped out the side door and clomped back to his pickup. Suzanna waved from the screen door as his engine growled and then stepped out of sight as he backed out of her drive. What brewed inside her? A puppy tossed in a ditch. Where was that ditch, and who had done the tossing?

Suzanna dug through the cardboard file box. Memories, long since packed up. Why had Daddy kept them?

A photo album of the orchard. He and Mother appeared together often, teenagers wrapped in the delight of youthful love. A worn hat, pinned with a note. *Fedoras never go out of style.* Mother's wedding bouquet, shriveled and gray, held together by a faded red ribbon. She'd carried roses. Two dozen long-stemmed red roses. Certainly, Daddy had bought them.

Their wedding picture. Suzanna had never seen it before.

A crinkled envelope stood in the corner of the box, jaundiced with age. It was addressed to Daddy in Mother's hand and bulged like an overstuffed suitcase. Dare she look? Everything personal and intimate may lie printed on those yellowed pages. The love of her parents, declared in the secrecy of their letters.

A love she'd never witnessed.

Would reading them help her understand?

She began to read, her hands trembling. Pain blended with anger as the pages opened, and words tumbled through her head.

At the age of seventeen, Mother declared undying love. At nineteen, she penned the same commitment, though qualified.

I cannot see myself as a pastor's wife. Michael, if that is your calling, evaluate it carefully. I was destined for a greater calling than to serve the ungrateful masses of a preacher's congregation. You know it would not be a life I could endure.

Suzanna's eyes bulged, and her throat felt swollen. Daddy hadn't gone to seminary until after she'd been born, but he'd been called as a teenager?

Her eyes burned as she studied the aged wedding photo. Mother's smile was perfect, set in her flawless complexion. It was a well-rehearsed expression, one Suzanna had witnessed often enough, though never at home. Daddy's smile reached only to the tips of his mouth. His eyes spoke of a torn soul. Maybe of a poor decision.

Their marriage had been a mistake. The revelation spiraled a new despair in Suzanna's soul. Did that make her entire existence a mistake as well?

Someone pounded on her kitchen door. She glanced to her watch. Almost two. Paul had come, just as he'd promised. Relief washed over her. His timing was perfect, rescuing her from the agony of the past.

She answered his knock with a smile, and he held up a DeWALT power drill.

"Got that cheater?" He pulled the trigger, and the bit squealed into motion.

Suzanna nodded. "In the garage." She slipped into her mud boots, which she'd discovered were necessary farm gear, and followed Paul toward the garage. Retrieving the winch system, she pulled it out of the open package. "I had it on, but I must have done it wrong. It wouldn't tighten like I think it's supposed to."

They walked down the road to her south pasture, and Paul took the cheater. He had it positioned and was securing it to the post before Suzanna could fumble with the not-so-informative insert.

"Are you up for a ride this evening?" He finished with the last of the screws and pulled the loop over the post. Stepping back, he let Suzanna close it.

"Horseback?" She cranked the handle, and the gate pulled tight. Easy enough. She'd tried to attach the cheater to the wrong side of the post. No wonder it hadn't worked. If only the thing had come with decent instructions.

"Yeah." Paul waited, one hand in his pocket and the other still holding the drill. "Supposed to be clear, I think."

Suzanna glanced at the sky, pale blue and cloudless all the way to the horizon. She hadn't been on the horse all week, allowing her backside to recover. Plus, to be honest, she wasn't sure she could saddle up on her own. What if she put the bit in upside down? Or failed to snug down the cinch properly? She wouldn't know the difference until it was too late, and by then she'd be on the underside of a twelve-hundred-pound animal. She could imagine the chatter in town.

Did you hear about that city girl? Killed herself with ignorance. Got run over by her own horse.

She couldn't let someone like Chuck Stanton have that kind of last laugh.

She slipped the cotter pin through the crank stop and turned back toward the road. "Where will we go?"

Paul fell into step beside her and shrugged. "Wherever."

Suzanna glanced up at him. His hat making his tanned face darker still. Kind blue eyes smiled into hers, and something warm spread through her core.

What was the rest of Paul Rustin's story? Such an amiable man could only be single by choice.

She forced her eyes from his, pressing her lips together. She had no right to feel any sort of attraction. Paul was better than most men and deserved more than she had to give. Which was, in fact, nothing at all.

"I've been wondering what's over that rise." She pointed north, past her house even as her stomach twisted. She shouldn't continue to latch onto his kindness, taking advantage of his generous spirit.

She pushed away the guilt. Certainly he was not in danger. Paul was settled in his life—content. He wouldn't look at her with anything more than friendly thoughts. She was alone in this growing attachment, and she could keep it appropriately concealed.

They reached his truck. "I'll be back around six, and we can go see." He tossed the drill to the passenger seat and turned back to Suzanna. "Why don't you try to saddle up on your own? I'll check it before we set out. Okay?"

She bobbed her head. *Do you want to come for dinner?* She held her tongue. That would be going too far.

CHAPTER TWELVE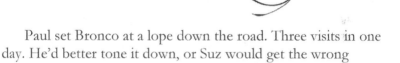

Paul set Bronco at a lope down the road. Three visits in one day. He'd better tone it down, or Suz would get the wrong impression.

What impression did he want to give?

Sort this one through. A pretty, single woman lands as his neighbor clean outta nowhere. No, somewhere. Fort Collins. How many single women pick up and move from Fort Collins to Podunk, Nebraska, on purpose?

None.

Singleness had settled with him. Well, he'd made peace with it anyway. Why would God switch gears on him when he'd accepted his lot in life?

How narcissistic could he be? Suzanna Wilton's move to Rock Creek had nothing whatsoever to do with him. He'd best get that set straight in his head right now, because from all indications, she needed a friend. An honest friend without any strings or deeper expectations attached. That's why he'd been chosen as her neighbor. He could do that. Content in the single life God had assigned for him, Paul could be that kind of friend.

He released a long breath and settled into the movement of his horse. Good. He felt like himself again. He didn't like feeling all discombobulated and upside down. He'd left that kind of nonsense behind a decade ago.

He crossed the creek, cleared the tree line and looked at Suzanna's barn. The little pickle hefted the bulky Western saddle over the blanket spread on the mare's back, her back arching against the strain. He ought to keep his eye out for a smaller saddle. Something with less bulk and weight but still equipped for ranch work.

She touched the mare's shoulder and reached for the cinch. Paul slowed Bronco to a walk and watched her secure it around the animal's belly. One loop, two. Three and up. Pull tight. Check the buckle. Through the D ring, back around and down. Tug and done. Executed perfectly. Paul smiled.

He rode up next to her and slid to the ground. "Well done, Pickle."

"Don't speak too soon." She pushed a few stray hairs off her face. "You'd better check to make sure. And I didn't do the bit. She tossed her head, so I wasn't sure I was going about it right."

Paul tugged the cinch strap and nodded his approval. He pointed to the bit. "Take it by the headstall, and let's have a go."

The horse shook away twice, but Suzanna stuck with it. Paul thought he saw her hands tremble, but she did it. Suzanna snapped her helmet on, and they both swung into their saddles. Paul wheeled Bronco around, heading back toward the road.

"Where are your boots?" He nodded toward her feet.

She tugged at her jeans, revealing her riding boots underneath. "I didn't want to tuck my jeans into them."

"How about sticking to the English getup?"

She tossed him a smirk. "Only so you could laugh at me?"

"I don't laugh at you." He liked the other outfit. Heat crawled up his neck. *Friend, cowboy. She needs a friend.*

"No." Sarcasm oozed from her voice. "You'd never laugh at me."

RECLAIMED

Paul chuckled but didn't trust his tongue enough to use it anymore. They turned north and hit a pasture gate.

"I worked on this one." Suzanna dismounted with the precision of an English rider—her back straight, her shoulders squared. Chin held perfectly under her riding helmet.

Paul tucked his lips between his teeth, holding back a grin. She shoved a shoulder into the cedar post, pulling herself toward the corner post. The gate reluctantly gave, and she smiled in triumph.

He set his smile free. Suzanna met his eyes and threw her hands up like she'd won a roping competition, laughing at herself. She pulled the slack barbed wire back, and Paul took both horses through.

She set the gate back into the bottom loop and smacked a hand against her thigh. "You get to close it."

"What?" Paul shook his head. "That's not how it works. You're already on the ground."

She cast a forlorn glance. "It took me six tries yesterday."

"Come on, girl." Paul nudged his chin forward. "You're not one to quit."

"Ha." She huffed and then stuck out her tongue. "Fine."

Paul waited for her third attempt before he slid from the saddle. She put her shoulder to it, and he pushed from behind. The loop slid over the corner post. Suzanna blew out a breath and backed into his chest. He caught her by the arms, just below her shoulders.

"Oh, I'm sorry, Paul." Her spine snapped straight, and she stepped forward.

He curled his fingers around her sweatshirt, squeezing arms that were thin, but capable. A strange jolt ricocheted in his chest, and he wondered what she would do if he pulled her back.

Where were these thoughts coming from?

Drawing a long breath in hopes to clear his reckless brain, he released his hold and patted her helmet. "Do we need a cheater for this one?"

"No." She shook her head, setting her ponytail swinging. "I'll get it. I'll just practice when I don't have an audience, and maybe try some push-ups in the mean time."

She moved toward her horse, tossing him a grin over her shoulder. Such a pretty smile.

Paul remounted, trying to ignore his undisciplined heart, and they set off for the northern rise. He needed something to ground himself, something normal to talk about.

Paul shifted in his seat. "So ... now that you've inherited two hundred acres of good grazing land, what are you going to do with it?"

That was harmless enough, right? Good grief, what was he, like fourteen?

Suzanna sat straight, cantering with her horse. "I'm not sure. I wanted to see what Dad had planned."

"Thus the notebook." His pulse returned to normal, and he felt like a grown-up again.

"Yes. The notebook." She looked over her shoulder opposite him, her eyes hidden from view.

Paul wondered what she saw as she scanned the scene around them. Rolling hills, prime for grazing? A vast emptiness, lonely and useless? How did this life look from her point of view?

Her attention came back, and he watched her profile.

"I was surprised to find cattle in it." She shifted and looked at her hands.

"In the notebook?"

"Yes."

He waited, hoping she would keep talking. She didn't meet his gaze, and her silence lasted too long.

"Didn't he ever talk about it?"

"No," she whispered.

Why did she hate talking about her family? Her face would go stone-cold when her mother came up. She seemed to have a soft spot for her dad, but she wasn't comfortable on that one, either. What was she burying?

"I was pretty wrapped up in my own life." Suzanna brought her gaze back to him. Her expression begged him to let it be. It was hardly an explanation. Pushing aside the questions she obviously didn't want to answer, he cleared his throat. "What did you think you would find in the notebook?"

"Trees." Life came back into her eyes. "We used to dream of an orchard, Daddy and me. I thought that's what he was aiming for. Maybe that's why he left me this property."

"Didn't he have an orchard?"

Her forehead wrinkled. "Yes. But he'd been called to the church, so he left it."

Paul nodded. Made sense... a little bit, anyway. Did preachers retire like bankers?

"He didn't want to leave the pulpit." Suzanna rushed to explain. "He just loved growing things."

"Like a hobby?"

"Sort of."

Still didn't make sense. Paul adjusted his hat and leaned back in the saddle. Mike didn't want to leave the pulpit, but he had. He wanted an orchard, but he was researching cows. He seemed to have been close to Suzanna, but he hadn't really talked to her much in six years. Maybe the man wasn't as stable as Paul had thought.

"Why did he leave the ministry?"

She shut down. Cold anger shadowed her expression, reminding Paul of the woman he'd first encountered.

Suzanna's jaw set hard as she looked away. "We don't plan some things in life," she whispered, her voice harsh. "They just happen, and nothing can be done."

Paul swallowed, but he couldn't break his gaze. Anger didn't complement her, but he longed to touch her skin, to hold her hand or fold her in his arms. Pulling back on the reins, he brought Bronco to a halt. The mare stopped as well, without Suzanna instructing her.

"I'm sorry, Suz."

Her shoulders slumped. Anger drained from her downturned face like sour water tipped from a dirty trough. Hadn't anyone ever offered her compassion?

She tipped her head up. "I thought he was planning an orchard. I don't know what he was up to now."

So, they were just moving on. Okay. For now.

"What do you want to do with it?"

"I don't know." She searched the plain behind him.

Please, God, let her trust me. There's so much more in there. I know there is.

"I was studying horticulture in college."

"Horticulture?" He couldn't restrain his surprise.

"Yes."

Her grin resurfaced. Paul's heart flopped again.

"Didn't know city people studied such things, did you?"

He chuckled. "It is surprising."

Her eyes grew distant again. "I didn't finish. I thought maybe it wouldn't matter out here."

Maybe not. Depended on what she wanted to do. Titles weren't necessary in the gritty reality of agriculture. Work and know-how did more good. The know-how part—that might be the hang-up.

"There's an ag school not far from here." He clucked to his horse, and they were moving again. "Degrees are just a piece of paper 'round here, but the classes would offer some practical knowledge."

Suzanna nodded, her expression thoughtful. "I suppose I'd better figure out what I'm aiming for, first."

The pasture dipped, and Paul shifted his weight back. Suzanna grasped the saddle horn, but her balance didn't waver. Sure-footed, the horses reached the bottom. The rise ahead would allow her a glimpse of her northern property line. With a glance to Suzanna, Paul nudged Bronco with his heel and set him to a trot. Together, they took the hill.

She was still gripping the horn by the time they crested, but she looked excited. He let her scan the panorama in silence, appreciating the view himself.

The sun lowered to their left, a ball of orange against the purple sky. Long grass waved until it reached the fence line, some thirty feet in front of them. Bales of hay, rolled tight and spaced like checkers on a checkerboard, dotted the hay field beyond her northern boundary. Cottonwoods, gold in their autumn glory, lined Rock Creek to the east.

Suzanna's face smoothed as she closed her eyes. A breeze carried the sweet smell of a freshly hayed field and ruffled her ponytail. She put her nose into it and inhaled, her lips tipping upward.

A woman who appreciated the small pleasures of country life. Satisfaction warmed Paul as the sun caught the blonde highlights in her hair.

Beautiful.

"Whose property is that?" Suzanna pointed to the hayfield.

Stop staring, you old fool.

He glanced toward the fence line, but, like a June bug drawn to his porch light, his eyes came back to her face. Skin the color of a wheat field in July set off those stormy blue eyes.

"Paul?"

Staring again. Good grief, he was pathetic. "Stanton's." He forced his attention back to the hay field.

"Chuck Stanton's?" Her jaw set, and her mouth pressed into a line. "He's my neighbor?"

"On a map, yes." Paul nudged his horse forward. "It's been in his family since the homesteading days. He doesn't actually live out here, though. Rarely even sets foot on his property. He leases out his pastures and sharecrops the hayfield. Some of the best grass in the county—it's naturally subirrigated."

"By Rock Creek?"

"Maybe. I'm not really sure. Might have its own little spring, or the aquifer is just closer to the surface here."

Suzanna dipped her chin, but her expression remained thoughtful. "He's never made a play for this property before?"

"Not until you moved in."

Rodewald

Paul sighed as the lightness of the evening crumpled under the weight of her troubles. She didn't really know how big they were. How far Chuck could cast his shadow.

CHAPTER THIRTEEN

The nutty aroma of a fresh brew beckoned Suzanna to her kitchen. Ten o'clock in the morning. She'd hoped Paul would drop by this morning. He was becoming quite a regular at her table. There must be magic in those coffee beans.

Suited her fine. She needed his help sorting out whatever Daddy had been after. She didn't know about bovines anymore than she'd known about cancer, but she could learn. This education promised to be much less demanding of her heart.

A blue truck passed by her kitchen window. A smile tickled upward, and Suzanna reached for another mug.

She glanced out the window again as she moved to the coffee pot. The truck was the wrong blue. She moved to the smaller side window and inspected the truck in her driveway. Paul drove a midnight blue truck. The one outside her window was electric blue, chrome shined to the point of vanity.

Chuck Stanton planted his glossy boots on her dusty drive. Sliding his hat over his slicked hair, he spat on her driveway as he made for her side door.

Guys like that ought to use the front.

Suzanna slid the mug back onto the countertop and scowled at the door. Waiting for Stanton's knock felt like waiting for a snake to strike. She wasn't about to.

She had herself outside and the door shut behind her before he made it to the gate.

"Morning, Miss Wilton." He smiled, his pack of chaw bulging in his left cheek. Another stream of spit blackened her sidewalk. "Thought I'd drive out to check on you. We are neighbors, you know."

She crossed her arms. "So I've heard."

"Everything all right round here?"

"Fine."

"Haven't run into anymore trouble?" His eyes flashed with malice.

She shifted, forcing her back straight. He wouldn't intimidate her. At least she wouldn't let him see it. "None at all."

He nodded, his grin making her flesh prickle. "Hope it stays that way."

Suzanna clenched her jaw. Something hard and hot caught in her chest, and she tried to swallow it down. "Don't see why it wouldn't."

"Can I come in?"

Absolutely not.

"I'd rather you didn't. The house is a wreck."

Chuck shifted, pulling his torso to its maximum potential. Goodness, the man was big. A shiver ran down Suzanna's spine.

"I think it's time you negotiate, Suzie."

Suzie? So much for endearing nicknames. She hated the sound of her daddy's pet name coming off his snarling lips.

"My friends call me Suzanna, Mr. Stanton, but Miss Wilton will work for you." She shoved her hands on her hips and stretched her neck. She couldn't match his build, but she sure wasn't going to crumble under his harassment. "The place isn't for sale. Just like it wasn't last month. And it won't be the next, either. I'm not moving."

He took a step toward her. "I'm not a very patient man, Suzie."

The darkness of his glare pressed down on her like granite. Sweat beaded at her hairline, and she couldn't slow her throbbing heart.

"It doesn't matter." She pushed the words past her closing throat. "I'm not selling."

Chuck dropped his eyebrows. He opened his mouth, but closed it when the sound of a truck kicking up gravel rumbled from up the road.

Suzanna's eyes darted toward the creek, and relief drained the rigid fear. Paul slowed as he approached her house, and the nose of his truck came off the road.

"We'll see about that." Chuck demanded her attention again. He backed away, clearing his throat as he moved.

Paul killed the engine and dropped out of his cab, slamming the door. "Morning, Suzanna." He pulled at the brim of his hat. "Chuck."

Suzanna forced her feet to stay still. She wasn't eight, and she couldn't run to Paul like she did to her daddy when the boys were mean to her in Sunday school.

But her heart sure wanted to.

Tractors are notorious for breaking down. All the time. Paul thought he had the parts he needed for his Deere, but he couldn't find the blasted hydraulic hose fitting in any of his backup supplies. Off to town he went, begrudging an entire morning wasted on the errand.

Maybe God had hid the spare part.

Pulling up to Suzanna's, Paul knew which wannabe cowboy was parked in her driveway. Towering over her like a cat over a wounded finch, Stanton was relentless. Why did he have his mind set on her property?

Water rights? What a flimsy cover. He didn't need them, and Chuck Stanton didn't give a salt's worth of care for the concern and well-being of his neighbors. He had them all gung ho to get rid of Suzanna under false pretenses. Convinced them she'd dam up the spring and divvy out the water according to a selfish whim. What was the motive behind his façade?

He caught Suzanna's eyes as he walked toward the pair, and a fireball burned in his gut. She looked like she did when she stood at the top of her basement stairway. Scared. Paul walked to the gate, positioning himself between Chuck and Suzanna.

"What brings you out this way, Stanton?"

"Thinking about Suzie here." Chuck looped his thumbs in his jeans and rocked back on his heels. "Came to see that all is well 'round her place."

I'll bet. Paul glanced down his shoulder at Suzanna. She held herself stiffly, and her chin came up.

"Bet you found everything's just fine." Paul crossed his arms. "Suzanna's right capable."

Chuck smirked. "Yep. Seems she's got all the help she needs." He pierced Paul with a cold stare.

Paul glared back, the muscles in his arms growing stiff. "I'm sure a busy banker such as yourself has plenty to do on a Monday morning."

"Plenty." Chuck sent a stream of black spit near Paul's boot. "Suzie, you have a good day now. Remember, my offer still stands."

He swaggered away and tipped his hat as he slid into his pickup. The engine roared to life, and he revved it before he backed out of the drive.

Scoundrel.

Paul looked back at Suzanna. Her eyes fixed on him, round and watery. He reached over the gate and pulled her shoulders against him. She leaned into his chest.

"What was his offer?" Paul rubbed her arm.

"It wasn't an offer." Anger punched her words. She straightened her frame, and her mouth formed a hard line.

Heat poured through him. Squaring to her, Paul gripped her arms. "Did he threaten you?"

She stared at his chest. "Not with his words."

Every muscle tensed. He wrapped her wooden frame close, wishing he knew what to say.

"Suzanna." Mrs. Rustin put a warm hand on her elbow. "How 'bout this. I was just thinking about you this morning, and now we're out shopping at the same time. Must be God."

No wonder Paul and Andrea were so kind. Their mother was a doll. Suzanna felt her smile lift her cheeks and smooth her furrowed brow. How long had her face been strained? Easing her frown felt like a spiritual lift.

"Thank you." Suzanna patted the hand still resting on her arm. "That's so sweet."

"Not sweet, I think," Mrs. Rustin said. "'Twas the Spirit. Pressed on me powerful this morning to pray for you. Was there a reason?"

Suzanna skimmed over the morning's events, and her smile faded. Yeah, there was a reason. She was terrified of Chuck Stanton. Now more than ever. What was the man capable of?

"I had a few hiccups this morning." Suzanna glossed over the confrontation. Anger had a way of seeping from her pores, and she didn't want lovely Mrs. Rustin to see it. What if she told her grown children to keep away because Suzanna Wilton was a bad apple? She'd lose her only friends in Rock Creek.

Not a price she could afford.

Mrs. Rustin nodded, her expression thoughtful. "I trust God ironed them out."

Had he? Was it possible Mrs. Rustin's prayer had sent Paul to her rescue at just the right time?

Since when did God come to her rescue? That was not the god Suzanna knew. She knew an aloof power who did not waste his efforts on the trivial, and not-so-trivial, struggles in life. A god whose heart didn't care about the people he'd made.

"It worked out." Was that a lie? Paul had rescued her—for the moment. Chuck Stanton was not going to let up, though, and his implied threats still rippled dread down her spine.

"Good. God is faithful, darlin'. Even when it doesn't look like it, He is." Mrs. Rustin squeezed her arm again. "Listen, sweetie. I'm meeting Andrea and the kids over at the park. I think you should come along. Andrea was just lamenting how she hadn't seen you all week."

Suzanna swallowed. She hadn't gone to church yesterday. She felt guilty about it, especially if Mrs. Rustin had planned on her for dinner, but she couldn't make herself go.

Two years. Jason's face swam across her vision. The face of the healthy young man who'd taken her to her senior prom. The face she preferred to remember.

"I'd love to come." Suzanna ignored the stinging in her nose. She could use the distraction. "What shall I bring?"

"Whatever you want, Suz." Mrs. Rustin smiled. "Dre was going to pack sandwiches for the kids. They're always hungry after school, and I was going to grab something from the deli for myself. It's a fend-for-yourself kind of picnic."

Suzanna nodded, a mild grin pulling at her lips again. Fend for yourself. She was pretty well practiced at that.

Mrs. Rustin pushed her cart on down the bread aisle, and Suzanna moseyed on her way. The fall afternoon was perfect for a picnic. Cool temps, the wind held to a mild breeze, and an autumn pallet promised peace.

Maybe today she would find rest.

"Do they always have this much energy after school?" Suzanna nodded toward Keegan, who chased his sisters over and through the monkey bars and down the slide across the playground.

"Not always." Andrea laughed. "But, come to think of it, usually. Thank goodness for nice weather."

"Will it hold for much longer, do you think?"

"Farmers sure hope so. Corn prices are high, and harvest looks good."

"Do you and Tom farm?" Nearing a month of friendship, Suzanna still wasn't sure what they did for a living.

"Tom's grandpa had some land in Kansas. Tom and his brother sharecrop it now." Andrea slid her hands in her sweatshirt pockets. "He'll be heading south in a few weeks for harvest. His brother's family lives down there, so he keeps Tom updated."

"But you don't farm up here?"

"Not really. We have about ten acres in alfalfa, and we run cattle on the rest, but it's a small herd." Andrea's smile embodied contentment. "Tom works with the Department of Natural Resources. That's how he knew your dad."

Suzanna nodded. A breeze stirred the trees by the creek, setting the golden-yellow globes in motion. The grass swept down and bounced back, stirring the aroma of the mowed field beyond the park boundary. Suzanna inhaled, savoring the clean, sweet smell.

Andrea laughed. "Paul loves that too."

Suzanna's head whipped to Andrea.

"The smell of a hay field. Paul loves it." Andrea held her eyes and then moved her attention to the field. "He smiles the way you just did when he catches a whiff of freshly mowed grass."

Suzanna blushed, but she wasn't sure why. She and Paul had been tossed together quite a bit. She didn't mind, except it wasn't fair to Paul. Either he thought he needed to babysit his inept neighbor, or he saw opportunity. Her gut twisted. He deserved better than her thin, worn-out heart. Maybe she needed to set some things clear.

But perhaps Paul, just like Andrea and their mother, was simply offering sincere friendship. Longing ached in her chest. Dear heavens—friends. Like a soft rain to her hard and cracked spirit.

"He's the reason we still live here." Andrea's eyes rested on the hayfield, distant and reminiscent.

Suzanna wondered where Andrea's memory had taken her. "Paul?"

Andrea nodded. "Did he tell you our grandparents left him their place?" She redirected her attention to Suzanna.

Shaking her head, Suzanna recalled the pieces Paul had told her. He'd ended his tale before his grandparents passed.

Andrea's smile was soft, and Suzanna saw the sincere fondness she had for her brother.

"He worked for Grandpa almost ten years. He didn't want to at first—sort of a last-resort situation, but he ended up loving it. Grandpa sold him some heifers at the end of his first year with them. Paul used them as a start, renting some of Grandpa's pasture. Did pretty well."

Andrea's grin grew. "Grandpa was pleased. Said if Paul wanted to, he'd help him with the cost of college at the ag school. Paul took the deal. He stayed on the whole time, working for Grandpa and building his own stock. When Grandpa died, he left instructions for Paul to take care of Grandma, which he did—quite well. She followed Grandpa only a year later, though, and Paul found out they'd left it all to him."

Andrea's eyes held Suzanna's. "They owned over three thousand acres—some of the best grazing land in the area. Grandpa wrote that Paul had proven his worth, and he was proud to leave a heritage to a boy who had become such a fine young man." Her eyes misted, and she swallowed hard. "I can't tell you what that meant to us—to our family."

Suzanna nodded, her eyes growing moist. "He told me he'd been quite a rebel."

Andrea laughed. "A rebel indeed. You want to know the thing that gets me though?"

Suzanna nodded.

"It was all his." Andrea sniffed and brushed a tear off her cheek. "The land, the cattle—everything was all his. Grandpa left it all to Paul, but he sold all of Grandpa's cattle and split the profit between Mom and Dad and Tom and me. Said he was sure Grandpa would want it that way. Then he gave us each one hundred acres of land. Told us to do with it as we wanted."

She took Suzanna by the arm. "People don't just do that, Suz. Tom and I couldn't have afforded what we have otherwise. We would have moved to Kansas, and I wouldn't have been able to help take care of Mom and Dad like I am now. Mom can afford to have full-time help for Dad. I can't begin to tell you what a relief that is for her. You may look at what Paul has now and think that was the least he could do, but it was, in fact, very generous. And it came from a heart of love."

Suzanna bit her lip. Paul had already proven himself to be far above the character of most men, but Andrea's testimony was astounding. Where did love like that come from?

CHAPTER FOURTEEN

"How goes it, Rodney?" Paul slid the sack of feed to the aisle floor and reached out his hand.

Rodney gripped it, though he looked to the ground. "Oh, I'm all right."

Paul stepped back and rolled his shoulders straight. Rodney was usually the talkative sort. Made him a good auctioneer. But as the moments ticked by, Rodney let silence hang between them. Something was wrong.

"Do you have that sale bill ready to post?" If anything could get him talking, it would be the sale barn. Rodney loved his work.

"Yeah, about that." Rodney pushed his arthritic fingers through his thin gray hair, refusing to make eye contact. "I'm afraid I have to cancel."

"The sale?" Something was definitely wrong.

"Yes." He shifted his weight from left to right. "Not just yours, all of them."

"Why?"

"I've run into a situation." The elderly gentleman swallowed, and his handlebar mustache twitched. "I'm gonna have to sell the business."

A situation? The timing was too parallel to be a happenstance.

Paul shoved his hands into his denim pockets. "I know I shouldn't pry, Rodney, but you mind telling me what sort of trouble you're in?"

Rodney scratched his neck. "I did something foolish a few years back. You know when I added that second pole barn, thinking the goat market was going to explode?"

Paul knew. The little building came in handy. Rodney often let the kids run mutton-busting contests there before the sales. And more than once, he'd seen youngsters practicing poles and barrels with their horses while their parents attended an auction.

"Yeah." Paul waited for the rest.

"I took out a second loan to do it. It's been called in—half due at the end of the month."

"Called in? Is that legal?"

Rodney grimaced, his eyes cast to the floor.

Paul shifted, moving closer. "Rodney, I don't think a bank can do that these days without a reason. Did you default on your payments?"

"No." His shoulders crumpled. "I didn't go through a bank. It was a personal loan from an individual."

Guess who? Paul's head snapped straight, and he pulled in a long breath. "How much do you owe Stanton?"

Rodney's eyes shot up. "How'd you know?"

"I know Chuck, and I know this town. How much do you need by the end of the month?"

"I can't take another personal loan to cover the last one that was a mistake." Rodney's gaze lowered again. "I've ruined myself. It's just the way it is."

Paul crossed his arms. "If you sell for me next Saturday, you can have it. All of it."

"All of what?"

"Every last dime that comes from those cattle." Paul rocked back on his heels. "Everything we talked about on the sale bill."

Rodney stepped back, his eyes widening. "I told you, I can't pay you back."

"This isn't a loan."

Confusion tugged on his expression, and Rodney stood dumbfounded. "Why would you do that?"

"Because I'm not going to let Chuck Stanton jerk the people in this town around to satisfy his greed."

Rodney's expression didn't clear.

"He's after me, Rodney." Paul pressed on. "It has nothing to do with you. Chuck's aim is set on me."

"Why?"

"Because I won't help him bully Suzanna Wilton out of town so he can buy her land."

Rodney's mouth dropped. "But he says that woman is planning to dam up the creek. Said she came into the bank looking for a loan on the project."

What? Paul felt a scowl gather his forehead, and his mouth pulled down.

"Look, Rodney. I've gotten to know Suzanna over the past few weeks, and I can tell you she wouldn't even be able to think up that kind of scheme, let alone carry it through. She's just living on the land her dad gave her and trying to find a place in our community."

"Are you sure?" Rodney's forehead wrinkled. "Why would Chuck lie about something like that?"

Paul looked across the store, not seeing anything but red. "I don't know." He moved his attention back to Rodney. "But I do know this. He's putting you out of business to get to me. Do you really think anything is beneath him?"

Rodney shifted like he was uncomfortable. Pulling in a long breath, he shoved his hands into his leather vest pockets. "No, I 'spose not."

Paul held his gaze with a sternness he hadn't felt in years. "Do we have a deal?"

Rubbing his neck, Rodney looked around. "What about you? Don't you need the money?"

"You sell what we talked about in a week." Paul rocked back again, hooking his thumbs in his pockets. "I'll go through my herd again, and we'll put together another sale bill for late November. You don't need to worry about me."

Rodney stood, clearly wrestling with the proposal. Two women came down the aisle, each carrying a sack of dog food, and Paul and Rodney stepped to the edge of the walkway. Rodney pulled at his whiskers and then slid his hand toward Paul.

"Okay, Rustin. We have a deal."

Paul's feet shuffled against the concrete as he waited for Suz to answer. He'd made a bad habit of knocking on her door too early.

She pulled the door open as he chided himself, her hair wet and her face makeup free. Yep, too early. Except this image of the little pickle tickled his insides.

He pushed away the pleasure. He had no business finding his friend perfectly adorable in her morning freshness.

"Hey, Paul."

Her smile warmed the spot he'd just told to behave.

"Looking for some coffee?"

His grin cracked. He didn't know what he was looking for, but coffee was a start. "Been a whole week since I've had Suzie's good stuff. It's addictive."

The coffee. He meant the coffee. His brain needed to start functioning like the thirty-seven-year-old grown-up he was instead of some giddy teenager.

She pushed the screen door open, and he stepped through, inhaling the sweet scent of whatever she used in her hair.

Behave. He shoved a hand into a pocket and tightened the grip he had on the notebook he'd brought.

"I was just about to set on a fresh pot." Suzanna led the way into her kitchen. "I was kind of wondering when you'd stop by again."

Pleasure zinged again. Paul couldn't stop his smile. "I've made quite a nuisance of myself, haven't I?"

"Not at all." She glanced to the counter top. "It's nice to have a friend."

There was something raw in her confession. Paul swallowed, holding his gaze steady on her.

She turned away to fill her coffee pot at the sink, her fingers touching something underneath the collar of her shirt.

"I was looking through your dad's binder." Paul moved toward the table. "I think he was looking for a breed he could finish on grass."

She pivoted back to him, her expression wrinkled. "What does that mean? Don't all cows eat grass?"

He dropped into a chair, pulling his hat off and resting it on his knee. "At some point in the process, yes, most cattle are set out to pasture, but there are different stages for beef cattle and different operations that specialize in those stages."

Suzanna dropped onto the chair opposite his side of the table and propped her chin in her hand. Her inquisitive eyes invited him to continue.

"So, you start with a calf." Paul leaned on his elbows. "It stays with its mama for six to nine months—we call them pairs. Pairs usually are put to pasture during the summer months and are most often separated in the fall."

Suzanna nodded.

"After the cows are sorted, the steers are sent to a feedlot. A feed yard will finish the cattle until they're ready to go to slaughter. Usually, they're finished on corn. It's a high calorie grain that will add fat quickly, and the beef will be tender."

Her forehead wrinkled. "But Dad wanted to finish cattle on grass?"

"That's what it looks like." Paul pulled out the binder he'd brought with him. "Look." He opened it and pointed to the first pamphlet. "Right here. These breeds are suited for grass finishing. They won't take as long as some of the others, and the meat will retain the tender quality, if they are finished properly."

Suzanna studied the information Paul had pointed out, but her expression remained quizzical. "Why would he do that?"

Paul shrugged. "Hard telling. There's a growing market for it in some areas. Supposed to be healthier—higher in omega-3 and naturally leaner. Sellers will claim it's a greener way to raise beef cattle. Maybe it is, I don't know.

"Anyway, if your dad had any connection with a health-conscious market, he may have seen an opportunity. He obviously knew how to grow grass, which is really what you're doing when it comes to raising grass-finished beef, so maybe it would have been a good fit for him."

Suzanna nodded, her eyes thoughtful. Paul watched while she chewed her bottom lip.

"So." He sat back. "Are you up for it?"

Her brows dipped. "Up for what?"

"Suzanna Wilton: cowgirl." He grinned. "Wouldn't that just put a bur under Chuck Stanton's preppy jeans?"

She laughed. "Maybe. Right up until I fail miserably."

Paul leaned forward against the table, shaking his head. "Pickle, I done told you. If you're strong enough to stand up to a bunch of bullheaded cowboys, you'll do just fine."

Her smile faded as she held his eyes. Something in her stare tugged at him. It felt like his opinion mattered. A lot.

"I'll help you, Suz." His voice dropped softly. "If it's what you want to do, I'll help you."

Her gaze fell. "I don't know."

She left the table, moving to pour the coffee. Somehow he'd upset her. He couldn't understand. Paul left his seat too.

"Suzanna..." He followed her to the counter and rested a hand on her shoulder. "What did I say?"

"Nothing." Her mouth tipped into a smile that contradicted her sullen eyes. "I just don't know what I want."

Paul studied her while his thumb brushed over her arm. It didn't seem like the truth—not all of it. But he'd no idea what else could have pulled the laugh out from under her.

"You don't have to raise cattle, Suz. You don't have to do anything. I just know that you can, if that's what you want, and I'm happy to help you, no matter what you decide. I'm glad to be your friend."

She looked back to him, and those beautiful, sad blue eyes pleaded in the silence. She needed a friend. She needed him to be it.

Paul tugged her into half an embrace, and she tilted her head into his shoulder. His heart whispered a promise.

Come what may, I'll be your friend.

CHAPTER FIFTEEN

Suzanna tossed beneath her grandmother's star quilt. Emotions rolled as her day replayed. Starting it with Paul felt like a new normal, a hopeful future. Something she'd given up on. She hated to feel needy, usually to the point of overcompensation, but with Paul ... well, he didn't seem to mind. He seemed, in fact, to like it.

Not neediness, per se, but that she was coming to depend on him. Maybe a little too much. Which was the drop in the ride. Didn't she tell herself she was done with the roller coaster?

But he believed in her. For no reason whatsoever, Paul Rustin believed she could do what she set her mind to. She'd starved the longing for that kind of affirmation a long time ago. Feeding it now flared resentment.

Find a dream you can actually accomplish, Suzanna. Work within reality.

Mother had never approved of anything. Her clothes, her hairstyle, her posture, her body, her choice in college studies.

Her marriage.

Nothing was ever good enough. Resentment and defeat became neighbors. Moving away hadn't changed anything on the inside.

Sitting under Paul's affirmation had set off a storm. The warmth of his friendly smile collided with the chill of the past, stirring up the anger she was trying so hard to calm. It shouldn't be so. Why couldn't she take his friendship, the approval he offered, and live with that? Why did she have to let the past interfere?

Tossing aside the star-patterned quilt, Suzanna set her feet on the cold wood floor. She glanced at her digital clock. Five thirty. She usually slept until eight on a Sunday, but closing her eyes allowed only images from years gone by to play afresh. She moved from her bed and set out for the kitchen.

She found the switch for the light overhead and flipped it on. Daddy's binder lay on the table. Reaching for it, Suzanna rubbed her eyes and dropped onto a chair.

Cattle. Who would have thought? Daddy running cows in an unknown corner of Nebraska. Suzanna cracked a tiny smile. Daddy had always been one for surprises. Birthdays and Christmas were special because he made them so. Even with Mother frowning in the corner.

Maybe she *could* do it. With Paul's guidance and some classes from the ag school, she could chase down this dream of her father's. There *was* a market for healthier beef. She'd been among them——the consumers who checked labels for things like *certified organic* and *heart-healthy*. Jason's strict diet required careful attention.

But what about growing fruit? That had been her hope since she'd been a girl. A dream she'd shared with her father. A dream her mother would not condone. Why had Daddy abandoned it?

Did it mean she had to let it go too?

"You going to my sister's today, Pickle?" Paul caught Suzanna before she escaped through the front door. Had nearly chased her down through the church hallway. How many people had noticed?

Suzanna looked at the floor. He understood. It'd been a chilly morning inside Rock Creek Bible Church, and that had nothing to do with the weather. It made him want to stand up and deliver a sermon of his own. Why were people acting so ugly?

There was only one reason. Paul intended to put an end to it. He'd catch Stanton before he headed home.

"I think so." Suzanna sighed and then summoned a smile. "You have the nicest family, Paul. You're lucky."

He dipped his head. Maybe he should just leave with Suz. She looked beaten.

Her gaze moved over his shoulder, and her eyes turned cold. "I'll see you later."

She did an about-face, her green dress twirling at her knees, then she moved across the rocks toward her Jeep. Paul checked behind him, catching a glimpse of Chuck striding the other way. His mind made up, he'd deal with it here, now.

"Stanton."

The man stopped and turned, his feet set like he was ready to go down into a three-point stance. Paul pulled in a breath as he moved forward, feeling like he was coming to the line of scrimmage against a guy who was known to take cheap shots. Maybe because he was.

"We need to talk." Paul rolled his shoulder straight and crossed his arms.

Chuck looped his thumbs into his pockets. "That so?"

"Yep." Paul held the man's stare, not even trying to push aside his irritation. "What's this I hear about Suzanna stopping up the creek?"

"Dunno." Chuck shrugged, his expression smug. "What do you hear?"

"Stop playing stupid, Stanton." Paul took another step forward. "You and I both know where that story came from and why. Put an end to it."

Chuck hiked up a brow and then laughed. "Put an end to it?" He shook his head, his steely eyes fixed against Paul's. "You're not understanding the situation, Rustin. You don't have position on me. This isn't going away, and it will only get worse. Whether you get dragged into it is up to you, so you'd better consider carefully before you cross the line."

"Line's done been crossed, Stanton."

Chuck moved closer, using his height to talk down over Paul. "Get this clear, Paul. There are advantages to having a wife with a loose tongue. It doesn't take but a few days to have a story spread all over town. From what I hear, you've been spending a whole lot of time over at Suzie's. Your truck's been spotted in her drive pretty early in the morning. Wouldn't take but a slip of the tongue to turn speculation loose."

Paul's stomach rolled as heat swept over him. "She's my neighbor and friend. There's nothing else going on."

Chuck smirked, and his laugh set Paul's neck hairs on end. "Rustin, a story doesn't have to be true to be told. The most prolific ones often aren't. Just think on that. What would that do to your perfect reputation? Aren't you up for elder right now?" He clicked his tongue. "Smear your integrity all over the windows of this quaint little church and break your mama's heart all over again. You want that?"

"You and I both know my reputation's far from perfect." Paul's muscles tensed as he balled his fists. "And lies always surface in the end. Leave Suzanna alone."

"Or what?"

Paul swallowed. His heart beat against his ribs, and the urge to employ his fists kept his body taut. "Just leave her alone."

Chuck's eyebrows rose again. Paul returned his cold stare until Chuck spat, landing blackened saliva on Paul's brown boots.

"Just so you know what you're getting into." He turned and sauntered away.

Paul watched him stride to his ridiculously tricked-out pickup. His jaw clenched until his face hurt. He couldn't protect Suzanna from this. He could only hope the people of this town, more importantly, the people of his church, would trust his honor more than they did Stanton's stories.

It didn't seem likely.

"I've gotta head south this week." Paul leaned back in the Adirondack chair, running a hand over his head.

"This week?" Dre sat forward. "I thought the sale wasn't until the thirty-first."

Paul sighed. The day had been overcast, fitting for his gray mood. The crisp air hinted snow, which would not work in his favor. Freezing mud was always miserable when it came to sorting and loading cows.

"I know. I've had to change my plans." He slid forward, leaning his elbows on his knees. "I need to ask if you guys can wait until the end of November to sell the head you had intended to have go this month."

Tom and Dre exchanged a glance.

"Sure," Tom said. "Not a big deal."

The crackling of the fire filled the night air. Paul stared at the flames as they danced in against the darkness. How bad would this get? He couldn't put out all of the flames Stanton was capable of lighting. And he couldn't protect Suzanna all of the time.

Next week, case in point. He'd be gone for at least four days. Stanton was sure to know it when he got wind of the sale on Saturday. Probably already did and was conniving something sinister.

Not to mention. . . Maybe he should bring it up with Tom and Dre. If nothing else, so they'd be prepared. Putting words to Chuck's threat made his stomach turn though.

Dre stood and refilled her mug. "What's going on, Paul?"

Paul bounced his fist on his chin, eyes still fixed on the fire. Might help for Tom and Dre to know how deep Suzanna's troubles ran. But he couldn't quite justify robbing Rodney of his dignity. Which would be exactly what would happen if word got around town about his situation.

"Stanton's dead set on Suzanna's place." Paul looked to Dre and then Tom. "He's stirring trouble, and he has a mighty big spoon to do it."

"Does she need money?" Tom scooted to the edge of his chair. "Is that why you're selling early?"

"No. Suz doesn't need the money."

Tom and Dre stared at him. He wasn't making any sense, and their worry was climbing by the moment.

"Look, this stays here, okay?" Paul stood, tossing his cold coffee onto the lawn.

"Of course." Tom answered, and Dre bounced her head.

"Rodney took a loan out a few years back to expand. He didn't go through the bank though. He went straight through Chuck. Chuck called it in this week. Rodney has to have half the balance in by the end of the month."

Dre dropped back into her chair. "What does this have to do with you or Suzanna?"

"Chuck's mad at me." Paul's skin felt hot, and his voice turned intense. "He doesn't want me helping Suzanna. I happened to drive by Suzanna's when he was paying her a visit Monday. He all but threatened her and wasn't very happy when I pulled up in the middle of it. Chuck doesn't have anything on me, nothing to take me by the neck, so he's going after the people I'm associated with. Starting with Rodney."

Dre reached for Tom's hand as worry turned to alarm in her eyes. "Is Suzanna in any danger?"

Paul jammed his hands into his hoodie pocket, wishing he knew. "I don't know how far Chuck will go. Right now, he's pretty underhanded. His reputation in town means maintaining his prime position at the bank, but he's also crazy over this. He's not letting it go, and I don't understand why. He's even started a ridiculous rumor about——"

"About Suzanna damming up the creek." Tom finished before Paul could.

Their gazes collided, and Paul knew Tom understood the situation.

Dre's questioning eyes focused on Tom.

"Jim Calloway came into the office on Wednesday all up in arms about it." Tom said. "Said if she carried through with it, he might just reinstitute the lynching code."

Even in the fading firelight, Paul could see her eyes grow huge. "Don't worry, sis. Suzanna has no such plans. There won't be any hangings in Cottonwood County. Chuck's just spreading lies to get people riled."

She leaned forward and scowled. "Sounds like it's working."

"I told Jim she couldn't do it, in any case." Tom tried to soothe Dre's fears. "It'd be illegal, and that would be that."

"But people will hate her just for thinking of it." Her voice cracked. "In fact, she pretty much got the cold shoulder in church today. Even Mrs. Blake failed to wish her a good morning."

Paul dropped back into his chair. He'd noticed that too. He was also certain Suzanna felt the snubs. She'd stayed pretty close to either him or Dre for the duration.

Dre's fine Sunday dinner soured in his stomach. Things had turned bad fast, but he had no choice but to leave town.

"I need you guys to check in on Suz while I'm gone." He caught his sister's eyes. "Okay?"

"I will." Her head bobbed slowly. "Tom will be gone most of the week, but I'll stop over for coffee."

Paul turned to Tom. He'd forgotten about harvest. The timing couldn't be worse. "When are you leaving?"

"I have a board meeting tomorrow, but I told Ben I'd be down by Tuesday night."

Rodewald

That left Andrea and Suzanna alone. Two women by themselves in the far reaches of the country. Out far enough where no one could hear a cry for help.

It didn't sit well at all.

CHAPTER SIXTEEN

Shattering glass ripped Suzanna from sleep. She bolted upright, gasping as though she'd been held under water. Her heart hammered in her chest as she searched for her cell phone in the darkness of her room.

She glanced at the doorway, listening for sounds of an intruder. Nothing stirred in the chilly night air. Gooseflesh rippled along her arms, and she lunged for her bedroom door in the eerie stillness. She shoved it closed, and set the lock with trembling fingers. Sliding to the floor with her back against the solid wood, she scanned through her contacts.

A quick check of her digital clock told her it was two. She couldn't call Andrea. What could the other woman do? Tom had left the night before, and Andrea was home alone with three kids. Paul was gone. That left...

No one.

Her throat swelled, and her eyes burned.

Daddy had a gun of some kind—a rifle maybe? She'd seen it in the back of the closet behind his box of memories. Suzanna had no idea how to load the weapon, let alone fire it, but she searched for it anyway. Maybe it would scare a predator. She didn't know what else to do.

Retrieving the long-barreled firearm and an oversized sweatshirt that had belonged to Jason, she slumped back down against the door. She slipped the sweatshirt on, hoping the warmth would calm her trembling body, and pressed her face into the extra length of sleeves. It didn't smell like him anymore.

Because he was gone. And she was alone. In the darkest hours of her life, she was always alone.

Suzanna laid her weapon across her lap, the cold metal of the barrel seeping through the thin fabric of her leggings, and rested a hand on the wooden stock. She tipped her head back as sobs quivered through her body. Tears ran down her face, dripping into her ears.

God, why do you hate me?

Heavy darkness lurked in the silence. Bitterness set a little deeper.

A hollow pounding startled Suzanna. Weak sunlight peeked around the roman shade, and her clock read seven fifty. She must have dozed. She rubbed her gritty eyes, which stung, and waited, hoping whoever was at her side door would go away. The knock sounded again, louder, more insistent.

Gripping the gun, she pushed herself off the floor. Her tailbone ached, and pins and needles ran down her legs. She shook both limbs, hoping the sensation would cease as she moved to her bedroom window. Pressed against the wall, she peeked through the crack of light. Andrea's truck sat empty in her driveway.

Suzanna moved to her bedroom door and unlocked it. A chilly breeze hit her face as she moved into the hall. The house was dim in the filtered morning light, and her curtains moved in an autumn breeze. Stepping with caution, she continued to the front room and halted. Shards of glass had scattered across the floor, and a rock the size of one of her shoes lay on the freshly scratched wood planks.

Who had done this?

She knew who. Why was he such a bully? And to her? He didn't know her, didn't have anything to hold against her, except this piece of land. It had meant nothing to him until she took up the rural-route address. Was Chuck really that stone-cold set against a city woman in his neighborhood?

Did Paul know why? He seemed pretty protective of her, seemed to know how much Chuck intimidated her. It was time to start asking some probing questions. If Paul knew more than he was letting on, she wanted in on it.

With her spine set straight, Suzanna tiptoed around the mess. She passed through the kitchen, and answered the door.

Andrea stood with her hand poised to pound again. Her eyes flared wildly, and she stepped back when she caught sight of Suzanna's gun.

"Suz, what's goin' on?"

Suzanna dropped her attention to the gun. Clamping her jaw, she set it in the corner nearest the door.

Andrea reached for her shoulder and gave Suzanna a small shake. "Suz, what happened? Why is your front window broken?"

"Don't know." The trembling returned. The sound of breaking glass echoed in her ears as she replayed the horrible moments over again. "Someone threw a rock at my house."

"Threw a rock?" Andrea stepped through the door, pulling Suzanna into the kitchen with her. "Like maybe a pickup kicked up a stone, and it broke your window?"

Suzanna shook her head and landed her attention on the rock visible from the kitchen table. "Don't think so."

Andrea released her hold and moved to the front room. "Good heavens, Suz." She turned back, pale and wide eyed. "That's no accident."

Suzanna held back the moisture in her eyes long enough for anger to smother the hurt. "No." She bit coolly. "No, it wasn't any kind of accident."

Andrea's gaze softened, and she stepped back toward the table. Suzanna stiffened when Andrea slid an arm around her shoulders, but Andrea hugged her anyway.

"Poor girl," Andrea whispered. "Must have scared you to death."

Silence, thick and heavy, hung in the kitchen. Suzanna swallowed back the urge to cry. She'd taken her mother's criticism, her parents' divorce, and had buried her husband without showing her tears to anyone. She could handle a rock in her house without crying in front of Andrea.

Strange. She'd cried in front of Paul. For something far less traumatic, she'd let the tears flow. Would she now—if he were here, would she let the pain spill over instead of capping it off with a seal of anger?

Possibilities not worth pondering.

"Listen, Suz." Andrea turned Suzanna's stiff frame to face her. "I want you to come home with me. Let's just throw some stuff in a bag, and you can stay with me and the kids. Heaven knows, I hate it when Tom is gone. I would so love for you to come—it'll be like a girls' getaway. I'll grab some chick flicks at the redbox when I go get the kids, and we'll eat junk and just hang out. Okay?"

Suzanna shook her head, her cold stare focused on the stone in her front room. "I'm not letting them push me out."

Andrea's shoulders dropped. "No, hon, you're not. We won't let them, either." She took her hand and squeezed until Suzanna turned her focus back. "I'm not talking about surrender. But I don't think you should be here alone this week."

"Why?"

Andrea's brows rose incredulously.

"Why this week?" Suzanna persisted.

"Paul's gone until Friday."

Suzanna scowled. "You don't think this would have happened if he were home?"

"I don't know." Andrea shrugged. "Timing's pretty suspicious, and Paul was concerned."

Suzanna jolted straight. There *was* more than Paul had told her. "Why?"

Andrea looked at the floor.

"Why does Chuck want my land?" Suzanna crossed her arms.

Andrea's eyes shot back up. "That I really couldn't tell you." She leaned against the table, honesty shrouding her face. "Look, I don't know what he's got in his back pocket, and neither does Paul, but Chuck's stirring up trouble in town, and it's not getting better. Paul's working on it, but he's worried that it's only going to get worse. For now, I really think it'd be best for you to come with me."

Suzanna turned her gaze back to the front room and scowled. Why hadn't Paul talked to her about any of this? If he were worried, why didn't he give her a heads-up?

"I need to clean this up." Suzanna gestured to the broken glass. "And I still have to work today. I'm already a few hours late, and I didn't even call."

Andrea's mouth pulled down. She studied Suzanna with eyes of compassion. Suzanna's stoic resolve almost melted. She swallowed, locking away the frailty of tears.

"I'll help you, then." Andrea conceded. "We'll need to board up that window until it can be repaired. Do you know if you have anything to cover it?"

Suzanna mentally searched the garage and the barn. Daddy had a canvas tarp and some cedar shakes stashed in the back corner of the barn. Maybe they'd make do. She told Andrea where they were, and the other woman turned on her booted heel to go after the supplies.

"Suz..." She stopped at the doorway off the kitchen. "Please come tonight."

Suzanna leaned on the broom she'd nabbed from behind her fridge. She held Andrea's eyes only long enough to feel the warmth of her friend's concern against the cold anger she maintained.

She dropped her stare to the floor. "I don't think so."

Andrea crossed the room and gripped her hand. "I won't sleep tonight knowing you're here all alone. Please?"

Suzanna was alone all the time. And she hated it. But hoping for something different. . .

Disappointment had proven far more agonizing.

"He did what?"

Sitting astride Bronco, Paul clutched his cell phone and nearly shouted into the speaker. Gone fewer than forty-eight hours, and the situation had already heated. Chuck didn't waste an opportunity.

Andrea sighed, her voice wavering over the digital air. "I don't know for sure it was Chuck, Paul. Suzanna didn't see anything. She was crazy-scared though. Answered the door with her daddy's .243 tucked under her arm."

His veins throbbed, and Paul struggled to see straight. Rumors were one thing—unpleasant, but bearable. Vandalism, bordering on threats of harm, was a new story altogether.

Paul tugged at his hat as though doing so would clear his thoughts. "Did you call Jude?"

Certainly the Cottonwood County sheriff should be notified. Even if he were a good buddy of Stanton's. Man, history got in the way.

"I called him before I called you." Andrea cleared her throat. "Said he had a little bit of paperwork to finish up from yesterday, and that he'd be out in the afternoon."

Figured.

How Jude Gilroy worked himself into the hearts of the Rock Creek citizens was a matter of pure amazement. He'd been the rollin' devil in charge of all of their idiotic pranks, the ones that had landed Paul in jail all those years ago.

Paul was hardly a man who could withhold grace, given his turn-around past, but Gilroy still wore a glint of mischief right alongside his government-issued badge. He'd taken an oath, though, to serve and protect. Paul had to hope he took that seriously, even if it did set him perpendicular to Chuck.

Paul pulled Bronco to a standstill and scanned the cows he'd been pushing. He was still nearly a mile from the working yard, and they had at least another day's worth of roundup before he could start sorting. It would take another day beyond that to finish and then load.

But he needed to go home. Chuck wouldn't have been so brazen with him just a mile down the road.

His mind worked over the situation. The calendar would flip to November on Wednesday. Rodney needed to make a hefty payment before then. The sale had to happen this weekend. Cal, Paul's land manager and trusted employee, was working as well as the two hands Paul kept on full time at the river property. They could probably handle it, but Paul had never been absent when it came to roundup. Didn't seem like a good idea. Things could go wrong pretty fast, and as owner, he needed to be on site if something went awry with either man or beast.

There simply wasn't a choice.

"Can you stay with her, Dre?"

"I planned on it." Andrea's voice sounded strained. "But I've got to go into town to get the kids after school. My bet, Jude will show up 'round about the time I gotta get. I don't like it. What's more, I asked her to come stay at our house tonight, but she won't."

Paul groaned. He tugged at his collar, turned upward against the chilly northern wind, and rubbed his temples. The little Pickle. Timid and fierce. She wasn't hard to figure. Scared to death, she was like a filly cornered in a pen. Fight or flight would always kick in.

Suzanna was one to fight.

Even through his righteous indignation and his frustration that Suzanna wasn't going to do the easy, sensible thing and go stay with his sister, a warm smile of admiration bloomed in his heart. Maybe she didn't know what she was up against when it came to Chuck Stanton. But Chuck sure didn't know what he was taking on, either. Suzanna Wilton was most certainly not the inept, wisp of a woman they'd all taken her for.

He knew her better, and she trusted him. Maybe she'd listen.

"I'll call her, Dre." Paul put a heel against Bronco, and the horse started forward. "Just hang out with her right now, and I'll talk to her. I'll give you a call in a bit."

She sounded relieved as she wrapped up her call. Paul set Bronco to a lope until he caught up with Justin, his hired hand.

"Everything okay, boss?" The twenty-something bachelor asked.

"No, not really." Paul sighed as he scanned his cattle again. Why did people—Chuck in particular—have to make life difficult?

Sin. Always the perennial answer. Sin.

Why had Paul made his parents' life miserable? Sin. Why had he been so awful to Dre growing up? Sin. Why had he been mean to Suzanna when they'd first met? Sin.

Chuck was just another man. Selfish and manipulative because he was sinful. But God's grace didn't limit itself to the white-gloved sinners.

Paul's mind echoed the words of Psalm 103, a favorite of his and one he worked to commit to memory.

He has not dealt with us according to our sins, Nor rewarded us according to our iniquities.

Praise God.

Paul branded the words across the forefront of his mind. He needed to keep them fresh as he dealt with the billowing issue of Chuck Stanton.

"Something wrong with the sale?" Justin pulled him back onto the range and into reality.

"No, we're still on." Paul shifted in the saddle. "My neighbor is in a bit of trouble, and I need to help her. Listen, I've got to make a few calls. Can you finish this push, and I'll meet you boys back at the yard?"

"Sure, no problem." Justin heeled his ride forward as though putting a seal on his commitment.

Paul's frown relaxed. He had good help. And Dre was with Suzanna. He couldn't be everywhere at once, but God had made provision, even for the things Paul could do nothing about.

He took up his cell again and found *Pickle* in his contacts. She answered on the fourth ring, and Paul didn't waste time on chitchat.

"Suz..."

Paul's voice beckoned emotion Suzanna thought she'd locked away.

"Tell me what happened."

Having had to retreat to her room to find her ringing phone, she dropped to her unmade bed. She gripped the edge of the quilt she'd flung helter-skelter in her panic the night before. Tears suddenly overflowed from the deep.

She sniffed and then wished she hadn't.

"Oh, Pickle."

The gentle tone in Paul's deep voice drew a sob, and Suzanna covered her face as though he were present. He waited, and in the silence she imagined him drawing her against his shoulder as he had after Chuck left her house the week before. The image washed warmth over her, and she felt guilty for clinging to the comfort.

But he was her friend. She shouldn't have to keep herself closed off from everyone in the world, should she? Certainly, he didn't carry any expectations as he offered her compassion.

Suzanna wasn't sure it would change her reaction if he did. Her starving soul couldn't help but cling to his generous kindness.

"I woke up to something crashing through my front window last night." Suzanna worked to control her wobbly voice.

"What time?" Paul's soft tone continued to caress her bruise soul.

"Around two."

"Were you hurt?"

Suzanna recalled the ache inside. It would have almost been a relief to have been injured; then she'd have something physical on which to blame the throbbing pain in her heart.

"No. I wasn't hurt."

"Suzanna... " Paul drew a breath, and the tenor of his voice took on authority. "I need you to listen to me, because I can't be there. I want to, but I just can't. I'm going to call Jude Gilroy so he understands the breadth of the situation before he comes to talk to you. Chances are Dre will have to go before he shows up, so I want you to call me when he pulls in your drive and after he leaves. I want to know what he says and what he plans to do about it."

Suzanna's tears dried quickly, and her back set straight. Her whole life, she'd longed for someone to protect her, to take care of her. She'd done most of the guarding and tending in her world.

But now, having Paul take over, she felt threatened.

If she let him be her shelter, she'd get caught defenseless. One time had been one time too many. She'd fortify her own refuge, thank you very much.

"I'll handle it, Paul."

He didn't heed the implication to back off. "I know you can, Suz, but you're not alone."

Her determination cracked. How did he know…?

"You don't have to walk the tough roads by yourself, Suzanna," Paul continued. "I don't know what life has dealt you, but it's time you let someone walk that path alongside you. Dre wants you to go and stay with her. I think it's a good idea. We're your friends, and you need to quit fighting us."

Suzanna swallowed, struggling against the urge to let her emotions spill out again.

Not alone… walk alongside you… friends.

Petitions she'd sent out to a deaf heaven. Could she trust the offer now?

"Suzanna?"

Her eyes slid shut.

"Please let us help you."

All the fight drained away. "Okay, Paul."

He exhaled, and she could almost feel the warmth of his breath as she again imagined his arms pulling her close. Was it wrong to tuck the image safely in her heart?

He made her promise, and then the conversation ended. Fingering the fabric star shaped by her grandmother's hands, she rolled to her side and curled into a ball. The floodgates released, and her silent cries matched those of two years ago. Days when she watched Jason wither into nothing as his body rejected the bone marrow.

"Promise me." He had rasped against the agonizing pain of death, refusing the morphine so he could talk to her with a clear mind. "I need you to promise me, Suzie. I don't want you to stay angry with God. His grace will sustain you, even in this. Promise me that you'll choose to live."

She pushed her face into the sterile bed linens at his side, afraid to touch him and increase his pain. "I will." She choked against sobs.

They were words spoken to ease her heartbroken husband as he struggled with the finality of his life. Words she couldn't mean. How could she not be angry? What kind of god put so many trials in one man's life and then brought it to a short and bitter end?

Jason wasn't bitter though. He of all the people she'd ever met had the most understandable reasons to be bitter, but he wasn't. Though he'd endured more than his fair share of trials, he lived with joy. And though in physical anguish, he'd died with peace.

It wasn't fair, and Suzanna was not going to let God forget it.

CHAPTER SEVENTEEN

"Kelsey, it's your night for dishes, sweetie." Andrea nodded to her oldest daughter as she pushed away from the table.

Suzanna watched as the girl, bordering on adolescence, dipped her head without a hint of complaint.

"Yes, Mama." She took up her plate, adding her silverware, and rose from the table. "May I take yours, Miss Wilton?"

Suzanna couldn't help but smile. She'd assumed such well-mannered children were all but extinct. "You may, but how about if I help you? I can rinse, and you can load. Would that be okay?"

Kelsey looked at her mother, who nodded, and then smiled in her sweet, shy way. Suzanna's heart puddled. The lovely twelve-year-old drew her in without pretense.

Kelsey cleared the rest of the dishes while the other children scooted off to put their clean laundry away. Suzanna helped Andrea put the leftovers in the refrigerator and then moved to the sink to work beside Kelsey.

"Mama!" Keegan called from the top of the stairs. "My drawer won't close!"

Andrea shrugged and grinned, moving to the stairs. "Spatially inept."

Her eye roll tickled a grin from Suzanna. Was this how families were supposed to interact? She set to work at the sink, trying to push away memories of heated outbursts followed by days of cold silence.

"Will you stay with us the rest of the week, Miss Wilton?" Kelsey asked.

"I don't know, Miss Kelsey." She handed a dripping plate to her shorter counterpart. "Your uncle seems to think it would be best, at least until my window can be fixed, but we'll see."

"I hope so. Mama doesn't like to be home alone—I mean without Daddy. I could tell she was excited to have you come. Kind of like when I get to have a sleepover with my friend Lizzy. We get to stay up late and watch movies and paint our nails. It will make the time special for Mama."

Suzanna studied Kelsey while she mulled over her words. She was more than a girl with her polished manners and insights of wisdom. Her mother was raising her to be a young lady, and she was well on her way.

Suzanna had always been told to behave as a proper young lady, but she hadn't really been raised to be one. Not on the inside, at least. On the outside, however, she was always to act refined. Prim and flawless.

We must present ourselves well at all times, Suzanna. Your father's congregation will look to us for the example, and we must set the standard.

She and her sister had scrubbed their nails and pressed their clothing. Their shoes were never scuffed and their hair was never disheveled. They sat stiffly on their pew, front row, right side, and never ran in the church.

No wonder the church members were shocked when the ugly truth came out.

Suzanna reset her thoughts. Movies and painted nails. She'd never had a girls' sleepover. People were not welcomed in their home for any extended length of time. They'd discover how imperfect the Wilton family really was if they'd hung around.

Suzanna shoved the memories back again "Tell you what, Kelsey. If you paint my nails when we're done here, I'll pack another set of clothes tomorrow."

Kelsey grinned. "I'll check with Mama."

"Check what?" Andrea dropped from the last of the steps and turned into the kitchen.

"Can I paint Miss Wilton's nails tonight before bed?"

Andrea's smile settled on Suzanna. "You bet."

Kelsey moved her eyes to Suzanna as well, a cheerful glee lighting her smile.

Suzanna gave in to the blissful tide. "One more thing." She passed another plate. "I would like it so much better if you just called me Suzanna."

"How's Suzanna?" Paul pushed down a taste of guilt. He was spying on Suzanna via his sister, but he couldn't let her struggle through this alone. Even if that was exactly what she wanted.

What made her afraid to let others in? Certainly, it must be fear. She was miserable in her loneliness. She wouldn't choose isolation unless she had a reason.

"She's with Kelsey right now. They're painting their nails."

"Really?"

Kelsey? His introverted, bookworm niece? That made for an interesting pair.

"Yeah." Andrea's smile carried in her voice. "I've heard Kelsey use more words tonight than I've heard out of her around anyone—including you, *Uncle* Paul."

"Wow, what are they talking about?"

"I don't know." Andrea huffed. "Did you expect me to eavesdrop?"

He chuckled. "No. Just curious. That's a twist, isn't it?"

Andrea echoed his laugh. "It is. I don't have the heart to tell Kels it's past bedtime."

"I'll call Suz when we're done, and you can tell her then."
Paul sipped his coffee, wishing it tasted more like Suzanna's. A
knot formed in his chest and began to expand. He inhaled
deeply, trying to dispel the feeling even while he worked to
identify it.

Homesick.

Homesick? For nearly two decades, the river property had
been as much of a home to Paul as the farmhouse had been.
He'd kept the cracker-box house that had belonged to his
great-granddaddy in good repair, and though nothing worth
showing off, it served him right well.

Andrea's voice, louder than it had been before, interrupted
his thoughts. "Hello Paul?"

"What?"

"I said, that'll work, I suppose."

"Oh, okay." What will work? Paul's mind scrambled to
remember whom he was talking to, let alone what he was
talking about.

*Andrea. You are talking to your sister about calling Suzanna. Crazy
guy.*

The pressure expanded against his chest. *Homesick.*

For the Pickle?

Oh boy. He was in trouble.

"Which one is your favorite?"

Suzanna leaned over to take in the loaded bookshelf.
Painted a soft pink, it held a variety of titles; some Suzanna
recognized, many she didn't.

Kelsey fingered a horse series whose spines all possessed
the telltale crease from multiple reads. "I've read all of these at
least three times."

A grin spread across Suzanna's mouth as she took in Kelsey's sweet face. Not a trace of world-weary heaviness etched her young skin. Her green eyes sparkled. She was a reserved girl—nothing at all like Kiera, who possessed her mother's and uncle's vibrant personalities—but her soft kindness beckoned Suzanna to draw near.

Suzanna sat on the floor with her legs crisscrossed and leaned her back against Kelsey's green-and-pink quilted bedspread. "Three times each, huh? You must love horses like your uncle."

"No, that's Kiera. She and Uncle Paul go riding almost every week." Kelsey shrugged. "I like them, but I'd rather look at them than ride."

There wasn't a hint of jealousy in Kelsey's voice or expression. Sisters, not set against each other. What a wonderful concept.

"So, what's your favorite thing in the world to do besides reading?"

"I draw."

"Draw?"

"Yeah." Kelsey's head dipped, but her smile lifted her cheeks. "Mostly pencil sketches, but sometimes I use chalk. My grandpa helps me. Well, he used to, anyway. The stroke took away the use of his right hand, but he still coaches me when I ask."

"I didn't know your grandfather was an artist."

Her head came back up, and her eyes lit with pride. "Come on, I'll show you."

She came to her feet and stuck a hand out to Suzanna. Suzanna took it while she pulled herself up and held on as they left Kelsey's room and stepped down the hall. They passed two doors, Kiera's room and a bathroom the three kids shared, and stopped short of another doorway at the end of the hall.

"This one is my favorite." Kelsey pointed to a framed picture—one Suzanna would have sworn was a costly print from a gallery.

The tall prairie grass almost swayed with the subtle movement of color and texture. A wide ribbon of water cut through the lower third of the canvas, the gray-blue ripples interrupted by the reflection of a twilight sky. The soft oranges and pinks echoed in the sky, the colors more intense as they gathered at the horizon. Staring at the scene, Suzanna felt herself there. Drawn into the oil pastel as if she'd stepped into a new reality.

She fingered the frame below the glass. "Where is this?"

"The river property where Uncle Paul works when he's not here." Kelsey's hand squeezed against Suzanna's. "It's so beautiful there. I hope you can go with us."

Longing climbed in Suzanna's chest. For the beauty captured in pastels. For the serenity that swathed Kelsey's world. And for the sense of belonging that teased her spirit. The Kents had fully embraced her, wanted her among them, with them. And she wanted to accept their welcome, to slide in as part of their family.

But things that are too good to be true...

And Paul? The man possessed something over her. A charm that promised to soothe the ache she kept buried beneath anger and resentment. A promise that certainly would prove empty.

Suzanna cleared her throat and gently pulled her hand from her young friend. She forced her gaze away from Paul's paradise.

"Show me your work, Kels."

Kelsey studied her, her young eyes hinting more understanding than a girl her age should possess. "I'm not as good as Grandpa."

"You haven't had as many years to practice." Suzanna smiled, relieved to move beyond the moment that had stirred the ache inside. "I would love to see, if you wouldn't mind showing me."

Kelsey's easy smile returned, and she nodded. They made their way back to her room, and she pulled an artist's sketchbook from her bookshelf.

"These are what I do on my own." She tugged another pad from the ledge. "And these are what I work on with Grandpa."

Suzanna perused both. Talent sprawled over page after page. A few horses appeared in graphite, well proportioned and realistic. Mostly, though, Kelsey's drawings took to organic scenes. Her mother's garden. The trees that lined the creek. A small pond that rested down the gentle slope from the Kents' farmhouse. And the river. Certainly a favorite subject as it made its way onto many pages.

The pieces Kelsey had worked on with her grandfather showed a more refined touch. The quality of the work spoke of the time she'd spent with a master artist.

"How long have you worked with your grandfather?"

"Forever." Kelsey's face wreathed with delight. "I've been drawing before I could write. Grandpa would sit and color with me. Our art sessions just grew from that."

"How often do you work together?"

"At least once a week, if he's up for it." A hint of sadness tethered Kelsey's voice.

Compassion flooded Suzanna's heart. Disappointment was something she knew well. "It must have been hard when he had his stroke."

Kelsey plopped onto her bed. "Yeah. I had a really hard time with it. At first, we thought he was going to die, and I was so sad. He's my best friend. But then, when he didn't, things got hard. He's not the same anymore."

Her eyes searched Suzanna, begging for understanding. Suzanna dropped beside her, silently waiting for Kelsey to continue.

"I hope you don't think I'm selfish. I mean, I'm glad he's alive, and we still have fun. He's just not the same though. I miss who he was."

Suzanna brushed the hair out of Kelsey's face. "I know exactly what you mean, and I don't think you're selfish." She swallowed as a rush of emotion nearly overwhelmed her. "I knew someone like that once. Well, sort of. He got sick, too, and he wasn't ever the same again. It was really hard. When you love someone, and you lose them, or even part of who they were, it hurts."

Kelsey's eyes came to hers and held fast. Tears pooled, making them shimmer and tugging at the ache Suzanna tried to keep smothered.

Kelsey sniffed as a tear spilled onto her cheek. "I've never talked to anyone about it."

Wrapping an arm around her, Suzanna pulled her close. "Me neither, Kels." She clamped her jaw and forced her own tears back. "I guess that makes you my new best friend."

CHAPTER EIGHTEEN

Paul tugged on the reins, pulling Bronco to a stop. He smacked his gloved hand against his thigh and pushed his phone harder against his ear. "Why do you keep pushing us to arm's length?"

Silence. Suzanna refused to meet his challenge. He sighed.

"Listen, it's not that far away, only an hour and a half, and you might enjoy seeing how some of this life works. We'll head back home that same evening. What do you have to lose?"

"I don't want Chuck to think I'm afraid of him." Suzanna's tone bit when she pronounced his name.

"Who cares what Chuck thinks?" Paul dismounted near the trailer. "He's going to do whatever he's going to do, whether you're there or not. So you might as well be here."

Paul thought he could hear her sniff, though it sounded like she muffled it with a hand over her phone. Something clenched around his heart, and he pulled in a breath. "Suz, what did I say?"

"Nothing." She sounded rushed. "Why would you ask that?"

"Because…" *Because I want to know why you suddenly shut down. Why some of the things I say and do push you to tears.* "I'm sorry, Pickle. I guess I'm being too pushy. I just thought you'd like it. It's pretty here, and I know Dre really would like for you to come with her, but no one will be mad if you don't."

A quiet pause hung between them, and Paul wished he could see her face. Not that seeing her was a guaranteed help. Suzanna was pretty good at keeping feelings shrouded when she didn't want her heart exposed. But maybe he'd know where he went wrong; maybe he'd understand her withdrawal.

"You're not too pushy." Suzanna let loose a long breath. "Truth is, I'd like to come. Kelsey showed me one of your dad's paintings of the river. I'd love to see it. I just don't want to intrude on your family. You're all so generous, and——"

"You're not an intruder." Paul cut her off. He waited for her to respond but was met with nothing. "It's not intruding to take someone up on an invitation. You're invited, Suzanna. I'd like you to come."

Bronco nudged his shoulder, impatient to be free from the saddle. Paul rubbed the horse's neck and counted the seconds before Suzanna spoke again.

"When did Andrea want to leave?"

A grin split his face. "Early. She's already called the school to excuse the kids. She'll hit the road before sunup."

·She'd have to put in some work hours on Sunday. She was short by at least eight for the week. Maybe she'd have to miss Sunday dinner, but as the sun crested the eastern horizon, highlighting the ripples of water with white-gold, Suzanna was certain it was worth it.

They'd driven southwest for over an hour, trekking almost to the Colorado state line before Andrea made a ninety-degree turn north. A mile off the highway, the sprawling plains transformed into a narrow cottonwood forest. They crossed the Republican and turned left onto a rough drive that curved through the trees before it gradually twisted its way up a hill. The trees thinned again, and as they reached the apex, Suzanna's breath caught.

The river had once bowed at this point, and though it now ran a straighter course, it had left a crescent-shaped body of water nestled against the hill. An ox-bow lake. Standing as a sentry, a small house rested below the top of the rise, protected from the northern winds.

Who would have imagined this little slice of rural paradise? Suzanna had detected nothing of it from the highway, or even as they approached the south side of the river. Paul's secret little haven was the kind you'd have to know about, and know how to get there, to ever see it.

"It's something, isn't it?" Andrea's smile made her voice dance.

"Wow."

"Is it like what you imagined from Grandpa's picture?" Kelsey whispered from the back seat.

"Not at all." Suzanna turned on her hip to face her young friend. "I thought it was the river, and I was trying to remember passing a section that was as wide as the one in the picture. But this is what he'd painted, isn't it?"

Kelsey nodded with a grin. "There's a little inlet over there." She pointed southwest. "That keeps the water from going green and slimy. And Uncle Paul keeps the outlet clear so the water will drain downstream."

Suzanna turned back. It wasn't really a lake, but it seemed too large to call it a pond. "Is it all from the river?"

"No, there's a spring." Andrea pointed toward the house. "Just like Rock Creek. My great-great-grandparents settled here. We're on the west side of the Old Texas Cattle Trail. They did pretty well raising beef. Over the generations, the land has been held, added to, and kept in good condition."

Andrea drove around the northwest side of the water's edge, approaching the house as the sun began to warm the earth. Paul appeared in the doorway, his grin reminding Suzanna he'd wanted her to come.

A surreal feeling overtook her as they pulled to a stop. She belonged. This family, these friends were *hers*, and they embraced her with sincere kindness. She'd felt that only with Jason, and even then, it was a lonely comfort. He was her real family, and even in the first few months of their marriage, she knew belonging would be a fleeting vapor.

He would go. They both knew it. He was sick, and a matching donor was a long shot. When the doctors found a partial match, five out of seven points, it was a last-ditch, slim-hope chance. They'd known the narrow odds, and he didn't survive them.

Suzanna's tongue pressed against the roof of her mouth as she pushed back emotion.

Andrea and the kids popped out of the truck as soon as she cut the engine. Suzanna stalled, trying to right her world. She couldn't, not completely, before Paul opened her door.

"What do you think, Pickle?"

She stepped out of the truck, forcing her mind back to the present while she watched Andrea's kids scramble down a dirt path toward the water. Keegan yelled something about fish, and the girls followed him, their giggles filling the chilly autumn morning.

"It's beautiful."

All of it. Not just the setting, which was, in fact, picturesque, but the moment. Kids secure in everything that surrounded them, running and laughing without burdens eating away their innocent joy. Andrea trailing after them—a lovely woman, a kind friend, and the sort of mother Suzanna had longed for during her own childhood. And Paul…

He'd slid a hand to her elbow as she stepped down from the truck. It still rested there, warming her arm and bringing that secure feeling back.

What if it lasted?

"I'm glad you came."

There was nothing intimate about his voice, but something inside latched onto his words. They set off a battle. Suzanna forced a smile and tipped a nod, but her spirit wrestled fiercely as she weighed comfort against agony. Pain always followed momentary happiness.

But maybe this time it would be worth it.

Suzanna looked cute in mud.

Standing in the middle of the working pen, surrounded by young steers and armed with a prod, she was caked from the knees down to her boots. Her hair was tied back and covered with a worn University of Northern Colorado ball cap. Andrea had lent her a flannel-lined denim coat, and her hands were safely covered with leather. Only the skin on her neck and her face were exposed, and they were streaked with filth.

Paul turned his back and moved toward the chute as a chuckle tickled his throat. His memory drew up an image of her sitting in mud several weeks ago. If he'd been honest with himself back then, he'd have thought the same thing. She was an attractive mess.

He stopped his stride next to the truck just as the steers started passing through the ramp. Loading cattle was a noisy affair—cowboys hawed as they sorted the herd, wood and steel rattled as the animals were loaded, and mamas called from the fence line, and the steers bawled back. It always touched a little sadness in Paul's gut, but it was part of the job.

He wasn't a disconnected supplier in the beef industry. He worked his cattle personally, whether he was down on the river property or up at his home base. When he lost a newborn calf, he felt genuine grief. When he had to put a sick cow down, he regretted more than the financial loss. And when he listened to the bawling echoes of mamas separated from their babies, he appreciated the sorrow of their sacrifice.

This time of year, and this event in particular, always stirred reflection. As the air filled with the chaotic orchestra of cows and cattlemen, Paul's mind drifted to a specific sacrifice. One made for all men. Necessary, and yet infinitely more grave than anything he'd witnessed on the ranch. God's Son, the jewel of heaven—rejected, beaten, and slowly put to death.

So men might live.

Stuart Townend's "How Deep the Father's Love For Us" rolled through Paul's heart. Not the song of a clichéd roundup. Maybe he wasn't the typical cowboy.

Dre's voice brought life to the melody in his mind.

Paul turned, catching Dre's smile as she continued to sing near the opening of the chute. He hadn't realized he'd been humming, but as Cal, a devout Christian man, added his tenor to her soprano, Paul continued to support their lyrics with his baritone. The kids, all three, joined on the parts they knew, making a choir out of his work crew.

They finished the song, and Cal moved into "Amazing Grace." They came to the end of the first verse before Paul realized Suzanna had moved to the far corner of the working yard, alone in her silence. He caught her staring, but she dropped her eyes as soon as their gazes collided, hiding them under the brim of her ball cap.

Moving toward her would embarrass her—and probably make her mad. She turned, her booted feet mucking farther away. Paul could almost read the invisible sign written across her stiff shoulders: *I don't want to talk about it.*

Showered and pleasantly exhausted, Suzanna dropped onto the porch swing hung from the rebuilt cover attached to Paul's small house. She was thankful Andrea had told her to bring a change of clothes.

The kids had all been sprayed down and were running around the house, shouting and laughing as they had been from the moment they'd first arrived. There was something magical about the place. Time seemed to slow, and the atmosphere could only be described as peaceful joy.

Everything about the Kents, and Paul, seemed peaceful. Tom and Andrea's home exuded peace from the front porch to the back patio. And Paul's river property… oh goodness. Life must be good here.

Paul appeared from around the corner, coming from the barn west of his house. He'd insisted the girls use the shower first. No doubt, his would be cold by the time it was all said and done. If he minded, it didn't show. Suzanna couldn't imagine that he did.

"Turned out to be a good day, don't you think?" He smiled as he took the two steps up the porch.

Suzanna felt her cheeks rise. "It did. Thanks, Paul."

He put a hand on the chain that held the swing. "I'm sure I still stink, but do you mind?" He nodded down to the seat.

Suzanna scooted over, and Paul dropped beside her. The chains moaned as he pushed off the floorboards, setting them both into a gentle rock.

Paul leaned back and exhaled, his shoulders dropping as he relaxed beside her. "Best seat in the house. Or out of it."

She nodded. "Spend much time out here?"

"At the river property or on this swing?"

Suzanna tipped her head. "Both, I guess."

"I'm here probably three months out of the year, but not in a row." He kicked his legs forward, stretching them as they continued to sway. "I'm down quite a bit for calving. We try to time it so I'm done up north before the season starts down here, but sometimes it's off. I have full-time hands down here, so it works out. This year I was here extra long in August because I had some fencing that needed more work before I

could move the cows onto fall pasture. And then this"—he
jerked his thumb back toward the working yards over the hill—
"takes a few weeks. Moving, sorting, loading."

"Sounds like it keeps you busy."

He nodded. "It's a life and a job all at once."

Suzanna laughed. "You love it."

Paul turned his eyes on her. "You can tell?" He chuckled,
not waiting for an answer. "Yep. I think I told you before, it's
the life I tried to run away from, and yet the life I love.
Grandpa told me before he died that it was in me. Not in my
blood, but in my head, my heart. I think he was right. I can't
imagine doing anything else."

Keegan tore around the corner with his sisters close
behind. "Uncle Paul! I saw a fish jump!" He hopped onto the
step. "Can we go down to the dock?"

Paul lugged himself up. "Sure, buddy."

"Yes!" Kiera pulled a fist down like a football player after a
touchdown.

The kids turned and sped through the yard. Paul stepped
from the porch and stopped, twisting at the waist to catch
Suzanna's attention. He jerked his head toward the water.
Suzanna laughed, but she didn't need to be asked twice.

The mowed grass ended fifty feet from the house. A worn
path cut through the native grass, which stood almost to
Suzanna's knees. The trek down to the pond felt like an
adventure through nature. She glanced at Paul as they navigated
down the slope. He looked like he'd shed about twenty-five
years, and she could picture him with a fishing pole and
overalls, skipping down the way. Something like Opie on the
Andy Griffith Show. It made her giggle.

"What's that?" Paul slowed his steps so she came parallel to
him.

"Nothing."

"Nope." He shook his head. "You laughed. Share the
joke."

"No joke." Her ponytail bounced against her neck as she shook her head. "Just an image. It's very Mayberry." She passed her hand in front of her as if the scene were a canvas.

Paul smiled. "I'll take that as a compliment."

Suzanna bounced her head and then studied him. They neared the bank, and the trail jetted left. A small dock bobbed on the water, its gray boards protruding into the reflection of the evening sky. Water rippled beneath it, lapping against the shore with a gentle smack. A cool breeze overruled the silent invitation to swim, though it could not halt the draw of the view.

"Why don't you live here?" Suzanna stopped where the path met the dock, turning her eyes back to Paul.

He grinned a little, and his head dropped back as he surveyed the scene. After inhaling deeply, his shoulders relaxed. Suzanna didn't need to ask; this was his favorite place on earth.

"It is something, isn't it?" His eyes fell back to her, twinkling with pleasure.

It wasn't much of an answer. She stared at him, her eyebrows pulling in.

Paul left the path and moved ten feet onto the bank before he dropped onto the grass. Not knowing what else to do, Suzanna followed, settling an arm's length away from him. He kicked at the dirt under his boot, freeing a pebble from the pale soil and tossing it into the water.

"Fish!" Keegan shouted. He dropped onto the boards of the dock, stretching himself on his belly and pointing to the water.

Kelsey and Kiera scrambled from their posts on either side of the dock to see Keegan's find. They joined him on their stomachs, and all three scouted the water's depths.

Paul laughed. "That's why." His head dipped toward the kids.

Suzanna's attention snapped from the kids back to the cowboy beside her, not understanding.

He met her questioning gaze, the smile crinkles around his eyes adding to the appeal of his handsome face. "I love it here, but it wouldn't amount to much without them"—his hands fluttered back to the kids—"without my family. I love that I get to see those kids grow up. I love that I can keep an eye on my parents, that I can help take care of them as age begins to take its toll. Tom was my best friend growing up, and being near him, watching him love and take care of my sister, means more to me than I can say. A pretty view can't replace that."

Mayberry indeed. Family devotion, born of honest love and raised with sincere affection.

The serenity of Paul's haven vanished like a thin fog over the mountains. A lonely reality sank heavy inside Suzanna's stomach. She moved her eyes from his, not wishing for him to see her unhappy regret.

His gaze didn't waver, and she could feel the intensity of his stare as it settled over her. Eyes that were gentle beckoned her back, confusing her with his kindness. It was safer to be angry than vulnerable. When she couldn't take the weight of his silent appeal, she came to her feet.

Paul remained in his place. "Why do you do that?"

She knew better than to meet his eyes, but her gaze wouldn't heed her warning. That silent promise called to the depths who she was, and who she didn't want to be.

Empty promises. He couldn't fill the loneliness life had carved into her soul. He would try, and he would fail, and she would be more broken than before.

Suzanna turned away, scanning the tall grass for the footpath back to the house.

Paul came to his feet, his movements calm and intentional. "Time to head back up," he called to the kids. "Your mama will be about ready."

Led by Kiera, the trio scrambled to their feet and left the dock at a run. Their short legs took to the path, and they bobbed through the prairie grass back up the hill.

With a last glance back over the water, Suzanna followed. Paul stopped her with a hand on her elbow.

"What do I say that makes you do that?"

She tugged at a seed head, twisting it in her fingers. "Do what?"

"Shut down."

Her heart began to throb. Refusing to look at him, she plucked another blade of grass, peeling it apart in narrow strips.

Paul stepped in front of her and stilled her fingers with his hand. "What is it, Suz? Do I offend you?"

Suzanna stepped back, pulling her hand away. "No, you don't offend me. It's nothing."

"It's something." He stood rooted, his frame blocking the path. "I can't figure it out. I thought maybe I was too pushy, but I wasn't demanding anything from you just now. How can I upset you in every conversation we have? Surely you know I don't mean to."

"I know."

A breeze dropped over the northern rise and stirred the trees, pulling yellowed leaves from their branches and setting them afloat over the air. Inspired by their flight, birds left their perches, dipping and turning as they waltzed with the leaves. Suzanna let her attention wander, envying the freedom to let go, to fly.

Paul waited with patient silence. Words built in her mouth and forced their way out.

"Being with your family makes me resent mine." Steamy tears burned against her eyelids. Her cheeks felt hot as shame tumbled in her gut.

Paul didn't flinch, didn't move. His eyes didn't grow in surprise or darken with disapproval. His silent appraisal didn't hint reproach. "Do you want to tell me about it?"

His low, soft voice felt like a warm cotton blanket on a cold, stormy night. A tear slid down Suzanna's nose as her heart grasped at the comfort.

"I don't know where to begin." Her throat closed over against a sob. She brushed at the stray tear with the sleeve of her oversized sweatshirt.

"Where's your mom?"

She cleared her throat. "Loveland, south of Fort Collins."

"Do you see her much? I mean, before you moved?"

"No."

"Why?"

It was too late to turn back. She'd allowed this conversation, and bottling it up again felt impossible.

"She left us." Suzanna could feel her face harden. "When I was eighteen she filed for divorce. She'd had an affair with her horse trainer for several years before she finally told my father she was leaving him. Said she'd done her duty, their kids were raised, and it was time she lived the life she wanted."

Paul slid an arm around her shoulders, pulling her close against his side. "I'm sorry, Suzanna."

She sniffed, but the tears could not be held. "It wasn't like we were an awesome family. It shouldn't have surprised me or hurt so much. I'd seen some things that weren't right, and our home life was rocky most of the time. But... but she just left. No remorse, no apologies. Actually, she felt completely justified, relieved that she could finally do what she'd wanted to do for years."

Memories pressed hard and replayed against her will.

"Stop acting like this is a tragedy, Suzanna." Mother's voice pierced as though the words were fresh. "I've sacrificed my happiness long enough. I raised you girls. You're grown now, and it's my time to be free. You need to grow up about this. God wants me to be happy."

"Were you close, you and your mom?"

Shutting off the memory, Suzanna snorted. "Never."

"How did your dad handle it?"

"He quit preaching." Suzanna stared past Paul into the horizon.

She hadn't expected her dad to stick around, couldn't blame him for leaving, but his retreat left her orphaned. A fresh rush of tears spilled from her eyes. "He said he couldn't expect to lead a congregation when he couldn't manage his own home, so he resigned and moved out here."

Paul stepped back enough to make eye contact. His blue eyes beckoned her to trust him, to spill everything. The agony of her family ripping apart and all of the things that followed.

And Jason.

Could she tell Paul about Jason?

"Did you ever talk about it?"

"No." She dropped her gaze. "Daddy just took it, swallowed it, and kept it buried deep."

He rubbed her shoulder with his thumb. "Kind of like his daughter?"

Suzanna had nothing for that. She stepped away and rubbed her eyes, forcing the rest of her tears back where they belonged.

Paul let her go and pushed his hand into his pocket. "Can I tell you something?"

She shrugged, waiting for the clichéd "God knows best" speech. She shouldn't have told him. The hurt was easier to manage when she didn't have to listen to how God planned all of this, and everything would turn out all right in the end. It wouldn't. There was absolutely no way it could. She hated her mother. For all the years of trying—and failing—to meet with her approval. For her unfaithfulness. And for blaming her unhappiness on her, *her daughter*, for heaven's sake.

And though she rarely admitted it, because it was a horrible truth, she resented her dad for leaving. He didn't even try to fight, if not for his marriage, then for his family. He didn't try, and the ugly truth was, he'd let them go long before any divorce papers had been signed.

Daddy knew about the affair. There just wasn't any way he couldn't have known. Mother wasn't that sneaky, and using her daughters' lessons as a cover to see her lover was a flimsy veil. The most expensive stables along the Front Range suddenly waved their boarding fees? And the owner, and prestigious trainer, Mr. William Pembroke, is suddenly willing to give not only Mother but both of her girls free lessons?

Doesn't happen. Not without some strings somewhere. Daddy knew, or he should have known, and he did nothing. For years, he did absolutely nothing.

It was a hard reality to chew on. Suzanna adored her father. He was her refuge from her volatile mother. He was her inspiration; they shared a common passion, a common dream.

And he became her greatest disappointment.

"Your father wasn't an angry man." Paul stepped beside her, his voice drawing her back to the present. "The man I knew was friendly and content. He was at peace."

Was that supposed to help? Suzanna crossed her arms, the muscles in her back growing rigid. But Paul was right. She'd seen it herself, and it made her angry. How could he not be mad? And worse, whenever they talked, Daddy spoke of being made new. He said God could make her new.

Was that the grand design? God would allow the disasters that shredded her world so her father could be made new? So that made her what? Collateral damage?

Awesome. She felt so much better.

Paul sighed, pushing his hands deeper into the denim. True to form, he was always saying the wrong thing.

Shouldn't it be a comfort to know your father didn't die in anger? That his life, his heart had been reconciled to God?

He had nothing further to say. All he had were those worn-out adages, but no matter how true they were, speaking them to Suzanna wouldn't help. She was set in her misery.

Paul's heart clenched. What an awful way to live. It'd be like waking up every morning with terrible pain throbbing through your body. *Depression hurts.* The med commercial wasn't lying, but surely there must be some way to break free, to heal.

Words reverberated in his head, his mother's tearful voice giving life to the memory.

RECLAIMED

He heals the brokenhearted and binds up their wounds. He determines the number of the stars and calls them each by name. Great is our Lord and mighty in power; his understanding has no limit.

Mother had whispered the Psalm even while sobs tore at her efforts after Dad suffered his first stroke. They'd gathered in the emergency room, shaken by his fall and not knowing if he were yet alive. Not waiting for Pastor Ron, as others might, Mother grasped the hands of her grown children and led them to their knees. She'd always been one to pray Scripture, and her memory did not fail in the moment of crisis.

Suzanna shuffled her feet and then started around him. Without forethought, Paul stretched his arm, catching her by the shoulders. She pushed against him for only a moment before her body sagged.

Fight or flight. Until there is trust. Anxiety released his heart as relief expanded in his chest. She seemed content to remain, though her stoic expression kept him from pulling her close.

Paul tipped his head to speak softly near her shoulder. "He heals the brokenhearted and binds up their wounds… His understanding has no limit."

Her body tensed again. Suzanna stared straight ahead.

Oh, how deep was that wound? Deep enough she wouldn't allow herself to feel it anymore. Deep enough to let anger cover the top.

Paul dropped his hold, and Suzanna marched up the hill. He followed her with only his eyes, and when she reached the crest, he turned to make his way back down to the bank.

Is anyone of you in trouble? Pray.

Paul didn't know what else to do.

CHAPTER NINETEEN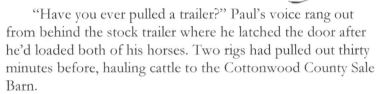

"Have you ever pulled a trailer?" Paul's voice rang out from behind the stock trailer where he latched the door after he'd loaded both of his horses. Two rigs had pulled out thirty minutes before, hauling cattle to the Cottonwood County Sale Barn.

Suzanna had tried to make herself useful while Paul had finished up the job. She followed Andrea into the house, collecting trash bags and wiping counters. Andrea had gone into the lone bedroom and stripped the sheets, but helping with such a chore felt too intimate for a friend. A handsome male friend.

What kind of friend was he? Paul poked into the deepest parts of her heart, stirring emotions Suzanna found she couldn't control. He made her angry by doing it, and yet she feared he'd retreat even as she pushed him away. She'd resigned herself to loneliness. Why, then, did she yearn for his presence, his concern?

"Pickle?" Paul popped a fist against the truck, grinning when she snapped to attention. "Yeah, you. Have you ever pulled a trailer?"

She snorted a laugh and shook her head. How could he go from the way-too-deep conversation they'd shared an hour ago to this playful rogue without really changing at all?

RECLAIMED

Paul leaned against Andrea's vehicle. "Today's a good day to try, don't you think?"

"To drive that?" She pointed to his Ford parked parallel to Andrea's.

Paul nodded, still smiling.

"Bad idea."

He pushed off the truck. "Why?"

"I can't even back a passenger car without hitting something."

He chuckled.

"Not kidding. Check my record... or the little Honda I have parked in the garage. Trust me, you don't want me behind the wheel."

"I have insurance." He snagged her elbow and pulled her alongside his easy stride. "Just don't kill my horses. I kind of like them."

He opened the driver's side and stepped out of the way. Suzanna looked at the steering wheel and then at Paul, her bottom lip going under her teeth. He tilted his head, nodded a silent "hop in," and charmed her with a smile. Suzanna searched the drive for Andrea, who had just finished herding her children into her own truck.

"Paul's a good teacher, Suz." Andrea rounded the nose of her vehicle. "You'll be fine."

Was this a conspiracy? Andrea hopped into her seat and brought the engine to life. There wasn't an out.

Suzanna set a boot on the running board and pulled herself up. "You might regret this."

Paul chuckled. "I doubt it."

The words were low, almost under his breath, but Suzanna caught them. Warmth bloomed in her chest and spread throughout her core before she could extinguish it with the reality of who she was... and was not.

Paul hopped into the cab and pulled the passenger door shut in one motion. "Okay. So first, turn the key; that starts the engine."

Suzanna caught his ornery grin out of the corner of her eye. "Who's the pickle?"

His shoulders shook with laughter.

"I could be done." She started the truck and squared her gaze on him, hiking her eyebrows.

He cleared his throat and sat a little straighter. Wiping the mischief from his face, he snapped his seatbelt in place. "Okay, I'm serious now. So, just pull out behind Dre, and we'll take it as it comes."

"Take what?"

"The lessons." He pointed to the right-hand turn out of the drive. "Starting with that. You're pulling a fifth-wheel hitch, so you've got to take the turns a little wide. The wheels of the trailer will cut a narrower path than the pickup's, so take that into account. You don't want to dump the horses in the ditch."

Suzanna stared at him, the engine rumbling. "Paul, seriously, I'll be okay if we skip this."

"Are you going to run cattle on that pretty little acreage of yours?"

She shrugged. "A couple, maybe. I was thinking about it, but—"

"Then you need to know how to do this. It's not a big deal, Suz. Just takes practice."

Paul kept his stare on her. Were his eyes always so blue, always so intense? She dropped her attention but not before her heart gave a little kick.

Not good. So not good. She needed Paul as a neighbor and a friend. She'd promised herself she would smother this attraction and keep it platonic. But every time he zeroed an open gaze on her, things tickled inside. Things she'd determined to keep dull and hidden.

She was determined still. Love had left her. Seemed like another lifetime ago, and she'd been a different girl. She couldn't be that girl again. Love had let her bleed to death.

Just remember that, Suzanna. Remember how searing it is to say good-bye. Remember the emptiness of sleeping next to a empty spot where your husband was supposed to lie. Remember... pain always follows. Always.

"Anytime you're ready." Paul reached across the cab and shifted the truck into *drive*. His mouth smiled, but his eyes were still warm and deep.

Was he trying to keep it light?

Imagination gone stupid. He didn't have to *try* to keep it light. She'd gone into the abyss of introspection on her own. Paul was the kind of man who made everyone feel special. Suzanna had no business making assumptions that would lead to expectations.

What was that saying? "Expectation is the root of all heartache." So true. Leave it lay, if you don't care, it won't hurt.

"Suz, the way this works is the tires have to start rolling, and then the whole rig moves."

What? Suzanna regained sensibility, discovering her hands white-knuckling the steering wheel. Andrea's vehicle was nowhere in sight, and amusement animated Paul's mouth. How long had she checked out?

Enough. She pressed the accelerator, and the engine revved. Tires spun against gravel, and she and Paul both jerked forward.

"Easy, cowgirl." Paul grabbed the handhold above the door. "This kind of setup doesn't peel out."

Sheesh. This was such a mistake. Suzanna glanced at Paul as the rig finally started moving.

The laughter left his expression. "Do you want to talk?"

Another switch. *How does he do that?* "About what?"

"Whatever. You have thought lines."

Suzanna wrinkled her forehead. "I have what?"

"Thought lines. Creases in your forehead. You get them when you're thoughtful."

"Is this a universal phenomenon?"

"I don't know. I just know you."

There it was again. A warm breath of life trying to arouse something she'd prefer stay dead.

"No you don't, and I don't have anything to talk about." She eased the truck into a wide turn onto the road.

She could feel his eyes beckoning, but she kept her focus on the dirt road.

Remember how much it hurts… and don't let it happen again.

Paul leaned against the backrest, exhausted, and yet his brain still worked. Too much. His head ached the way it did when he put pencil to paper to run figures. Math really wasn't his strength.

Neither were women.

He closed his eyes as the end of the afternoon replayed.

"You know what I think?" Dre had helped him load the horses after they'd sent the kids with Suzanna to pack up.

Paul shrugged. It'd been a good day. He'd been excited when Dre had suggested they come down for the last day of loading. It had worked out well.

"I think you done got bit." She hung her arm over the fence and stared straight at him.

Huh? Paul looked his arms over, which were safely covered in flannel. His hand brushed over his neck, checking for welts.

Dre's laugh settled in the small valley. Her merry eyes danced with delight as she shook her head. Her booted foot slid off the rail, and she pulled away from the fencing.

Paul stared at her back as she moved toward the rise. She didn't mean…?

"Hey, Dre." He called, and she turned back.

Her hands rested on her hips, her smile wide as the high plains.

Paul sailed over the fence and set his stride toward her. "What are you saying?"

He knew good and well, even though Dre hadn't answered him with anything more than a twitch of her amused brow.

And she was right.

The realization should have sent spirals of pleasure through him, not fissures of concern. Yet, pondering the truth while sitting next to the woman who had captivated his attention left him anxious.

Not the nervousness of a boy hoping the girl would say yes. He couldn't even ask at this point. Something was not right with Suzanna. She struggled with something serious and troubling. He needed to know what it was, but she refused to open up again.

The hum of the tires against asphalt had long since settled in the cab. In the hour they'd traveled together, she'd said only five words—all in response to his instructions—*okay, turn here?* and *this one?* He could have tried harder, but a guy can get shot down only so many times in one day.

And that day was about done.

"Suz, do you mind if we stop at the sale barn? I need to take care of some last-minute stuff with Rodney."

"Sure." She bobbed her head. "It's the first building when you come into town, right?"

"Right."

Now they had a conversation. Super. What if he offered to buy her dinner? Paul examined her as she leaned over the steering wheel. Even focused on the road, she looked like a lost puppy begging to be cared for. Yet, every time she was offered a compassionate hand, she snarled and bared her teeth.

He *would* fall for a wounded pitbull. Thirty-seven years on his own, and his heart went for this one. Why couldn't he ever, in his life, pick an easy path? Clear cut, no bumps, smooth sailing the whole way. Nope. Not this headstrong cowboy. Nothing about a relationship of any variety with Suzanna Wilton would be easy. To start off with, how did he begin? Suzanna kept herself locked away in a fortress, guarded by anger and fed on pain. How did a guy scale that?

Susanna sat up and glanced at him.

Caught. Staring right at her.

She scowled. "What?"

Paul pressed his lips together. What if he told her what he was thinking?

She'd freak out, clam up, and probably walk home. Or make him hitch a ride. Yeah. That was probably closer to the truth. The woman had a temper.

Hmm… was that an attractive quality? Paul pushed a hand over his hair and rubbed his forehead. No more thinking today.

"Paul, are you okay?"

Concern crinkled the skin around her eyes, drawing attention to the blue pools. Oh boy. That about summed her up. One minute she was snappy and about as inviting as a porcupine, and then, after two breaths she could puddle his heart with a tender look and a kind word.

Complicated. That was what she was. Layers of confusing, intriguing, angering, mesmerizing complexity. Which was why, of course, he liked her. Easy reads were boring. And usually fake.

"I'm fine. Just a little headache." He met those cool sapphires, and his breath caught when she held the connection. His fingers twitched, longing to brush her skin. A fear of hitchhiking, however, kept him sensible. "Thanks for asking, Pickle."

The day had given way to a cold night by the time they pulled into Suzanna's drive. She'd slid into the passenger's seat while Paul talked to Rodney, her shoulders achy from tension. Driving Paul's truck with his horses in tow had been nerve wracking. She didn't want to take on the fifteen miles of dirt road.

She'd had a hard time keeping her eyes open after Paul turned off the pavement. He must be tired too. He looked it. His eyes had lost their mischievous glint, and though his mouth still curved upward, his smile looked thin.

Well, he'd earned his exhaustion. She had no idea what the rest of his week had looked like, but if he worked as hard every day as they had today, he was overdue for a nap.

Suzanna rubbed the muscle in her thigh and was rewarded with dull pain. Both legs ached. And her arms and her back. Oh, and let's not even think about her backside. She wasn't sure she could walk from her drive into the house. She glanced back at Paul as he threw the truck into *park*. Her imagination ran through a quick scenario of her asking for a piggyback ride, and Paul hauling her into the house in his arms instead.

Heat rushed into her face. She'd keep her tender backside to herself. Sheesh. What was wrong with her?

Paul left the truck, still as agile as an eighteen-year-old. Suzanna pushed her door open but didn't make it to the dirt before he was at her side. She couldn't help but lean into the hand that cupped her elbow, and a groan escaped before she could cap it.

"Sore?" He shifted so one hand slid around her waist.

Suzanna cast her eyes upward, certain her face was flaming. "Don't ask."

His laugh moved through his chest, which brushed against her shoulder. "We all are, Pickle. It was a day."

He guided her forward, and she was more thankful with each muscle-screaming step that he held her upright.

"You're still walking like a biped," she said.

Paul laughed again. "I ride just about every day. Certain anatomy is a little more accustomed to use, but if it makes you feel any better, my calves are burning something awful. Trudging through the mud is hard work."

He released her so she could unlock her side door, and Suzanna suddenly wished the trek were a little longer. She pushed open the steel door and reached inside the entry to flip on the outdoor light. A yellow glow flooded her yard. She blinked, trying to understand what had just been illuminated.

Trash. Everywhere. Garbage littered the grass, the sidewalk to the front door and the small flower bed she'd kept weeded. Soreness aside, she jolted straight.

"What on earth …?" Paul said.

It took about three seconds to do the math.

"Chuck," she hissed.

Suzanna walked into the yard, tight muscles hobbling her gait. The garbage was hers. She recognized the yogurt cups and dinner-for-one microwave meals.

Paul followed, alarm painting his voice. "Maybe coons, Suz."

"No." She marched, as well as her tender legs would let her, to the trash bin on the other side of the house. "I keep it locked. Daddy told me once about coons getting into the trash, so I always make sure I've got it closed up."

Coming to the cage her dad had set up for the garbage, Suzanna picked up the chain that should have held the door secure. The carabiner hung at the end of it without any sign of damage. The slide lock had been opened. The whole process required more intelligence and dexterity than even a raccoon was known to have.

Chuck did this. Just like he'd sent a rock through her window. He did it, and she'd had enough.

Suzanna spun on her heel and set off for the front yard again, scooping trash up along the way. She snagged a half-torn Hefty bag and began stuffing it with the unsavory mess. Without a word, Paul followed suit, finding his own ripped bag.

When she'd packed as much as her sack could hold, she marched toward the garage, stomping across the drive.

"Whoa, whoa, whoa." Paul dropped the trash and jogged to catch up. "What are you doing?"

"Going to return the favor." She kept her pace, tossing her reply over her shoulder.

Paul caught her from behind with one arm wrapped around her waist. "No, you're not."

She pushed his hand, but his fingers gripped the fabric of her jacket.

"Let me go."

"Suzanna, don't do this." His mouth dropped close to her ear. "We'll clean it up, and I'll talk to Jude. Don't seek your own revenge."

"Jude?" She spun to face him, anger setting her voice hot. "Jude Gilroy did absolutely nothing about my window. Nothing! I'm not so completely ignorant that I can't figure why. And do you know what they're saying about me in town?"

Paul caught her shoulders with both hands. "I know, Suzanna, I know, but you can't retaliate. It won't end there, and this will continue to get worse."

"It *is* worse." She forced the burning tears to stay out of sight. Why was Paul so calm?

Because it didn't affect him. He'd go home tonight and crash in his safe little house, secure knowing the people in town liked him just fine, and nobody was trying to run him off his land. He didn't understand.

"I'm through with the small town politics." She jerked her shoulder free from his palm. "I'm not going to be liked here. For whatever reason, the people of Rock Creek have decided I'm unacceptable. Why should I play nice with people who are so mean?"

Paul pulled her back. "Not everyone in Rock Creek, Suz. Just Chuck, mostly. His lies will surface sooner or later, and if you've behaved well in spite of his harassment, you'll come out clean. Just give it a little more time."

Those blue eyes, full of earnest concern, took her captive and removed the heat from her boiling rage. Suzanna swallowed, dropping her gaze to stare at his chest. Daddy would preach forgiveness. Mother would fly into a nasty fit. Who did she want to resemble most?

Paul shifted and took the trash bag from her hands. "I'll talk with Jude face-to-face. Let me take care of it, okay?"

Her fingers uncurled from the plastic. Having Paul talk with Gilroy again wasn't going to fix anything, but disappointing him, going against his judgment, felt foolish. No, it felt impossible. She could endure Chuck's antics. Live through the townsfolk's cold treatment. But to fall short in Paul's opinion? Wasn't going to happen. Not if she could help it.

CHAPTER TWENTY

"That's it?" Paul's pulse pounded in his forehead. "Jude, you're not trying. You and I both know who did this. He's not even denying it." He turned to Chuck, his fists balling at his sides.

Chuck dropped his boots off his desk, his smirk tempting Paul to violence.

"You're getting a little too wound up about this, Rustin." Chuck sauntered next to Gilroy and placed a large hand on the sheriff's neck. "Just harmless pranks, boy. That's all. Didn't need to drag Jude's uniform in here to make a big fuss. No harm done. Right, Gilroy?"

Jude ducked his eyes for a half a second. Cornered. The man was stuck. How had Chuck managed to position every man of influence directly in his back pocket?

"It's not worth the paperwork, Paul. They were just pranks, and nobody got hurt"—he glanced up at Chuck—"and it ends here, right?"

"Just pranks?" Paul stepped forward and focused his scowl on Jude. "She had to replace a window, and she's scared. That's all harmless?"

Chuck moved as though he were guarding Jude, protecting his investment. "I recall the three of us pulling all sorts of shenanigans back in the day. Nothing ever came of it. Let it roll, boy. You've let that woman get you wound up too tight."

"Nothing ever came of it for *you*, Chuck. I spent the night in jail the time we shattered the windows at the old factory."

Chuck shrugged. "Your old man could have bailed you out, same as ours."

"Might have done you some good if your daddy hadn't been so worried about his political image." Paul crossed his arms. "Actions have consequences, Chuck. You'd think that after a couple of decades you'd have that figured out."

Gilroy's cell phone beeped. "Listen, boys, I've got a day ahead of me. I don't want to hear anymore about this." His eyes darted from one man to the other.

Chuck raised an eyebrow as though he'd just been challenged. Oh good grief. He was like a little boy on the playground telling everyone that the swing was his. Gilroy took the call and scurried out of Chuck's office, a pathetic look of relief smoothing his expression.

Maybe he should have let Suzanna trash Stanton's yard. Civility was going nowhere.

"Seems to me you're really not understanding this whole situation, Rustin."

Paul turned his attention back to Chuck, his hands dropping to his hips.

"Line's been drawn, and you're standing on the wrong side." Chuck narrowed the space. "I'd think real careful about where I leave my boot prints."

"As I recall, we already had this conversation, Chuck. Your spineless antics haven't changed my mind."

Chuck grunted. "Just wanted to make sure you remembered that talk"——he squinted and folded his arms over his chest——"because I haven't forgotten it. Let me make this real clear. I can make life pretty dang miserable when people stand in my way. And little Miss Priss is in dead center of that path. I won't have it."

"What is your deal with that? It's a piece of dirt, Chuck. A little bit of ground that never belonged to you, to any of your family or even to a close friend. Why are you so crazy over this?"

"That woman doesn't belong here. I'm sick of Colorado money coming in and claiming things they have no right to claim. They turbocharge inflation and fling their money around like they're better than everyone else. She's an outsider, and she'll always be an outsider. It's just that dadgum simple."

Paul shook his head. "That's not it at all."

Chuck cocked an eyebrow. "No?"

"Nope. You don't think that deep. She told you no, and you can't stand it."

A flash of heat sparked in Chuck's eyes. Bull's-eye.

"You're just a ten-year-old bully, Stanton. You may have the ears of everyone in this town, but it won't be long until everyone sees you for who you really are."

Paul pivoted on one boot and set off toward the exit. Chuck's voice, low and cold, stopped him at the door.

"One way or another, I'll get that woman out of Rock Creek, Rustin."

Paul glanced over his shoulder. "You'll have to go through me first."

Chuck nodded, his smirk resurfacing. "You've been warned."

Paul hadn't skipped Bible class since... well, he wasn't sure since when. But Suzanna didn't typically go, and he wanted to be sure she didn't walk through those church doors alone. He read through Matthew chapter twelve over coffee until it was time to leave for the service.

He slowed his pickup before he reached the creek, pulling off the shoulder at the tree line. He could see Suzanna's garage from that position, but unless she was really looking, she wouldn't be able to see him. Pulling at his collar, he tried to smother unease. He felt like a sneak… or some creepy old man, spying on his beautiful neighbor. Following her. But shielding her took priority over dignity.

By now, loose lips were flapping like a slack tarp in the wind. He couldn't let her walk into the shunning alone.

Paul gripped the steering wheel, and his shoulders tightened. Dad-gum-it, Chuck. Not only was his heart rotten, his timing was cruel. It'd been years since Paul had met a woman he was interested in. Interested? Well, that was an understatement. He was pretty sure he was done gone. Suzanna had tossed a lasso around his heart, and Paul had no desire to struggle free. Now this. How could he pursue something deeper with her and not make Chuck's manufactured tale look like truth?

What could he possibly do?

Dressed in dark blue jeans and a flowing teal top, Suzanna breezed from her doorway. She turned, locked the steel door, and scanned her yard. Checking for trouble. Paul never had to lock his door—worry-free departure was part of the charm of rural living. He blew out a breath. Suzanna probably had less trouble living in the city.

Apparently satisfied, she strode to the old yellow Jeep. Her hair bounced against her shoulders, strands of golden-brown catching in the light fall breeze. She'd curled it this morning. He'd never seen it fixed that way. Did she have a reason to look special?

Paul drifted back to yesterday afternoon. The morning hadn't started well, with Jude being so pathetically apathetic about Suzanna's predicament, but the sale had gone well. He had stopped by Suzanna's afterward and asked her to go for a ride.

She looked tired, but her smile brightened her eyes, and she agreed. They rode in her west pasture until her stomach growled, and then she invited him to stay for supper. Chicken-salad sandwiches. Paul wasn't much for chicken, and the croissants made it seem like girly food, but it sure tasted good sitting across from a pair of pretty blue eyes.

Dare he hope she'd curled her hair for him?

Schoolboy. Paul laughed at himself but sobered with the next breath. It didn't matter whether she did or not. She'd probably keep him a good lariat's length away after today.

Suzanna backed out of her drive and set off for town. Paul waited to put his pickup in drive until after she took the first turn. *God give me wisdom. Today could be awful.*

Suzanna parked on the road beside the gravel lot belonging to the church. She had to steel herself, just like all the other Sundays. Her stomach rolled as she flipped the sun visor down. She met her reflection in the tiny mirror with a scowl.

"Fake." She muttered. "He'll see through you one of these days. What happened to indifference?"

She wrapped a barrel-rolled strand of hair in between her fingers and let it slide through her grasp. She hadn't curled her hair since... when? Long before Jason's transplant. Time became irrelevant after that.

Jason had loved her hair. Curly, straight, up, down. Whatever. He'd played with it every chance he could. The first time he'd touched her, he slid a tress between his fingers. They'd been kids, but even then, as teenagers, they really only had each other. How could a loving God take him?

She balled her fists. He wasn't a loving God. It didn't matter what Daddy had said.

A truck pulled up behind her and parked, drawing her glare away from the white church building. Glancing in her rearview mirror, she was surprised to see Paul sliding from the vehicle. She fixed a pretty mask and snagged the Bible Daddy had given her on her twenty-first birthday.

"Hey, neighbor." He sauntered toward her.

Her heart did a clippety-clop when he stopped near enough for her to smell his mild cologne. What was he wearing? It was light and crisp and smelled happy. Appropriate. "Kind of late, aren't you?"

Paul shrugged and tapped her elbow with his index finger, a hint of an escort to the church building. "I was slow getting after it this morning."

He kept a leisurely pace, his boots scuffing against the rocks. Suzanna hadn't seen him drag his feet before. Almost as if he were dreading something.

Church? Not likely. Paul, like his sister, loved church. His face illuminated with peace and joy—which was true for all the other days of the week too—but especially on Sundays. Suzanna often caught herself gaping when he'd raise his hands during a song or when she'd sneak a glance at his earnest face while he pored over some passage in the Bible. What exactly moved him so that he would become so enviably undignified? What stirred him to read an old book with such devoted hunger?

Daddy didn't worship that way. And she'd never seen him study like that. His face, while kind, always looked stern, almost grim, when he studied the Bible. Did Paul know something her father didn't? Or maybe it was the other way around.

But today, this first Sunday in November, Paul looked tired. Unenthusiastic. Yes, reluctant even.

Her hand fluttered to his arm. "Are you feeling okay?"

Contact. The muscle under the cotton sleeve tensed beneath her fingertips. A current of energy raced through her hand and down her arm.

Paul stopped, and his eyes settled on her. He covered her hand and attempted a smile. Where was his zest?

"I'm okay, Pickle." His voice was low, tentative.

He most definitely was not okay. She'd seen dread in a man's eyes before.

"What is it, Jase?" *They'd been waiting for the doctor to release him for far too long. His arm had been set and wrapped in a cast for hours. Why were they running all these tests? What had the doctor told him when she'd gone to get something to eat?*

Paul had that look. Her breath caught as panic clamped down on her lungs.

"Let's go." Paul dropped his hand and nodded toward the door.

She bit her lip and pulled her eyebrows in.

Paul sighed. "Suzie..." He stared at the building.

Suzie... She liked the way her dad's name for her came off his lips. Almost as much as she liked when he called her Pickle.

"We're friends. No matter what Chuck does or says, you and I are friends." Paul turned his eyes back to hers. "I just wanted you to know."

That was strange. And cryptic. She pushed a curl behind one ear. "Okay... is there something I should know?"

Lines creased his forehead. Thought lines. He put a hand to her elbow and set his feet in motion. "We're going to be late."

Suzanna had a strong suspicion he didn't want to go at all.

He should have warned Dre and Tom—Suzanna, too, for that matter. It would have been better, but Paul hadn't been able to form the words. Walking in together, his hand wrapped protectively—possessively—around her arm hadn't been the most helpful move, either.

"Need to talk to you." Tom leaned in as they shook hands. "Now."

Paul nodded and then glanced at Dre. She caught his eyes and answered his silent plea. She'd stay with Suzanna.

When they were safely alone in a classroom, Tom cut to the chase. "There's a rumor ablaze."

"I know." Paul rubbed his neck.

Tom studied him, his eyebrows low.

Paul dropped his hand and stood tall. "You know it's not true."

"Yes, I know. Dre and I both know. But—"

"But you were afraid maybe it was?"

Tom dropped his eyes. Heat put color in his sun-weathered cheeks. "Not really, but… well, maybe just a little." He pulled his face back up. "It's gotta be hard. You've been single for so long, and well, Dre and I can see you like her."

"I do"—Paul pulled at his collar and forced a deep breath—"but I've never even held her hand, kissed her, anything. She doesn't even know I want to. Now I can't. This will shred every little scrap of trust between us. Trust that I… that we… you, Dre, and I have had to work to win."

"Why doesn't she know?"

"How was I supposed to tell her?" Paul spread his hands wide. "Hey, you know that guy you can't stand who's been horrible to you and I wouldn't let you trash his lawn? Well, here's a heads-up. He's telling everyone we're sleeping together."

Tom chuckled.

"Clearly, I'm not a wordsmith," Paul said.

"Well, that maybe would have worked, but that's not what I meant. Why doesn't she know you're interested in her?"

"Um, have you met Suzanna Wilton?" Paul cocked an eyebrow. "She's complicated."

"Most women are." Tom clapped him on the shoulder. "I've been out of the game for a while now, but I'm pretty sure it still starts with a date. 'Suzanna, can I take you to dinner?' Or maybe you should call her Pickle. She seems to like that."

She did? So far off the subject. "Well, thanks for that, but now I can't, so it's not helpful."

"Why?"

"Hello? Why did you bring me in here to chat?"

"You're really going to let Chuck control your life?"

"It'll look bad—worse than what it looks like already." Paul rubbed his head. He could only imagine what kind of story Chuck had fed to Shelby. *Hear that your pickup has been spotted in Suzanna's drive pretty early in the morning.*

How did he know that? The only people who would drive out that way at that time of day were Tom and Dre. Clearly, they weren't raising suspicion.

"The way I see it"—Tom interrupted Paul's thoughts—"it can't get any worse. In the end, people always believe what they want to believe. Might be helpful to Suzanna to know you care. Maybe she wouldn't feel so alone in the world."

"I'm going home." Suzanna wouldn't allow her lip to quiver. She cleared her throat, demanding her voice behave.

Andrea reached for her hand and squeezed. "Please, Suz. At least come out for dessert."

Shelby Stanton burst from the church arm in arm with a woman Suzanna recognized from the bank. She caught their contemptuous looks as they crossed to their cars. Forcing her eyes away, she took in the earnest face of her friend. They'd been so kind. All of Paul's family. And she hadn't deserved it.

Especially Paul. She'd been absolutely horrid to him. Now his reputation was charred. Blackened by a friendship he'd never been obligated to extend in the first place.

Disobedient tears burned her eyes and slithered down the side of her nose. "I can't, Dre." She wiped at the stream. "I can't do this to your family."

Andrea pulled her into an embrace. "You didn't do this. We know Paul. You haven't done anything wrong."

But you don't know me. God, why do you dangle love in my face only to rip it away? Why do you hate me?

Suzanna clenched her jaw and pulled away. "I'm really not up for anything today. Thank you, Andrea. I'm going home."

CHAPTER TWENTY-ONE

Paul's intent to stay by Suzanna's side throughout the whole miserable morning was sabotaged. Pastor Ron wanted a word with him. Man, a juicy piece of slander traveled faster than a spooked horse. Before Paul could trail Suzanna out of the sanctuary, Pastor had a hand on his cuff.

"There's a story spreading around like a prairie fire." Pastor spoke with questions in his eyes.

"I know." Paul shifted his Bible, anger nipping his words.

"I assume there isn't any truth to it, but I wanted to ask straight out."

"None. We're not even dating."

Pastor nodded, but his gaze still puckered. "Something is going on though."

Paul's spine snapped straight. "What does that mean?"

"You've been at the top of the most-admired-bachelor list for a long time, Paul." He dropped into his cushioned desk chair and leaned back to gaze up at Paul. "I mean no offense and understand why you're upset, but something had to have provoked this tale."

Paul shoved a hand into his pocket. "Someone's mad at me, plain and simple."

"Want to talk about it?"

"No, I don't think that'll help. Makes me no better than him."

Pastor cocked an eyebrow.

"Look, I'm sure you've heard other stuff about Suzanna—about how she planned to dam up the spring at her property line?"

He nodded, his look growing more concerned.

Paul eased into the chair across from Pastor's desk. "Well, that one isn't true, either. Anyway, I stood by Suzanna when this guy tried to intimidate her, and he's mad about it. It's all very junior high."

Pastor scowled. "What does this person have against Miss Wilton?"

Paul's jaw went tight. "Greed. Green and ugly and as old as sin itself. He offered to buy her land, and she said no."

"Surely there's more?"

"Don't know." Paul rubbed his eyebrows as a dull ache expanded in his head. "I thought so for a while, but now... well, I think it's just plain old selfishness. Wants that green piece of pasture and can't stand that she said no. He doesn't hear that very often."

Pastor Ron folded his hands and laid them on his desk. His eyes drifted to the side window of his office, and his expression remained thoughtful.

"Don't know Suzanna Wilton beyond her face—I haven't had a chance to visit with her. Need to, but with my dad moving into a care facility, and the time spent driving to make sure it all goes okay—well, I just haven't done what I need to do around here."

Strange response. Sort of sounded like an excuse. Why would Pastor Ron need to offer an excuse?

Pastor's attention came back. "Seems a shy woman."

"Life has dealt her some tough blows. She comes across as cold. But—"

"She's not."

Paul nodded. "She's pretty much alone in the world. I think it makes her guarded, but she's actually kind, and under her armor, she has a good heart."

"Is she a believer?"

What was with the interview?

"I think so. Her dad, Mike Wilton, had been a pastor before he moved here."

Pastor Ron pulled on his chin. "Yes. I knew Mike. We visited often."

The office suddenly went still. Paul was missing something—something important. He shifted uncomfortably, trying to figure out how to ask about something he couldn't identify.

"You seem to have a bond with her, Paul."

Huh? Oh, back to Suzanna again. Where was Pastor's aim in all this?

Paul cleared his throat. "I'm her neighbor."

Pastor's head dipped slowly. "Yes."

Quiet resettled between them. This was getting more uncomfortable with every breath. Paul put his hands on his knees, ready to rise and retreat.

Pastor reached a hand across the desk. "Paul, I'm sorry. That must have come off as an accusation, which was not my intent. Actually, I was thinking you shouldn't let this rumor hinder something deeper, if there are feelings between you two. But... well, to say it plainly, be sure first. Like I said, I knew Mike, and he talked a bit about his daughter. You're right; life's taken her into the ring a few times. It wouldn't be fair for you to pursue her if you weren't sure about where you were going."

Twice in one day? He must read like a Dr. Seuss book.

Paul took to his feet and accepted Pastor's outstretched hand. "Thank you, sir."

"No need." Pastor squeezed. "And just so you know, I'm still endorsing your candidacy for elder. It'll come from the pulpit next week, and people will see where I stand in this messy little story." His head moved in a firm nod while he held a steady gaze.

Paul left the empty church, looking across the lot. His pickup sat alone. If only Suzanna had a community for support. For now, he and his family were it.

Suzanna yanked at her closet door as if she intended to rip the thing off its hinges.

Who knew such an average-looking tramp would be the undoing of Paul Rustin. All those years of overcoming his past, and a little city-girl reject comes along to soil his sheets.

One would think a beautiful woman like Shelby Stanton, all dressed up in her clean white skirt and navy top, wouldn't say such horrible things, especially not in church.

Why would people listen to such a story? Paul's hometown. People who knew him best and were supposed to love him most. How could they latch on to such a bald-faced lie without so much as a doubt sending up a caution flag?

But they did. Almost everyone, except his wonderful family. They ate the lie and let it sink into their guts. Let it sour their faces. Harden their stares.

Oh, Paul. If you'd known this was where all this would have landed you, would you have troubled yourself with a little pickle like me?

Tears fell, cooling her hot cheeks and blurring her vision. Didn't matter. She had a lot to do.

Suzanna wrapped her arms around the clothes hanging to her right. Lifting, she removed them, hangers and all. She should have gotten rid of most of them the first time she moved. She'd donate them this time. Surely she could afford some new outfits once a sale went through.

She hefted the load to her bed and dropped it, not caring about the shirt that had slipped off its hanger, or about the pair of jeans that lay strewn on the floor. Returning to the closet, she ducked under the horizontal pole and moved to the back. Boxes lined the floor, and she dropped to her knees.

She'd labeled them with a sharpie. *Daddy's. Jason's. Wedding. Funeral.*

Strange brandings for a girl all of twenty-seven.

Her fingers traced *Jason*, and a sob welled up from the depths of her stripped soul. She didn't want to look, but her hands moved as if compelled by something beyond herself. The box was opened, and her life sat revealed on the closet floor.

His uniform. Blue and yellow and smelling like musty cardboard.

No. It was supposed to smell like Speed Stick and Old Spice. Like Jason.

His cleats. Not even broken in. He'd bought a new pair before training camp. Only wore them twice. She hated that he'd thrown his older pair out.

A hospital bracelet. A plastic strip that became jewelry he rarely removed.

Their picture.

Suzanna sat back against her heels as she caressed the frame. She'd been eighteen, and they were happy. He wore his UNC hat, and his arm draped around her shoulders, his glove dangling near her elbow. He was the good in her life. Despite all the upheaval at home, all the animosity between her and her mother, and all the disappointment in her father she'd tried to push away, she'd still believed life could be good because of Jason.

Even at that, she hadn't known she'd be married within six months or widowed by the age of twenty-five.

Widowed. Such an ugly word. It sounded like an accusation or a label of scorn.

There's Suzanna Cumberland. Did you know she's a widow? Felt like she was to blame.

She returned Jason's treasures to their coffin, smiling portraits and all. The box was already packed. She didn't need to redo it. She had plenty of other sorting to do.

Paul scanned his sister's table. No Suzanna. Should have known. Her Jeep wasn't in the drive. It'd been featherheaded of him to hope she'd ride over with Dre.

"Wouldn't come." Dre stepped to his side and spoke in a low whisper. "She looked like she wanted to cry and scream and stomp her feet, but all she said was she was going home, and then she just left. You'd vanished, and I didn't know what to do."

He looked down at his little sister, her face contorted with worry. *Dang it, Chuck. Didn't you know how this would affect everyone?*

'Course he did. He went for the gut. That's how he got what he wanted every time. Wonder why it took so long to catch on. Chuck had been a selfish manipulator since the time he talked Paul into stealing old man Barkley's Farmall and parking it in front of the entry doors at the high school.

Harmless pranks. That's what he'd called all those stupid tricks. Except Paul had stripped the gears and the school had to call a tow truck to get the thing out of the way before classes could start. And old man Barkley was stuck with the bill. Paul was sure two days of sweat labor hadn't covered the damage. Chuck never did have to put up any kind of restitution.

"You okay, Paul?" Tom stepped in front of him, his eyes darting from Dre to Paul.

"Not really." Paul swallowed. "I need to talk to Suz. I should have warned her."

"Warned her?" Dre moved from Paul's side to Tom's. "How did you know?"

"Skip it." Paul ran a hand over his head. "I really need to talk to her. Go on ahead and eat."

He turned to leave, and Dre matched his stride. "Bring her back later, okay? We'll have homemade ice cream..." Her shoulders slumped.

Homemade ice cream fixed a lot of things, but this wasn't one of them.

Dre tugged on his elbow as if she were willing him to understand. "I need to know she's okay."

Paul squeezed her shoulders. "We'll see."

Three miles never felt so far. What if she'd taken off? Gone somewhere he didn't know anything about and just vanished from his life. Unacceptable.

He flipped his cell and sent the call. Six rings later, her voice tickled his ear.

"This is Suzanna. I'll call you back later."

Yeah, she would. He hung up and hit *Resend*. Same drill. He called her three times before her house came into view.

Paul parked and left the vehicle with a cloud of dust billowing around him. He set off toward the garage and opened the side door. Relief. Her Jeep sat next to her Honda. She was home.

He shut the door and moved to the house. Suzanna didn't answer his knock. He tried the front door. She didn't respond to the doorbell, either. He took a turn about the house. Nothing. Maybe she was in the basement.

Probably not.

Sleeping?

Didn't matter. He wasn't waiting.

Paul pushed on the side door, and it gave way.

"Suzanna?" He leaned against the frame as he called into the house.

Silence. Good grief, that woman was stubborn. He had a love-hate appreciation for that little quality of hers.

"Suzanna Wilton!" He stomped into her kitchen. "I know you're here."

Something rustled down the hall. Paul stopped and leaned against the counter.

"Come on, Suzie." Did his voice just crack? "Talk to me."

Hinges squeaked from the hallway, and her footfalls muffled against the wood floor. She appeared after five steps, her lovely, curled hair tousled around her shoulders, and her blue eyes red rimmed and bloodshot.

Looking at her hurt. It actually hurt. She'd been crying, and she was a total mess. Paul closed the space between them and pulled her close.

"I'm so sorry, Paul." She trembled, and her voice was ragged. "I'm so, so sorry."

His arms tightened. "You didn't do anything wrong."

It was Chuck. All Chuck.

Her warm tears seeped through his cotton shirt. Setting aside his indignation, he smoothed her hair. "It's going to be all right. Just let this ride, Pickle, and it'll be okay."

She pushed away, shaking her head. She raked a hand through her hair, setting the curls into a loose frenzy. Paul itched to run his fingers through the same path.

Not now. It could make everything worse.

He lifted his eyes and took in the house beyond the kitchen. *What the——?* Her computer was gone. Cords were left sitting on her desk, looking like mouseless tails in some kind of bizarre collection. Boxes were scattered across the wood floor, and her coat closet stood open like an empty tomb.

"What are you doing?" He waved to the mess.

She sighed. "Does your offer still stand?"

"What offer?" His heart skipped, and his skin grew cold.

"I know you'll give me a fair price, Paul."

She stepped away. He snagged her by the elbow and pulled her back. She looked up into his eyes, those sad blue puddles begging him to understand. This was hard, too hard. It was selfish to ask her to stay.

"You're tougher than that." Okay, so maybe Chuck wasn't the only selfish man in this county.

She lowered her gaze. "You're an honorable man, Paul. No one will question your integrity when I'm gone."

This was for him? His heart dissolved into warm goo. He slid his hand down her arm until he found hers and then squeezed. "I'm fine, Pickle. Honest. I knew this was coming, and I'm okay."

Her head snapped up. "You knew?"

Uh-oh. Yep, he should have warned her. He nodded, certain he looked like a kid caught in a lie.

She pulled her hand away. "Why didn't you say something?"

Good question. He'd hoped, unreasonably so, Chuck was bluffing. He'd hoped nobody would listen. He'd hoped it wouldn't touch her. He'd hoped for a whole lot of foolishness.

Paul shrugged.

The spark of anger in her eyes dwindled. It didn't matter now. She turned to face her packing disaster, once again moving out of his reach. "I can't stay here and ruin the life you've reclaimed."

Paul rubbed his neck. What would she do if he stepped behind her, wrapped her in his arms and begged her to stay? For him.

Probably not helpful at the moment.

"Let me ask you something." Paul forced his hands to stay at his side. "Why didn't you sell before?"

Suzanna spun on her socked foot, facing him with a bewildered expression. "I didn't want to."

"Why? You had several offers—some pretty good ones from what I hear. Why were you so set on staying?"

She held his gaze for a breath, and then her attention drifted to the window. The fields were brown, dormant as they waited for winter's blanket of white. The big cottonwood in her front yard stood against the cool blue November sky, its branches a skeleton without leaves. Not much appeal this time of year. What would a city girl see in a place so remote and vacant?

"My daddy found peace here." Her voice cracked. She pulled in a shaky breath. A sob.

Paul watched the strength of a determined woman fracture under the weight of rejection. A weight he'd known well.

His throat felt thick; a whisper was all he could manage. "And you wanted it too?"

She nodded, her lips quivering. "I was mad at him. Mad that he could be happy again. But…"

But she ached to be happy again. Paul moved close enough to take hold of her shoulders. "I think God has you here for a reason, Suzanna Wilton. And I'm praying you'll find that the Great Physician specializes in peace."

She searched him, perplexity in her eyes. "What does that mean?"

"Means I'm not buying your land." His thumbs traced circles on her shoulders. "If you want to sell, it'll have to be to Chuck."

Life reentered her expression. "Not happening."

"Good." Paul dropped his hands against his will. "I kind of like having you for a neighbor. It's like having my own personal coffee shop."

A smile lifted her mouth, followed by a laugh. A laugh. Paul could have kissed her.

Not now. Small steps. He'd take a smile.

CHAPTER TWENTY-TWO

"What is that one?"

Suzanna moved to her kitchen table and leaned against Kelsey's shoulder, following the girl's finger to the printed picture in the nursery stock catalog.

Prunus fruticosa x Prunus cerasus

"It's a cherry bush. Carmine Jewel." Suzanna smiled down at her friend. "A fruit grower named Dr. Bors has been working on some new varieties of sour cherries. They're supposed to be quite cold-and-drought tolerant, and sweeter than most pie cherries."

"Are you going to grow some?"

"I was thinking about it. What do you think?"

Kelsey tapped her chin with her finger. "Yes." She tipped a definitive nod. "Grow lots of them."

Suzanna laughed. She'd been in town, trying to make herself as inconspicuous as possible when she'd run into Andrea. Kelsey had just finished with piano, but Kiera still had lessons. Suzanna offered to take Kelsey home with her, suggesting Andrea pick her up when they were done.

Suzanna couldn't express what it meant to have Andrea stop to talk to her in the middle of the store, out in the open where all of the town could see them. She couldn't put words to what it did to her heart to have Andrea trust her with Kelsey. To have her publicly uphold their friendship in spite of the chatter buzzing in the streets.

Paul had said it would blow over, but her ears had been burning for two weeks now. The storm done raged on.

Done raged. Suzanna grinned. She'd started talking, thinking like Andrea. She liked that.

In the middle of the storm, Paul's constancy anchored her. He stopped by his "personal coffee shop" almost daily. He'd been doing some more research on the cattle Daddy had been looking into, and they talked beef, pastures, fencing, and anything else related to the topic.

And lots of things unrelated.

"If I guess your favorite color, you owe me a donut from Big Bat's."

Suzanna had laughed at his out-of-the-blue audacity.

He grinned with confidence. "Green."

"How'd you know that?"

"You studied horticulture, right?"

Clever. She laughed again. "How much is a donut?"

He crossed his arms and shrugged. "Don't know—depends on what I'm hungry for."

She stood and opened a drawer near her refrigerator. "Here's five dollars. Certainly that will cover enough donuts to make you sick."

Paul's mouth sagged. Clearly, that wasn't what he had in mind. And honestly, she would have loved to go with him, even if it was only to the local gas-and-shop. But public appearances together were out of the question.

"I'll bet I can teach you to lasso," he quipped another morning. "You'll be swinging a lariat in less than an hour."

Suzanna shrugged while she tried to swallow a laugh. He'd become adorably random. Had he always been so quirky?

"Okay."

"Okay?" He leaned on his elbows. "That was a bet, darlin'. Whatcha got?"

"What do I have?"

"Quit with the college grammar. Toss me something. What do I get when I done show you how to rope?"

Suzanna raised an eyebrow. "My admiration?"

Something light and deep flashed in his eyes, like maybe that was what he was going for. He shook his head. "Nope. Tangible." He snapped his fingers. "Lucky Charms."

"I do *not* buy Lucky Charms."

"You bought me a donut two days ago."

"Did not." She shook her head. "You done bought that yourself."

Paul chuckled and scooted from the table. "Let's go. It's on. I teach you to rope, and then we're off to town for a box of Lucky Charms."

He caught her gaze before he turned for the door. Swallowing hard, she shook her head. Disappointment oozed from his pores as he silently held her gaze. His ploy surfaced.

"Don't live like this, Pickle." He stepped back to the table and leaned on the back of his chair. "Don't let him lock you away. You've got nothing to be ashamed of."

She couldn't. Just couldn't do it. Not to Paul Rustin. Talk would never die down if she were always traipsing around town at his side.

"We were roping, right?" She forced a smile, certain he knew how fake it was. "I'll go to town tomorrow for your yucky cereal."

Which was why she had been in town today. Buying Lucky Charms.

"Uncle Paul says you're looking into cattle." Kelsey thumbed through the pages of Suzanna's catalog. "Why aren't you going to grow these instead?"

Suzanna shrugged. Opportunity spread right outside her front door, and fear had slithered around her ambition.

Dreams are the food of envy and the sustenance of discontent. A strange comment coming from her mother. It never left Suzanna's memory though.

"Well," she said, her hand going to the ring beneath her tee shirt, "those cherries have been successful in Canada, which is quite a ways north. No one really knows how they'll do in this climate, with the summers being so hot and quite a bit longer."

"Would it hurt to try?"

Simplicity in logic. A child's gift.

"Mama always says she'd rather be wrong than to never know." Kelsey smiled. "I think she read that somewhere. Says they're words to live by."

Such a different perspective. Failure was the worst possible outcome in the Wilton home. Never mind their family was a total failure.

A cloud of dust billowed on the road, its tail visible from the window. Suzanna stood, painting a smile. "Must be your mama. Don't you tell her I spoiled your dinner with Lucky Charms."

Kelsey grinned, and laughter bubbled in Suzanna's chest. Ha! Paul thought he had her pinned, but she could play ornery. Step one: give away the fuel for his sugar addiction. Step two— okay, she hadn't gotten that far. Something would hit though. Just give her time.

"Hey, Pickle," Paul called from the doorway, "got my cereal?"

What was he doing here?

Kelsey's mouth spread with a sassy grin. "That was for me, Uncle Paul."

His boots smacked against the tile in Suzanna's entry, announcing his approach. "Were not." He stomped into the kitchen, his shirt peppered with dust and his hat rimmed with sweat. "You better not have given away my Lucky Charms, woman."

Kelsey giggled. "I done ate them all. They were gooood."

Paul feigned a glare, first at Kelsey and then at Suzanna, his mouth twitching with mirth. "That's it. I've a mind to paddle you both. Starting with you."

He stuck a finger in Kelsey's face, and she squealed as she spun away. Kels tore off toward the front door, and Paul took off after her, winking as he passed Suzanna.

Her stomach fluttered. Flirting? Was he actually flirting with her? Had he been flirting this whole time?

Suzanna watched him as he ducked through the front door. A grungy cowboy, built tough but loved tender. She could see it in how he treated his sister. How he treated his nieces and nephew. They adored him. Due in large part because he loved well.

Could he love her? Suddenly, it seemed possible. Except... except there were parts of her he didn't know. Secrets she couldn't bring herself to share.

Paul caught Kelsey before she cleared the front gate. He hauled her in both arms and dipped her upside down. She squealed like a toddler tossed into the air. Laughter erupted from his belly. Kelsey normally didn't squeal. She didn't roughhouse or cut loose like Kiera and Keegan. She wasn't that kind of kid.

But when she was with Suzanna... well, she was a kind of normal the rest of the family didn't see. Something special bonded them.

Warmth spread through his chest. Two little puppies, sweet and vulnerable. They needed each other. How good of God to set the match.

"Suzanna..." Kelsey called between giggles. "Suzanna, help!"

With one eye on the lookout for Kelsey's backup, Paul tickled her neck, and she began to squirm like a calf.

"No, Uncle Paul!" she gasped, pushing at his hands. "No tickling! Suzie, help!"

He glanced at the front door. No assailant. Where was she? "Looks like you're on your own, kiddo. The Pickle's afraid of me."

No sooner had the words left his mouth than a pair of arms flung around his shoulders from behind.

"Am not." Suzanna threw herself full force at his back.

Caught off guard, Paul rocked forward and then to the side. Balance gone, he tumbled to the ground, and Kelsey wriggled free. She popped to her feet and then flew against Paul, laughing so hard she cried.

Gravel stirred from the dirt road, and a honk from Dre's white pickup ended their tussle. Too bad, it was about to get interesting.

Suzanna pulled her leg free from where he'd landed on it and pushed him away. He glanced over his shoulder to catch her expression. She smiled, but she wouldn't meet his eyes as she moved farther from his reach, her retreat looking almost like humiliation.

Paul's heart suddenly felt smaller.

"What are you doing?" Dre slid from her pickup and popped her hands on her hips, but her smile betrayed amusement.

"Your daughter done stole my cereal." Paul hopped to his feet and messed up Kelsey's hair. He kept track of Suzanna out of the corner of his eye, hoping she'd regain the confidence to be a part of this family. To live in delight.

"Did not." Kelsey grinned back at him. "Wasn't yours. They were Suzanna's, and she gave them to me."

"Nope. They're mine." Paul crossed his arms and aimed a wink toward Suzanna. "Won them fair and square. Now you owe me, Kels."

Kelsey laughed and pushed him away.

Dre giggled, pulling Kelsey close under one arm. "What are you doing here, anyway, Paul?"

Paul bent to snag his hat that had come loose when they'd all gone down. "I stopped to get my Lucky Charms." He shoved it on his head and turned his eyes to Suzanna.

She lifted her gaze to meet his, soft pools of blue timidity. Shy? Was that why she'd retreated? Air jammed in his lungs. Paul imagined taking her hand, pulling her close. Telling her she was wanted. Kissing away apprehension.

Bad timing. She wasn't allowed to look at him like that when they had an audience.

"Well, what the hay bales were you thinking?" Dre yanked him back to earth, her natural sass cutting off the deliciously awkward moment. "Don't you know better than to go calling on a woman looking like you've been wrestling cattle all day?"

Good grief, Dre. Paul felt heat race up his neck and dump into his face. Unable to resist another peek at Suzanna, he found her eyes on him, still soft and so alluring. A wonderful pink touched her smooth cheeks, and her shoulders moved with a silent giggle. Humiliation worth suffering.

Suzanna shifted her attention to Dre. "Situation normal. He's always the rough cowboy."

Paul's mouth opened, and he grabbed his chest as though it hurt. "Ouch. Poisoned by my sister's impertinence." He dropped his hand and lunged for Suzanna. "That's not going unpunished."

She yelped as he snatched her by the legs, tossing her over his shoulder without much more effort than he'd used with Kelsey.

"Paul Rustin, put me down!" She pushed against his back, trying to right herself.

"Nope. I haven't inspected that "big tub for the horse" in a while." He moved toward the barn. "I think we should go make sure it still holds water."

Suzanna kicked with both legs. "Don't you dare drop me in that tank."

Paul laughed, his stride set on a mission.

"Andrea!" Suzanna called, still squirming. "Help!"

He could hear his sister laugh, though she sounded as though she were moving away. "He's ticklish, Suz. That's all I've got. Good luck with it."

A car door slammed, followed by another, and then her pickup rumbled to a start. Dre was leaving. How intuitive of her. He always did love that girl. Okay, not always, but he'd keep her for sure.

Suzanna traced a line from his hip up to his arm, brushing over his sensitive ribs. Maybe he'd been overly generous with his affection toward his sister. The snitch. He jerked away from Suzanna's evil touch.

"No." He reached around his back with one hand and caught her torturous fingers. "No tickling."

Suzanna's sinister laugh set his skin tingling as she went for his other side. He danced away again and shifted her around his shoulders. Though she was more intelligent and agile than a calf, he had her secured and defenseless before he made it to the corral.

"Please, Paul." Suzanna still wiggled, her breathless voice brushing his neck. "I had to break ice in that tank this morning. Please don't throw me in."

Paul stopped at the gate. "How much is it worth to you?"

A kiss. A long, deep kiss that redefines what I am to you.

He stared into her eyes, her face resting on his shoulder so near he could feel the warmth of her sweet breath against his jaw. Laughter sifted away, and he felt her heart kick against his shoulder.

Maybe the redefining moment was now.

The chain around her neck slipped, and the gold of whatever was on the end peeked from her collar. Her gaze darted to the ground, but he caught the alarm before she could hide it.

Maybe not now. Not ever? Heaven help him.

Paul lowered her to the ground. Setting her securely upright, he forced his hands away. Difficult command to master. He craved the warmth of her breath against his skin, the rhythmic beat of her heart near his own, and the fulfilling comfort of her frame filling his arms.

Fanciful wishes. Hand to her throat, she took a subtle, but telling step backward.

A dull pain gripped his insides. "I wouldn't do anything to hurt you, Pickle."

No freezing water tanks. No stolen kisses. Hopefully, she understood both.

CHAPTER
TWENTY-THREE

"I can't come Thanksgiving." Suzanna sighed as she slumped against Andrea's kitchen bar stool.

She'd wanted to taste the holiday with the Kents. To experience a full stomach alongside a spirit of joy, rather than indigestion born of resentment.

"What do you mean?" Andrea poured two mugs of coffee and brought them to the island.

"Something came up..." Suzanna fingered the ring hidden against her skin.

Andrea looked at her with an unvoiced question.

"It has nothing to do with the rumor."

Nearly a month gone by, and the thing was still as hot as a potato out of an oven. No doubt Shelby kept it fresh in everyone's mind with her gift of gab and stores of misinformation.

How on earth did the woman know how often Paul stopped for coffee? And that he was often at her house sometime before eight in the morning? Where was she getting that stuff?

The truth didn't look good, innocent though it may be. Suzanna wondered when Paul would change his habits, though it made her sad to think that it was inevitable.

"Really?" Andrea sounded less than convinced.

"Really." Suzanna settled her mind on the conversation at hand. "My mother called. She'll be out Thursday and plans to stay the weekend."

Andrea sat up, her eyes round. "That's wonderful. How long has it been since you've seen her?"

Wonderful? Not really. Suzanna's stomach had been queasy since she'd gotten the call two days ago. She hadn't spent a holiday with her mother in years.

"My father's funeral."

Half-truth. No, not really. She'd *seen* Mother there. It shocked her, but there she sat, back left corner, her giant ice rink of a rock contrasting just so against her proper black suit. Had she married her wealthy lover yet? For a woman who preached propriety since before Suzanna could understand what the word meant, she sure lived scandalously.

There was that indigestion. A full two days early. Ugh.

"Will it be nice to get together again?" Andrea grinned, certainly thinking of her own mother-daughter relationship. The one where her mama still called her Bumpkin, held her hand when they talked heart-to-heart, and embraced who Andrea was with admiration and cheer.

Add envy to white lies for the day's sin count. How did God work that, anyway? Certainly by now, His list marked "the hopelessly stained Suzanna Wilton Cumberland" had run out of room. Who could stand before a God who kept track?

Her stomach burned.

"I'm not sure why she decided to come." Suzanna carefully removed the edge from her voice. "She has a busy schedule, so it is a surprise." ·

"How nice." Andrea punctuated her approval with a nod. "Will we get to meet her?"

Good land of grain, she hoped not. Mother could find something wrong with Pollyanna Whittier. Suzanna would do her utmost to keep her beloved friends from Mother's scrupulous evaluation.

Suzanna couldn't put that nicely. She shrugged and searched for a new topic.

"My brother didn't really throw you in the horse tank, did he?"

Thank goodness. How did Andrea always know when to switch gears?

"No, he didn't. Made me promise cinnamon rolls in exchange for dry warmth and dignity." Suzanna smiled, trying to block the heat moving toward her face. "Ruthless, isn't he?"

Andrea held a silent stare, locking eye contact with Suzanna. A hint of a smile lurked on her lips, matching the suggestion of laughter in her eyes. "Little boys never do grow up."

What did that mean? Suzanna tried to stop the question as it formed in her head, as well as the answers that tagged along with it. Paul hadn't pursued anything with her as the week had passed. He still came, still teased, still drank her coffee, but since he set her down next to the corral fence, he hadn't touched her. At all. Not a brush of their fingers when she passed a mug to him. Not a squeeze of her shoulder when he thanked her and set out for the day. He'd been noticeably careful, in fact, with any physical contact—which was to say there was none.

Her heart sank into her upset stomach. She should have listened to her more sensible self. Indifference doesn't hurt. Hope is brutally disappointing. When had she cultivated that cruel sapling of misery?

And here Andrea was, trying to add sunshine to that weed of destruction that needed——Cut. Pulled. Buried. Better yet, burned.

"What is Kelsey working on these days?" Avoidance was a much easier solution.

Andrea cleared her throat. "I'm not sure. She and Dad were hard at it Sunday afternoon." Her smile resurfaced, genuine and pretty. "Thank you so much for taking an interest in her. She has bloomed under your attention the past few weeks. I can't tell you how often I've prayed for a friend for her." She laughed. "God certainly does surprise me with His answers. He's so good."

Apparently a comfortable conversation was simply not in the cards this afternoon.

"I enjoy Kelsey very much."

There. That should steer things in a clear direction. Simple. True. And it left out Mother, Paul, and God.

Paul took his chair between Kiera and Keegan, his regular seating arrangement for any given holiday. In years gone by, he didn't dwell on it, even as other couples in the room paired off and inevitably shared how thankful they were for their partner as the corncob passed from hand to hand. This year, however, he'd recklessly nourished a far-off hope that Suzanna would take the seat by his side, and he'd be able to, at the very least, state how happy he was she'd become his neighbor. And if things had gone more to his preference, he'd have been allowed to squeeze her hand, to whisper later how happy he was she'd become so much more.

Fruitless daydreams. Kiera and Keegan were certainly worthy dinner companions, and he was most definitely thankful for them.

Kelsey dropped onto the chair across from him. "I wish Suzanna could've come today."

She looked him dead on, her eyes communicating knowledge that went beyond her twelve years.

"Me too, Kels." Paul leaned on the table with both arms.

She leaned in too. "Do you think she's having fun with her mom?"

Doubt it. He recounted her reaction every time the woman came up in conversation: stiff spine, tight mouth, cold stare. No, Suzanna's Thanksgiving was most likely miserable.

"Hope so." He couldn't manage a smile.

Kelsey looked at her place setting. She pressed two fingers along the fold of her orange cloth napkin and drew in a long breath. "I painted something for her." She tipped her face back to him. "Do you think we could go over later so I could give it to her?"

Sunshine parted the dreary fog in his mind. "I think that's an awesome plan, Kels. She'll love it. We'll go after dinner."

Kelsey smiled, and Paul felt gratitude light his heart. He'd worked for years to gain the same kind of closeness with Kelsey that he had with Kiera and Keegan. She loved him, he knew that, but their bond wasn't as tight. Now, with Suzanna in the mix, he shared something unique with Kelsey.

They were alike, Suzanna and Kelsey. A striking epiphany. Kelsey retreated into herself, and she was guarded, especially when it came to something painful. Like Dad's stroke. Kiera had cried openly. She'd crawled into his lap and sobbed for her grandpa. Keegan had held his hand with tears running freely. Kelsey had sat alone in the hospital chair—stiff, staring at nothing. She'd come across as detached, but it was hurt, not indifference, that kept her from the others.

Suddenly he knew them both. Understood them both. Kelsey handled her broken heart with distance. Suzanna's sharp edge kept guard over a whole lot of pain.

Paul reached across the table, brushing Kelsey's knuckles. She hesitated but then lifted her fingers to curl around his. Through the innocence of her open gaze, he caught a glimpse of her heart. Precious and lovely.

A tiny smile settled on her lips as if she understood what had just happened. Certainly she did. It wasn't everyone she'd let in like that. The privilege made his heart swell.

"We should go out for Thanksgiving dinner."

Of course we should, Mother.

Suzanna ground her teeth as she pushed her mitted hands into the hot oven. Never mind I put this bird in at five this morning. Never mind I spent a small fortune on a ridiculously extravagant dinner because you called to say you were coming.

How could she be surprised? Nothing ever suited Mother. The woman could rave about the color purple, and Suzanna would wear a lavender sweater, only to hear how the weave was too thick—it made Suzanna's wide shoulders look masculine. And food? Why had she bothered?

Did you use real butter on the potatoes, Suzanna?

Option A: Yes.

That was foolish, my dear. You'll never get down to a 4 with those kinds of eating habits.

Option B: No.

Sparing expense should only be done on the side. One must use the best when it comes to something front and center.

"We can't go out, Mother." Suzanna slid the roaster onto the hot pad waiting on the island. "This is a small town, and nothing is open for the holiday."

She peeled the foil back, and a curl of turkey-infused steam rolled up to her face. Juice bubbled around the golden-brown bird. Perfect.

"Such a large bird for only the two of us." Mother tsked. "I've taken to Cornish hens, dear. They're a much more reasonable size for a woman without a family."

Two jabs in one sentence. Awesome.

"I can freeze the meat in smaller portions. Jason and I used to do it often."

Mother frowned. "Certainly, Jason's dietitian told you fresh food is always better."

Good heavens. Why was she here?

"I've fresh green beans." Suzanna tried to keep her voice a cheerful tone. "We'll steam them. And I picked the apples myself the last of October."

"Did you ask the farmer if he grows organically?"

No, that would be rude. "They came from a friend's house. She lives down the road, and her family is the picture of health. I'm sure it's fine."

"Well"—Mother slipped onto a chair—"I suppose asking would have been awkward, but really, you should grow your own produce out here. These farmers' wives are always dumping some sort of chemical on their plants to win a silly ribbon at the fair. You simply must be careful."

Suzanna stared at her mother. Insulting her, that was one thing. Taking a cut at her friend?

Mother met her gaze with a raised brow. "What?"

She swallowed and focused on carving the turkey. The knife cut in deep, and more than once she got it caught in the bone.

"Well, I see I'm not being helpful." Mother came to her feet and drummed her manicured fingers against the back of the chair. "William's show will be on in a few minutes. I'll just go see what channel."

"I don't have a satellite dish, Mother."

"I should hope not. They're ever so expensive, and I know the burden Jason left with you. Cable carries RFD-TV."

"I live fifteen miles from town." Suzanna covered the meat slices with foil and turned to the beans. "Cable doesn't make it out this far."

"But it's a new show." Mother slid her hands to her tiny waist. The one she'd been so excited to show Suzanna the second she stepped from her Lexus LX. *"Tada!" She gushed as if it were a wonderful surprise for Suzanna. "Compliments of the* Rock It Like An A-lister *diet plan. I've brought you a copy."*

Indigestion set fire in Suzanna's chest. Miserable from the first hello. Whatever did the woman want?

"I'm sorry, Mother. I'm sure William recorded it, and you'll be able to catch up."

Mother groaned, and her foot scuffed the floor. A grown-up version of stamping her foot. This was her mother. "Oh, phooey. William will ask what I thought; he'll be so disappointed." She stepped closer to Suzanna's work area. "We fought about me coming out here, you know."

Suzanna glanced up as she continued to wash the beans.

"Oh yes. He was quite against it. Such a long drive for a woman by herself, and for what? There's nothing out here. But, no, I said. My little girl is out there. I couldn't let you spend another holiday alone."

Sure you could. Did it last year just fine. And I only lived thirty minutes away.

"I'm sorry you fought, Mother. You shouldn't have on my account. I would have been fine."

"Oh..." Mother's shoulders sagged as if sandbags had been lashed to her arms. "I just couldn't, Suzanna. This has gone on long enough. It's time for some things in your life to change."

Really? What things? If Mother was involved in her life at all, it was only to launch a full-fledged, meddling takeover.

Suzanna pushed a smile. "I'm glad to know you think of me."

"Yes." Mother spread her hands on the counter. "It's time we had a talk."

How pleasant. Should be a warm heart-to-heart. That was about enough. Heat climbed from her gut to her throat, and her hands began to tremble. "Mother, I'm—"

A hollow knock sounded from the side door. The hinges squeaked, and boots smacked against the tile.

"Hey, Pickle," Paul called before he passed through the kitchen door. "Happy Thanksgiving."

A happy intrusion. Suzanna was tempted to hug him. Kelsey trailed a step behind, her shy smile also a welcome reprieve and an appropriate target for her relieved affection. She wrapped both arms around the girl.

"Hey, Kelsey." She kept her close. "How's my best friend?"

Kelsey squeezed back, careful not to squish the package she'd brought with her. "We missed you at dinner." She stepped back. "I have something I wanted to give you, and Uncle Paul agreed to bring me over."

"I'm so glad." Glad was an understatement. Could she pirate them for the rest of the day? How about for the entire long weekend?

"I painted this for you." Kelsey held out the cloth-wrapped package. "Grandpa helped me."

Suzanna grinned, knowing a canvas rested under the protective cloth. "Can I open it now?"

Kelsey nodded. Suzanna felt her smile grow, and her vision collided with Paul's. His warm expression made her stomach feel like a freshly uncorked bottle of champagne; a thousand tiny bubbles popped delightfully in her middle.

Suzanna pulled at the wide green ribbon, and it slipped away like silk. She unfolded the plain cotton and turned the waiting canvas to discover Kelsey's work.

An orchard. Row upon row of shrub cherries in full bloom stretched over a small rise that met a pale blue horizon.

Vision. Purpose. Excellence.

Kelsey had used a careful script to place the three words in the light blue sky.

Tears suddenly threatened to choke Suzanna. Her dream— her vision captured by Kelsey's talent. How did she know what it would look like?

"I looked up some orchards online." Kelsey explained. "This was so pretty, it made me think of you."

Suzanna's eyes caressed the portrait. So very well done by a wonderful kindred spirit. "I don't know what to say, Kels." She couldn't draw her eyes away from the picture as she whispered, "Thank you."

Kelsey's arms wrapped around her waist, and Suzanna leaned to give her a proper hug. Mother cleared her throat. Oh yes. How could she forget? Suzanna fixed her posture and stepped back.

"Mother, this is my neighbor Paul"—she touched his shoulder—"and his niece, who happens to be my best friend, Kelsey." She slid an arm around Kelsey's shoulders.

"How lovely to meet you both." Mother held a stiff hand out while keeping a noticeably awkward distance. "I am Katrina Pembroke."

She was? So, they'd married. When, exactly, was that going to come up?

Paul stepped forward, closing the ridiculous gap Mother had maintained. "It's a pleasure, ma'am."

Mother eyed him with cool reproach. How dare he enter her circle of hallowed space without permission? *Oh, Mother.*

Paul turned his attention to Suzanna, resting a hand on her shoulder. "We won't keep you from your meal, which, by the way, smells really good, Suz." His eyes caught hers and looked deep. Questions lay in them. *Are you okay? Can I help?*

No, she wasn't okay. If only he could help.

"Dre sent over a pie and a plate of cookies." His fingers curled around her arm above her elbow. Stability. "They're in the pickup."

No offer to bring them in. Bless you, Paul Rustin.

"How nice. Tell her thank you."

She moved to the door with her arm still draped around Kelsey and Paul's warm hand near her elbow, ushering her away for a moment of peace.

Mother didn't move. Suzanna could feel her sharp stare driving shards of disapproval into her back. She'd hear about this. Hopefully, the scolding would wait until Paul and Kelsey were gone.

They reached the truck, and Suzanna pulled Kelsey closer. "Thank you so much. I can't begin to tell you how much I love it."

Kelsey hugged her back before she hopped into the truck. "Will your mom be here all weekend?"

Suzanna shrugged. "I don't know her plans for sure."

"You could bring her over. I know Mama wouldn't mind."

Sweet little thing. Suzanna shut the door, keeping her eyes on her hands that rested on the open window frame. Paul came around from the other side, quietly waiting for Suzanna's response.

"Perhaps." She'd sooner set a badger loose in the Kents' home.

Paul handed her a pie tin and a covered plate. He stepped toward the tailgate, and Suzanna matched his move.

"Everything okay?"

She tried to smile. It didn't work. "Nothing ever changes."

"Should we have stayed awhile?"

Suzanna met his eyes. "No, but thank you."

Paul's eyes trailed to the house, settling on the kitchen window. Without a doubt, Mother would be standing lookout. Glaring.

His attention came back, and a grin pulled on one side of his mouth, puckering a tiny dimple. "I haven't felt eighteen in a while." He slid a hand under the pie and brushed her fingers. "Thank your mother for me."

He winked, and Suzanna giggled.

"Bye, Pickle. I'll see you Sunday."

For the first time in a month, Suzanna looked forward to church.

"You've put me off long enough." Mother dabbed her mouth and then scowled at the paper napkin. "Look at this." She waved the offending item. "This is the nicest restaurant in town?"

Sheesh. Like they needed to be eating out, anyway. Suzanna had stores of leftovers jammed in her refrigerator. She swallowed, her tongue raw from biting it multiple times over the past three days.

Almost done.

She need only make it through this lunch, and Mother would be gone. And tomorrow was Sunday.

Was she still looking forward to that? Pastor's endorsement of Paul's candidacy for elder had helped. Well, it had eased things up for him at least, which counted for something.

"Back to the issue." Mother smacked the napkin onto the table. "When are you coming home?"

Home? What home?

"Mother, *this* is my home. I'm not leaving."

"Just like your father. Stubborn to the point of stupidity." She leaned in, her eyebrows stuck together. "What's out here for you? How will living here gain you a life? Suzanna Korine, you have an opportunity to start over. Sell your father's pathetic little farm and get a life you can be proud of. Go back to school; major in something useful."

Suzanna's chest quaked inside like the seismic tremors preceding a volcano. She cleared her throat, willing away the steamy tears that blurred her vision.

"I'm sorry I can't meet your approval, Mother."

The woman cocked her head and raised an eyebrow.

She met her mother's cold gaze. "You always demanded perfection, and I could never attain it."

"Stop feeling sorry for yourself," she snapped. "If you'd stop pining for a dead man and moping about things you can't change, you would see the opportunity sitting in front of you. I know for a fact you've had offers. The banker himself told me your property would be easily sold if you would put it on the market."

"The banker?"

"Yes, Suzanna, the banker." She shook her head as though she thought Suzanna daft. "I know my way around business. Do you think I'd discuss this uninformed?"

Smoldering heat exploded. "You have no business here, and we have nothing to discuss. This *is* my life, and I'm not leaving because you don't approve. Fact is, Mother, you've never approved of me, of Jason, or of anything else I've done."

Mother gripped the table and leaned in. "My judgment has proven right," she hissed. "What did your marriage accomplish? You're worse off now than you were before. Buried in debt and running from memories. And *horticulture*? I warned you that you could do nothing with such an obscure study. Even if you had completed your degree, it would accomplish nothing. It's time you start listening to your mother."

"Yes, because your life has gone so smoothly."

Mother sat back, her sharp brown eyes cold and calculating. "This is because of that farmer, isn't it?"

"Farmer?"

"Your neighbor. I saw the two of you by his truck, shamelessly flirting in front of the child. And you, using her to win his affection."

Suzanna raised an eyebrow and breathed a scornful laugh. "Paul? He's not a farmer; he's a rancher, and there's nothing shameful about him."

"That's not what I hear."

Oh good. Chuck made sure she was fully informed. Why was she surprised?

Suzanna crossed her arms. "You lived half your life in church. Surely you know how gossip works, Mother, and you're hardly qualified to condemn. Shameless indeed."

She held her mother's challenge, her heart pounding and hands trembling against the building fury.

"He will lead you to ruin." Mother snatched her purse. "Middle-aged men who are single are in that condition for a reason. Mark my words, Suzanna. You will regret this." She jumped to her feet, knocking her chair backward. "Don't call me to bail you out." Mother stomped away, a fine ending to her perfectly dramatic scene.

Suzanna stared at the toppled chair. "I never have."

Another pleasant family holiday.

CHAPTER TWENTY-FOUR

"Will you hang around?" Paul rubbed his neck, wanting instead to take Suzanna's hand.

Chatter rumbled through the hall of the church, Sunday churchgoers discussing their holiday festivities and plans for the upcoming week. Dinner would be served in a few minutes, a tradition practiced before every quarterly business meeting.

Suzanna's face darkened. "I don't think so, Paul." She cast a glance at the floor. "It wouldn't be good. They vote today, don't they?"

"Well, yes, but—"

"I'm not a member anyway." She looked back at him. "It wouldn't look good, and I want you to have a fair chance. Pastor Ron's approval shouldn't be wasted, and I'll only stir suspicion."

He stepped to her side, blocking any spectator's view of her face. "But I want you here."

She raised her eyes, timid and wounded. Scratch propriety. He reached to pull her close.

Suzanna shrank away. "Paul, I know you're on my side. You don't have to prove it here."

She stepped backward and pushed against the glass-paneled door. It gave way, and she scurried down the sidewalk. Paul followed, emotions so stirred he labored to breathe.

"Ah, the infamous Ms. Wilton." Trish Calloway stopped Suzanna's flight from the other end of the walkway. "Are you not joining us for our meal?"

The woman's smirk made Paul's chest tighten. He covered the gap between them with three quick steps. Suzanna's spine snapped straight, and her cold glare was set as she glanced back at him.

She leveled her stare on Trish. "My business is finished here."

Oh, Pickle. You don't melt ice with frost, darlin'.

"Surely you'd like to stay to support your ... neighbor."

Suzanna stepped forward. Unsure of her motive, Paul caught her arm. She stiffened at his touch but did not acknowledge him.

"Paul is entirely capable all on his own, despite the black lies set against him."

Trish fluttered her eyelashes. "Whatever could you mean?"

Paul could feel her draw a long breath. *Good heavens. Please don't let her lunge.*

"You know exactly what I mean," she growled. "As you and Shelby Stanton reign as the town gossips, you've maintained this invented scandal, but I'm not beaten. How much lower do you intend to sink?"

Trish's thin mouth set in a rigid line. "Keep it up, Miss Wilton, and you're bound to find out." She adjusted her fitted coat and rolled her shoulders straight. "Give in now, city girl. You're not welcome here. That will never change, no matter who you wrap around your crooked little finger."

She looked at Paul, seething with contempt. "Mr. Rustin,"——she nodded——"I look forward to our meeting. Should be very interesting, don't you think?"

What did that mean? The woman stepped around them, her head tipped back as though looking at them was not to be tolerated.

Was that a verbal catfight? Yikes. Wouldn't it be easier to deck the other person and move on with life?

Suzanna didn't move. She stared straight ahead, her face stone, but he felt her tremble under his hand.

"Suzanna…" He stepped closer, dropping his voice to a whisper.

She remained still. "Go inside, Paul."

"No."

"You're making it worse." Her voice cracked, but her face remained hard.

"You'll never overcome this by throwing stones back at them."

"What?"

"All they see is this." He waved his free hand over her. "You only let them see anger. They never get to see the beautiful woman I know."

Paul gripped her shoulders and forced her to face him. She locked her eyes on his chest, but he could see the working of her jaw. He traced the side of it with his thumb. "A soft answer turns away wrath."

She pulled in a breath, and for a moment, he thought she'd crack. He longed for it. But when her eyes flew to him, they smoldered, and she pulled away from his touch.

"You'll not win like this." Suzanna pushed his outstretched hands away. "Go. Reclaim your spotless reputation. Don't waste it on me."

She abandoned the sidewalk, her angry stride quickly covering the ground to her vehicle.

Paul looked at his boots. Win? An appointment as an elder? The responsibility, though an honor, was fairly low on his priorities. He'd much rather win her heart.

Agnes Blake stood slowly, her weight pressed upon her aluminum cane. "I think we deserve an explanation. Paul's character has been cast into doubt, Pastor Ron. Is this something the board intends to ignore?"

Heat washed over Paul, from the tips of his cropped hair to the ends of his well-worn boots. So, it'd come to this. Perhaps it was as it should be. Diligent members would be prudent to guard who they allowed to shepherd the congregation. It was time to clear the air.

Pastor Ron put a hand on Paul's shoulder. "I don't believe that is the board's intent, Mrs. Blake." He looked over, catching Paul's eyes. "I've personally investigated the rumors flying about, though I found them to be quite questionable from the beginning. There is nothing of any truth to the scandal you're concerned about. It's time Paul cleared the air for himself."

Pastor squeezed his shoulder and took a half step back. Where to begin? Was Paul supposed to tell the whole story? He cleared his throat.

"Suzanna Wilton is my neighbor"—*Good plan. Begin with the obvious*—"and, because she didn't receive a very warm welcome from our community, I made it my business to see that she was okay."

Several people squirmed against their pews.

"In spite of the efforts of some to make her otherwise, she's doing all right. She's a good woman, and she would like to find a life here in Rock Creek. And she's never had any intention of damming up the spring." Paul paused, making eye contact with Jim Calloway and Rodney. "We have since become friends. I've no shame in that because there isn't anything inappropriate in our relationship."

"Can you explain your constant presence at her home, then?" Chuck rose, slowly unfolding his six-foot-six frame as though he were Goliath rising against his miniature foe.

"I'm not sure what you mean, Stanton." Paul resisted the urge to pull at his collar, sure steam would rise from the vent. "I have a place to run, a rather large one which demands quite a bit of time. Thus, I am not *constantly* at Suzanna's home. I do check on her when I can, but—"

"Come now, Paul. You're not a very good liar." Chuck crossed his arms. "I know for a fact your blue Ford is parked in her drive pretty early most mornings."

Patience eroded. "When do you begin your day, Chuck?" Paul grasped the podium in front of him. "Because mine starts around five. If you'd bothered to get to know Suzanna at all, you'd know she starts hers about the same time because her job operates on Eastern Standard Time. I stop by for coffee somewhere between seven and eight because that's when we're both ready for a break, and to be perfectly honest, she makes a darn good cup o' Joe. Another detail you'd know if you'd been at all kind to her."

Paul stepped around the podium and down the two steps from the stage. "I don't know how you're getting this information—spying comes to mind, which is—but you're certainly misconstruing it."

Chuck unfolded his arms. "Nothing wrong with checking on a neighbor, as you're so vehemently claiming. As to misconstruing information—everyone here knows you've got a thing for that woman, Rustin. We're not blind. Suspicious behavior lends itself to doubt."

Everyone knew? A rush of adrenaline set Paul's fingers tingling. Maybe so, but Suzanna was still holding him across the fence. How had this become so complicated?

"Her name is Suzanna, Chuck. Try it; it's not difficult." He moved toward Chuck. "And while I might have an interest, there's no scandal in it. She's a single woman. Nothing has come of it though. Even if it had, or does, I wouldn't smear her integrity. Character matters to me. It matters to this church family, and I work to uphold it."

Chuck snorted. "This from a graduate of Boys Town." His mouth twitched as though he were stifling a grin.

The low blow. Paul's gut clenched and pain rippled from it. He didn't want to admit it though. God, his family, and most of his church had forgiven him. It'd been so long ago, but he'd been a rebel, a heartbreaking disappointment. The sting of that shame never completely went away.

"Yes." He forced his voice to work, though it was low and quiet. "Some stains are never forgotten. I know that very well."

Paul looked at his hands, trying to ignore the cool moisture in the corners of his eyes. He cleared his throat, but he couldn't force his eyes to the crowd. "You all know who I am. I haven't hidden anything from anybody. Do with that as you will."

He walked to the rear of the sanctuary. Andrea's face was the only one he caught as he made his exit. Tears glistened against her cheeks, but she reached a hand to him as he passed, the gentle squeeze on his arm a reminder of his family's love. A reminder of things more important than popularity.

Suzanna pulled the fleece blanket close to her chin, although her brain told her to get up. If she napped any longer, she'd never go to sleep at night. Rolling to her back, she forced her eyes open and rubbed at the salty grit. It stung, beckoning the tears that had stopped rolling when she'd drifted to sleep an hour ago.

She shouldn't have stayed in Rock Creek. Moving would have restored Paul's reputation. But he'd wanted her to stay, lending her a hope she'd no business borrowing.

She sniffed, catching a tear with her fingertips before it rolled to her ear. The weekend had been awful. Thank God it was over. Back to normal life.

Perhaps not. It was time for a change. She needed to have a talk with Paul about his visiting habits for his sake and for the security of her heart.

Suzanna sat up. Life would go on. It always did. She slid to the edge of her bed and set her feet on the floor. The closet door stood slightly ajar, and she caught a glimpse of Jason's box against the back wall. Her hand went to her chain, tugging his ring free from her collar.

Loneliness clawed at her throat, threatening to choke her resolve. She'd lived through hospitals and chemo and hospice and funerals. She would survive this. Her eyes slid shut against the miserable promise. Survival was an agonizing existence.

Enough. Her jaw clamped hard, and she pushed away from the bed. After stomping to the kitchen, she reached for the coffee pot. If survival was all she could expect out of life, she wasn't going to let it hurt. She filled the pot and set it to brew and then threw open the cabinet door. Her blue mug, the one she usually handed to Paul, teetered on the edge of the shelf and fell, hitting her nose before she caught it. Warm pain shot from the spot of impact and throbbed into her eyes.

"Dadgum it!" She covered the injury with one hand and gripped the offending object with the other. With the form Jason had taught her when they'd still been teenagers, she threw the mug against the far wall. Shattered, porcelain littered the floor.

Ignoring the mess, she marched to the bathroom for a cool cloth, though her nose didn't really hurt anymore. Anger made a pretty good analgesic.

CHAPTER TWENTY-FIVE

Paul pushed pasta around his plate wondering why he'd heated it at all. The clock said seven, so he'd figured it was time to eat, but being hungry had nothing to do with it.

Soft rain plinked against the tin roof of his covered back porch. The rest of his house lay quiet, normal for a Monday evening. He usually flipped on ESPN for Monday night football. Denver was playing. Manning was putting on a show, no doubt, but his television sat black and quiet against the wall above his fireplace.

Paul gave up on food and abandoned the kitchen. Bypassing the living room, he pushed through the back door. The air smelled cold and clean, a hint of snow settling behind the drizzle of rain. His breath puffed white, drifting lazily on the calm air. He shoved his hands into his pockets as he leaned against the porch rail.

The previous day replayed. Suzanna had acted... tired. He'd asked about her mom's visit, and she'd shrugged.

"She left yesterday."

That was it. He guessed it was a relief, but maybe there was disappointment too. Church started before he could ask more about it, and after the service, things had gone south rather quickly.

The moment she pushed him away played over and over in his mind like a scratched disk. Rejection had an unforgettable sting. She was trying to protect him, but it still shot an ache in his chest and stirred up memories he'd rather stayed settled.

He ran a hand against his hair as if he could clear away the recollection. It didn't work. He involuntarily pictured his grandmother's ring nestled safely in a small black box tucked in his top dresser drawer, exactly where he'd replaced it seven years before.

I can't marry you, Paul. You're a good man, but I just can't.

Female language. Translation: I don't want you.

He shut his eyes and groaned. He'd laid that one down. Washed his hands of it and walked away. Why'd it spring up on him now?

Because Suzanna stirred all sorts of things deep inside. Some he liked. Others? He'd prefer to live without them. Bottom line: she was driving him nuts.

Risk rejection or march toward insanity? Maybe Tom was right. It was time to show his cards. If only he could read Suzanna. One minute she'd smile at him like he could be her forever after, and his heart would trip and turn into mush. The next, she'd scowl at him, pushing him away and draining hope right out of him.

Dre would say it was better to know than to guess. Sounded wise, except Tom had been head over heels in love with her since the day she had come back from Baylor looking like a woman rather than an awkward teen. What did she know about rejection? Knowing you're not wanted is not better. Than anything.

Except maybe insanity. Paul strode back into the house, holding his shirt to his nose to take a whiff. He'd showered when he came in for the day, but a clean shirt couldn't hurt. And an extra dash of deodorant.

Set on a mission, he changed and left the house before his determination could dissolve. One short mile and a quick sentence or two, and he'd find out.

He might regret impulse.

His pickup came to life, rain glittering in the headlights. Bad timing. The road was bound to be soft, and it was already dark. Ms. May's would close in fewer than two hours. He should pick another day to exercise courage.

He shifted into reverse and backed out of the drive.

The drizzle continued as he pulled up to Suzanna's. The roads weren't bad yet. He could say he just wanted to check on her—peek in the basement, pretending to check for signs of water leaks. Because it'd been raining all of an hour.

So pathetic. This could be why he was still on Rock Creek's very short bachelor list. Suck it up and stay the course. What's the worst that could happen?

She could look at him with "no" plainly written in her eyes as she tried to find a kind way to let him down. Their friendship, as they knew it, would be over, and the highlight of his days—morning coffee at her house—would become too awkward to continue.

She could reject him, and that really would hurt. He swallowed, his grip tight on the steering wheel.

God, I'm flat-out in love with her. I sure could use a shot of strength here.

The light over her side door flicked on, sending a beacon to his pickup. Too late to turn back. Paul turned the key, and the pickup died. He slipped his hat over his head and stepped into the rain.

Suzanna met him at the entry, a smile on her lips and questions in her eyes.

"Surprise." She held the door open. "You weren't out working in this, were you?"

Paul stepped over the threshold but stopped two feet inside. "No."

She pushed the door closed and faced him. A small red welt crossed the bridge of her nose. He reached to trace it with his fingertips. "What's this?"

She ducked away, covering it with her hand. "Nothing. I caught a mug with my nose is all."

"Wasn't mine, I hope."

She looked back at him. "Yes, it was."

Why wasn't she smiling? Paul glanced at the floor and shuffled his feet.

"Do you want to come in?" Suzanna stepped toward her kitchen.

"No." The word came out too abrupt. "I mean, well... actually, I wondered if you wanted to go to Ms. May's. She makes a fierce pie, and I thought..."

Thought what? What in the great big universe had he been thinking?

Suzanna stared at him, her sky-blue eyes growing larger with each breath, making his heart thud as though he were working in the round pen with a high-stepping filly.

Her lips parted, and the thought lines on her forehead crinkled. "Like a date?"

"No... yes. Maybe?" His face burned unmercifully. "Only if you're okay with it. Otherwise... well, I owe you for a month's supply of coffee anyway."

She didn't blink. Didn't move. Didn't answer. She just stood, her gaze fixed on him as if he'd just landed from Mars.

This is why he'd given up on dating. Nothing made him feel dumber than standing in front of a woman with his heart hanging out in the open while she tried to figure out what the hay bales she was supposed to do with it.

"Wow." She took a half step back. "That's awkward."

Great. Paul backed away, aiming for escape before the smoldering flames of this disaster set off the fire alarm.

Suzanna's solemn face broke, a giggle surfacing with her grin. "Paul." She snatched his arm. "I'm kidding. I'd love to go."

Good grief. His heart took a dip and then restarted. "That was cruel, Pickle." He recovered enough to laugh.

"Paybacks for almost throwing me into the horse tank." She slipped her feet into a pair of flat, girly shoes sitting by the door.

Paul reached for her coat, which was hanging on a peg on the far wall. His brain whirled, and he was unable to come back with something witty. He held the coat by the shoulders, waiting for her to insert her arms.

Suzanna moved to do so, but she paused when their gazes collided. Questions. Concern. Hesitation. They mingled in her eyes, and doubt began to tumble in his stomach again.

Maybe they'd still recover if he let her off the hook. He could just show up in the morning, expecting coffee and easy conversation, and they could pretend this never happened.

She tipped her head, a tiny smile nudging the corners of her mouth. "So, it's a date?"

"You tell me." *Please say it is.*

She smiled, her head dipping a slight nod.

Paul's lungs expanded as if he'd just remembered to breathe. Suzanna slipped her coat on and slid a hand to his elbow. He felt a full grin break the tension in his face, and he escorted her through the rain.

"Did you want to drive?" See, he could still be ornery. She hadn't completely melted his brain.

"Um, no."

He opened the passenger door, and she settled in. Taking the wheel, Paul started out of her drive, congratulating himself that he could still operate the vehicle. Proof he wasn't a blithering idiot after all.

"Do you always wait until it's raining to ask a girl out?" Suzanna couldn't resist a playful jab. It helped to drown the spinning arguments in her head.

What was she doing? She'd made up her mind just the day before. She and Paul needed some distance. So, the best way to accomplish that was by going on an official date? He'd been too cute though. What girl would reject such an adorable offer, and from Paul Rustin at that?

"Yep." Paul's grin looked boyish. "It comes off more pathetic that way. Almost always guarantees a yes."

"Really?" Laughter tickled her chest. "How often have you tried this method of manipulation?"

"Counting tonight?" He slipped a glance her way before he guided his truck around the curve.

She nodded.

His grin spread full. "Once."

"Nice." She let her laugh roll free right along with his.

Maybe it'd be okay. After Sunday, maybe the whole rumor thing had cleared away.

"How did the meeting go yesterday?"

"At church?"

Suzanna nodded, trusting he could see from his periphery.

He shrugged. "Fine."

Figures. Men were always good at relaying details. Get out the towrope. Time to drag out some info.

"Fine? So, that means you're the newest member of the board?"

"No." His jaw worked.

"No? Why not?" Dumb question. She knew the obvious reason. Why'd he say it was fine, then?

"Just wasn't voted in, that's all."

"That's all?" She stared at him. "Two months ago they wouldn't have bothered counting the results. Don't tell me it's not a big deal."

Paul shifted in his seat, sighing before he answered. "Suz, it's not like a high school royalty gig. It wasn't a popularity vote. I trust each member took it seriously, and right now, I'm not the right guy for the job."

"That's not true, and we both know it."

Paul's lips pushed together as he rubbed his jaw. "Look, I'm not going to get upset about it. God still sits on His throne, and for now, He's said no about this. I can accept that. It was an honor to be nominated, to have someone ask me to consider it. And the way it worked out, I was able to clear the air about some things... about you and me. I think that was a good thing. As for the rest... well, it's done. I'm not going to lose sleep over it."

Suzanna's pulse sped up, her blood heating with his every passing sentence. She met his eyes, and though his words were sincere, her anger continued to build.

"How can you say that?" She twisted in the seat to face him. "How can you just dismiss the injustice, ignore their cruelty?"

He slowed the vehicle as they neared an intersection. He would turn onto the highway, and they'd be in town in fewer than five minutes. That put them approximately fifteen minutes into their first date, and she was already upset. Not good.

Paul shifted into park after at the stop sign. He reached across the cab and brushed her jaw with his thumb. "I'm sorry this whole thing has been so hard on you." His hand dropped, and he leaned against the console between them. "I haven't dismissed the injustice, and I know they've been cruel, but it's not for me to demand restitution."

Why? If he didn't, who would?

"So, it doesn't bother you at all?"

"I didn't say that. It does bother me, mostly for you." His hand moved again, this time to wrap around hers. "But I'm not going to hang on to my mad. It doesn't do anyone any good."

Hang on to his mad? Mad clung to her like bugs splattered on her windshield. Why did he get to have a choice about it?

His stomach growled, and he squeezed her hand. "It's done, Pickle. Close it up and put it in the ground." He let go and put his thumb against the corner of her mouth. "Find that pretty smile."

He turned back to the wheel and put the truck in drive. If only she could switch gears as easily.

CHAPTER TWENTY-SIX

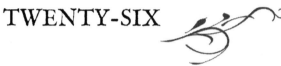

Ms. May's Café was dead. Only one other patron on this rainy November night——old Mr. Whitney who kept a hobby farm north of town. Paul held the door for Suzanna and took her coat, hanging his own beside it on the rack near the entry.

"Hey, Paul, what are doing out on this dreary night?" Alice, Ms. May's daughter, greeted them from the dining room where she was wiping down tables.

Paul scolded the heat that threatened to color his cheeks. A grown man could take a woman out for a slice a pie. Didn't need to be self-conscious about it. "Had a taste for your mama's apple pie. Have any left?"

Alice grinned. "Come on in. Sit wherever you'd like."

Paul glanced at Suzanna. She was biting the inside of her bottom lip, looking anywhere but at Alice. It was time she ended this cold war with the townsfolk.

He slid a hand to her back and moved toward the table nearest Alice. "Alice, have you met Suzanna Wilton?"

"I haven't officially." Alice left her rag on the table and wiped her hands on her apron. "I've seen you here and there but haven't had the decency to introduce myself. Forgive me. I'm Alice."

Suzanna's rigid spine gave a little. She slipped a hand forward to meet Alice's, and Paul exhaled. Progress. Progress was good.

"It's nice to meet you." Suzanna's words sounded rehearsed, like she'd said them a million times over the years.

All part of the preacher's kid gig, Paul was sure, but she wasn't fixing a blank stare or exuding cool indifference. It was a start.

"Go ahead and have a seat." Alice chirped, either ignorant of or kindly overlooking Suzanna's stiff greeting. "Can I get you some coffee to go with that pie?"

"You know me." Paul pulled a chair back for Suzanna.

Alice smiled. "Never turn a cup down."

"What about you, Suz?" Paul took the seat across from her.

Suzanna's eyes shifted from Paul to Alice. She suddenly looked more unsure than aloof, like a little girl trying to fit into a roll she wasn't comfortable with.

"Coffee would be nice." She forced a small smile. "Do you have decaf?"

Alice stepped closer to Suzanna. "Sure do. What else can I get you?"

"Do you have cherry pie?"

"You bet." Alice nodded. "À la mode? The ice cream is homemade."

Suzanna looked at Paul.

"You don't want to miss Ms. May's homemade ice cream." He winked, hoping she'd crack a real grin.

Success. Her smile bloomed, making his grow.

"Ice cream on both. Got it." Alice stepped away with a nod. "I'll be right back with your coffee."

Suzanna unrolled her napkin and fiddled with the silverware. She kept her attention on the table.

What happened? They could chat and tease like a pair of ducks on the creek when they were sitting at her kitchen table.

Why had she clammed up and gone awkward on him? His thoughts drifted back to the ride in and settled on how upset Suzanna was about the church. Upset for him, which was sweet. But it made him wish all the more he could have figured out how to prevent the whole thing.

"Why are you still single?" she asked.

Her voice hinted amazement, which made him laugh. Paul leaned against the back of his chair. Some superhero he'd turned out to be. Everything he'd dreaded had happened, and here she thought he'd done her some kind of favor.

"Seriously"—she said, folding her hands and shifting toward him—"a man like you should have been snatched up at least a decade ago."

"Thanks?" He grinned and raised an eyebrow.

"You know what I mean. Didn't you want to get married?"

Paul sighed, setting his elbows on the table and using them for support. "I did. Almost a decade ago." He felt his mouth twitch as her cheeks shaded a rosy pink. "I was engaged, actually, about eight years ago."

Suzanna's face drained of the flush he'd found enchanting, and her eyes widened with pity.

An intro like that demanded the rest of the story. She may as well know. Now was as good a time as any to tell it.

"Her name was Hailey. We dated on and off through high school. She was a couple of years younger than me, and when she went away to college, I didn't see her for several years. She came back for what she called a short-term visit, and I was ready, I thought, for something of a real commitment. We dated for almost two years, and then I proposed."

He stopped, sorting through those years. Yes, he thought he was ready, and had they married, he'd have made it work. As much as it had hurt in the midst of it all, it was for the best they hadn't. Not just because he was sitting across from Suzanna Wilton at the moment, but because he and Hailey had been a bad fit.

"What happened?" Suzanna whispered.

Paul took a pull on his water. "She called it off and moved to Denver. I found out later she'd met someone—one of those Internet match sites, which hit pretty hard. I guess she wanted to see what type of guy she'd be matched with, and it went further than she thought. She didn't have the heart to tell me about him, but it was probably a good thing she ended it when she did."

Suzanna stared, her eyes glossy and tender. "I'm sorry, Paul. I can't imagine—"

"Here we are." Alice stepped next to the table with a tray. Two slices of pie and a pair of steaming mugs settled in front of them in quick order. "Can I get you anything else?"

Paul looked to Suzanna. "You need anything?"

She shook her head, so he thanked Alice. The woman smiled and left them to their conversation.

Suzanna dug her fork into her pie. Red filling oozed over her plate, bleeding with the white of the vanilla ice cream. She blended the two, turning the concoction an appealing shade of pink. She seemed absorbed in her food. Avoiding him?

Pretty deep topics for a first date, but this wasn't a typical first date. Had he pushed her away by showing her his deepest scars? Certainly that couldn't be so. Suzanna wasn't put off by the battle scars of life—she had some of her own.

"Do you miss her?" She kept her eyes focused on her plate.

Ah, there it was. He should have guessed. Who wouldn't worry about the imprint of a first love?

"Not now." Paul took up his own fork and buried it in the pastry and hot apples. "I did the first year after she left. I spent a lot more time down at the river property. Even thought about moving. There wasn't a spot in this town that didn't hold a memory of her and me together, and I thought I'd go crazy staying here. But my sister and those kids… I learned quite a bit about love as well as pain during that time. Found out that love runs deeper."

Her eyes flickered to his. He'd hit something. She held his gaze, studying him as if she were searching for something to latch onto. She lowered her eyes, and Paul rubbed the back of his neck. It was like she wanted the more in their relationship that he longed for himself, but every time she'd creep to the threshold, something pulled her away.

"Do you ever talk to her?"

"Not since the day she said good-bye." Eight years was a long time. He'd let it go. Apparently, Hailey had too. Was Suzanna going to?

She picked at her pie and nursed her coffee. Quiet settled around their table, making Paul feel like a failure. Where was the chemistry that had kept him coming back day after day?

Oh, there was chemistry. He'd felt the energy every time they'd locked eyes, every time he brushed her skin.

He slid a hand across the table and traced her knuckles. Sparks of pleasure tingled through his fingers. Definitely chemistry. Just not conversation.

That wouldn't do.

"So…" He wove his fingers in hers.

She looked first to his hand, knitted with hers and then to his face. Those eyes softened into a cozy shade of blue, and Paul's chest expanded. He drew an easy breath before he finished his thought. "I was wondering about the picture Kelsey painted for you."

She smiled and leaned against her chair. "That was sweet of her."

"Sugar runs in the family."

Suzanna rolled her eyes, and Paul laughed. They were on the road back to normal. He rubbed his thumb along hers. Better than normal.

"I was asking about the subject she painted, not whether you liked it. What was it?"

Her smile softened. "An orchard. Cherries."

Yes, he'd gathered that from their conversation. He was asking the wrong questions and not getting anywhere in the process. "Why did she paint that?"

Suzanna set her fork down and drew her hand away. "She knew I liked orchards."

Studied horticulture. She and her dad had dreamed of an orchard. The math was coming together. Good grief, he was slow. "That's what you want, isn't it?"

She shifted in her chair. Her hands fell to her lap, and she refused to meet his eyes.

Why would she be ashamed of that?

"Suz, if that's still your dream—what you want to do—then why have we been talking about cows for the last six weeks?"

She shrugged. "I don't know. Nobody around here does anything like that. My dad didn't even try it, and it was his passion first."

Not even thirty and the woman had given up. How unacceptably sad. Hope, cut short and left frayed. How had that happened?

"People grow fruit trees here." He set his fork down and leaned against the table. "Dre has an apple tree in her backyard."

"I know, but an orchard is different." She sighed and then lifted her gaze to meet his. "It's risky. I could lose everything in a single season, and it's not like Rock Creek has the population base to make a big draw for a you-pick farm. It's just more complicated than sticking plant stock into the ground and hoping it'll produce."

Paul couldn't argue with that. Agriculture in general was way more complicated than it appeared. He didn't set a cow loose on the prairie and then turn around and sell at a profit the following year. Raising beef cattle was work. Hard work. He wouldn't doubt that growing fruit would be the same.

But he loved the work he did. There weren't many who could say that with sincerity. He knew how privileged he was to chase down a dream and live it every day.

"If you don't try, you'll never know."

Life lit her eyes for a skip of the heart before it faded, leaving her silent.

"Maybe this is what your dad wanted for you." Paul moved his chair closer to her. "He loved you. Maybe he wanted to give you an opportunity to try."

A sheen of tears suddenly covered her eyes. "If it doesn't work, that means I let him down."

He shook his head and reached for her hand again. "I think he'd have been more disappointed if you didn't give it a go."

Thought lines creased her forehead while she mashed her lips together. Paul made up his mind. He'd make this possible for her. Whatever she needed, they'd make it happen.

"You've thought about it," he said. "I know you have. Kelsey wouldn't know to paint that picture otherwise."

One side of her mouth poked upward. That was all the encouragement he needed. "Did you have a spot in mind?"

A silent laugh set her smile in full bloom, which made him grin, even if she still refused to meet his eyes.

"I'm not sure." She sipped her coffee. "I saw a couple of spots that looked promising. But the soil needs to be tested, and I'd need to get a topo map to make sure the ground isn't in a flood plain."

Paul nodded. He settled back against the chair and took a long draw of his coffee. He'd have her show him. They could go on horseback, and he'd fan that tiny spark of enthusiasm.

Alice made her way back to the table. "How is everything?"

Mr. Whitney had long since paid his bill and left the dining room to Paul and Suzanna. Paul flipped his wrist to check his watch. Five after ten. Man, time got away.

"Oh, I'm sorry, Alice." He pulled his wallet out and handed her a twenty dollar bill. "I'm sure you're ready to get home."

"No problem, Paul." She smiled. "We're glad for the business." She shuffled through some bills she kept in her apron.

Paul held up a hand. "Keep it."

Alice looked like she'd argue, but Paul stood, effectively closing the conversation. He moved to the entry to retrieve their coats and held Suzanna's open for her.

"Paul"—Alice followed them and spoke as Suzanna slid her arms through her sleeves—"I just wanted to say I'm sorry about the way things worked out at church yesterday. It wasn't right, and there are some of us who know what's really going on." She shifted her eyes to Suzanna. "We're not all blind sheep, and some of us know firsthand just exactly how sharp Shelby's tongue can be."

Paul followed Alice's attention to Suzanna. She pulled in a long breath, and her chin came off her chest. Her expression softened with gratitude, and Paul laid a hand on her back.

"Thank you, Alice." He caught her eyes again and held them, hoping she understood how much that really meant to him. For Suzanna.

Alice's soft grin had a knowing quality. She held a hand out to Suzanna and brought her into a hug after Suzanna took it. "It's nice to finally meet you. You stop on in anytime. We'll get to know each other and be fast friends, I'm sure."

Paul flashed a grateful smile. One more friend for Suzanna. Bit by bit, she'd find a place in Rock Creek. And with every little victory, Chuck's charade would become less and less effective.

CHAPTER TWENTY-SEVEN

Suzanna snapped her seatbelt as Paul pulled onto the highway. The streets were dotted with puddles, but the rain had turned to snow. White speckles drifted in the streetlights, turning the quiet town into a winterscape suitable for a Norman Rockwell painting.

She savored the tender warmth of Paul's hand on hers, but her mind wouldn't settle on that small joy or on the enchanted scene just outside the windshield. It spun like one of those crazy whirling contraptions at a theme park. She hated those rides. They always made her stomach twist into nauseating knots.

Which may explain why her stomach hurt.

Engaged. Paul had been in love, engaged, and then jilted. Was that really possible? What woman in her right mind would leave Paul Rustin?

He'd been so open about it. Which left her with guilt souring in her stomach. She had the perfect opportunity to say what she needed to say, and she'd ignored it. Why was it so hard to tell him she'd been married? She hadn't done anything wrong... well, sort of, but she hadn't been ashamed to become Jason's wife.

The words just wouldn't come out. She'd toyed with the right way to say it.

So, since you've told me, I may as well tell you; I was married. That was pathetic. *You should probably know I'm a widow.* She hated the word—it summoned images of spiders and made her feel horrible.

For the lack of the right thing to say, she said nothing at all. Her stomachache got worse. She forced her mind to something else.

"Alice seems nice." Bad switch. Paul would know jealousy when he saw it.

Paul glanced in her direction, but she couldn't make out his expression in the dark. "She is."

He turned onto the dirt road, which gave beneath the weight of his tires. Suzanna gripped the door handle, and Paul released her hand to take the wheel with both hands. The dirt had turned to greasy mud, slick and tricky to navigate. Paul leaned forward and switched to four-wheel drive as the truck swayed.

"Should I be worried?" Silly question. She already was. Fifteen miles of fishtailing through wet clay? Sheesh, what had they been thinking?

"Naw, I've driven through worse."

She could make out his grin by the flash of his teeth. Dre was right—little boys just don't grow up. She forced herself to sit back, but she couldn't remove her death grip from the handhold. Why, she couldn't figure. It wouldn't help if they went spinning off into a ditch.

She didn't pursue the topic of Alice. Paul needed to focus on keeping them between the pastures. It was probably for the best, anyway. He didn't need to know how thin her heart truly was.

"Alice went through some stuff." Paul broke the silence. "She knows a little bit about being the topic of discussion."

Awesome. She'd opened a book, and now he felt like he had to explain himself. Should she tell him he didn't have to? That her jealousy only came from a deep-rooted thorn of insecurity?

Sheesh, tell him all that and then add Jason into the mix. They'd never go on a second date.

"What happened?" She felt obligated to ask.

"She got pregnant her junior year in high school."

Screech. Didn't see that coming. That sweet woman? She'd looked so pure and unscathed. Suzanna had pictured her with Paul, and the image seemed completely wholesome. No one would have guessed either had the histories of the heathen.

Paul shifted forward as they started down a hill. The back of the truck slipped, but he righted it with practiced precision.

"She's waitressed for her mama since she was sixteen. She was always the friendly type. Some cowboy on the rodeo circuit came through town and swept her up in a whirlwind romance. Promised her the moon after he won in Las Vegas. Left her a single mom before he even made the pro circuit."

Suzanna caught the edge in Paul's voice. Couldn't blame him. Evidently scoundrels exist in all forms and in all places. Even wholesome Mayberry-type towns.

"Did she have the baby?"

Paul's hat moved with his nod. "She did. A pretty little. Named her Grace, which is what Alice longed for and should have received. Town talk struck her like a prairie rattler, and she withered from the poison. There were a few who loved on her, including her mama. Grace is sixteen now. Honor student and as sweet as they come."

And here Suzanna had been sure she'd been picked on because she wasn't local. Was she really that self-absorbed? The pain in her gut got worse.

What did Paul see in her?

"She'll be an honest friend, Suz." Paul disturbed the silence.

How did one go about making friends? With Paul, she'd done everything wrong, but here they were. Beyond him and

Dre and Kelsey, she didn't have any friends. Hadn't had any, except Jason. Just didn't come naturally.

Neither had piano, but she'd learned. Practiced—by threat of a sore backside— for years. Now she could still plunk out a recognizable version of "Amazing Grace."

Practice. A woman who named her illegitimate daughter Grace would surely be a good place to start.

Suzanna turned to Paul. "Does she drink coffee?"

He reached across the cab and rubbed her shoulder, returning her look with a proud grin. She leaned against his arm, and he stretched it further to pull her close.

The tender moment was ill timed.

The final curve before her house suddenly came within the reach of his headlights, and Paul hit the brakes, turning the wheel left. Had the road been dry, it would have been a sharp, but manageable turn. But muddy roads being what they are, the truck slid across the slime and settled in the ditch.

Suzanna's heart took to a sprint and didn't settle nearly as quickly as Paul's truck.

"You okay?" Paul spoke just above her head. She didn't realize she'd been clutching his arm until he pulled it free to wrap her with it.

She pulled in a long breath and released an equally long exhale. "I'm fine." Aside from adrenaline setting her limbs to tremble and her heart, which was still off to the races. "Are you?"

He nodded and revved the engine, but the truck didn't move. He shifted into reverse and tried again, but the tires only sent mud splattering on the windshield.

A moment skipped by in silence, and then Paul laughed. He moved away from the steering wheel, and his head dropped forward, but he kept laughing. "It's been an interesting date, hasn't it, Pickle?" ·

She pushed her hair out of her eyes and snickered. "Quite unforgettable. You do know how to show a girl a good time."

His laughter continued to bubble as he reached toward the half-seat in the back. "It's about to get better. We're stuck. I won't be able to move the pickup until the road dries." He produced a pair of rubber mud boots. "Put these on—they'll save your city-girl shoes."

"We're walking?" Suzanna tried but couldn't fake indignation. Her smile just wouldn't cut back.

He pulled a flashlight out of the console and left the cab without answering but was at her door within three seconds. He opened it and held out a hand. "Can I interest you in an evening stroll, Miss Wilton?"

Suzanna giggled while she shoved her feet into Paul's boots. They were at least three sizes too big, and they'd probably get sucked in the mud, leaving her barefooted, but it was sweet of him to think of it.

She took his hand, and he led her out of the ditch. She almost lost a boot as she climbed onto the road, but she managed, with curled toes, to keep it in place.

Snow fell with quiet determination, wet and heavy and lovely. The glow from Paul's flashlight set the white flakes sparkling, and aside from the clomping of her boots and the squishing of the mud, it was a charming stroll.

Her house came into full view, and within five minutes they'd reached her drive. Paul held the screen door open while Suzanna unlocked the solid one.

She pushed it open and stepped inside. "Are you going to come in and dry off?"

Paul followed her in but only far enough to shut the door. "Naw, I'd better keep going down the road."

Suzanna pulled her feet free from the mud-laden boots and straightened to meet Paul's gaze. "You're not walking the rest of the way home."

"It's only a mile."

She stared at him. "Take the Jeep." A grin tugged on her mouth. "It's a straight shot from here, so you should be okay."

Paul chuckled, rubbing his neck. "I don't think that's a good idea. However Chuck knows what he knows, he'll have it published by nine tomorrow morning that your Jeep stayed the night in my driveway."

Ah, the real world. The one where she and Paul weren't going to work because people in town didn't want them to. Suzanna glanced away.

"Hey..." Paul put a hand to her arm and squeezed.

Suzanna made herself look at him.

"I had a good time." Warm blue eyes took hers captive.

"Me too."

He swallowed, the heat in his gaze growing more intense. "We're pretty good friends, aren't we, Suz?"

What? He wasn't giving her the "let's just be friends" speech. How was that possible? She nodded, unable to find words, while disappointment lodged in her chest.

He settled his other hand on her shoulder. "If I kiss you, we may never be able to go back."

Her pulse began to throb as warmth spiraled inside her stomach. "That's true," she whispered.

His fingers trailed along her neck and brushed her jaw. He traced her mouth with his thumb as his head dropped closer. "I really want to kiss you though."

"I really want you to." The words tumbled out breathlessly.

His hand slid over her cheek and to her neck as he pulled her close. Her eyes closed as his mouth brushed over her lips, his kiss soft and tender.

Oh, sweet breath of pleasure. She slid her hands along his arms, following them to his shoulders. He moved a hand to her back, pulling her against his chest. Bliss warmed her limbs as he claimed her lips again.

He pulled away, leaning his head on hers. She opened her eyes and found hesitancy staring back. Fear?

He'd been rejected before.

Never, Paul Rustin.

She lifted her mouth to his, and he returned her kisses with building passion. When he pulled away again, he stepped back.

Suzanna's heart pounded as their gazes held. A smile tugged on his mouth, beckoning hers.

"Does this mean we can't be friends anymore?" She raised an ornery eyebrow.

Paul chuckled but grew serious again in the next breath. He caught her hand and pressed it to his lips. "You're my best friend, Suz." He kissed her palm again and let her go, opening the door to leave.

"Paul." She caught his arm, and he paused. "Just take the Jeep. Otherwise, I'll worry."

He looked outside and then back at her. "Keys?"

"They're in it."

He nodded and then leaned to brush a kiss against her head. "Good night."

Suzanna watched him trek back into the snowy night, mud caked up to his knees. Mud seemed to jell them. That being the case, she'd take the rain.

CHAPTER TWENTY-EIGHT

Paul finished measuring grain and lifted the bucket to take it through the first stall. The snow had cleared, and the early morning sun was chasing the remaining shadows of night across the prairie. His breath puffed white in the pale light as he whistled "Oh! Susanna," which made him chuckle on the inside. Giddy was such a happy, juvenile feeling. He'd forgotten how it tickled.

Bronco nuzzled his shoulder before he dumped breakfast in the trough. Buck nipped at the other horse, demanding first dibs. The pecking order stood. Took something pretty significant to shift the lead in a herd.

True to life. What was it going to take to turn things in town? Even if the magical vision of Chuck didn't catch the fact that Paul and Suzanna had gone out last night, which was highly unlikely, it wouldn't take too long to figure out they'd become more than neighbors, more than friends. Because Paul wasn't going to hide it.

"Morning, Paul."

He spun around. Tom strode toward him from the house.

"Didn't hear you pull up." Paul hung the feed bucket on a post and moved to hop the corral fence.

"Too busy whistling." An eyebrow arched as Tom grinned.

Paul grunted a laugh, hoping the chill of the morning air had already made his face red before the blush crept into his cheeks.

"Everything okay?" Tom shoved his hands into his coat pockets. "Saw Suzanna's Jeep out front."

"Yeah, everything's fine." Paul started to the house, and Tom fell into step. "Could use your help though. Are you heading in to work?"

"I am, but I can call in late if you need something."

Paul cleared his throat. Good grief, Tom would hang on to this one, and Paul would never live it down. "My pickup's stuck in the ditch."

Tom's eyebrows climbed up his forehead while a knowing smile spread across his face. "How'd it get there?"

Paul kept walking.

Tom chuckled. "It's been at least fifteen years since you've put anything in a ditch."

"Yeah, so?"

"Didn't have our neighbor with you at the time, did you?"

Paul took the three steps up his back porch and turned to Tom. "Are you gonna help me?"

Tom folded his arms over his chest. "Did you take her out?"

Paul rolled his eyes and tried to tuck his grin. "Good grief."

"'Bout time." Tom slapped him on the back and laughed. "Did you kiss her?"

Paul shook his head. "What are you? Fifteen?"

Tom continued to laugh, taking Paul by the shoulder and moving toward the back door. "Come on, old man. Let's get Suzanna's vehicle out of your drive before Stanton's all-seeing eye catches sight of it."

"Yeah, about that——" Paul pushed the back door open. He moved toward the front entry and snagged Suzanna's keys from the hook on the wall. "Do you know where Chuck gets his info?"

"Not sure. Dre and I were talking about that Sunday. The Hansens still lease his ground out this way, but we only see Jake pass by once a week or so."

"He's got to have something set up somewhere. Something that gives him a daily report." How bizarre. And creepy. "Which means he probably already knows about Suzie's Jeep."

"Probably." Tom sobered entirely. "It won't look good."

Suzanna's fingers fumbled over the computer keys. Her typing pace was just sad this morning. *Focus, girl. This isn't rocket science.*

Maybe if she'd slept the night before. Why did she continue to chase a futile point? What was done was done. She'd kissed Paul. Really kissed him, with every emotion she'd been fighting against for the last month. And he'd kissed her back. There wasn't a way to undo that, and she wasn't about to backpedal on it. He'd been heartbroken once. She wasn't going to be the next source of pain in his life.

She couldn't be. This was so much more than a crush on her handsome neighbor.

Her hand moved to her neck, and she tugged on her chain. Jason's ring slipped from beneath her collar, and she slid it over her finger. *I was married, Paul.*

She had to tell him. She'd slipped into his arms under false pretenses. Surely, it wouldn't change how he felt—he wasn't shallow. But he should know about it.

She blinked, realizing she'd been staring blankly at the computer screen. She'd missed at least two minutes of data. Great. Now she'd have to start over. Warning—long day ahead. The caution warranted a fresh pot of Joe. Then she'd start over.

Paul parked Suzanna's Jeep in her usual spot and hopped from the vehicle. He walked to Tom's pickup and waited for Tom to roll his window down. "Be right back. Just gonna tell Suz."

"Make it quick." Tom teased. "I don't have all day."

Paul shook his head and bumped the pickup with his fist. Good grief, how long was this going to last? Oh, just wait 'til Dre got the word. The blunt little fireball was sure to have him heated like a wood-burning stove for a good week.

Whatever. Could be worse. Scratch that—it probably was going to be worse. Seething whispers of fornication were bound to double in town. Supported by the fact that he was, indeed, smitten with the object of their scorn.

He'd handle it, but shielding Suzanna from it didn't look possible. Talk was bound to touch her, and she'd jam her little back straight and take it all on with cold anger set hard in her soul.

Pain squeezed sharp inside his chest. She sure had an armor of steel, but it wasn't who she really was deep down. If people could only see the beauty beneath. See her endearing expressions when she opened up, see the way she loved Kelsey with tender understanding. See the way pain really affected her underneath the mask of rage.

The mask needed to come off. Removed completely and destroyed.

Paul knocked on the kitchen door but didn't wait for an answer before he pulled it open. "Suz?" he called, poking his head in the entry. "Brought your Jeep back. Going to get my pickup."

She stepped in the archway that separated the kitchen from the entry, her hand clasped around whatever she kept on the end of her necklace. "Do you want some coffee first?"

"Naw." He smiled. "Tom's helping me, so I'd better get. I'll be back though."

She tucked the chain back under her collar. Something gold flashed before it disappeared. A locket? Perhaps a picture of her dad.

"Tell Tom he's welcome to stay for a cup when you're done."

"I doubt he will," Paul said. "He's bound for work."

She nodded, her little smile tickling his heart.

"Hey…" He caught her before she stepped back into the kitchen. "You look beautiful this morning."

She looked to the floor with a shy smile while her face shaded a lovely pink. Dang, if that didn't make her completely kissable. Things to do, cowboy. Things to do.

But he'd be back for some coffee and sugar.

Suzanna dove into her work with fresh energy. Who knew how long it'd take Paul and Tom to drag the truck free from the ditch, but she needed to get at least one file done before they got back. For heaven's sake, she'd be typing until dark if she didn't get something done.

Coffee with Paul had become a new normal weeks ago, but her anticipation of it now felt different. More intimate. She remembered breakfasts with Jason when they were first together, how special they felt. How it made her feel like they were family. She missed that.

And now she might have it again. With Paul. For keeps?

Please, God… I cannot beg you enough. If you're listening this time, please let me have this.

Daft woman. Hope is dangerous. It cuts to the marrow and leaves a jagged wound. Except… it hadn't with Paul. Maybe this time would be different.

Paul kicked his boots off just inside the door and cuffed his jeans so mud wouldn't flake onto the floor. He stood, inhaling deeply. Oh, Suzie's magical brew. A man could get used to that.

One date sealed it. He was definitely gone, and he was after this for keeps.

"Did you get it?" Suzanna called from the other side of the house.

Must still be working.

"Yep." He made his way through the small entry and met her as she walked into the kitchen. "Made a heck of a mess out of the ditch, but we got 'er done."

Suzanna looked him over, and a smile lit her face when her eyes reached his sock feet. "Made a mess of more than the ditch, I see."

He chuckled as she moved to the cupboard. She pulled down two mugs and carried them to her coffeemaker. Paul followed her, and wrapped his arms around her shoulders, pulling her against his chest. He felt a sigh leave her body as she rested her head against him. His eyes slid shut as he curled her closer.

"Every day for at least a month." He spoke softly against her hair.

"What?" She tipped her chin up so she could see him.

"I've sat in that chair and watched you pour coffee, wanting to do this for at least a month."

Her eyes left his face, and she stared across the kitchen, still settled against him. "I thought maybe you decided against it." Her voice drifted. "You seemed to pull away after... after the horse tank."

Paul loosened his hold and turned her by the shoulders, leaving both hands to rest against her arms. "I couldn't read you." He swallowed, waiting for her gaze to meet his. "I gave up on romance awhile ago. But with you——this is what I want. I'm sure, Suzanna. Is it what you want?"

A smile tugged on the corners of her mouth. "Yes."

Warmth flooded his core as he moved to kiss her. Years of waiting, he knew she was the one. A pickle for sure, but she made life interesting. He loved that.

Suzanna gnawed on her lip as she stared out the windshield. Paul turned onto the highway. They'd be at church in fewer than five minutes.

I'll pick you up for church in the morning.

That's what he'd said last night after dinner. She'd grilled chicken and served it with salad. Paul cleaned his plate but turned down seconds. He'd had two slices of her frosted carrot cake, devouring them as though he were still hungry.

I don't usually go in for classes. She'd tried a subtle tactic.

I think you should try. We're going through Genesis right now. It's really interesting.

What could she have said? No, she didn't want to? Truth, but it wouldn't have gone over well. Actually, the real truth was she didn't want to arrive with Paul because flaming tongues would devour any fuel in their path. And their joint arrival would be like pouring gas on a house fire. But saying that to Paul... well, he'd argue, they'd fight about it, and she'd feel terrible. She really didn't want to be at odds with him. Ever.

So, she'd shoved away the panic clawing in her throat and nodded her head. Now here they were, almost to church the first Sunday of December. Her heart raced as invisible hands closed around her neck and squeezed.

Paul, what are you doing? Don't you understand cause and effect?

He glanced her way and lifted a grin, reaching for her hand. His felt warm and rough and large, encasing her with a feeling of protection, but it wasn't herself she was most worried about.

They turned into the gravel lot, and Paul parked by Tom and Andrea's Expedition. He released her hand, killed the engine and was at her door just as her feet hit the rocks.

Shutting her door with one hand, he reclaimed hers with the other, and then started for the building.

The invisible hands squeezed tighter. She tugged her hand away.

Paul stopped walking. She met his eyes for half a breath and then shifted so she didn't have to hold the contact. "I know you like me. You don't have to do this." Her cheeks burned.

He took her hand again and held it tight. "I'm not hiding this. I'm not ashamed of you, and we've done nothing to hang our heads about."

His thumb traced her knuckles, and then he lifted them to his lips. Suzanna raised her eyes to his face, and the depth in his expression sparked an electric jolt through her system.

He loves me. Dear God, let it be true.

Joy zipped through her, making her head light. But just as the euphoria lifted, reality settled hard.

He doesn't know everything.

She dropped back to earth with a thud.

"Kiera asked me if we could go riding today." Paul flicked the blinker to turn onto the dirt road. "Do you want to come with us?"

Suzanna forced her mind to keep up with Paul. Tough to accomplish. In her head, she was still sitting in church. Joy, pastor Ron's wife, had just invited them for dinner Tuesday night, which had lured a smile to her lips. They agreed, and Suzanna had breathed in relief. Joy had moved away when whispers settled in Suzanna's ears, setting them aflame.

"About time, I'd say." Trish Calloway must have only been three rows behind them. "Hopefully, they'll set them straight, now that they've brought their rebellion out into the open."

Didn't that woman have anything else to occupy her thoughts?

"Doubt it'll help," Shelby Stanton hissed. "He's already sold himself to the Devil."

The spear hit its aim, ripping through her chest with searing pain. The wound had yet to stop throbbing.

"Pickle?" Paul squeezed her shoulder. "Do you want to ride with us?"

"No." She forced a smile. "No, thanks. That's special between you and Kiera. You should keep it that way."

He glanced her way, tender appreciation gleaming in his blue eyes. His hand slid around her, and he pulled her into his shoulder over the center console, pressing a kiss into her hair. "Will you hang out with Kelsey this afternoon?"

"Planned to after I visit with Andrea. Kelsey was going to show me how to draw Mickey Mouse." That beckoned a real grin. Ah, Kels. Such a darling friend.

Paul chuckled. "Hope Dre lets you. I'm sure she'll have plenty to visit with you about."

About today? A lump swelled in her throat. It was old. This whole thing was getting so old. She watched him, his smile still wide. That couldn't be what he meant.

Again, he looked at her. Must have read her confusion. "I haven't talked to her all week, but I'm sure she got a story from Tom on Tuesday, and she'll want details." He raised an eyebrow as though issuing a warning.

Suzanna let herself smile. "No details?"

His brow hitched higher. "That's just weird. She's my sister."

Good point. Very weird. She giggled. But the lightness vanished as quickly as it'd come. Suzanna returned her view to the endless pastures, harsh words replaying against her sore heart.

"Will she approve?" she whispered, her eyes still pinned on the view outside.

"You have to ask?" Paul slid his hand to her neck and massaged it. "She's been scheming since... well, since before I started calling you Pickle."

Since he started calling her Pickle? As far as she could tell, that was from the moment she'd breathed fire on him at their first introduction. Andrea hadn't known her then. Was he placating her?

Paul's hand shifted to her back, and he rubbed small circles over her spine. Her silence must have shouted her doubts. "Honestly, Suz, my family adores you. You have nothing to worry about."

She leaned into his touch, trying to absorb confidence from it. Nothing to worry about? *How will they feel when I finally tell you all of my story?*

CHAPTER TWENTY-NINE

The December sun sank toward the western horizon, its orange rays bouncing light off the dusting of snow covering the pasture. Suzanna gave a light tug on the reins, and Sugar came to a halt. She let her eyes drift over the rolling hills, white and clean, and a smile lifted her cheeks. Inhaling, she let her eyelids slide shut, and something lovely and warm glimmered in the deep part of her soul. The part that was normally dark and cold.

Did love do that? She'd loved Jason with all her heart—loved him since they'd been little more than children. But it didn't feel like this.

It could be because of Paul, who sat astride Bronco a few yards ahead. She'd known she was tumbling into that same place with him for weeks now. Could love for this man feel so different—like this? Like light was calling her, whispering *draw near.*

In this moment, this beautiful foreign feeling spoke to those depths. Not with a language heard by her ears, but one discerned in the caverns of her heart.

Draw near and find life...

Lightness filled her being as though the law of gravity had been shattered. Was this love? *Dear God, if it is, don't take it away.*

Suzanna inhaled again and opened her eyes. Though the idea was unfathomable, she expected to be floating in the purity of a light not known to man.

The sun neared the land beyond, its hues growing more intense as it bid the day farewell. She was still grounded on the earth, sitting in a saddle with her land sprawling before her. Disappointment pulled her chest in but didn't plunge her to despair. The echo of that voice still whispered in her heart.

Draw near...

"I love that about you, Pickle." Paul sat, leaning against the saddle horn, watching her. "You don't miss an opportunity to savor God's creation. It is a marvel, isn't it?"

Is that what she'd been doing? That voice—was it the voice of—surely not. God hadn't wanted anything to do with her. Ever.

God loves you, Suzie doll. Daddy's voice had sounded more like a plea that day at the park.

No sir, she'd thought, He doesn't love me at all.

Suzanna silenced the memory. "It is beautiful."

Paul's smile widened as he turned his mount back toward the creek. "Show me the place."

"What place?"

"You said you had somewhere in mind to plant an orchard. I want to see it."

Back to that? He was relentless, but it was nice. She turned Sugar south, and they rode until they were nearly halfway between her house and the creek.

"Right here. If I'm allowed to use some water from the creek, it would be easy to irrigate, and the small slope faces north, which would be good so the plants don't bloom too early."

Paul dismounted and held a hand out to her. She slid to the ground and accepted his offer. Leaving the horses, they walked into what she envisioned as her orchard.

"I can see it," he said, his eyes grazing the scene. "Kelsey's picture come to life right here. Not just cherries, but apples, maybe some peaches, right? It'll be beautiful, Pickle."

"How did you know that?"

He leaned down near her hair and inhaled. "You smell like apples. When you picked over at Dre's last month, you looked like you'd died and gone to heaven. And the peaches—well, for your dad, right?"

Warm laughter tickled in her chest. How well he understood her.

"Tell me what you need." Paul pivoted to face her, his face bright with excitement. "Whatever it is, we'll get started. Test the soil, plow the rows. When you're ready, we'll plant them. One by one, we'll set their roots in the ground."

His enthusiasm rushed over her like a long-awaited rain on the hot, dry prairie. It overwhelmed her, amazed her. "Why would you do all that? Maybe it's just a silly dream."

He tugged on the hand he still had wrapped in his own, drawing her close. His lips brushed over her forehead, and then he framed her face with both of his work-roughened hands. "It's not a silly dream. It's your beautiful dream, and I'll work with you to make it happen. Because I want to."

His thumb traced her mouth, and his eyes narrowed as he leaned in close. His voice dropped soft and quiet. "Because I love you."

She forgot how to breathe. Electricity tingled over her as she moved to meet his mouth. His gentle kiss lingered, and she leaned into him. Desire plunged them deeper, and she clung to him as he held her tight.

The sun had met the land far off by the time he slowly pulled away. Breathless, he rested his forehead against hers, his hat tipping back. She opened her eyes to find his still closed, though a tender smile crinkled the skin near the corners.

"God, thank you for Suzanna Wilton." His deep whisper rasped husky. "I'd stopped believing, but You knew all this time."

Was that true? Did God know? Did He care? A new longing took hold. Who was this God Paul knew so well?

Paul opened his eyes, their blue depths confirming his proclamation of love. A fresh ripple of joy tumbled through her. Maybe that was enough.

He brushed another kiss across her lips before claiming her hand. They returned to the horses and rode along the creek bank as it curved around the house.

"Whoa." Paul tugged Bronco to a stop and squinted into the trees before he turned to face her. "Have you given anyone permission to hunt?"

"Huh?"

He came off his saddle. "Has anyone stopped and asked to hunt on your property?"

Hunting? We went from *that* kiss to hunting? Must be a country boy thing. "No."

He moved to a tree, looking up the trunk with curious intent. "Did your dad hunt?"

"Don't know." She dropped from her saddle. "Why?"

Paul looked over at her and then back up the tree. "There's a trail cam up there. A nice one."

Trail cam? What was that?

"Come here." He waved her over and then squatted. "Climb on my shoulders. You should be able to reach it."

"It's not mine. Are you sure we should bother it?"

He took off his hat. "If it's not yours, then someone is poaching. It's illegal to hunt on private property without permission."

Suzanna sat on his shoulders, and he stood. She reached for the box strapped to the tree trunk and unsnapped it, then handed it down to Paul. In one smooth motion, he knelt back down, and she returned to the ground. "I don't understand. What does this have to do with hunting?"

Paul looked from the box in his hand to the tree and back again. "Maybe nothing. That was set up too high for deer."

She rolled her eyes. "Paul, *what is* it?"

"A video camera." He pushed his hat back over his hair. "Hunters use it to gauge activity in an area. To see if there are any deer."

A video camera? A *video* camera? Suzanna glanced over her shoulder in the direction the box had faced. Her house sat in plain view.

Chuck. She felt violated. Every time she'd been home, every moment she'd been outside, she'd been watched. For how long?

Paul stepped closer, his hand on her elbow. "Have you noticed anyone coming by on a regular basis?"

"You, Tom, and Dre, and that white pickup that passes about once a week."

"The Hansen boys." He frowned. "They lease Chuck's land."

Suzanna looked up to his face. "But I never see them stop here."

"Did you notice my pickup parked behind the tree line a few Sundays ago?"

"What?" Her voice climbed an octave.

His cheeks darkened. "I waited for you after I knew what Chuck was saying. That's why we got to church at the same time. Did you see me?"

"What on earth?" She scowled. "Do all country boys go through some kind of spy class in high school?"

"Not necessary. We've been hunting since we were six. Keeping out of sight is part of the gig."

Cute. She has some Peeping Tom keeping tabs on her, and the man who'd just declared love for her was making light of it. She glared at the box in his hand and then stomped away.

"Suzanna"—he came after her—"I'll deal with this." Paul pulled her to a stop.

"I'm coming with you."

He looked down at her, his face dark under the brim of his hat. "Don't think so, Suz."

"What?" Fury buzzed in her head. "Why not?"

Paul sighed, his hand clasping her shoulder. "I told you. This is all they know of you in town."

"What does that mean?"

"Name three people who've seen you smile. Tell me who, other than my family, has had the pleasure of a calm, friendly conversation with you?"

She crossed her arms over her chest and glared. This was helpful? Never mind that he was right. There were good reasons for it. Namely, they were *mean*. Whose side was he on, anyway?

He took her by the other shoulder and stepped closer. "Hon, listen." He rubbed her arms as though that should settle her anger. "I know. I really do. You haven't been treated fairly. Chuck's been as nasty as a blind rattler. Even if you're justified in your anger, if you go and unleash, no one will ever see past it. Your reaction will mark you, for better or for worse." He lifted a hand and ran his knuckles over her cheek. His voice dropped to a whisper. "Please. Let it be for the better."

How did he posses the power to disarm her? Better question, why did he bother? He should be wrapping his arms around some sweet woman with a gentle heart. He didn't deserve her soured spirit.

Tears dropped from her eyes as she hung her head. She was unworthy of this man's love, and yet he poured it over her, protected her. Not only from the slanderous meanies in town, but from herself, from her lack of good judgment.

He gathered her in his arms, his cold Carhartt coat smelling like the outdoors and hay and horse. Like Paul. She snuggled into his chest and secured her arms around him.

He loved her and made her feel it with every touch, every word.

And yet, she knew no peace.

Paul pulled into town with steam ready to billow from his ears. *Spying? What the heck, Chuck?*

He didn't let Suzanna see the full extent of his anger—she didn't need any fuel to add to her already massive bonfire—but he was blazin' mad. He took the trail cam home to check, just in case it had been Mike's, and he'd jumped to some irrational conclusions. Nope. The disk was new. That skunk had set an eye on her. The creep.

The bank would have just opened. Paul hoped Stanton was in, and that he wasn't in a meeting. Hope? Naw, that's the wrong word. Stanton would rearrange his day for this. Paul would see to it.

He marched across the marbled lobby and past the reception area, letting himself in Chuck's office.

"What, Olivia?" Stanton snapped. "I just got here. What couldn't wait until I'd at least had a cup of coffee?" He looked up, and his face registered surprise.

Paul glared from his spot at the door.

"Come in, Rustin." Chuck recovered, sitting straight and meeting Paul's stare with one of his own. "Do we have something to discuss today?"

That smug face. Does he know how quick I can take down a 200-pound calf?

Paul marched across the room and didn't stop until he was leaning over Chuck, who was still sitting in his oversized, leather desk chair.

"Recognize this?" He slammed the trail cam against the desk, cracking the lens.

Chuck glanced at the box and then swallowed.

"Thought you might. Thought you'd want it back. I looked it up." Paul whistled. "That baby wasn't cheap." He picked it up, opened the back, ripped the disk out and then dropped the camera on the floor. It clattered against the marble, cracking the casing.

Smacking the disk on Chuck's desk, Paul bent until he was right in the other man's face. "You won't want to miss this week's recording. I kissed her. Right out there in the pasture.

Good and long, because I love her. I'm sure you can spin something scandalous out of that."

Chuck's eyes widened, his smirk momentarily replaced by a flash of fear. His arrogance returned in the next breath though. He stood, pushing Paul out of his space. "You think this means something, Rustin?"

"The game's up, Stanton." Paul stepped closer. "You lose. She's not leaving, and you've run out of leverage."

Chuck held Paul's gaze, his eyes cold and unyielding. "I don't lose. Ever."

"Let it go," Paul growled. "Just let it go."

CHAPTER THIRTY

Suzanna pulled the cookie tray from the oven. Ginger and nutmeg drifted to her nose, and she closed her eyes as she inhaled. Ah, warmth and... Nope. Not peace. Bummer. But it did smell good.

Where was peace? Why did it elude her? Paul loved her, stood up for her. As far as she could tell, had taken care of the Chuck issue. Still, her heart felt as restless and as abandoned as ever. Perhaps peace was only an illusion, something poets wrote about, but no one ever possessed.

No, that couldn't be right. Paul had peace. Said so. Lived so. She saw it every time she gazed into those wonderful blue eyes. Dare she ask him?

That would mean telling him she still didn't have peace. He'd be disappointed like Jason had been. Jason had believed they were on the same page, believed the same things. Maybe she had at one point, but the loving God thing didn't ring true. She couldn't understand why Jason still believed it after everything they had gone through.

Maybe he'd had to believe. In the dwindling glimmer of his life, he'd had to believe in a God who cares. What other option did he have?

This was why she couldn't have peace. She relived the past every single day. It clung to her like the ring dangling on the chain around her neck. To take it off would be to betray Jason's love, but wearing it kept her from having peace.

An engine rumbled outside the kitchen window, drawing Suzanna from her gloomy thoughts. Suzanna hoped Paul liked gingerbread cookies. They weren't as sugary as his normal fare, but Jason had loved them, and they were one of very few things that stirred her sweeter memories.

Except, perhaps not today.

Paul slipped inside Suzanna's side door, the smell of cookies filling his nose. *Gingerbread.* So good. "Hey, beautiful," he called, "are you baking cookies for me?"

Suzanna appeared in the kitchen, her grin complemented by a lovely rose tint on her cheeks. Paul stamped his boots and wiped the snow from his pant legs, eager to kiss the cook.

"Christmas has done passed us by." He slipped an arm around her waist and pulled her into his side. "What's the occasion?"

She shrugged and then snuggled into him. "Just sounded good on a snowy day. Work's slow. I was done with the morning data by eight."

Paul smiled, mentally placing her in his house, as his wife. His grandmother's ring flashed through his mind. He'd intended to take a knee and slip it over her finger on Christmas day, but something deep and strong said no. Maybe just not yet. Neither made a whole lot of sense because he knew she was the one—except that perhaps it was too soon. For Suzanna. She had yet to say that magic phrase.

Brushing away the little sting that came every time he thought about that small disappointment, Paul bent to capture her lips. She leaned up to him, welcoming his kiss as always. It felt like "I love you." She just didn't say it was all.

Molasses and sugar lingered on her mouth, tasting so much better, he was quite sure, than any cookie. He combed his fingers through her hair and trailed them down her neck. His thumb caught on the chain she wore. Pulling away only enough to see her clearly, he gave the necklace a gentle tug.

"You always wear this," he said. "What is it?"

Her hand flew from his chest to her neck, catching the piece of metal before he could make it out. Panic flashed in her eyes, and she drew away from his touch.

Paul's head began to swim. What was she hiding? "Suz?" He reached to touch the hand she had clasped around her trinket. His heart kicked, sending a tremor of pain through his core when she cowered away.

She drew a long breath and then met his gaze. Her look begged him for... something. Forgiveness? He clasped her hand, rubbing his thumb over her knuckles.

"It's my wedding ring," she whispered.

Paul froze. He couldn't breathe, couldn't move. His chest felt suddenly heavy, like he'd been pinned under one of his bulls, and his hands began to shake. He tried to swallow past the swelling in his throat.

"You're married?" *Dear God. I'm in love with a married woman.*

His heart hammered against his ribs as he tried to draw a calm breath.

"Was, Paul."

Dropping his hand, he backed away. "Where's your husband?" His low tone was dark, and she shrank farther away.

Tears dropped onto her cheeks. "He died."

Paul shut his eyes, trying to process what she'd just said. She'd been married. Widowed,

and she hadn't told him about any of it. He opened his eyes, fixing them on her. "But you go by Wilton, same as your dad."

She wouldn't look at him. "It was easier."

Easier? Lying was easier? His blood turned cold as the betrayal sank deep. "Were you gonna tell me?"

"Yes." Her voice wobbled.

"When?"

She still wouldn't meet his gaze. What else was she hiding? How could she not tell him about this?

"Paul, I didn't know we'd end up here."

Anger swirled in his gut and burned in his chest. No wonder she never said those words—she was still in love with another man. "We've been *here* for a while. I told you everything about me. Everything, Suzanna. How could you hide this from me?"

She sniffed, reaching for his hand. "I didn't know how to tell you."

He moved away from her touch.

"Please, Paul. I love you. Please don't reject me now."

I love you. He'd ached to hear those words from her lips. Every time he'd whispered them to her, he'd felt a needle pierce his chest when she didn't echo the bond. *Now* she said them? Hailey had done that, used those words to manipulate him.

Please, Paul. I love you. I just want to be with you. We don't need to spend so much time with your family. Please, Paul, I love you. I want us to have a new life. Not here. Let's start over, just you and me somewhere far away.

"Don't do that." He nearly growled. "Don't tell me that now, like this."

"Paul"—she choked on a sob, wrapping her arms around herself—"I do love you. I know I should have told you. It's been killing me, but I couldn't get it out."

Confusion slithered around his heart. It hurt. The squeeze nearly made him vomit. He needed to get away, needed to think. Walking to the door, he passed her as another sob trembled through her frame. He stopped short of leaving, raising a hand to lean against the door frame.

God, I can't think. Everything hurts, and I can't think straight. She sniffed, and he closed his eyes. Suzanna didn't often cry. She got mad when pain struck at her heart, and this ache may be why. It ran deeper than he'd ever imagined.

"How 'bout now?" He dropped his hand and turned back to her, his voice hoarse.

Her eyes finally met his, begging him to understand.

He took a step toward her. "Can you tell me about it now?"

Another cry shook her frame, but she nodded. Paul pulled a chair from the table and held it until she sat. He sat across from her and then stared at his hands in his lap.

The moment had come. It was more horrible than she had feared. Never would she forget the horror on his face. *You're married?* Why hadn't she told him? Her silence had made things so much worse.

Wiping her face with the sleeve of her sweatshirt, Suzanna cleared her throat. "My name is Suzanna Korine Cumberland." She drew a ragged breath. "I was married for almost six years."

His brows pushed up. "You were young."

"Very." She swallowed. "I was eighteen. He was twenty."

"What was his name?"

"Jason." She closed her eyes, and Jason's face lingered in her memory. So different from Paul's. Jason had been shorter, his skin darker, and his thick hair nearly black, but their characters were well matched. Paul would have liked her husband. They shared a common steadiness and a good heart.

"We met when I was fourteen." Suzanna drew a breath. "Jason came from a rough home. His dad left when he was too little to remember. His mom is a meth junkie. He lived in an apartment next to a young couple from our church. Mr. Larson would see Jason out on the lawn with a baseball and go play catch with him. He invited him to church once, and Jason came every Sunday after that. He was a baseball player—a good one, and Mr. Larson and Daddy worked out some kind of scholarship so he could come to our school. They won state both his junior and senior years in high school, and he had scholarship offers from four colleges. He chose the University of Northern Colorado because it was close."

"To you, you mean?" Paul asked.

Suzanna nodded. "He had a hard time when he transferred to our school. It was a different group—you know, a bunch of church kids, and his background made him stick out."

"And so you befriended him."

"Sort of, but it wasn't really like that. We were both the odd ducks. I was the pastor's kid, and he was the drug addict's kid. Anyway, we became close. He graduated a year before I did, but he knew what life was like at my house. He didn't want to be far away.

"His freshman year in college went perfectly. He was an all-academic student athlete, and he led his conference in RBIs. Everything was going well until he started feeling off during the summer. He thought he'd caught a bug, maybe West Nile, until he went to training camp in August. They were fielding grounders, throwing them in from left field, and his arm suddenly snapped. It was a throw he'd made a million times, but his bone just snapped in half."

Paul's shoulders slumped. "Cancer?"

"Leukemia."

Paul's eyes settled on her, the warmth slowly returning to his expression. "So you married him."

"Yes"—she looked to her hands as her face burned—"but we were already basically living together." Tears began to roll again as she relived their first night together.

"I'm sorry, Suzie." Jason buried his face in the pillow. "It's my fault. I'm so sorry."

She traced his shoulder and then combed her fingers through his hair. "Don't say that, Jase. I love you, and I know you love me. This is where I want to be."

His head came up, and his face hovered over her, guilt dulling his eyes. "You should go home, Suzie. This isn't right."

"Please, Jason." Tears slipped from the corners of her eyes. *"Please let me stay with you. There's nothing for me at home."*

He traced the wet trails on her face, his expression torn. Slowly, he pulled her into his shoulder, and she clung to the comfort with every bit of her strength.

Suzanna couldn't look at Paul. "Jason felt guilty about it. We knew it wasn't right, but he loved me—wanted me. My home life was a cold existence. My mom left us. My sister and I never got along, and my dad… he just sank. Jason was all I had."

Paul remained still. His silence felt like disappointment. Like rejection. She was losing him because she wasn't who he'd thought she was. The ache surged straight to her soul.

He stood up, turning his back to her, and walked to the door. Was he leaving? He groaned, moved back to the middle of the kitchen and laid both palms against the counter. This was tearing him up. She'd known it would. Did he understand how dark her world had been? Did he know how much she hurt?

Paul returned, dropping back into his chair. "What happened?"

"We tried chemo, but the cancer came back. Doctors said his best chance was a bone marrow transplant, but finding a match took awhile. When they did, it wasn't exact, but they still said it was his best chance. His body rejected it."

Paul slouched forward, leaning his elbows against his knees. "When did he die?"

The last of her tears dried against her face. "Two years ago September."

Silence sat heavy between them. Waiting for Paul's reaction twisted Suzanna's insides.

He hung his head, both hands rubbing over his hair. "Do you still love him?" He didn't raise his face to hers until the question was out.

Her heart squeezed until it was hard to breathe. How could he possibly understand? "I'll always love him, Paul."

She couldn't read his eyes. They seemed stormy but not angry. Hurt and yet tender.

"Is that why you can't love me?"

"Oh, Paul." The tears turned on again. "I do love you. Have since the day you pulled me out of the mud."

"You never say it."

She looked to her hands and twisted them in her sweatshirt. "I couldn't... because I hadn't told you everything."

Frustration darkened his eyes. She'd waited too long to tell him, making it all the more difficult. He stood and began pacing again.

"You don't believe me, do you?" She felt like a tiny, helpless mouse caught in a trap.

He faced her. "Why would I think you made that up?"

"No." She stood, edging closer to him. "I meant you don't believe I love you."

His shoulders sagged, and his expression softened. "I don't understand, Suz. I'm trying, but I don't understand how you could love me and yet not be honest with me."

Silent cries shook inside her chest. She couldn't stand the look of betrayal on his face, so she shut her eyes. She felt his hand on her arm, his touch tentative. He stepped closer and wrapped her in an uncertain embrace, one that felt more like a good-bye than forgiveness.

"I'm sorry you went through something so heartbreaking," he whispered against her hair.

Clinging to him, she buried her face in his flannel shirt, but he didn't tighten his arms. *God in heaven, please don't take him away. Help him forgive me. Please, God, don't let me lose him too.*

Paul straightened, dropping his arms. The move made her heart rip. He was leaving. Saying good-bye.

"I need to think, Suzanna." He lifted her chin, forcing her eyes to his face. "I just need some time to think. Okay?"

No. It wasn't okay. Her throat was too thick for words. She gripped his hand, desperate for his loving touch.

He brushed at her tears with his fingers and leaned to graze her forehead with his lips. His voice quivered as he whispered against her skin, "Just give me some time."

CHAPTER THIRTY-ONE

Suzanna slipped onto a bar stool in Andrea's kitchen, not able to paint a happy face over her heartache. "Does Paul usually go to the river property this time of year?"

Andrea stacked cookies on a plate and set them on the island counter before she sat across from Suzanna. "It's a little early, but moving the cattle to a closer pasture for calving is typical." She pushed the plate closer to Suzanna and leaned on an elbow. Silence buzzed between them, and Andrea's furrowed brow deepened. "What's going on, Suz?"

He didn't tell them. Paul wasn't the gossiping type, but telling his sister didn't seem like gossip to Suzanna. It seemed like… counsel. They'd find out, anyway, especially if Paul decided he couldn't handle it.

A wave of nausea passed over her, and Suzanna dropped her head in her hand. "I haven't been completely honest, Andrea."

Sitting still, listening calmly, Andrea waited.

"I was married. My husband died"—the words rushed out—"and I didn't tell Paul until Tuesday."

Andrea leaned in, her expression nothing short of gut-felt sympathy. "What happened?"

Hot tears threatened to spill over, but Suzanna sniffed them back. "Paul asked about the chain I always wear." She pulled the ring from beneath her shirt collar. "I have my wedding ring on it. So, I finally told him. He's upset because he told me everything—about Boys Town and Hailey—all of it, but I hadn't told him about Jason."

She fingered the ring, drawing a shaky breath. "I knew I should, but I couldn't make the words come out. When he left Tuesday, he said he needed to think. Then he stopped by yesterday and said he was going south. Wasn't sure when he'd be back. Something told me this was out of the ordinary."

Andrea's eyes glazed, though something like disappointment lurked behind her compassionate tears. She stood, wrapping her arms around Suzanna's shoulders. "I'm sorry." She tightened her hold. "I'm so sorry, Suzanna. Will you tell me about Jason?"

Where was the anger? She hadn't been truthful. She'd hurt Andrea's brother deeply. Why was she so kind?

Andrea took her silence as a no. "Does it still hurt too much to talk about it?"

Sort of. But for more reasons than the death of her husband. Suzanna swallowed and cleared her throat. "No, it was just easier to start over as Suzanna Wilton. Easier not to have to explain my life and my decisions. Easier to let it stay in the past." *Really? Is that where it all stayed?*

"I can understand that." Andrea scooched her stool closer and sat near enough to keep an arm on Suzanna's back.

Her touch, though warm and loving, felt odd.

"I've hurt Paul." Tears swam over her vision and she huddled to herself, trying to keep her broken heart inside. "I don't think he can forgive me."

Andrea rubbed her back. "You know better than that."

Paul's face flashed through her mind—betrayed and then distant. No, she didn't know better. She knew reality. She leaned forward, running her hands over her face before she peeked at Andrea. "He looked like I'd shoved scissors into his chest. And when he left on Wednesday, he didn't … didn't kiss me good-bye."

Andrea leaned back and moved her hand to cover Suzanna's. "Here's the thing about my brother, Suz. He's human. He's a wonderful man and has outgrown a lot of his flaws, but not all of them. Insecurity, particularly with a woman he's let close to his heart, is a tender sore that is easily aggravated. Give him time."

How much time? He'd left indefinitely. What was she supposed to do, supposed to think while he was gone? Hope had once again proven itself to be an agonizing traitor. Was she supposed to continue writhing within its grip?

"I think it's time to go back to Colorado." Suzanna talked more to her hands than to Andrea. "I can't stay here. It'll be too hard—for everyone."

Andrea breathed a small laugh through her nose. "Don't jump ship because of a small clap of thunder. Wait this one out, Suz. Paul's got some scars too. When pressed just so, they still hurt. Give him some time."

Okay, so maybe it would take more than a couple of days, but every hour of silence felt like forever.

What did Paul feel? Besides betrayed, what was he wrestling with?

"Did he love her?"

"Hailey?" Andrea looked out the window. Her silence stretched as contemplation played over her expression. "I don't know how to answer that for sure without giving you the wrong impression. Paul wouldn't have proposed to a woman he didn't care about, but he wasn't like the way he is with you. This isn't going to make sense, but he wanted her to be the future he'd planned. When she left, it was the loss of those plans, and rejection in general, that hurt more than the pain of broken love."

"Are you saying he was settling?" That didn't make sense. At all.

Andrea tipped her head to look at Suzanna. "I'm saying they were both settling. They didn't fit together. Paul seemed to think it would just all work out. Hailey discovered Paul wasn't going to change. They wouldn't have worked. They wanted different things, different lives. Neither one was willing to drop those desires to see to the other's happiness. They didn't love each other like that."

Paul Rustin? Must have been a different man. Suzanna stared across the kitchen, trying to imagine a lesser version of Paul. Wasn't possible.

"He loves you, Suz." Andrea spoke as if she knew Suzanna's unvoiced musings. "You got to him the first day you met. He came here that morning all frayed around the edges because you'd stood up to him. Granted, it was undeserved, but Paul doesn't get frayed often. There's more at work here than boy meets girl. God has plans for the two of you. I know it. So, give it time. He'll be back."

Hope again. Darn pest. Persistent as a thirsty mosquito. If only she could smack the thing dead.

Then what? Peace? Foolish notion. Peace fills. Without hope, she'd be completely empty.

Paul stretched his back before he poured a mug of fresh brew. Out of habit, he inhaled the bold scent. Wasn't Suzie's. The sore spot in his chest kicked out a fresh fissure of pain. *Homesick.* Yep. For the Pickle.

He forced his feet across the old carpeted floor and out the front door, grabbing his Carhartt coat on the way. Trading the mug from hand to hand, he pushed his arms through the sleeves and dropped onto the porch swing. The cold, dark night draped around him, offering only an empty chill rather than familiar comfort.

His cattle had looked at him about like his foreman had when he showed up yesterday morning.

You're about six weeks early, boss. What are you doing here?

Probably wasn't hard to figure out. The last time he'd landed here out of the ordinary had been at the doings of a woman. Same song, second verse.

No, not at all the same song. Heartaches come in different tunes, different keys, different depths. And this one had plunged deeper than he'd thought possible.

She'd lied. Suzanna Wilton was not Suzanna Wilton, and by all indications, she wasn't ever going to tell him about her marriage on her own. How could he reconcile that? Thus far, he wasn't having any luck with it. Didn't change the fact that he loved her with every corner of his heart, which, at the moment, smarted pretty good. Love and trust were supposed to go together. Right now, they were at war.

If it were possible to pick a side, which one would he want to win?

A vehicle rumbled past the southern tree line, and a pair of headlights flashed upon his home. People only showed up at this house on purpose. Paul shoved a lid on his internal battle, wondering what Cal wanted.

The engine cut as soon as it stopped in the drive, and a door slammed. Paul stood and moved to flip on the porch light. Pushing the door open, he paused when he caught sight of Tom heading for the front porch steps.

Tom stopped at the top and shoved his hands in his coat pockets. He didn't say a word, but his look said it all.

"Dre sent you." Paul said flatly.

"She's worried about you."

Paul puffed a small laugh, rubbing the back of his neck. "So I guess that means she's talked to Suz."

Tom nodded. Paul pulled on the screen door, and Tom followed without the need for an invitation.

"Coffee's fresh." Paul waved toward the small kitchen.

Again, Tom nodded and then moved to fill a mug. Paul sat in an overstuffed chair in the front room and waited until Tom returned to sit in the middle of the worn couch. Awkwardness filled the room like a sudden chill from a northern gust of wind.

Paul leaned his elbows against his knees. "So... what did she say?"

"Suzanna?"

Paul nodded.

Tom leaned back. "That she'd been married, and her husband died of cancer two years ago. That she hadn't told you until earlier this week, and you were pretty upset."

Well, that was the *Reader's Digest* version.

"Dre thinks I'm being ridiculous, making too much out of it, doesn't she?" Because, really, he was. And this wrestling match he had going on inside was undoubtedly killing Suzanna. Why couldn't he just accept the whole deal and move on? Offer the comfort he knew she longed for and promise forever like he'd intended to in the first place. Why was that so hard?

"No." Tom held a steady expression. "No, she doesn't think that at all. Like I said, she's worried about you. Both of you. I'm not here to fetch you back. Just wanted to make sure you're okay."

Silence settled again. Tom had been his best friend for more than twenty years. He shouldn't have been surprised to see him pull up, to have him sitting here now, waiting to hear whatever Paul needed to say.

"I know she didn't mean to lie to me"——the words tumbled out of his mouth, taking him by surprise——"but it felt like a gut shot to hear her say she'd been married."

Tom took a sip of his coffee. "She probably should have told you awhile back. I imagine it's just not the kind of thing that sits on the tip of your tongue."

Paul's eyes slid shut, and the horrible moment replayed.

It's my wedding ring.

He felt like puking all over again.

"The thing about it isn't just that she didn't tell me. It's that she's been married. I wanted her only ever for myself. Now I know she's been with another man, loved another man."

He looked at Tom, certain that he would be disappointed in him, because he was disappointed in himself. It was selfish. True, but selfish. He dropped his gaze and wiped a hand over his face.

"That's gonna be a tough one to wrestle down." Tom spoke with a quiet hint of understanding.

"What if Andrea had come to you that way. Would you have had a hard time with it?"

Tom pulled in a long breath and set his mug on the coffee table. "I came to her that way."

Paul's emotions seemed to fall to the floor. What did Tom just say? He had been the straightest arrow of any of their peers, and he'd had a tender spot for Paul's little sister for, well, almost forever. It went from a teenage crush to full-blown love in a matter of weeks after Dre had finished college. How could Tom mean what Paul had understood?

"You weren't the only one tangled up in rebellion, Paul." Tom's voice brought him out of confusion. "I just wasn't as brazen with mine. Trust me when I tell you Dre had a pretty hard time with it—and not just for a little while. Even a couple of years into our marriage, she struggled with insecurity."

Good heavens. Things were definitely not as they appeared. Paul had only seen them happy. The perfect couple blessed with the perfect marriage.

Tom cleared his throat. "Dre thought maybe it'd be too awkward for you to talk to her about this, but she wondered if it wasn't part of your struggle."

Paul rubbed his hair. Yeah, talking to Dre would be weird. Really, really weird. But part of him wished she were sitting here now. "What did she do?"

"Love keeps no record of wrong." Tom shifted against the couch. "That was her anchor, and she stayed by it. Doesn't really apply to your situation per se, but that passage is loaded. Love is a high calling, and not an easy one at that."

Love... bears all things, believes all things, hopes all things, endures all things. Love never fails.

God, I'm failing now. I know the right reaction. I know it, but I don't feel it.

That was the thing about emotion. It didn't always lead true. Could lead to disaster. Wasn't that the reason he wouldn't let Suzanna confront Chuck? Because her anger —her emotions—wouldn't serve her well?

So, there it was. The right answer. Move on. Love her and let the past rest. Why, then, did he still feel miserable?

Suzanna rubbed her temples, wishing away the throbbing pain. Sleep would have helped. But just like Paul, it had left her for five days. Oh, it taunted her here and there. She'd drift off, only to wake up more tired and restless after a couple of hours. Teasers. Kind of like Paul's short texts.

Hey Suz. Thinking of u 2day.
Morning Suz. Praying 4 u 2day.
Miss u.

He missed her? *Then come home.* Why would he stay away so long unless he couldn't forgive her? If he couldn't forgive her, then why did he keep her hanging on?

A strong surge of anger made her head hurt worse. She should have left. Wait? For what? To sit on a wire while Paul dabbled in indecision? She'd been widowed. Where was his compassion? Where was the man she thought she'd fallen in love with? Not here and apparently not down on the river property, either. The Paul Rustin she loved had a bigger heart, a kinder spirit. The Paul Rustin she loved was not the man torturing her right now.

Suzanna ripped her earbuds out and slammed her fists against her keyboard. Her wrist bone smacked the desk, and the impact raced along her nerves all the way up her arm.

Ouch. *Sheesh, Suzanna. No wonder the man can't decide.*

Anger dissolved into tears. She wished she had just stayed mad.

CHAPTER THIRTY-TWO

Paul's cell phone chirped before he remounted Buck. After double-checking the gate he'd just closed, he checked the ID—Dre—not Suzie. She didn't respond to his texts. Hadn't tried to call him once. Where was she?

He should call her, but every time he pulled his phone out and started to pushed *Send*, he pictured her face before he'd left. A mask of stone. He couldn't handle that kind of detachment over the phone. He wouldn't be able to tell if anger or hurt chilled her voice without looking at her.

They needed to talk face-to-face. Which meant he needed to go home, but he'd started a job and didn't intend to leave it half done. One more day's worth of work, and he could take off.

He answered Dre's call just before it went to voice mail, expecting her to ask when he was coming back.

"Hey, Dre. I've got a couple more pastures to ride tomorrow, and then I'll be done." He pulled himself up into the saddle.

"Paul, you need to be done today." Panic animated her voice.

His stomach twisted. What had Chuck done now? "Is Suz okay?"

"It's not Suzanna. It's Daddy." She stopped, tears cutting her voice short. "I'm on my way to the hospital now. You need to come."

Suzanna parked her Honda on the street across from the school and stared out the windshield. How do you tell three little kids their grandpa had been rushed to the hospital?

Is he dead? They would ask. Suzanna didn't know. She hadn't heard from Andrea in a couple of hours. It didn't sound good though.

Can we see him? No answer there, either. She'd asked Andrea if she should bring them to the hospital, but Andrea hadn't been sure. It was a little more than an hour's drive, and Andrea didn't want the kids there unless there was a reason—like to say get well or good-bye. Not to stare at a dead body.

Her phone buzzed, indicating a text.

Daddy's in ICU. Do you mind bringing the kids?

Suzanna typed a quick answer and then left to weed out the Kent children from the tangle of school kids pouring from the building. Kelsey saw her first and lit up with a smile. Suzanna's heart ached, hating that the news she was about to share would crush her young friend.

The drive had been nearly silent, and the air felt heavy as Suzanna pulled into the hospital parking lot. Andrea's Expedition was easy to find, and spotting the truck parked next to it made her heart even heavier. How would Paul react to her bringing the kids—to her being here? She locked her worry away in a far corner of her mind. Didn't matter right now. Andrea asked her to come, and Kelsey needed her.

Good God, anchor my mama's soul.

Paul held her small, wrinkled hand. It trembled.

"I'm sorry, Mrs. Rustin. I have to ask you to make a decision." The young doctor sat across from them, his elbows on his knees, hands clasped, and sympathy written in his dark eyes. "Your husband's lack of brain activity indicates he will not recover."

God, why couldn't you have just taken him quickly? How is Mama supposed to make this decision?

The stroke, or series of strokes, had chipped away at his father for several years. Even if he lived through this, which didn't sound likely, life would be that much harder. How much more could his mother take?

"He who believes in me, though he may die, he shall live." Mother's voice quivered as she whispered the recitation. She turned her tear-laden face first to Paul and then to Andrea and then pulled both their hands into her chest. "Your daddy's eternity is secure in the hands of Christ." She paused as a sob tore through her frame. "It is time to let him get to it."

Paul's chest lurched, and his lips quivered. He gathered his mother close, pulling Andrea in with her, and they cried.

The doctor rose, catching Paul's eyes and tipping a nod. "When you're ready, I'll meet you in his room."

Saying good-bye felt like what he'd imagined it would be like to be hit by a truck. Pain burned in his chest, and it hurt to talk, to breathe. Paul said his good bye, waited for Dre and then pulled her under his arm until he delivered her safely to Tom, who waited in the hall. She huddled against her husband's chest, and Paul turned back to the open doorway of his dad's room.

"Thank you for the wonderful life, Clyde." His mother's words came broken and soft. "I'm so blessed to have shared it with you. But now Jesus is calling you home, and I won't stand in the way." Her cries trembled through her frame, and she buried her face against his chest. "I love you."

Paul turned away as the intensity of the emotion sliced at his heart.

Suzanna sat next to Kelsey, who stared across the family waiting room with an empty expression. Tom had come twenty minutes earlier to tell kids he wasn't going to live, and then they had been allowed to see their grandpa. They'd been taken to say good-bye and returned to Suzanna's care. Kiera and Keegan clung to their father, their sniffles filling the room. Kelsey sat by Suzanna, her eyes moist with unshed tears.

Reaching for her hand, Suzanna understood all too well the girl's soundless retreat.

Kelsey clasped Suzanna's fingers and raised her pale face. "Mama says you were married, but your husband died."

Suzanna swallowed as her lips began to tremble. She nodded.

Kelsey leaned against Suzanna's shoulder. "Will it always hurt like this?"

Pain overcame every shred of anger, every determined resolution to keep it at bay. She pulled Kelsey close under one arm and tucked her head close.

A masculine hand pushed a tissue into hers. She took the tissue, and his fingers wrapped over her hand. Paul kneeled in front of them, pulling them both close to his chest. He pressed a kiss against Suzanna's forehead and then moved to kiss Kelsey. He held them, and Suzanna felt a foreign sensation of safety even as her tears fell.

Kelsey's question continued to swim in her heart. She didn't have an answer.

Please, don't let it always hurt like this. I want to live.

Compassion suddenly flooded the spot that had been angry with Suzanna. Is this what it had been like for her? Did she still live with this agony?

Paul sniffed and released the girls from his hold. He moved to the chair next to Suzanna, taking her hand in his.

Dre came through the door, her face splotchy and eyes red rimmed. "I think it's time to get the kids home," she said. "Paul, will you stay with Mama?"

Paul nodded. Tom rose with his two younger children still wrapped in his arms. Kelsey slid from her seat but didn't move forward. Suzanna shifted and tugged her hand away from Paul's to reach for his niece. The pair clung together in a silent embrace, and gratitude sat next to the ache in Paul's heart. They needed each other, those two.

Tom and Dre waited until Kelsey was ready, and then the Kent family left the hospital. Suzanna sat at Paul's side, her eyes dry. He reached for her hand again, and she willingly took it, but their estrangement remained heavy.

"Is this what it was like?" Paul whispered.

She bit her lip as her forehead puckered. She was fighting against her emotions. But closing it up wasn't helping her. Wasn't helping them. He let go of her hand and pulled her under his arm. "I'm sorry I reacted badly, Suzie." He leaned his head against hers. "I really do want to be the man you need."

Her body trembled. Suddenly she was huddled against him.

"Does it still hurt like this?" he asked, holding her tight.

"No"—her voice cut out—"sometimes."

Warm tears seeped through his shirt as his own fell against her hair. Sliding her arms around his neck, she turned on her hip to hold him.

"I'm sorry about your dad. He was a good man."

Paul buried his face in her neck.

"We'll get through this, Suzie," he mumbled against her hair. Sitting up, he brushed the light wisps away from her face. "All of it. We're going to be okay."

RECLAIMED

Suzanna tugged at her awful black wrap, hating that she had a reason to wear it again. Clyde Rustin's funeral was a tearful celebration. It felt odd. She glanced at Andrea, wondering about her lighter colored dress. The family didn't focus on death. They talked of Mr. Rustin's life, his impact on his family and friends, and of the wonderful heritage he had left. They spoke as if this were a temporary good-bye that would soon be overcome by reunion.

Of course it would. Death and then life. That's what the Bible taught. Everyone died, but then they'd be in heaven. That was the gospel, right? Suzanna had known it all her life, but something about it didn't seem right. Why would an uncaring God offer heaven to people in whom He didn't have any interest?

Some people thought Christianity was folklore, nothing more significant than the Greek and Roman myths, not any truer than the Grimm brothers' fairy tales. Suzanna was more and more disposed to believe that.

Except at a funeral—especially Clyde Rustin's. The people there seemed to live in a peace fairy tales didn't offer. She must have missed something somewhere, but that didn't seem likely. Her father had been a pastor, after all. She'd grown up on a steady diet of Bible stories and Christian traditions.

Paul handled grief with an odd mix of courage and vulnerability. He never closed his heart off. He seemed to embrace the ache of loss while accepting the comfort of love. He carried his father's coffin with unashamed tears, tenderly held his mother while she bid her final farewell, and when it was all said and done, he leaned in Suzanna's arms with a peaceful resignation.

No strife. No anger. Just open grief and an acceptance of her meager offering of comfort. Nothing at all like her experience with death, neither her husband's nor her father's. Why did he get to have peace at all times?

Healing crept into Paul's heart as the winter days drew out. From the grief of his father's death and from the anger and disappointment in Suzanna's revelation. They pushed through it together. The lighthearted euphoria he'd known at the beginning of their relationship didn't mark it anymore, but the surge of love ran strong and deep, sometimes almost painfully so. Through it, he had to believe the fun, easy days they'd shared would come again.

Time. They both needed time and healing. Hers was long overdue.

He hadn't been able to dislodge the picture of his mother's final good-bye, and it often faded into an image of Suzanna. His mind's eye saw her beside her husband's casket, alone. Standing at his grave, alone. Maybe it was his imagination, working off assumptions, but it seemed to explain a lot of her wounds. It broke his heart.

"Was anyone there for you, Suzie?" He'd taken her into his arms on a late January evening, resting in the soothing power of her warm embrace.

She pulled away, her hands resting on his elbows, and her eyes searched his The walls were gone, completely broken down, and he could see into who she really was.

Her gaze moved away from his, landing on his chest, and she sighed. "My family came to Jason's funeral, but they aren't like yours. We don't love like you do."

That would be a no. His assumptions had been right—— she'd been abandoned to the misery of bearing the loss on her own. "What about his family? Were they around?"

She shook her head. "His mom was in a women's correctional facility when he died. She was allowed to come to his funeral, accompanied by a guard of some sort. I haven't seen her since."

Utterly alone. *Puppy tossed into a ditch.* How awful. No wonder she armed herself with anger.

Paul tugged her back against his chest, the ache of her heart making his hurt.

Healing, Father. I beg of you, bring healing.

Sketch paper and pencils covered the table in front of Suzanna. Kelsey shaded the apple tree she'd outlined, showing Suzanna how to fade the colors into a realistic shadow. She tried to apply the technique, but only Kelsey shaded. Suzanna just colored. Artistic talent was not a shared trait between them. But they connected in so many other ways.

"Are you going with Uncle Paul to the dance?"

Huh? What dance? Suzanna quit coloring and looked up. They had the kitchen all to themselves, so Suzanna didn't feel self-conscious about Kelsey's faux pas. She waited for the girl's explanation.

She tipped her chin and tapped it with a pencil. "The second weekend in February Rock Creek always holds a barn dance."

Paul hadn't mentioned it, probably too emotionally worn out to even think about it, not to mention physically. Calving season carved exhaustion into his handsome face.

"We'll see. Paul's been pretty tired. Maybe he's not up for it."

Kelsey's eyes gleamed as she shook her head. "He always goes. Kiera and I get to dance with him. He says it's a good break from the doldrums of winter."

Okay, so there goes that theory. Suzanna pushed against the insecurity flooding her brain. Maybe he didn't want to go because of her. Because of what people in town thought and said. Disappointment pressed against her. She didn't want to be a drag on his life.

"If you marry Uncle Paul, you'd be my aunt." Kelsey had gone back to shading. She glanced up, her expression hopeful.

Heat flood her cheeks. "It would work that way."

Kelsey stopped her pencil again and looked at Suzanna with deep intent. "I would like that very much."

Suzanna stood and moved to hug Kelsey from behind. "It doesn't matter either way, Kels. You'll always be my best girlfriend." She sat in the chair next to Kelsey. "That's pretty special, because I've never had one before."

Kelsey leaned her head against Suzanna's shoulder. "Promise?"

Suzanna laid her cheek against the girl's hair. "Promise."

Paul took Suzanna's gloved hand in his as they set off down the road toward her house. He picked her up after he and Kiera had finished riding, and she suggested walking home from his house. His head ached from fatigue, and a late Sunday afternoon nap sounded good but not at the expense of time with her.

That seemed to be a luxury these days. He'd never really paid attention to how much free time he didn't have during calving season. He liked staying busy, but he missed the extra moments with Suzie. He'd gain a whole lot more of them and be happier if she were his wife.

"Keys mentioned the Valentine's dance today." He set aside the uncertainty that always niggled at his gut when his thoughts turned to marriage. "Asked if we were going. I told her yes before I realized I hadn't talked to you about it."

Suzanna gave a small laugh. "Kelsey mentioned it today too." She looked up at him, her eyes warm. "It's okay if you don't want to go. I know you're tired these days, and with things in town…"

He tugged on her arm and pulled her close to his side. "I do want to go. With you."

She smiled, tipping a small nod before she snuggled closer. They walked along in easy silence. Paul pictured her as she was when he'd brought Kiera back home this afternoon. Paper and pencils and erasers and oil pastels had covered Andrea's dining room table. She sat across from Kelsey, coloring as they chatted away like lifelong friends.

The image made him smile, and he squeezed her close. "Looked like you were having fun today."

He couldn't see her face, but he felt a smile in the way she sighed. "I always have fun with Kels." She glanced up, her expression merry. "With all of your family. I feel like…" Tears made those blue eyes shine. "Like I belong."

Paul's throat felt thick. "You do," he whispered. *Belong forever. With me.*

He wanted to say it. Desperately. Why couldn't he?

CHAPTER THIRTY-THREE

Paul and Suzanna stepped off the dance floor and found Dre with her girls just as Shenandoah's "I Wanna Be Loved Like That" came over the speakers. Bummer. He'd have liked to two-step with her to that song.

Suzanna picked up her plastic cup and sipped her lemonade, her face bright from the swinging they'd just done. She was having fun. Paul felt a smile clear down to his boots. She had danced and laughed, talked with Alice May, Joy Hurst and Dre. She'd taken Kelsey onto the floor when he'd gone with Kiera and even managed to sweet-talk Keegan into a dance.

Perhaps everything had smoothed itself out.

"Mama, I need to be excused." Kelsey had to raise her voice to be heard above the music.

"I'll come with you." Suzanna's hand slid from Paul's, but she caught his eye and smiled before she reached for Kelsey. "Be back."

Paul grinned as he watched Suzanna and his niece move through the crowded barn hand in hand. She did fit. So perfectly. Maybe it was about time to make it official. Permanent.

Wait. Just wait.

Where were those whispers of insecurity coming from? He didn't feel insecure. He wanted Suzie to be his wife. So, what was with the hesitation?

"Hello, stranger."

Paul froze. The sultry, feminine voice rippled up his spine. He turned, his gaze colliding with familiar brown eyes belonging to a beautiful woman he'd known quite well.

"Hailey." The air emptied from his lungs. "What are you doing here?"

She cocked her head, and her eyebrows toyed upward. "You didn't really think I'd stand you up." Her painted lips parted into a smile. "Certainly you know I've been looking forward to this for weeks."

What the—— His jaw went slack as he stared.

Hailey laughed, sliding her hand over his arm. "Come on, handsome. You remember how to dance, right?"

Her fingers trailed his sleeve and then wrapped around his hand. Before his brain could restart, Paul found himself on the pine-planked floor, moving in rhythm with Hailey. She sidled closer than he was comfortable with—actually he wasn't comfortable with her within five feet of his personal space—and her gaze lifted to him with an intimacy that set off alarm bells.

His arms stiffened as he pushed her to a more appropriate distance. "Hailey, I really don't know what you're doing here."

Her eyebrows dropped, but then she looked at him as though he were a tease. "You were always such a sarcastic flirt."

Paul stopped moving, taking another step back. "I'm not flirting with you. And I'm not teasing, either. I had no idea you were coming, and I really don't know why you're here. Don't you have a life in Denver?"

Paul moved his eyes from Hailey and scanned the crowd. Suzanna stood stone still at the other end of the barn, her heated glare clamped dead on him.

Please let her be reasonable.

"We've been talking about this for over a month, Paul"——Hailey's response commanded his attention. Honest confusion—and hurt—stole over her expression—"and you know exactly what's going on in Denver. Todd and I aren't working. We've talked about this. You were willing to give us a new start."

"Stop it, Hailey." Paul snapped. Had the woman gone crazy? "I haven't spoken to you since the day you left. My life has moved on, and you and I don't have a future. At all."

He looked again for Suzanna, catching sight of her back as she fled from the barn. Dre was close on her heels, though she looked back at Paul with horrified incredulity. He felt like someone had just drop-kicked his heart.

Leaving Hailey in the middle of the dance floor, Paul set off for the exit. Chuck stepped in his path as he neared the back door. "Playing ball on two fields, Rustin?" He crossed his arms and smirked. "Didn't know you had it in you."

Paul's blood boiled. Stanton most definitely had a hand in whatever was going on. Suzanna was blazin' mad, so he couldn't deal with Chuck right now. "Get out of my way," he growled, clearing Chuck from his path with one firm shove.

He could feel stares burning into his shoulders as he made his way out. What a scene. What a horrible, scandalous scene.

Voices drifted from across the road as Paul continued over to the vacant lot where he'd parked. The evening had been so fine. Suzanna looked beautiful in the red striped dress she'd bought especially for this dance. They'd laughed together, and things between them had felt more like they had before Christmas, before everything went deep and dark and solemn.

What the devil was Hailey doing here?

"Just take me home." Anger edged Suzanna's voice, though he knew by the subtle crack in it that tears lay just beneath her fury.

"Please, Suz," Dre begged, "let's wait for Paul. This has to be some kind of misunderstanding."

Paul moved around his sister's Expedition, and both women looked his way. Andrea stared at him, her eyes wide. Her mouth closed, forming a thin line, before she turned and walked away.

Suzanna balled her fists and then crossed her arms. Paul wasn't sure if it was the February chill or her raging anger that had her shivering. She glared at him, her blue eyes making accusations that speared him in the chest. He stepped toward her, and she backed away. He continued moving in measured steps until her back hit the door of his pickup. Resting a hand against it, he leaned down to her ear.

"After everything we've been through, Suzanna Korine Cumberland," he growled, "don't you dare go doubting my heart."

She snapped straight, drawing herself up to all of her five-foot-five inches. "Why would I do that?" she hissed. "Just because you tangled your arms around some beautiful woman—who you happened to have almost married—right in front of the whole town? That shouldn't matter a bit, should it?"

Frustration pulsed hot in his veins, feeling more like anger with each passing breath. "You know better than to think what you're thinking. I had no idea Hailey would be here, and she dragged me onto the dance floor before I could figure out what was going on."

"Well, that makes me feel so much better." She lilted the words with sarcasm. Her eyes pinched as she scowled. "The pixy just smiled, and you were putty in her perfectly manicured hands. And don't tell me you didn't know she was going to be here. She quite obviously thought that you expected her—wanted her."

"Paul?" Dre's soft voice drifted from behind.

Paul jerked upright.

"Here." Andrea handed Suzanna's coat over the small distance and turned to disappear into the night.

He held the coat open for Suzanna, but she snatched it away and shrugged into it on her own. She wasn't going to ease up. Fine. He didn't feel like backing down, either. He reached for the door, opening it enough for her to fit through.

"We're not doing this here." He glared at her until she'd climbed her pretty little self into his pickup. He slammed the door and stomped around to the driver's side.

The frigid silence in the cab could have hung icicles along the windshield. Paul took the dirt road a little fast, setting the bed of the pickup into a small fishtail. Memories of their muddy expedition flashed across his mind. Getting stuck in a ditch wouldn't be nearly as much fun tonight.

He eased up on the gas pedal, and the miles rolled by under their frosty impasse. Suzanna sat straight and stiff, her mouth set hard, until he passed her house.

"You missed your turn." Her voice cut over him.

"No, I didn't." He matched her edge. "We're not done with this, and if I take you home, you'll march your infuriated little self into that house and slam the door in my face."

She turned to him with a defiant stare. *Nailed it. Do I know this woman or what?* Within two minutes, he pulled up to his house and killed the engine.

"I'm not going in." She set her stare out the windshield.

"Fine. We can have it out right here."

She glowered at him again and then opened the door. Marching over the driveway, she pounded up the front steps and waited for him by the door, her arms crossed over her chest. If he weren't so blasted hot with her right now, he would have laughed. She had one heck of a temper. The Pickle.

Paul drew a deep breath, and his pulse began to settle. *Takes two, Rustin.* He slid from the pickup and walked to the house, forcing the whirling in his head to slow down. Opening the door, he let Suzanna pass through and then moved to hang his hat on the peg beside the entry.

"Suz"—he sighed, running a hand over his hair as he turned to her—"why would you think I would do that to you?"

She had decidedly *not* settled down. "What am I supposed to think when I walk into a room, and you're wrapped up in the arms of your ex-fiancée?"

Her voice had a bite that sank in deep, and the accusation had him coiled up and ready to strike. "You're supposed to know I love you," he barked. "You're supposed to trust me."

"Trust you?" She shouted. "Trust you in her arms? You almost *married* her, Paul!"

Fire snapped between them as he stepped closer. He held her livid gaze, silently imploring her to stop treating his devotion with skepticism.

"I never loved her like this." He clasped her shoulders, wanting to shake her. "Not even close. Did you know she begged me to move? I wouldn't even talk about it. But if you told me tomorrow you'd decided to set off for Tanzania, I'd put a "for sale" sign in the front yard before the day was done. Because I *love* you, Suzanna. Hailey was a vague hope of something I didn't understand. Had I been a wiser man, I would have known she and I didn't have a future, but I *know* my future is with you. Whatever it looks like, however it plays out, I'll be happy, as long as I'm with you."

A degree of coldness melted from her eyes. Her shoulders drooped, and she looked to the floor. Her head shook ever so slightly, and her voice still sounded hard when she spoke. "That's easy to say, Paul, because you know I'd never ask you to leave. I know how much you love your life right here."

Dadgum it, Pickle. He'd just laid his heart at her feet, and she toed it with as much care as one would handle a mangy pup.

"You're not going to let this go, are you? He tipped her chin, forcing her to look at him. "There's nothing I can say. You're just gonna stay mad because you want to be mad. Because you're afraid to feel anything but anger."

She stared at him, her jaw set like granite. She blinked several times, undoubtedly to force back the tears that glistened in her eyes. "Good night, Paul Rustin." She brushed past him, her heels smacking an angry rhythm on his floor. The door shook on her exit, and Paul squeezed his eyes shut.

Thoughts whirled again. Resentment still throbbed hard, but a sudden flash of his grandmother's ring set everything tipsy. Man, they had some issues to work on. *This is why I can't marry her now, isn't it?* The house settled quietly, the familiar creaks and moans suddenly sounding painful, making him think of time and wear—of life beyond this moment.

Was it always going to be this much work? Feeling love and doing love were not at all the same. Sometimes loving that feisty little pickle made him want to howl. Then again, he was pretty sure at the moment, she didn't feel all warm and fuzzy about loving him, either.

Creaks and moans. Wear and tear. Did they have what it would take to last?

Paul's eyes moved to the door, and he remembered it was both dark and cold outside. Taking long strides, he dug his keys out of his pocket and set off for the pickle.

Why hadn't Paul mentioned his almost-wife had been a knockout?

Wasn't his fault she was gorgeous, but, sheesh, did he have to go and dance with her in front of the whole town? She'd literally draped herself in his arms, and he just let her as they swayed to a country love song. What was he thinking? As if there wasn't enough juicy gossip about them oozing into the streets.

Maybe she shouldn't have taken a swing at his head, so to speak. Or, probably more true, his heart. Did he really love her like that?

Why did he take that cheap shot at the end?

You're afraid to feel anything but anger.

It unnerved her that he saw into the very depths of who she was. Into all the rottenness.

What if someone knew all of the wounds in my heart, all of the bitterness stored up there and loved me anyway.

She'd thought that, longed for it months ago. Now she had it in Paul.

Headlights lit the road ahead as the sound of a vehicle crawled behind her.

Paul.

She sped up her pace while an argument erupted in her mind. The vehicle stopped, and the sound of an opening door cut into the night.

Apologize and end it. He didn't do anything wrong.

Shore up the defense and keep him out. This will only end in heartache.

Heartache was inevitable, but did it have to end that way?

"Suzanna, stop." Though softer, his voice still held a hint of frustration. She heard his boots scuff against the dirt as he jogged to catch up. "Get in the pickup."

Not happening. Stubbornness won the round. She pulled her shoulders straight and kept her feet moving.

He snagged her elbow. "I mean it, Pickle. Get in. I'll take you home."

She lifted her chin. "I'll walk."

He pulled her to a halt. "Don't make me toss you over my shoulder."

"You wouldn't."

"You wanna find out?"

She held his eyes, the heat of his emotion burning into hers.

Why did she continue with this? He was the best thing going for her. Did she really want to push him away? What if he gave up on her?

Better now than later.

The thought startled her. Was that how she really felt?

He tugged on her arm again, and she took a step toward him. His hand slid down her arm, and she was surprised when he wrapped hers in it. She followed him to the pickup and climbed in without a sound.

Their silence felt more uncomfortable than combative as he took her home. Parking in the drive, Paul leaned over the steering wheel and sighed.

"Suzie, let's end this."

"End this?" Her voice cracked. The stone wall around her heart began to crumble as tears slipped onto her cheeks.

"The fight, hon." He turned to look at her, his eyes tired—discouraged.

Oh. Wiping the tears, she nodded.

He reached across the cab and pulled her head into his shoulder, brushing a kiss over her forehead. "It's just a fight, Pickle."

CHAPTER THIRTY-FOUR

Suzanna's room felt unusually cold. Didn't really have to do with the thermostat though. She shivered in the lonely darkness, staring at the ceiling. Where was sleep? Tucked away far from her reach in the happy place where peace and hope weren't at war.

Rolling to her side and gathering the quilt closer to her body, she trembled to remember what it had been like to roll into Jason, to soak in his warmth and to snuggle into his arms. Even then, though warm and not so lonely, she didn't know peace—only the fleeting comfort of his heartbeat, the temporary relief his love provided against the feeling of abandonment.

The comfort of Jason's love had left her cold, deserted and forever in turmoil.

A tear slipped from the corner of her eye, making a damp trail along her face until it splotched her pillow. Jason had filled the void for a time, but the hollow places in her soul had never been satisfied. Never. Why had she hoped Paul would be able to accomplish what Jason had failed?

He couldn't. They would fight, and though it would be just a fight, it would grow those tender holes. Make them larger and carve the emptiness deeper.

Paul was right. She didn't want to feel the pain.

God, where are you? If you love me, like Daddy claimed, then where are you?

The chill of solitude—absolute and impenetrable—pressed in closer. No, Daddy was wrong. God didn't care at all.

Paul went to the door in a white tee shirt and his flannel pants—certain it was Suzanna. Who else would show up on his front porch at five in the morning? He scrubbed his hand over his face but not really to remove the sleep. There hadn't been any. It was more to push away the anxiety.

He pulled the door toward him, and Suzanna stood in her sweats, her puffer coat wrapped tight around her frame. "Did I wake you?"

"No." He stepped back to let her pass. "I went out to check cows around four and never made it back to bed."

Small lie. He hadn't made it to bed at all. Foreboding kept him up. Praying. Searching for answers.

He shut the door and turned back to where she waited in the narrow hall. She looked at him through timid eyes, puffy from lack of sleep and most certainly tears. His heart ripped, leaving regret.

Don't let the sun go down on your anger.

They should have worked this out last night. Stepping across the hall, he reached to pull her close.

"I'm sorry, Paul." She sniffed. Her arms locked around his waist, her hold strong. Almost desperate.

Paul curled around her, cuddling her close. His throat felt too thick to speak, and so he just held her, swaying slightly as though a distant melody played a healing tune. He closed his eyes as he leaned his head against hers, trying to shut out the images of her anger. Such a thing to think about in a moment like this, but it wasn't something he could ignore. Something needed to change.

He stepped back, putting space between them while he anchored his hands on her arms. "Suzanna, we need to talk."

Her lips trembled, and she looked down at her feet. "Do what you need to do," she whispered.

Still unconvinced. What could he do to make her understand? He lifted her chin, his thumb tracing her jaw, until she locked with his gaze.

"I'm not breaking up with you, Suzie. I hope someday you hear me when I tell you I'm in love with you."

She shuddered as a cry ripped through her body. Paul pulled her across the small distance, securing her once again in his embrace. She rested her head against one of his arms as the cries continued to escape from the depths.

Bottomless pits he could not plunge.

"Why would you want me?" she gasped between cries. "Why would you want this ugly, scarred heart of mine?"

He took her arms again and moved so he could speak into her eyes. "Baby, those aren't scars. Scars don't ache like this. They don't continue to bleed. These are still wounds, and I can't fix them. I can't fill the holes in your heart, but I think you're hoping I will."

She covered her face with both hands as sobs took over completely.

Where are you, God? Why haven't you healed her?

Because she wouldn't let Him. Just like she pushed Paul away, she pushed the healing hand of Love away. The revelation shattered his heart, and he couldn't contain his own tears.

"Hon, you've got to let God in. He'll heal you if you'll let Him, but you've got to let Him."

She moved away. "I don't know God like you do, Paul. Your God is with you, loves you." She shook her head, agony in her eyes. "The god I know doesn't care about my pain, or if he does, he can't do anything about it. He doesn't love me, doesn't want me."

Paul's stomach knotted hard. She didn't know Him at all. All this time, he had thought she'd just been mad at Him, kept Him at a distance. But she really didn't know Him.

Oh God. I'm in too deep. Please don't do this to me.

His hands trembled at his side, and Paul drew a deep breath. "If that's what you believe, then you don't know Jesus."

Her eyes came up to his face, but her brows drew down. "I'm a preacher's kid, Paul. I know all about Jesus."

"That's not the same as knowing Him."

Her shoulders drew back. "Are you trying to tell me that I'm not a Christian?"

"I don't know, Suzie. Are you?"

"Of course I am." Her eyes narrowed.

"Why?" He slid a tiny step forward. "Why do you think you're a Christian?"

She looked at him befuddled. "My daddy was a *pastor*. I was baptized as a child. I was confirmed as a teenager. That's what Christians do."

Oh God, no. Please, Father, don't do this.

"Suzanna, those are all good things to do, but they don't make you a Christian. Only Jesus makes you a Christian. Only Jesus saves."

Suzanna huffed. "Well, of course I know that."

"Do you? You didn't say it."

"Okay, fine." She blew out another breath. "Jesus is the Savior of the world. Now do you believe me?"

Paul covered his forehead with his hand, rubbing his temple. "Hon, I'm not trying to pick a fight with you, but I have to ask, is Jesus *your* savior?"

Her lips parted, and she looked at him as though he were speaking Latin. "What do you mean? I just told you, He's the Savior of the world. You know, like God so loved the world that He sent His only son to save it."

Yeah. Close. And yet so not right. Paul sighed. "Do you know the rest of that verse?"

She held his eyes, defiance hardening her expression. "Is this a test?"

Paul ran his hand over his face and pressed it against his mouth.

She's not going to listen. God, what do I do?

"No." His shoulders slumped as he moved down the hall toward the kitchen. He opened a cupboard and reached for the coffee but only set it on the counter. Leaning against it, he felt tired. Weak. Helpless.

Suzanna trailed him after a few moments, her eyes dry, but her expression upset. "I'm sorry, Paul. I don't know why I snap like that."

He lifted his head and swallowed. *Because you won't let anyone in. Not God. Not me.*

"What does the rest of that verse say?" She asked softly.

"My Bible's over on the coffee table." He nodded toward his living room. "You can look for yourself."

She nodded and moved toward it. She stopped halfway and turned to him, guilt showing in her posture. "I don't know where that verse is."

Paul breathed deep and then nodded, pushing away from the counter. He walked toward her and took her hand, leading her to his couch. Flipping to John 3:16, he held his Bible so she could read it.

"Okay," she spoke slowly, raising an eyebrow. "So, I'm still not understanding your point. I believe in Jesus. Do you still think I'm not a Christian?"

"Suzanna, a general belief in God, or Jesus, isn't the same thing as saving faith. James says even the demons believe in God, but it doesn't make them saved."

"James?" Her tone got snippy again. "Who is James?"

Paul felt his shoulders drop again. "James, the half brother of Christ. He wrote the book of James in the Bible." He sighed, not knowing what else to do.

"Look, to be a Christian means you are a follower of Christ, that you have a relationship with Him. Salvation is personal—kind of like marriage. Andrea couldn't just say she's a Kent because she knows about Tom. She's a Kent because she married him. She committed to him, follows him. *Knows* him. There's a big difference."

Suzanna smacked the Bible shut. "I don't know what you're talking about. I never heard my daddy talk like this. Are you saying if I don't know Jesus like you want me to, then I'm not saved?"

Paul groaned, wanting to shout. "No. It doesn't have anything to do with what I want. I don't make up the salvation rules, Suzanna. Jesus said it. He said there will be many who say Lord, Lord, and He will turn them out, saying He never *knew* them."

He turned to her, leaning his hands against his knees. "I don't know what your daddy believed, what he preached, but I do know you came here searching for something he found. Maybe it wasn't in the land or the town or anything else you have here. Maybe he found truth, and it gave him peace. Maybe he found *Jesus.*"

Suzanna jumped up. "My daddy knew truth. He spent his life preaching the Bible!"

Paul closed his eyes, trying to stop the spinning in his head. He stood slowly and wandered back to the kitchen.

Suzanna stayed in her place until he reached the counter. When she turned to him, the anger had drained from her face. She moved toward him but stopped on the opposite side of the sink.

"This is a deal breaker, isn't it?"

A deal breaker? Was that as deep as she thought his heart went? A deal, like a handshake over the sale of a cow? A contract for a purchase? Paul swallowed, emotions crashing over him so strong he trembled.

"Jesus is at the very core of who I am, Suzie. If you don't know Him, you'll never really know me." His voice cut off as his throat closed over.

"What does that mean?" Her eyes gleamed with tears.

He pushed a fist against his head. What was he to do? His heart felt like it was slowly ripping apart, and he found it hard to breathe.

God, I can't do this.

"I don't know." He choked. "I don't know what to do."

Suzanna wrapped her arms around herself. Her voice came broken and hoarse. "Why can't you just love me as I am?"

Agony spilled onto his cheeks. "I do, Suzanna. This is the problem. Right here. How many times have I told you I love you? I keep pouring love into you, and it drains from your heart like water through a cracked tank. I can't fix that. I love you, more than I can find words for, but I can't fix what's wrong on the inside. I could try, and you would end up resenting me, because I will fail."

He could see her begin to tremble as she cried in silence. Tears blurred his vision, but he forced himself to finish. "I'll always love you, Suzanna. That will never change, but I want you to be whole. To have peace. I can't do that for you."

Wanting desperately to go to her, to take everything back, Paul leaned against the counter, his heart writhing with every silent moment.

Suzanna pulled herself straight and sniffed. Brushing her tears away, she fixed a glare on him. "That's it then."

Her angry tone cut deep. She moved out of the kitchen, and the front door slammed two seconds later.

Paul dropped into a chair at his table, his head falling into his hands. *God, why?*

CHAPTER THIRTY-FIVE

Suzanna raced up the creepy basement stairs, her large suitcase in tow. Paul had stored it in the basement for her so she wouldn't have to try to be brave on her own. He wasn't there to retrieve it for her now. He wouldn't ever be there again. Her tears refused to be bottled.

If you don't know Him, you'll never really know me.

She tried to turn his voice off, but it refused to be silenced. Refused to be ignored.

Jason had said something similar. Only weeks before he went into hospice, he'd forced a similar conversation—wanting her to *know* Jesus. Over the years of their marriage, as Jason struggled through treatments and pain and fatigue, he turned more and more to his Bible. Became more and more religious. Except he hated it when she said that.

It's not religion, Suzie. It's a relationship. I need Jesus every day— like I need you. I need to talk to you, to spend time with you. He's everything to me.

Everything? They had spent more time in the cancer center than they had in church. He spent more of his life sick than healthy. What kind of relationship was that? Where was the fairness in it all?

Suzie, you and I need to face reality. I'm going to die.

He had quit——given up the fight, but she couldn't surrender as readily.

Jase, don't talk like that. There's still chemo. We can try that again. This doesn't have to be the last effort.

Lying in his bed, pale and thin and weak, he had reached to cover her hand.

Baby, I'm ready. Heaven is calling, and I'm ready to go. But I don't want to leave you not knowing whether or not you're saved.

Why did the men in her life question that? Didn't they think she was good enough? Granted, she didn't match their character. Neither one—not by a long shot. They were both tremendously good men, and she knew without a doubt she didn't deserve their love. But did she deserve hell?

I'm a good person, Jase. You wouldn't love me if I were completely evil. Why wouldn't I go to heaven?

He'd stared at her, real fear playing over his face.

What if your good isn't good enough?

What if… what if they were right? Where did that leave her? And her father? He didn't preach relationship. He preached living, doing. Religion. Wasn't that the real deal? Didn't Jesus teach about doing good? Serve the poor. Love the orphans. Go to church. Get baptized. Take communion. Jesus said to do all those things. Daddy taught that. Where did Jason——and Paul——get the idea that it wasn't enough?

She tugged two pairs of jeans from her closet and threw them into her bag.

I'll always love you. That'll never change.

Jason had promised the same thing. It was a beautiful sentiment, but it didn't do her any good. Jase was gone, and Paul had drawn a line he would never cross. Both had left her alone. Just like Mother. Just like Daddy.

Just like God.

She continued to rummage through her clothing, tossing sweaters and socks into her bag without any rhyme or reason. Anger regained its hold, and her tears dried against her hardened face. So, she was to be alone. Fine. *Never again.* She wouldn't let anyone that close to her heart again. *Ever.*

She flipped the top of her suitcase shut and was zipping it when her doorbell rang.

Paul?

No. He wouldn't use the front, probably wouldn't even bother to knock. He'd just step in the side entry and yell *Pickle* to announce his arrival.

The doorbell rang again.

Stopping at her bedroom mirror, Suzanna brushed at the trail of dried tears and gathered her hair into a ponytail. She looked awful. It was only seven in the morning, so she could claim bed head, if pressed.

She went to the door, and Shelby Stanton and Paul's beauty queen stood on the other side. Her back stiffened. "What do you want?"

Shelby put a hand to the other woman's elbow and pulled in a long breath. "This is Hailey, Suzanna. We wanted to talk to you—to explain—and apologize."

Come again? Suzanna stared at them.

"Hello, Suzanna." The chocolate-eyed woman spoke.

Was she supposed to talk back?

"I'm busy." She stepped back, not sure if she really had it in her to close the door on them.

"Please, Suzanna." Hailey stepped over the threshold. "I do want to apologize. I didn't know Paul was seeing someone—you. Honest. It was all a big mistake."

Shelby stepped forward, and suddenly both women were in her house. She should have shut the door. Was she expected to offer them coffee too?

"You were set up. Both of you," Shelby said. "Andrea and I figured it out last night after you and Paul left. Hailey and I have kept in touch over the years, mostly by Facebook these days. She got a message from me in November, saying Paul had been asking about her. Only I didn't send it. There's only one other person who has access to my account, so it didn't take too long to figure things out."

Chuck.

Shelby nodded as though Suzanna had said her husband's name out loud. "Hailey has been having an ongoing conversation with someone whom she *thought* was Paul. Dre insisted Paul wasn't on Facebook, so Hailey showed us the page on her phone. Except, well, it was established about the same time Paul started seeing you. Most of his messages to Hailey were between seven and eight in the morning—and all of us know that's when he's usually here, having coffee with you. We figured it out. And trust me when I tell you, my husband is in all kinds of trouble."

Relief should have draped over her. It didn't. Because it didn't matter now. Paul had seen the ugliness inside her and had deemed her unworthy. They were done, no matter what Chuck did or didn't do.

Hailey twisted her hands together. "I should have known better, anyway. I should have known Paul would never encourage me to leave my husband. He wouldn't have suggested... what Chuck suggested. That's not him—he's too honorable to do that. I was just desperate... well, anyway, you don't need to know all my troubles. But you should know Paul wouldn't do that. He just wouldn't, and I'm sorry for the scene I caused."

Silence edged into the room and needled Suzanna. What was she to do with all of this?

"I hope you can forgive me," Shelby spoke softly. "I believed everything Chuck said, and now I know it was all a lie. I said horrible things about you—and Paul. I'm so sorry."

Forgive? How does one do that?

Paul finished settling the orphaned calf in a stall in the barn. He hated this part of the job. Not just because the motherless babies were so hard to keep alive at this age, but it touched his heart. And that area ached enough today.

How could he have let this happen? He and Suzanna had done battle, plunged to uncharted depths and resurfaced together. How could he have overlooked the most important part?

How could she not be a believer? No wonder forgiveness came hard for her. She hadn't experienced it for herself. No wonder anger was her perennial response. She didn't know peace.

She didn't know peace, and yet she longed for it. Ached for it with every stitch of her soul. The pain in his chest constricted.

God, please give her peace.

"Did you lose one?" Tom's voice came through the stall door as he stepped onto the straw.

"Yeah." Paul came up off his knees. "About an hour ago. Don't know if this little guy will make it."

"I'm sorry." Tom shoved his hands into his pockets. He toed the straw and leaned back against the stall wall. "Are you and Suzanna okay?"

Paul rubbed his jaw, trying to clamp a firm hold on his shaky emotions. "No. We're not."

"Wondered. That's why I'm here. There's some stuff you need to know. Hailey came under false pretenses. You were both set up by Chuck. Seems he pirated his wife's Facebook page and then set up one in your name. Hailey thought the two of you had been talking for the past three months. She didn't know anything about Suzanna." He stuffed his hands into his pockets. "Anyway, the whole thing came spilling out at the dance, and now everyone in town knows the truth. You can both move on with your lives—Chuck's done."

That was great. Except it didn't matter. Paul looked the other way and then stepped out of the stall.

"Paul?" Tom tailed him.

Paul swallowed, searching for words. They came out surprisingly simple. "Suzie's not a believer."

He didn't want to know Tom's reaction. It didn't matter. At the moment, nothing was going to change the fact his heart was broken. He didn't want to share that. With anyone.

CHAPTER THIRTY-SIX

Suzanna turned toward her car as a Chevy truck pulled in across from her. Sheesh. One gas station in town. She couldn't even make a silent escape.

Pastor Ron dropped from the driver's seat and reached for the gas pump. "Hey there, Suzanna Wilton."

"Hi." That was pathetic.

Who cared? She wouldn't be back.

He removed the gas cap and started filling his truck. "You doing okay?"

She kept her attention on the gas pump. Surely the man would take a hint.

"Look a little tired. Been a day?"

Guess he couldn't. Her eyes moved back to him, almost of their own accord, and something deep inside latched on to his sincere concern.

"Did you know my dad well?" *Say what?* What happened to *it didn't matter?*

"I did, actually." He smiled, his expression warm, honest.

Since when did she trust people, especially people in this town?

Pastor seemed to ignore her discomfort. "He and I spent quite a few mornings together over coffee."

Suzanna nodded, stifling her voice with a closed mouth lest anymore mutinous words set themselves free. She turned back to her Honda. Why the dickens was it taking so long to fill the tank?

"Did you want to talk about him?" The man's voice came from over her shoulder.

Yes.

No. Nothing good would come from it. The more she'd opened up about the past, the worse her life had become. But Daddy had found something here—something she longed for with a desperation that pressed near insanity. Yearning welled up so strong that the tears managed a rebellious escape. She hardened herself against the rush of emotion.

"I can't. I'm on my way out of town... to visit my mom." Back to lying. That should work well.

"I think we should," he continued softly. "I know there were things your dad wanted you to know."

She froze, her back still to him. The demand for answers overcame her resolve to run. She *had* to know.

"Joy was putting some cinnamon rolls in the oven when I left." Pastor came around the gas pump and stood a respectable distance to her side. "Why don't you stop in for a bit? Colorado will still be there when we're done."

She nodded, unable to raise her eyes.

"Good. There're some things I've wanted to tell you. I have a feeling they may change the way you see life."

Doubtful. What made him so sure?

The smell of cinnamon and freshly baked bread swirled around Suzanna as she dropped into a chair at the Hursts' table. Joy offered coffee, but out of the norm, Suzanna declined. She didn't intend to stay.

What on earth was she doing here? Escape had been her only aim. How did she get so easily sidetracked?

"How's calving season going for Paul?" Joy asked——innocently, Suzanna reminded herself.

"I…" Maybe she should have accepted the coffee. At least a mug would have been some kind of distraction. "I'm not sure. He's busy, so I guess that's good."

"I know how that feels, not knowing exactly what my guy's up to, but knowing whatever it is takes up a whole lot of his time."

My guy? Not anymore——thanks to God. He must really hate her.

"Your dad was looking into cattle before he died." Pastor sat across from her, speaking as though the conversation shouldn't be uncomfortable. Maybe not for him. His family still breathed.

Suzanna nodded. Cut to the chase and hit the road. "He was a pastor. Did you know that?"

"I did." Ron grinned as though he were truly acquainted with the man. "He and I had many talks about the years he spent behind a pulpit."

Joy brought a plate of cinnamon rolls and set it in the middle of the table. She passed out plates and forks and then settled herself between her husband and Suzanna.

Uneasiness was pushed over by a demand for answers. "Paul has a different idea about heaven than my dad did. We…" She looked to her hands. "We fought about it."

Pastor Ron shifted in his chair. "That's bothering you."

Uh, yeah. Silence settled in the room, and Suzanna fidgeted with the sleeves of her sweatshirt. How could she get out of this?

"If what Paul says is true, then I don't know if my dad is in heaven." Holy buckets. Did she just say that?

Pastor leaned back against the chair. "Why don't you tell me what Paul said."

Suzanna swallowed. It may as well all come out now. Wouldn't matter much anyway since she was leaving for good within the hour.

"He says not every person goes to heaven. That you have to be saved personally. He called it having a relationship with Jesus."

Pastor nodded slowly and then tipped his head. "Paul didn't make that up. The Bible says it. John wrote that the person who has the Son—Jesus—has eternal life. But the one who does not have the Son does not have eternal life, but the wrath of God is upon him."

Anger surged like a high-pressure fountain. "My daddy preached for nearly twenty years. He *never* talked like that. If God is going to offer heaven, and if He's fair, then He would give it to every basically good person, without condition."

"His offer is for everyone, whether they think they're basically good or not, and there's only one condition. Belief."

"I do believe in God!" Her heart rate doubled. "Paul doesn't think that's good enough."

The older man held her gaze with kindness. "Your dad and I had a couple of conversations similar to this, Suzanna."

He what? Perhaps her father was trying to straighten these narrow-minded people out.

"He was restless and angry." Pastor Ron leaned an arm atop the table. "Mad at God because he didn't feel like God had kept the deal they'd made."

Daddy made a deal with God? Not likely. Okay, maybe. That's how life worked, right? Good deeds resulted in a good life, except Daddy's fell apart. It wasn't fair—he had good reason to be mad. So did she. Why did God deal kindly with some but gave others the cold shoulder?

But the last time she'd met with Daddy, he wasn't angry. He was content. Peaceful. It had made her hot with anger, especially since he kept insisting God would make her life beautiful again.

Beautiful? How did you take muck and make it pretty? Why did Daddy keep telling her to put her hand in God's? She'd been about to bury her husband. Her parents had made a shredded mess out of their family. Her sister had abandoned her entirely. God had failed. On every side—*failed*.

"Your father had quite a tale, Suzanna. And I know for a fact he wanted you to know it. He hoped the truth would release you from the bondage he'd put you in."

"You're wrong about whatever it is you think you need to tell me." Bitterness hardened her voice. "My daddy didn't put me in bondage. God did. He allowed our family to rip apart. He took everything I loved and put it through the shredder. That's the truth."

"Your father told me about you." He leaned closer, his eyes ever steady, ever kind. "About your husband. And about your mother. I know why you see God as cruel. The truth is, you see Him that way because you don't know Him. Your dad felt responsible for that."

"Responsible?" Her voice rose. "Everything I know about God I learned from my dad. You're not making sense, and I think you're speaking out of turn."

"Do you know why your father went into the ministry?"

She sat back hard, not even trying to hide her annoyance. "Because he was called."

"No. That wasn't why he went to seminary nor was it the reason he preached. He did it because he thought it would appease God. He thought he could make a deal with Him."

"Why would he do that?"

Pastor leaned back again. "Because he couldn't stand the guilt he carried around."

"Guilt? Over what?" She glowered at Pastor Ron.

"Your mother got pregnant before they were married. When they were seventeen."

"Ha." She rolled her eyes. "That's quite an invention. My sister was born when they were twenty-two."

"Your mother aborted the baby." Ron held her with a long stare. "She did it on her own. Your dad didn't find out until after it was all said and done. Guilt set hard on him, even after they were married. He thought preaching and teaching all the moral laws of the Bible would satisfy his guilt. It never did."

Suzanna's ears rang as if the man had just smacked her. It wasn't possible... couldn't be true, except... those letters she'd found in Daddy's box demanded an explanation.

Pastor Ron's soft voice filled the sharp silence. "He knew about your mother's affair, but he couldn't confront it because he couldn't get away from the guilt rotting inside him. When she filed for divorce, he felt not only the failure of his marriage and the collapse of his family, but also failure in his attempt to please God. Everything he'd believed, everything he'd preached throughout his ministry was thrown into question. And the final straw was you. Actually, no, it was Jason. That was your husband's name, right?

Suzanna nodded. She wanted to leave, but she sat paralyzed like she was stuck in a bad dream.

"Your father loved Jason, and not just for your sake." Pastor continued his story. "He said he watched the young man come alive, watched him bloom out of a pile of ashes. He couldn't reconcile why God would afflict Jason, of all young men, with leukemia. He would come in my office raging at the unfairness, and then our talks would turn to theology. Who is God?

"Over time our discussions continued. Your dad didn't know the God of the Bible. He knew the "thou shalts" and the events recorded in the Bible, but he didn't know God. Coming to terms with that was both heart shattering and bondage breaking. He found a God he could love. A God who loved him without reservation, without condition. He found salvation through faith, not by works. He found peace in Jesus. Shortly afterward, he went back to Colorado, not long before your husband died. Do you remember that?"

Suzanna nodded again. The emotion of the memory and the overwhelming story Pastor Ron had told held her tongue in silence.

"He came back knowing he needed to tell you all of this—feeling like he had led you wrong. He wanted to but not at that time. Not when your husband was dying. But he didn't get the chance, did he?"

She bit down into her lip, tasting blood but not feeling the pain. How could this be true? How could any of it be right?

"He wanted you to know." Ron leaned forward, sympathy in his expression. "He wanted you to find the Jesus he came to know——came to love. Your dad wanted you to have peace."

Suzanna pressed her hand to her lips and stared across the room. Everything about her life seemed to shatter, and she couldn't think, couldn't take it all in.

"I have to go." She stood, and her legs trembled.

Ron looked at his wife, and Joy laid a hand on Suzanna's arm. "You're safe here, Suzanna. Please don't leave just yet. Let this sink in. Truth——God's truth will set you free. Don't run from it."

Truth? She wouldn't know what that looked like. She turned toward the door.

"Suzanna, wait." Pastor Ron stood. "I have something to give you."

He disappeared down the hall, returning a minute later with an envelope. "I found this in my desk last week. Your father wrote it a few weeks before his heart attack." He pushed the letter across the space between them. "He asked me to look it over, but he died before I got it back to him. I'm sorry to say that until I saw you at the dance the other night, I'd forgotten about it."

Suzanna stared at the paper. Too many mysteries. Too many things she didn't really want to know. She fought the temptation to crumple it up. Not returning his look or even speaking to say good-bye, she turned on the ball of her foot and headed out the door.

CHAPTER THIRTY-SEVEN

Paul trudged up the hill, his breath puffing white in the February morning. His orphaned calf didn't survive. Disposing of the carcass only added to his gloom.

Pastor's pickup sat in his driveway. Paul sighed. He liked the man very much, but he wasn't up for company. Hadn't been all week.

"How do, Paul?" Ron dropped from the pickup and held out a hand.

"All right." His voice felt rusty. It'd been a long time since he'd squirreled himself away from people. Probably wasn't the best plan now, but he couldn't bring himself to get about the town. Despite his desire for isolation, hospitality was still required. "I was just going for something hot. Come on in."

Pastor stepped beside him, and they moved toward the house. "Missed you in church Sunday."

Should have known. You don't fail to show up after a scene like last week's and have it go unnoticed. Had Suzie gone?

He ached to talk to her. Had her number up and ready to push *Send* more times than he could count, but he couldn't think of what to say. Things weren't going to change, and it hurt too much to talk about.

Paul rubbed his neck as he led the way to his kitchen. "Just felt the need to stay here—it's been busy."

Ron accepted the excuse without a hint of rebuke. The pause between them felt like it was supposed to have meaning. Maybe it was just foreboding. Paul wouldn't know the difference.

Ron cleared his throat. "Talked to Suzanna on Monday before she left town."

Left town? Whoa now.

Had she told Dre? Who was taking care of her horse? What about Kelsey—did she talk to her?

"I take it you didn't know she'd left." Ron said.

Paul turned, reaching for a cabinet without knowing what he was after. "No."

"Paul, I know why you fought—that it wasn't just about Hailey. Suzanna told me you told her she needed a relationship with Jesus."

He couldn't turn around. Swallowing wasn't working, and blinking didn't clear the moisture in his eyes.

"I can't imagine how hard this must be, because I know you love her." Ron spoke quietly. "Are you doing okay?"

Paul's hand trembled as he ran it over his head. He turned back to Ron and leaned against the counter with both palms, and his head hung low. "No. Not really." His voice turned gravelly.

"I thought maybe not."

Paul couldn't move, hating he'd crumbled before another man. "I don't know how I let this happen. I *know* her—and I knew she had some stuff to work out. Who doesn't though? We talked about everything except the one thing that should have mattered most."

"It happens." Ron said. "Probably more often than you think." He sighed and Paul glanced at him. "I don't know how to help—don't know that's even possible, but I did want to tell you I had spoken with her. She's searching, Paul. I don't want to give you false hope, but she hates all the anger and bitterness she can't cut away. She wants to be free. I believe that longing is God calling to her."

"She's too stubborn to admit it." Paul pushed away from the counter. "Even if she weren't, admitting she needs Jesus will put her dad's eternity into question. She won't do that. He's the one good memory she has of all her growing up. She won't cast his eternal life into doubt."

"She and I talked about her dad." Ron leaned against the counter with his elbow. "Mike and I were good friends, and he was a believer when he died. A fairly new one, but he was saved. I'm sure of it."

Hope glimmered a faint shaft of light, and Paul latched on to it. "Did you tell her?"

Ron dipped a slow nod though it looked like he wouldn't go into detail. "It was a long story, and she listened. All I mean to say, Paul, is she has a lot of things pushing her to truth. That isn't to say she's not a fighter—we all know she is—but so is the Hound of Heaven. I have hope Love will not fail."

Love never fails.

God's doesn't, but that doesn't mean the Pickle will accept it. Paul kind of wished Jesus were more the beat-it-into-you type rather than the wooing type. He knew from experience how much work the latter really was.

Suzanna turned her car onto Eleventh Avenue and followed it through the UNC campus, wishing the familiar street, the old buildings, and the college culture would distract her from the empty canyon gouged into her soul. Memories played one after another. She and Jason had walked the campus paths many times. They'd studied at Michener Library together, sat at the campus coffee shop, lived in the student housing. He'd held her hand as they walked the campus after sunset, lights strung in the trees and the vitality of eager young minds setting the darkness to life.

Good memories. They made her cry as pain carved the valley deeper.

Why had she believed this would be an escape? You can't escape from something that's on the inside. Paul had been right. The wounds still bled. They'd never healed. So, what did that mean? She was sentenced to a life of bitter agony? She'd rather not live at all.

No. Those thoughts led to a condemning sin. No matter how good a person you were in life——murder, even of oneself, is unforgivable. Unforgivable? So, what was forgiveness all about, then? What needed forgiveness? What could be forgiven? Did it even matter?

Jason talked about being forgiven. That he'd been forgiven. That didn't make any sense. Jason was a good person. Despite his horrible circumstances, he was a good person. Why did he think he needed to be forgiven?

Suzanna followed Twentieth Street toward the baseball field. She parked in the Admissions lot and walked toward the sports complex. She'd spent many afternoons stretched out in the late spring sunshine, watching practice from a distance. He loved the game. She didn't know it well enough to appreciate the long hours of scoreless innings interrupted by brief moments of action, but she could see his passion for baseball every time Jason picked up his glove. It made her happy to see him succeed.

Promise me you'll choose to live.

A bitter wind tugged at her crocheted scarf. Jason's life had been a brief flash of light to hers.

Paul's love had been a fleeting blanket of warmth over her freezing soul.

Neither brought anything lasting. Neither gave her peace. She spun an about-face and returned to her car. Visiting the sites of memories had been a bad idea.

She set her car west on Twentieth Street, merging with traffic without a plan. Ten minutes passed, and she found herself parked at the cemetery. Another bad idea. Yet, her feet took her out of the car and down the rows of headstones.

Jason Allen Cumberland

His headstone was plain, sunk into the ground because it was cheaper—and the caretakers preferred them that way. Easier maintenance. Nice. She'd buried her beloved husband in a manner of convenience.

Live, Suzanna. Promise me.

She dropped to the cold ground, the February chill seeping through her jeans.

How? What kind of life is this, Jase? Every time I start to breathe again, I get another blow.

Her eyes squeezed against the ache aggravated by her confession. He wanted her to find life, but she felt buried by his death. Buried by hope's plunge into disappointment. Buried by her tumultuous life.

"Jase, I tried. I really did. I even met someone. He's a good man, but we don't agree about God, and he can't live with that." Her mumbled words came out in broken cries. "He thinks like you." She doubled over as pain ripped hot down to her core. "I don't know God like you—or like Paul. Jason, why can't I know Him? Why does He hide from me? Hate me? You said He loves me. Daddy said it too. And Paul. But I don't feel loved. I feel rejected."

You're afraid to feel.

Paul knew her. Better than she understood—like Jason had. But they didn't understand. If it weren't for anger, all she would know is heartache.

Draw near.

The voice that whispered to her soul seemed familiar. Her eyes slid shut. She saw an image of a snow-covered field set to glow by the sinking sun on a cold December evening.

Draw near and find life.

The skin on her arms prickled, and she gasped as the memory continued. It had been the purest moment she'd ever known. The voice was the kindest, most inviting sound she'd ever heard. No—not heard. Felt.

Her lips quivered. "God?"

Draw near and find Love.

Love? Love didn't last. Death came. Conflict destroyed. Love failed.

Love never fails.

She'd heard that—it was in the Bible. Suzanna vaguely remembered her father reading it on her wedding day. But love had failed.

Draw near and know my peace.

She turned her face to the sky. "Who are you? How can I love what I do not know?"

Draw near and find me.

She crumpled, her hands covering her face. "I don't know how." An image flashed behind her closed eyes—an envelope, unmarked and unopened. Daddy's letter.

Suzanna pushed off the ground and turned back toward her car. She'd stuffed it into the glove box, not wanting to see it or to think about the things Pastor had told her, but she needed answers. Maybe Daddy had given her some.

She landed in her car and barely had the door pulled shut before she had the glove box open. The envelope waited— called. She shivered, begging the Voice not to let her find more disappointment, and then tore it open.

> *Suzie doll,*
>
> *There is so much I need to tell you. I've made a lot of mistakes in my life. Mistakes that robbed your mother of the life she'd dreamed of. Mistakes that have left both you and your sister*

*wounded and lost. I'm sorry, my little girl, so sorry. There were
many things I didn't understand. I need to tell you about some of
them.*

*The first is about your mother. I know the two of you
clashed—usually violently, and I regret that. You need to know
her anger comes from a deep pit of pain. Unfortunately, something
you can relate to far too well. Suzie, I don't mean this
maliciously, because I do love your mother, and I always will, but
you are on a path much like hers. You have let the root of
bitterness take hold of your soul. Baby, I love you, and I need to
warn you the weed will strangle you. It will rot in your heart and
leave you empty. Hopeless. Don't let that happen.*

*I taught you that if you lived a good life, did what the Bible
says, God would love you, and you would have a happy life and
then go to heaven. I was wrong.*

*Suzie, God loves you no matter what. Life gets hard. I'm sad
to say you know that better than most. That doesn't necessarily
mean God is mad at you. His love is constant. There's nothing
good enough you can do to make Him love you more, and there's
nothing so bad you can do that will make Him love you less.*

*Heaven is a gift He gives by way of faith in Jesus Christ. He
offers it to all of us—to you, but you have to receive it. I led you
astray to make you think you could earn it.*

*I think you resent God, but God is good. He is kind and
righteous and just, but merciful. There is a Psalm that says taste
and see the Lord is good. I've finally tasted that heavenly
sweetness, and I found God is a God I can love because He loves
me.*

*Please, baby girl, please—seek this God. He will be found,
and you will know Him. That is my heartfelt cry for your life. He
will heal your wounds, set you free from anger, and give you peace.
Seek Him, and you will be His.*

"How?" Suzanna cried to the empty park beyond her
windshield. "God, I want to know you!"

Draw near.

Tears soaked her face, and she leaned back against the headrest of her seat. "I don't know how."

"Will she ever come back?" Kelsey pulled her knees to her chest as she sat against the wall on the far side of her bed.

A gust of anger stirred inside Paul. Leaving him without a word? He got that—things being what they are. But Suzanna done just up and took off without explaining to Kelsey what was going on, without giving her a hug or even saying good-bye. Friends don't do that, and Suzanna should know better. She knew how it felt to be abandoned.

"I don't know, Kels"——Paul lowered himself on the foot of the bed, feeling old, really old and broken—"but this isn't because you did anything wrong. Suzie's got some stuff to work through, and she must have felt like she couldn't do it here."

Kelsey examined Paul through sad, dry eyes. Dry because the only person he'd seen his niece cry in front of was Suzanna. "Did you have a fight?"

He sighed, rubbing his neck. "Yeah, we did."

"Because you danced with that pretty lady last week." Her tone rang of accusation.

How do I explain this to a twelve-year-old?

"I didn't handle the whole thing very well, Kels. We did fight about that, but that's not why she left." He examined his hands.

Do I tell her the truth?

"We found out through that fight Suzie and I don't agree about God."

"I don't understand. You went to church together."

"Yeah, we did, and I thought we believed the same things, but we don't." Paul looked back at Kelsey. "I can't marry a woman who doesn't share my beliefs because God warns against it and because it usually turns out to be a bad decision. I love her, but I love Jesus more, and in this situation, I had to choose. It wasn't fun, and to be honest, Kels, my heart really hurts over it."

Kelsey's expression softened. "Because you wanted to marry her?"

Raw emotion swelled against his chest, and he had to clear his throat to speak. "Yeah, I do."

Staring at her hands, Kelsey drew a long, slow breath. "I wanted you to, too."

CHAPTER THIRTY-EIGHT

Suzanna stared at the Gideon Bible she'd found in the bedside table. Reading it made her head hurt, especially as she attempted to wade through the list of impossible names in Genesis chapter five. Desperation filled her. She needed answers.

Reaching for her phone, she debated. Paul? Or Andrea? Both were bound to be upset with her. She'd left without a word and had been gone for over a week.

Maybe she wouldn't call. She set aside the phone and returned to the Bible.

All the days of Methuselah were nine hundred sixty and nine years: and he died.

Nine hundred years and then he died? Where did he go? Did he know God? If he did, how?

She fingered the pages. Sheesh, there were a lot of them. She'd get lost in it all. She *was* lost in it all. Returning to her phone, she found *Andrea* and pushed *Send. Please, don't be mad.*

"Suzanna?" Andrea sounded breathless.

Just the hint of her emotion made Suzanna's throat thick.

"Suzanna, you'd better start talkin', girl." Andrea spoke in her "mother voice." "Where are you? Are you okay?"

"I'm in Colorado—Greeley"—she cleared her gauzy throat—"and I'm... okay."

"You don't sound okay, Suz." The bite in Andrea's tone softened.

Suzanna stared at the Bible. "I need answers, and I don't know who else to ask."

"Okay," Andrea spoke slowly, "I'll do my best. Shoot."

"How do I know God?" Suzanna pushed the words out before she could change her mind. "Paul says I don't. Actually, I know I don't, not like he does, but"—her voice cracked—"but I want to."

Silence stretched over the phone. What if Andrea told her she couldn't help? That only special people got to know God? What if it were like an exclusive club in Hollywood—VIPs only?

"You know Him through Jesus, Suz," Andrea finally answered. "By trusting Jesus as your savior, and by studying His word."

Suzanna dropped back against the bed as frustration poured over her. "I've been trying to read the Bible. It's not helping."

"Okay, so it's a big book, and there's a lot to take in." Andrea began to sound like herself again. "What are you reading?"

"Genesis five."

Andrea breathed a small laugh. "Yeah, I could see how you could be frustrated. Although, if you keep reading, Genesis six will give you a picture of salvation."

"What's in Genesis six?"

"Noah."

Noah? Like the guy with the big boat stuffed full of animals? That was actually in the Bible? Suzanna thought it was a story to keep kids entertained during Sunday school.

"I know that story. Why is it a picture of salvation?"

"Because God told Noah He was going to destroy the earth, and the only way to be saved was through the ark. God tells us now that life will end for all of us at some point in time, and the only way to be saved eternally is through Jesus. It's a true story that points forward to another truth."

"Okay." Suzanna sighed.

"I think for now you should start with a gospel. John. Read the gospel of John. Watch Jesus as He lives and interacts with others throughout the book of John. You'll hear His offer of salvation as He speaks with a man named Nicodemus. You'll see His compassion as He speaks with a Samaritan woman, offering a life that will satisfy her longing for love. You'll see His power to heal. You'll know His desire for a relationship when He says to abide in Him, and He will abide in you. You'll weep as you watch Him die."

Andrea's voice wavered, but she continued. "You'll see He is indeed God when He defeats death. Watch the Son, and you will know God."

"John?" Suzanna felt like a timid mouse. "That's in the New Testament, right?"

"Yep." Andrea didn't sound the least bit condescending. "Right after Luke. Matthew, Mark, Luke, John."

Suzanna rolled to her side and propped her head on her hand. She traced the damask pattern on the hotel duvet with her finger as she tried to put words together. "I'm sorry I left without telling you," she whispered. "Please tell Kelsey I'm sorry."

"I will." Andrea's voice became quiet again.

"Is she okay?"

The pause over the line was telling. "She's trying to understand. Paul stopped by earlier today to talk to her before he left for the river property. He'll be gone for a few weeks—calving."

Paul.

Longing stirred in her heart. "Is... how is he?"

Andrea sighed. "Suzanna, don't take this wrong, but I don't think you should worry about Paul right now. This is between you and God, not you and Paul. It needs to stay between you and God."

Paul sat up and shivered in the darkness. Soaked in a cold sweat, he reached for the hooded sweatshirt he'd tossed over a chair before he climbed into bed. His hands trembled as he pulled it over his head, and his heart raced like a Thoroughbred.

He couldn't help her. The vivid images of the nightmare still replayed, though he was awake. Suzanna had been caught out alone in a violent storm. Sheets of rain shrouded her, and the wind tore at her voice, but he could hear her scream. She begged for help as thunder clapped and lightning ripped through the sky, but he couldn't reach her. Couldn't save her.

It wasn't the first time he'd dreamed the dream. Two weeks running, she'd called out to him in his sleep, and he found himself helpless. Except to pray.

Save her, Jesus. You calmed the waves and made the winds cease at the sound of Your voice. Please save Suzanna.

Suzanna met her work quota and closed her laptop. She sat in her lonely room at the Residence Inn with nothing but her thoughts to keep her occupied. Wet, heavy snow fell in huge flakes, measured in feet the first week in March, keeping her away from the college fields and Linn Grove Cemetery. Early spring snowstorms are common in Colorado and sometimes paralyzing to the Front Range.

She fingered the remote for the television, but her glance found the Bible tucked near her pillow. She'd read through John, like Andrea suggested. There was a lot she'd never heard before. Did Jesus really offer living water to a woman who had five husbands and was living with a man who was not her husband? Did He really blast the religious leaders for making too many rules? Had He stood between a shameless woman and an angry crowd?

Who was this Jesus? He was not the crabby old man in the sky she'd imagined—the one who sat forever frowning, waiting for her next blowout mistake. Reading the stories, she imagined a man with kind eyes and a gentle smile set off by a strong jaw. A man capable of great power like when He cleared the temple, but one who was uncommonly gentle to the weary and brokenhearted.

A man very much like Paul Rustin.

Was that sacrilege? Paul wasn't God, and he couldn't save her. He made that perfectly clear, but he said he knew God—that Jesus was at the core of everything he believed. Maybe Jesus was the reason Paul was the man he was. If that were so, then Paul had been right. She was wrong about God. She wanted—no needed to know this God.

She opened the pages and returned to John eleven. The scene had captured her heart and held all of the emotion she felt. A man was dead. Two women grieved, not only his death, but because he'd left them alone. Crowds gathered, but they were more noisy than helpful. In the midst of it all, Jesus finally showed up.

Jesus said to her, "I am the resurrection and the life; he who believes in me, will live even if he dies, and everyone who lives and believes in Me will never die. Do you believe this?

She said to Him, Yes Lord. I have believed that You are the Christ, the Son of God, even He who comes into the world.

Sitting on the bed, Suzanna read it over again twice, and Jesus's words took on life. The Voice spoke again.

Do you believe this?

"Yes, Lord." She trembled, and a cry surged through her body. "Yes, Jesus, I believe you." She fell facedown against the mattress, sobbing. "I want life. Save me."

Paul stamped his feet on the porch and removed his boots before he went inside. Six inches of snow spread over the river property, looking clean and fresh and new. He stopped at the big picture window in his front room and examined the western horizon. The clouds had cleared, leaving a cool blue sky that set a backdrop for the warm oranges and intense purples of a prairie sunset.

Suddenly he wasn't in his grandparents' living room. His mind traveled back several months to a chilly evening in December. The sun lit the sky with glory, and he and Suzanna were riding her south pasture. She stopped, turned her horse to take in the display, and then she was gone somewhere else. Her face glowed as her eyes slid shut. He'd been sure by the light in her expression she'd had a moment with God.

Paul expected the darkness of his nightmares to crash upon his moment of reverie. Usually did when he thought of Suzanna these days. Maybe because he missed her so much sometimes it was difficult to breathe, but on the chance that the dreams were God's way of reminding him to pray, he would do exactly that.

The darkness of those nightmares didn't fall. Paul leaned an arm against the window frame and watched while the sun bid the day farewell, and still the gloom didn't descend. He closed his eyes, and an image replaced the vision outside his window.

Mike's pasture as it was six years ago. A feedlot. Destroyed ground—muddy, packed down, infertile. Useless. With a love no one understood, Mike tilled and amended, tilled some more, and planted. Before Paul's eyes, the sterile dirt sprouted green life. Color spread over what had looked like death until it filled every lifeless patch of mud. The land had been reclaimed. Saved.

Love never fails.

The picture seemed like a promise.

Suzanna turned her car in the drive and waited at the gate. She gave her name and sat with knots tying a mess in her stomach. The man in the black hat opened the metal gate and waved her through. Too late to turn back.

Mother opened the door, dressed like a woman of wealthy English breeding. Suzanna was surprised a housemaid hadn't greeted her instead.

"Security claimed it was you. I couldn't believe it." Mother spoke as if she were explaining her presence at the door.

Seemed fitting. Mother looked her over, reproach lurking in her eyes. Maybe Suzanna should have done some clothes shopping before she showed up.

Tugging on her hoodie, Suzanna cleared her throat. "It's me."

Mother pushed a smile onto her face. "I'm glad. Won't you come in?"

"Just a sec, Mother." Suzanna dropped down the front steps of the massive Tudor-style stone house. "I have something in the car for you. Let me get it."

She turned to the car, rubbing her hands along her jeans. *Jesus, I don't know if I can do this.*

It was a must though. She opened the back door and pulled out a three-gallon potted plant. Careful not to catch her skin on the thorns, she settled it against her hip and returned to the house.

"What is it?" Mother scowled.

Suzanna steadied her emotions. "A David Austin rose. This one is William Shakespeare. You told my neighbor at Thanksgiving you were Katrina Pembroke. I must have missed that you got married. I wanted to get you something—to say congratulations."

Mother's lips parted, and her eyes rounded. Something soft overcame the sharp edge of her demeanor. For the first time Suzanna could ever remember, her mother had nothing whatsoever to say.

"I can plant it, if you want me to." Suzanna went on in a timid voice. "I thought the old double-bloom style would fit well in one of your English gardens."

Mother's mouth closed, but her face didn't harden. "That's okay, Suzanna. We have a gardener for that." Her eyes perused the glossy green leaves and soft crimson blossoms.

Was there approval in her appraisal?

"Thank you, Suzanna. It will fit quite nicely." Mother cleared her throat. "Would you like to come in? I can have some tea made."

Tea with my mother. Who would have ever thought? "Just for a bit. I'm heading out of town today."

Mother's lips moved as though there were a question on them, but she stilled them and nodded. Suzanna followed her into the travertine-tiled entry, leaving the potted rose on the front step.

She'd never been in Mr. Pembroke's house. His stables were on the other side of his estate, and so she'd driven by it many times, but never had she laid eyes on the interior. Never had she wanted to.

She felt like a filthy beggar, walking around in her canvas tennis shoes and worn-out jeans. She expected a rebuke for it at any moment.

"Are you going back to Nebraska?" Mother settled herself in a satin-covered, wing-back chair.

Suzanna looked around. The ornate couch was cream colored. The opposite wing-back chair matched its light blue twin. She'd taint either one with her street clothing. Should she sit on the floor? "I am."

Mother seemed not to notice her standing with her hands tucked into her kangaroo pocket. "What brought you out here for such a short visit?"

She tried not to gulp. "I've been in Greeley for three weeks."

Mother's eyebrows arched. "Oh."

Was that disappointment?

"Are you moving back?"

Mother didn't like her. Never approved of her. Why would she want her here?

"I…" Suzanna twisted her hands together. "I'm not sure. I had some things I needed to work through, and I couldn't do it in Rock Creek, but——"

"There's something between you and that farmer——rancher. Sorry." Mother sat back against the chair.

Suzanna let her gaze drop from her mother's face to the gleaming mahogany floor. "He's a good man, Mother," she whispered.

She waited in the silence, preparing herself for the onslaught of disapproval.

Mother sighed. "Well, if things don't work out, William has the apartment above the carriage house. You're welcome to land there, if you want."

Holy buckets. Really? No lecture and a kind offer all in one breath? Suzanna's eyes flickered back to her mother's.

Mother offered a strained smile. She settled her eyes over Suzanna again, and she sat up. "Is he good to you, Suzanna?"

"Yes." Her breathless whisper squeezed past a fresh wave of ache. *He's too good for me, Mother, but he loves me.*

"Good." Mother managed another forced smile.

Suzanna accepted it, amazed she'd gotten one at all.

Paul wiped his feet against the bristled doormat on the porch before he let himself inside. Done. Calving was done, and he could go home. He'd close things up and take off in the morning. The prospect seemed bittersweet. He missed the kids and needed to see his mom to make sure she was doing okay. Wanted to share a meal with Tom and Dre. But driving past Suzanna's empty house…

Worries for another day.

He flipped on the kitchen light and headed for the sink when something sitting on his table stopped him cold. Lucky Charms. Doing an about-face, he set his stride back out the door. He moved to the end of the porch, in the opposite direction of the barn, and peered around the corner of the house. A black Honda sat empty in his drive. His heart did a jump-kick and then began to throb.

After an about-face, he moved back to the door. Reaching back into the house for his coat, Paul scanned the property. The pond lay peaceful in the gathering dusk, but a lone figure stood on the end of the dock, facing the water. A smile bloomed in his chest before it tickled his lips.

When his boots hit the wood planks of the dock, she turned, her eyes timid but lovely.

"Someone brought me a new box of Lucky Charms." He stopped in front of her.

"Yes"—her smile made the homesick feeling go away—"there's no accounting for taste."

Paul chuckled, locking eyes with her. Those blue gems danced with life. With peace. He slid a hand along her jaw and then cupped her face. "You found it," he whispered.

Tears made her eyes sheen, and she nodded as though she knew exactly what he was talking about. "He found me, actually. Had been there all along. I just couldn't see Him."

Something wet fell on his cheek. She reached to brush it away, and he held her hand against his whisker-shadowed face. "Love never fails." The whisper started in his heart and left his lips with absolute wonder.

Suzanna nodded, her lips quivering with a small cry, and he pulled her in close with both arms. Her voice shook against his chest. "Praise God."

Praise God indeed.

EPILOGUE

Suzanna sat on a step of Paul's covered back porch, watching the evening settle over the pond beyond his backyard. The small purple wildflowers of early May blended into the silver ripples of water. A canvas of peace. Something to smile about, especially considering it was only a tiny stock pond.

She stretched her arms and leaned back as the delicious ache of sore muscles whispered accomplishment. Two hundred shrub cherries in the ground. Twenty-five apple saplings lined her little orchard. With Paul digging at her side, she'd planted every single one. The daring step felt like flight, and the thrill made her giggle.

Paul came out the screen door, and she listened to the rhythm of his boots clicking against the decking. He dropped down on the top step behind her, one booted foot landing on either side of her seat. His arms wrapped around her shoulders, and she leaned against him.

"There's an understated beauty in this Nebraska of yours." She smiled, though she doubted he could see it. "Something you can't see or know while flying down a highway at sixty-five."

He chuckled, the rumble coming through his chest and tickling her ear. "Yep. Don't tell anyone though. We like to keep it a secret. Keeps those city slickers out."

She bumped his knee in a playful rebuke, and he tightened his arms around her.

"So," he spoke just above her ear, "I've been thinking, but I'm a little hesitant to ask because I'm not wearing a helmet, and I know how dead set you've been about staying in your daddy's house, but…"

Her heart leapt into a run as he drew out the pause. "But what?"

"Well, I was wondering if you'd consider relocating."

She grinned. "Where would I go?"

"Just down the road is all. There's a bigger farmhouse there. Recently remodeled. Pretty view out back."

She tipped her face to his. "Does it come with a blue-eyed cowboy?"

His smile made his eyes dance. "Package deal, but we'd have to get married first. I'm kind of old-fashioned like that."

His eyes grew deep and sincere.

"Is that a proposal, Paul?"

He unfolded his arms and opened a fist against his knee. An antique diamond set in a white-gold band rested in his rough palm. Suzanna fingered it as tingles raced through her body.

"Well?" He suddenly sounded breathless.

She turned her attention back to his face. "I'm gonna have to hear the words."

He grinned, slid the ring onto her ring finger and tipped her chin.

"Just say yes, Pickle."

She barely had the syllable out before his mouth found hers.

For I will pour out water on the thirsty land,
And streams on the dry ground;
I will pour out My Spirit on your offspring,
And My blessing on your descendants;
And they will spring up among the grass
Like poplars by streams of water.
~Isaiah 44:3-4~

RECLAIMED

Dear Reader,

Thank you for taking a journey with Suzanna and Paul. I hope their imaginary lives blessed your real life. When I write, I am ever-mindful—and prayerful—that these stories speak hope and life to whomever may be reading.

I have to confess that the town of Rock Creek is completely fictional. I named it after a park my family enjoys. When I began this story, I had a real place in mind, and pictured it throughout the telling, but I couldn't bear the thought of painting, in any degree, any of the wonderful towns in my rural area with a shade of malice or snobbery. As a small-town transplant from a big-city upbringing, I can say there is always a fear coming into a little town that the new girl will be snubbed, that she won't fit in or be welcomed into the already-established social groups. That wasn't the case in my move, and as I've visited other little towns, I have found there are always kind hearts who welcome just as sure as there will be ones who are cold and closed. I hope you'll forgive my liberty in making a place up!

Reclaimed is my second novel and there are more to come! If you missed my debut novel Blue Columbine, I invite you to step into Andrew and Jamie's world, hold on tight as they wrestle with loyalty and addiction, and ultimately rejoice in the reflection of God's redemption. Also, watch for the release of The Carpenter's Daughter, releasing in 2016.

I'd love to meet you in cyberspace! Please visit me at www.authorjenrodewald.com or connect with me on my Facebook page, Author Jen Rodewald.

As always, I'm shamelessly begging for your review on Amazon! Please take the time to tell others what you thought of Reclaimed.

Thank you again for reading! You have blessed me.

For HIS glory,

Jen

About the Author

Jennifer Rodewald is passionate about the Word of God and the powerful vehicle of story. The draw to fiction has tugged hard on her heart since childhood, and when she began pursuing writing she set on stories that reveal the grace of God.

Jen lives and writes in a lovely speck of a town where she watches with amazement while her children grow up way too fast, gardens, and marvels at God's mighty hand in everyday life. Four kids and her own personal superman make her home in southwestern Nebraska delightfully chaotic.

She would love to hear from you! Please visit her at authorjenrodewald.com.

Made in the USA
San Bernardino, CA
12 August 2020